LOCKED IN A BATTLE FOR THE FUTURE OF THE FREE WORLD

Major Aleksei Bodnya—Hero of the *Rodina*—the Motherland—whose mission is to deliver the first crippling blow to the U.S. in what will become the Third World War.

Ensign Pavel Kovpak—Brutal and cunning, he is Bodnya's right-hand man.

Richard "Jinx" Jenkins—One of the CIA's finest—and most exasperating—he's most at home with a gun in his hand and his ass on the line.

B. J. Kirkley—Recon team leader, specialist on the Soviet army and a genius with a map. He's the only man who can pinpoint the location of the Soviets' attack.

★ WWIII: Behind the Lines ★

WWIII: BEHIND THE LINES

TARGET TEXAS

James B. Adair and Gordon Rottman

BERKLEY BOOKS, NEW YORK

WWIII: BEHIND THE LINES
TARGET TEXAS

A Berkley Book/published by arrangement with
the authors

PRINTING HISTORY
Berkley edition/March 1990

ISBN: 0-425-12046-5

A BERKLEY BOOK® TM 757,375
Berkley Books are published by The Berkley Publishing Group,
200 Madison Avenue, New York, New York 10016.
The name "BERKLEY" and the "B" logo
are trademarks belonging to Berkley Publishing Corporation.

PRINTED IN THE UNITED STATES OF AMERICA

10 9 8 7 6 5 4 3 2 1

*We dedicate this book to the
United States Army Special Forces,
which introduced us both to a lifetime of adventure.*

When history cannot be written with a pen,
it must be written with a gun.

—Farabundo Marti

Acknowledgments

We wish to thank Jim Morris, our editor at Berkley, for his never-ending patience and encouragement.

We would also like to thank the 5th Directorate of the Main Intelligence Directorate of the General Staff (GRU), whose continuing deployment of Spetsnaz troops in the United States and around the globe has provided us with invaluable inspiration in spinning this tale.

All characters and political organizations in this book are fictitious. The military units are not, nor are their aims and missions.

★ Prologue ★

On his best days, Ivan Alexeyevitch Gortov, the new President of the Soviet Union and General Secretary of the Communist party, looked like a kindly old grandfather. This was clearly not one of his best days, for today he looked like a Siberian bear prematurely awakened from hibernation. As he entered the large, high-ceilinged room, he scanned the faces seated at the long, polished table. Light from the tall windows on both sides of the room gave it a churchlike appearance. The ornate decorations, left by the dead Romanovs, accentuated this cathedral atmosphere. Gortov had often thought of this room as a church for the worshipers of power.

All permanent members of the inner circle of the politburo were in attendance; not surprising, since a missed meeting could cost a man his career. In the past two years, the General Secretary and his closest ally, Kirill Gerasimov, Chairman of the KGB, had bullied and hounded the politburo into a flock of docile sheep.

The triangle of power that controlled and "balanced" the Soviet Union had been shattered by Gortov's predecessor, Mikhail Gorbachev. Gorbachev had centered all power to himself to promote his vision of glasnost and perestroika. After Gorbachev's mysterious demise in the crash of an Aeroflot IL-76, Gortov had wielded this increased authority with a will and a purpose that would have made Ivan the Terrible proud. Of the politburo members under Gorbachev, only Gerasimov remained.

1

The lesser politburo members, the candidate members, were not present, nor had they been invited. As he walked slowly to the head of the table, Gortov studied each wary face. Most were blank or mildly curious. Only Gerasimov and Mikhail Valerian, the Minister of Defense, knew the purpose of this emergency meeting.

"Comrades," Chairman Gortov began, "we are at a watershed point in history. We are here today to discuss the future of the *Rodina mat*, our motherland, and, indeed, the future of the world."

Gortov smiled, seeing the effect his words had on the suddenly concerned ministers.

"We are beset with political and economic problems, some of which have been created by the greed and jealousy of the Western powers and some," Gortov paused for effect, "that are due to the failures of those whom the *Rodina* has entrusted with its very life."

The effect he had paused for was instantly forthcoming. Every minister, except for Defense and KGB, took on the look of souls doomed to the Hell whose existence Marxism denied, a look that Molotov had once called "dead men talking."

The Chairman continued, his expression changing to that of a wrathful father scolding errant children. "These problems are more serious and far-reaching than ever before. My predecessor's attempts at glasnost and perestroika merely opened up our nation to the problems that have confounded the West for years: drugs, protests, discontent. In the name of democracy, he bought disaster for our *Rodina* and the revolution. Today we will deal with that disaster."

Tension soared among the assembled ministers. Many began to taste the coppery taste of fear. Without doubt, someone's head would roll, maybe several heads. Those ministers whose organizations had failed to produce as expected, especially Agriculture and Energy, were pale and perspiring.

"From without," Gortov went on, "we are beset by economic war. The illegal satellite antennas sprouting up in our cities and collectives, to which we have so recently turned a blind eye, are making the people restless as they see how Westerners live. Our people greedily seek consumer products like those produced in the West. What they get are inferior products, worse even than those produced in other Warsaw Pact states. To get these inferior products, they wait in line for hours for the few items available.''

At the mention of the satellite antennas, Gerasimov shook his head in amusement. He had loudly opposed the distribution of the devices, worried that they would contaminate the masses with dangerous Western ideas. This reference by the General Secretary was his validation.

''They cannot understand,'' Gortov went on, ''that the luxuries served up by the gangsters who rule the West are only an anesthetic, numbing the people to the decadence and corruption of capitalist society. My recent predecessor's experiments only confused the people more.''

The Chairman paused again as he cast his flint-hard eyes on the gray face to his right. ''The harvest has failed for the third year.''

Hearing this, Ilya Kuzov, the recently appointed Minister of Agriculture, bowed his head like a man making peace with his maker, just prior to meeting him.

''Our people wait in lines for the few food items they can get. Each year we fail to produce enough food, and we are forced to buy the Americans' *surplus* wheat! The most popular food in Russia today is vodka, despite all efforts to discourage drunkenness. Once again, *she de kasha pischa nacha*, boiled cabbage and oatmeal are our daily food.''

As the Chairman listed these deficiencies, the ministers from the various failed ministries took on the ashen look of corpses dug from the frozen earth after a winter offensive. There were no protests. Each knew that their respective organizations had failed miserably to meet their goals for years, but the blame had always been put on the capitalists, or recidivists, or some other convenient scapegoat. This time it was on their own heads. The Chairman next turned his withering stare on the Minister of Transportation.

''It is increasingly difficult to maintain our economic warfare efforts to defeat the West. We operate our merchant ships at a loss in order to underbid the West for Third World shipping customers. America now operates fewer than two hundred merchant ships because we have driven them from the market, but we cannot continue to operate in such a manner.''

Ivan Strecklin, the obese, turgid Minister of Transportation, started to speak, but a look from Gerasimov froze the words in his throat.

"From within, also, we are seeing more political unrest," Gortov went on. "There have been more demonstrations in the Central Asian republics. The Poles are as restless as ever, the Estonians seek independence, and, as a result, the other Warsaw Pact states are feeling more independent, especially Yugoslavia. Hungary and Romania cling to their 'most favored nation' status, Poland continues its economic overtures to the West, Czechoslovakia and the German Democratic Republic are both increasing their trade with West Germany and Austria; only our loyal Bulgarian comrades have maintained their efforts to obtain the goal of true Communism—and Bulgaria is the most economically depressed of the Warsaw Pact states!"

Gortov paused again, as much to let the ministers catch their breath as to catch his own. He put on a look of exasperation as he continued the litany of despair.

"On our Eastern borders, the Chinese have deviated even further from their twisted form of communism by becoming increasingly capitalistic. Their new friendship with America enables them to modernize their armed forces at an alarming rate, with technology rivaling our own."

"My predecessor's ill-advised pullout nearly led to the loss of Afghanistan. There, too, we have had to go back in to undo the damage done in the name of perestroika. The *Basmachi* counterrevolutionaries still resist the inevitability of socialism. Fortunately, their stubbornness has greatly increased the number of combat veterans in our armed forces."

It was lost on none of the ministers that no hard looks had been directed at either the Minister of Defense or the KGB. Gortov shuffled his notes for a second, making the ministers wait for the next victim to be selected.

Gortov smiled wanly at Vladimir Bokoy, the Minister of Energy.

"We have reached the straining point of energy production. It will not be long before we cannot meet the demands of heavy industry, transportation, agriculture, and construction."

Bokoy noted to himself that the demands of the armed

forces were not mentioned, since it was their *right* to whatever resources they desired to ensure the security of the *Rodina*.

"Fortunately, there is some good news to report!" A few of the ministers seemed to relax slightly. Perhaps there could be a reprieve.

"The Armed Forces of the Soviet Union have never been stronger!" the Chairman shouted, pounding his fist on the table to emphasize the last three words. "Never has the world seen such might as the Soviet Union has now to defend herself against the Forces of Darkness."

The use of the phrase "Forces of Darkness" gave many of those attending this cloistered meeting a hint of what was to follow. The Chairman invariably used the phrase when he spoke of military responses to a global situation.

"Our comrades in the military, industry, and all branches of science and technology must be congratulated on their unceasing efforts to make the *Rodina* strong," the Chairman said, beaming at the respective ministers, "as well as the Committee for State Security, whose efforts to acquire new technology from the West have been invaluable."

Essential, you mean, you old goat, thought Gerasimov to himself as he nodded and smiled back at Gortov.

"Perhaps the Minister of Defense would like to elaborate on our current military status?" Gortov asked, taking his seat for the first time.

Rising to his feet, Mikhail Valerian, a Marshall of the Soviet Union well into his sixties, placed his papers to one side and fixed the ministers with the smile of a fox entering a henhouse.

"Comrades, in the past two years, the Armed Forces of the Soviet Union have obtained a level of ability to defend the *Rodina* not possible since the 1960s. We have expanded and modernized both our nuclear and conventional forces and are prepared to defeat our enemies in any form of warfare. We constantly deploy increasingly capable weapons systems made possible by new technology obtained from the *glavny rag*—the main enemy." He nodded at Gerasimov, who returned the recognition with a slight bow.

"These new weapons include both ballistic and cruise missiles, air defense systems, fighter aircraft, attack helicopters, ground weapons systems, and submarines. Our Ground Forces maintain a high state of training and the new weapons systems for them have been issued to our forward deployed forces. The troops are politically prepared to defend the *Rodina*. They are at a fever pitch of loyalty and possess a desire to sacrifice not seen since the Great Patriotic War. We need only to be given the order to do what we must!''

With that he nodded to the Chairman and sat stiffly back into his chair.

Gortov stood again, looking up at the ceiling. His expression changed from dark to inspired, as if he had just seen a vision of salvation.

''Comrades,'' Gortov said, dropping his voice so that the ministers all had to lean forward to hear his words, ''to ensure the survival of the *Rodina*, we must eject the Americans from Western Europe and control the region economically. We must ensure our supply of petrol, and curtail the flow of it to the West. We must bring the other states of the Warsaw Pact back under our firm control. The history of the Revolution will hinge on our decisions here today. We have the power to save the *Rodina*—if we but have the courage.''

The tension in the room changed perceptibly with these words. The way to personal survival was now clear. Those who supported the chairman's plan, whatever it was, would survive the day. Those who opposed it might never leave the building.

Gortov nodded at the Defense Minister, who rose again as an aide hastily set up a large map of Europe on an easel. The map had three large red arrows curving from the East German border toward the English Channel.

''We will begin with diversionary attacks on selected American military targets, both in Europe and in the United States, followed by a coordinated land and air attack on NATO forces in Europe,'' the Minister began, as chins dropped all around the table, ''to disrupt and destroy the American–NATO control of Western Europe.''

''The ground attacks will take three separate routes through West Germany,'' Valerian continued, pointing to the red arrows on the map, ''and will be preceded by air and missile attacks with persistent chemical weapons on NATO commands, communication centers, and troop concentrations.

The goal of these attacks is to overwhelm the NATO forces and occupy all of Western Europe before the Americans can mount an effective resupply and reinforcement.''

''In the event that our forces encounter impenetrable enemy opposition in this pursuit, we will use the low-yield tactical weapons of mass destruction to break the enemy's strongpoints.''

Seeing the wild expressions on the Ministers' faces at the mention of nuclear weapons, Valerian added, ''Since the signing of the treaty removing all American intermediate-range nuclear weapons from Europe, the NATO countries lack any means to attack the Soviet Union with nuclear weapons. We do not believe that the Americans will commit to a full-scale nuclear exchange simply to save their European allies.''

''Once we have superiority in Europe, the second phase will begin. Its objective will be to secure and occupy the oil-producing areas of the Middle East, primarily Iran, Kuwait, Saudi Arabia, and Libya, and deny their use to the West. Our initial action will be against Iran, as their pool of available military-age men and their stock of weapons and supplies has been reduced to near zero by their interminable war with Iraq. The Iranians have broken themselves against the rock of Iraq. There will be no Afghanistan in Iran. Once we control the Straits of Hormuz, the entire Persian Gulf will be in our grasp.''

So there it is, comrades—war, thought Gortov as he watched the various ministers for their reactions. Apart from the initial surprise, all of them quickly altered their expressions to reflect the greatest enthusiasm for the plan, since the plan was obviously not being presented for discussion, only for affirmation.

The Minister of Energy, in his astonishment, nearly opened his mouth to ask how these two huge plans could succeed on the meager stores of fuel currently available, but caught himself before he spoke. No sense dying now, he assured himself, there will be plenty of time to die later.

★1★

13 September

"But Comrade Capitán, what if the agent is correct?"

"Then you will have saved the lives of fifty soldiers of the revolution, and shown the Contra mercenaries to be killers of children and enemies of the beloved Catholic church," Sprickereit slowly replied as if he were speaking to a dim-witted child. "You will score a propaganda victory and avoid a military defeat."

"Sí, Comrade Capitán."

"Why is it so hard to explain revolutionary conduct to these people?" Hauptmann Rolf Sprickereit, East German National People's Army, wondered to himself as another cloud of dust drifted over him from the narrow road. "It's as if they cannot see anything past their next plate of beans and rice. What do the Americans call these little countries—banana republics? An excellent description!"

In truth, Sprickereit despised the Nicaraguans. He had not yet adjusted to the mañana attitude of the Central Americans, and their laziness rankled his Prussian sensibilities. It was hard to tolerate laziness, even in a country where the sun burned your brain and the daily downpour soaked everything.

The previous evening an agent from one of the refugee camps in Honduras had reported that an ambush was being planned, perhaps for the next day. Sprickereit distrusted the quality of information these agents obtained. They were frequently wrong, or their information was too sketchy to be of any real use. Nevertheless, it would be easy to test this story.

The local Catholic school regularly made trips down the same road. Today they would trade buses with the *Batallón de Lucha Irregular*, the Irregular Struggle Battalion, of the Sandinista Popular Army; one of eighteen such units formed to combat the Contras. Since the Catholic church was a major thorn in the side of the revolution, anyway, today he would use Sister Mary Elizabeth and her little brood as "Polish mine detectors". If they died in a Contra ambush, so much the better.

Jesus H. Christ! How the hell many road ambushes have I done? Jinx wondered. Two hundred, five hundred? Christ, I can't even remember how many, but I've done 'em in a dozen countries against the toughest mothers in the world, and none of 'em was a disaster like this one. How I got talked into this Nicaraguan cluster-fuck, I'll never know. At least the screaming has about died down.

I really need to paint this K again, he mused, turning the old submachine gun over in his large hands, wanting to think about anything but what was happening around him.

He had been delighted to find that the Contras had dozens of the old Carl Gustav m/45b submachine guns. He had first used one in Vietnam, where they had been called Swedish Ks. Although they were thirty years old, the men who used them swore by them, because they were simple and they always worked.

Sixty meters away, the bus lay on its side, smoldering. The bodies of two dozen young girls lay on either side of the road, their white blouses stained in ugly red and black patterns from the mud and their own blood. The luckier girls sat shaking and crying in a small group several meters from the bus, their faces white with terror.

Half the Misuras were throwing up behind the trees where moments before they had hidden to ambush the bus. The others were milling around trying to decide what to do.

I should be down there looking for wounded kids to save or at least trying to pull these half-wits together, Jinx thought, but right now I'm so mad at them I would probably end up shooting that jerk Pablo, and then all hell would break loose.

Like most disasters-in-the-making, the mission was supposed to be simple. Every day, the Sandinistas bused a pla-

toon of militia from Sisin to the fortified camp compound
eight kilometers away and returned with the previous day's
group.

The plan had been for Jinx's Contras to set up a simple
road ambush for the bus, knock off the platoon, move a klick
up the road, and then hit any rescue effort mounted from
Sisin. No sweat, can do easy, G.I.

Movement to the ambush site had been uneventful. The
gently rolling grasslands were home to the Misura Indians,
whose people had farmed and fished there for hundreds of
years, and they knew the trails by heart. Misura stood for
Miskito, Sumo, and Rama, the three tribes whose homes in
Northeastern Nicaragua had been destroyed by the Sandinistas. The lodgepole pines and tall grass reminded Jinx of North
Carolina. The terrain made movement easy, even for the Misura, whose movement in the woods reminded Jinx of a Gypsy
junk band.

The ambush was laid out like a textbook problem at Ft.
Bragg. The bus had come down the road about an hour early;
unusual, but not impossible. The windows had been so covered with dried mud and dust that the ambushers could not
see that the passengers were not troops, but schoolgirls.
Schoolgirls in white blouses and navy blue skirts.

The command-detonated mine buried in the road had gone
off behind the left front wheel, pitching the bus onto its right
side, and setting it on fire. By the time the children had gotten
the emergency door in the back of the bus open, smoke from
the fire had just about covered the bus. As the girls ran out
of the smoke, they ran into a Claymore mine that had been
planted off to one side. Victor, the Misura who fired the mine,
had only seen running figures; he squeezed the handle before
he saw the first white blouse and blue skirt. The Claymore
fired its seven hundred steel ball bearings like a scythe, waist
high and seventy feet wide. The girls caught in that fan of
steel had twitched and jumped like puppets in a whirlwind.
Now Victor sat by his tree, sobbing.

The other troops had fired wildly at the bus when the mine
went off (fired wildly was redundant, really, since it was the
only way they ever fired) and many of the girls had made it
out of the bus and into the road before they were cut down.

Pablo, the Misura lieutenant, had already gone down to

the road. Jinx was still sitting with his back to the grass-covered mound from which he and Pablo had directed the ambush. Although he wore the same blue-green Texaco suit uniform as the troops, it was easy to see that Jinx was no Misura. At five feet eleven inches, he was not tall for an American, but he towered over most of the Indians. Only Manuel Nixon, the RPG gunner, was taller, doubtless due to the genetic influence of the English sailor who was Manuel's ancestor. Jinx's fair, sunburned skin and hazel eyes were a real contrast to the dark, almost black, Indians.

I guess I better get down there, Jinx thought as he slowly rose to walk down to the road. God, I feel tired; old and tired.

As he emerged from the tree line, Jinx called to the Indian lieutenant, "Pablo, better send a squad down the road to watch for *Piricuacos*. We don't want to get caught here with our pants down."

"Señor, I—"

"Forget it, Pablo. *C'est la guerre—Así es la guerra.*"

Pablo got a squad on its way to watch the road, and began to gather up his troops. Most of them were wandering around like zombies, horrified by what they had just done.

Some of the girls in the small group of survivors were wounded, and the Indian medic was trying to bandage them. Many were so terrified, they wouldn't let him touch them. Others just sat and stared, their faces like chalky masks.

Jinx walked around to the back of the bus to check for more wounded. The bus driver, a short, plump nun, lay across the broken windows. She had been killed by a piece of the bus frame that hit her under the left kidney and lodged in her right lung. There were a couple of girls still in the bus, but they weren't moving, and the bloody, ragged holes in them said they never would.

As he walked past the survivors, one of the older girls was crying over and over, "They made us take the bus, they made us!" She seemed to be trying to explain, almost like an apology for being there.

"*Muchacha, por favor*, who made you?" Jinx asked in Spanish, kneeling beside the terrified girl. "Who made you take the bus?"

"The soldiers, the soldiers," she said, the words tumbling

over themselves as she spoke. "They made us take their bus, and said they would take our old one. Sister Mary wanted to leave earlier, but they made us stay and take their bus!"

An old, sick feeling started in Jinx's guts. Their accident was starting to look like something a lot worse.

"*Pobrecita*, the soldiers, were they Nicaraguan army or militia?"

"Army, with a gringo just like you, too!"

"A gringo?"

"*Sí, un flaco*, thin, tall, with blue eyes and white hair."

"A setup, a Goddamn setup!" Jinx thought. "They set these kids up to take a beating and then—what? And how did they know it would be today?"

"*Señorita*, I'm very sorry, *lo siento mucho*. Understand?"

She just stared, tears running down her face.

Jinx stood and called to Pablo, "Better saddle up, amigo, this could be a bad trap!"

As Pablo formed up his troops to move out, it began to pour rain. They had counted on an afternoon shower to hide their trail after the ambush, but now the rain just made a sorry scene even worse.

It will take forever to get these guys back to being soldiers, Jinx thought. Every time they look down that rifle barrel, they're going to see little girls in white blouses.

Considering how long it had taken to train them in the first place, this was a depressing thought.

That thought was cheerful, though, compared to what awaited him personally when he got back. The Sandinistas would make an international incident and propaganda show of this, and Jinx's superior would probably have an out-of-body experience! Jinx had tap-danced his way through plenty of shitstorms in the past, but this one would need breakdancing.

As the Indians moved back into the trees, Jinx made a last check of the ambush site. He could hear the radio crackling, the security patrol reporting trucks loaded with regular troops coming down the road a klick away. Pablo was telling the patrol not to engage, and to meet at the rally point.

The rain was soaking the girls' thin cotton blouses, which became almost transparent where they stuck to their adolescent chests. The sight was disturbingly erotic, a sensation that both surprised and annoyed Jinx as he turned away to follow the Indians into the trees.

"I've been in the woods way too long," Jinx muttered to himself as the trees behind him slowly hid the sordid sight of those pathetic, used children.

At the rally point, Jinx stopped to gather up the security squad, sending the ambush party on. Behind them, the sound of truck gears grinding could be clearly heard through the rain-soaked forest.

Pablo should be back here, Jinx thought, as he and the security squad caught up to the swiftly moving platoon. Normally, a patrol leader should be near the point, but under the circumstances, he thought Pablo should be here in the rear where contact was most likely.

Jinx grabbed Hennesey, Pablo's second-in-command, and quickly led him up to the point.

"Pablo, we need you in the rear! Leave your number two up here to lead the platoon. Let's go!"

Pablo looked very skeptical, but gave Hennesey some quick instructions and stood with Jinx until the end of the column came by. He and Jinx fell in with the last squad.

"Those Sandinistas are going to be pissed off no end, *Teniente.*" Jinx explained as the platoon came to a shallow but steep-banked stream. "They are going to be out for blood, and will probably come charging down the trail. We're going to use that for our advantage."

As the last squad crossed the stream, Jinx held them on the far bank. Making certain that they had an M60 machine gun and an M79 grenade launcher, Jinx placed the reluctant rear guard in concealed firing positions on the crest of the steep bank. The M60 and M79 were positioned to fire back down the trail.

With a practiced eye, Jinx gave the stream crossing a quick once-over and told the squad leader to keep everyone in place.

Jogging up the trail, Jinx caught up with another machine gunner and took him in tow as he made his way back to the rear guard and found the Indian lieutenant.

"Pablo, I want you to stay in the platoon's rear and keep pushing them. One squad and I will wait here to surprise the *Piricuacos.* Leave me this M60."

"*Sí, señor, con mucho gusto!*"

The relief on Pablo's face as he sped off after the column was matched by the sudden concern on the face of the reluctant machine gunner.

Returning to the stream crossing, he was mildly surprised to find that most of the press-ganged squad were in fairly good positions. He placed the second machine gunner twenty meters south of the crossing and sighted back up the stream. Moving rapidly from man to man, making final corrections to their concealment, he told each, "*Esta vez, no habra niñas piqueñas,* there will be no little girls this time! Fire everything you have, throw a grenade, and go back up the trail to our friends!"

Jinx took up a firing position a few meters north of the trail, where he could see down the trail on the far side of the stream. Now, if no one gets too jumpy, he thought to himself, we might just pull this off.

It seemed like only seconds before he heard the whisper of wet vegetation, followed by a muffled voice. A head appeared, disappeared, and reappeared as a bearded figure in a faded camouflage uniform and the obligatory Sandinista red-and-black scarf emerged from a screen of brush between Jinx and the trail. Pausing for only a moment, he slid down the muddy bank. Another soldier appeared, slid down after him, and the two began to cross.

Two more men followed them down and more heads appeared. All were armed with AKM assault rifles and they were clearly in a hurry.

Jinx placed his K's sights on the third man's crotch. No sense aiming at the point man since every Contra probably would. Waiting for the fourth man to align himself with the third man, Jinx slowly squeezed the trigger, letting the weapon's natural climb walk itself up the man's belly and left chest, spinning him to the side. The 9mm bullets tore into the fourth man's sternum and face.

Jinx was only now aware of the hammering of the two M60s, one firing a continuous stream of lead down the trail, the other slamming two of the enemy into the mud bank, making them almost vanish in gouts of mud as they slid down into the water. The M79 thumped and was followed by a subdued bang down the trail. The Contras emptied their AKs and G-3s into the brush on the far side as fast as the weapons would fire. In less than ten seconds, most of the rifles were empty.

Jinx fired a final brief burst of his few remaining rounds into the brush, ejected the thirty-six round magazine, and snapped in another. The M79 thumped again. The first hand grenades exploded on the far side, thrown by the riflemen.

There was little Sandinista return fire. Wiggling to the rear, Jinx rolled behind a large tree, and, bent double in a crouch, double-timed through the brush with the Contras passing him on either side as they hurried to rejoin the main group.

These people move like cattle, Sprickereit thought, as the column pushed its way through the wet foliage. The Indians will get away if we do not press this pursuit faster.

Ahead, the point team paused and softly said, 'Rio,' then slipped out of sight down the steep bank. The patrol slowed as the men in front slid down, one after another, toward the gurgling water.

"Rapido, rapido," Sprickereit muttered as he neared the drop-off. He was twenty-five meters from the edge when the enemy opened fire. The Sandinista lieutenant in front of him turned to flee, but Sprickereit's rifle butt in his chest stopped him.

"That way, fool," Sprickereit hissed, pushing the panicky Sandinista backward with his AKM. "The enemy is that way!"

Turning back toward the stream, the Nicaraguan officer took only one step before an explosion hurled him back into Sprickereit like a broken doll. The firing from across the stream was suddenly much heavier. Two soldiers broke out of the brush in front of Sprickereit. One turned to fire, covering his comrade. As he fired, a long burst of machine gun fire ripped across his stomach and his fleeing comrade's back.

Dropping to one knee, Sprickereit called to the forward element to pull back. Only one voice replied.

"These Indians must have some American help with them today," Sprickereit thought to himself. "Too bad all I have to work with are these bean eaters, we could see who is the better soldier. Maybe another time."

Jinx's once-reluctant rear guard proudly tramped past the still soaked and weary remainder of the platoon, which was strung out on both sides of the trail. Most of the platoon had frankly not expected to see the squad or the American again, and were surprised and impressed to see them catch up, alive and victorious. The squad members had the tired but smug look of returning heroes.

And rightly so, thought Jinx. They did OK under the circumstances. They only had one man slightly wounded, and he may have been clipped by his own buddy. They had bagged six of the enemy in the streambed, and probably another three or four on the trail. The Sandinistas had broken off the pursuit, but Jinx could not let the Indians feel too secure at this point. They could get fatally lax all too quickly. A subdued Pablo snapped to attention as Jinx approached.

"Let's get them moving, amigo, they still want our blood."

With little of their usual grumbling, the platoon got to its feet and stumbled down the trail after the disappearing squad of heroes.

Maybe we'll pull this off yet, Jinx thought as the rain began again. If they got back to Honduras alive, Jinx had two pressing missions: first, to find the Sandinista spy in their camp, and then to try to cover his own butt, if possible. Pulling his poncho over his head, he smiled at a remembered phrase: just another shitty day in paradise!

★2★

14 September

The black Volga from the Ministry of Defense sped down the special VIP lane on the Leningradskiy Prospekt. As it turned into a gate between two of the Kremlin's eighteen towers, it stopped for the first of three identification checks. The young soldier in the royal blue collar-tabbed uniform of the Kremlin Guard Regiment waved them on through. Another check by more KGB troops followed in the inner courtyard parking lot of the General Staff of the Soviet Army and a third check at the building's entry foyer.

Most of the guards recognized Maj. Gen. Sergey Pavlovskiy. His trim, muscular build was unusual in an army where generals usually ran to fat. No less recognizable were his scarred face and pale gray eyes. Looking into those eyes brought thoughts of one-way rail passes and Siberian skies. He was a frequent visitor to the offices of the General Staff these days.

Pavlovskiy was ushered into one of the many ornate briefing rooms for his twice-weekly meetings with Col. Gen. P. G. Tolubko. Despite his tank troops insignia, Tolubko was, in fact, the GRU's liaison with the General Staff. He stood at his desk, attired in his sea-green dress uniform, a color that in another time was called czar-green, when Pavlovskiy entered.

Tolubko immediately dropped into the overstuffed, throne-like chair and pointed to another for Pavlovskiy. As he sat down, Tolubko's ever present aide, a rat-faced, anemic little

17

signals major named Tret'yak, hovered about with *zahuski*—
hors d'oeuvres—and vodka. The Colonel General consumed
both in large quantities. Pavlovskiy had often wondered how
much Tret'yak's father, a minor Party official, had paid for
his son's commission.

Tolubko was typically gruff and to the point. "The status
of Summer Harvest, Sergey?"

"All preliminary preparations have been made, Comrade
General. The assembly point for the troops is ready. The
equipment has been collected. The training camp in Nicaragua is completed. The *zamorozhenniye agenty*—frozen
agents—in Texas have been alerted, as has the agent in the
sanctuary movement group. Coordination is completed with
the special operations staff of the Military Transport Aviation
for the movement of the force to Cuba and Nicaragua, as well
as the special aircraft needed for insertion. The preparation
staff is even now conducting rehearsals for briefings and training sessions."

Tolubko, constantly munching on *zahuski*, nodded at each
aspect of the operation. "Tell me again about this sanctuary
movement, Sergey," he said between bites. "I am still confused about its function."

"The sanctuary movement," Pavlovskiy began, "is a pe-
culiarly American phenomenon—"

"One of many!" snorted Tolubko through a mouthful of
vodka, which trickled down the corner of his mouth.

"Yes. The movement was begun by religious groups in 1983
in"—Pavlovskiy paused, consulting his notes—"Arizona. Its
purpose is to aid illegal refugees fleeing from American-backed
imperialist regimes in Central America."

Pavlovskiy searched for a moment for a comparison that
Tolubko could relate to, the concept of illegal immigrants
being unheard of in the Soviet Union.

"These immigrants might be compared to the *zhidy*—dirty
Jews," adding the derogatory connotation he thought appro-
priate, "desiring to leave the Soviet Union for Israel, except
they are driven by poverty to flee oppressive American puppet
regimes to seek work in America under slave labor conditions. The sanctuary movement spread from Arizona to New
Mexico and then to Texas within two years. The head of the
state of New Mexico declared the entire state a sanctuary in

1985. Millions have entered the country. The authorities have done little to stop the flow. The sanctuary movement operates in almost total defiance of the government.

"Can their FBI and border troops do nothing about this?" asked Tolubko skeptically. "It does not seem possible for a government to have so little control over its borders and to permit infiltration by foreigners!"

"The FBI has little actual power in such cases, Comrade General. They may harass their own citizens or place them under surveillance, but they do not possess the protective powers of the KGB—fortunately for us. Additionally, the American Border Patrol is not a military force such as our own KGB Border Troops, but a civilian police force that seeks only to hunt down and return refugees to the poverty of the American satellite regimes."

"Truly a strange country!" remarked the general as another *zahuski* disappeared into his mouth.

"Some of the movement's supporters have been jailed or fined, but such actions have failed to intimidate them. The particular group we selected to infiltrate is the Concerned Citizens for Latin American Peoples. It is based in Austin, the capital of the state of Texas."

"Is this a wise choice, Sergey? Would this particular group not be under closer surveillance being located in a state capital?"

"This is an unusual case, Comrade General. While the citizens of Texas are generally reactionary and militant in political outlook, the state capital is unusually liberal. In fact, the city mayor, a Democrat opposed to Reagan's racist immigration policies, attempted to declare the city a sanctuary in 1986. This effort was suppressed by reactionaries on the city Soviet—oh, what do they call it—city council. Another factor is the presence of the state's largest university, the University of Texas. American university students are traditionally more enlightened to the inevitability of world socialism."

The General only shook his head and drained his glass, which was immediately refilled by his aide.

It's hard to explain the idiosyncrasies of the American sociopolitical system to a man whose whole life has been spent in the most rigid social system in the world, Pavlovskiy thought. I spent nearly five years in New York, and I hardly understand it myself.

Pavlovskiy had worked in one of the Soviet intelligence-gathering front delegations to the United Nations. Social trends in America were impossible to predict. The American military was different. All planned operational, organizational, and equipment developments were well publicized by the news media. The American military called it public relations, the GRU operatives called it prepackaged intelligence reports. Pavlovskiy recalled one operative who hated serving outside the Soviet Union, but hated to leave because the Americans were so accommodating to his work.

"There are other reasons the Austin group was selected, Comrade General," Pavlovskiy continued. "This group is well established and has many contacts which will be beneficial to us. The group has previously assisted Eastern European defectors, from Poland and the German Democratic Republic. They are, as the KGB calls them, very useful fools. And Austin is only one hundred kilometers from Summer Harvest's target, less than one and one half hours' driving time."

"When will Summer Harvest's commander be selected?" asked the General.

"The choice is among three candidates. In two days, the Tasking Committee will conduct the final interviews and make the selection."

"Sergey," the General said emphatically, "we need a killer! Someone who can organize the mission, operate in a strange environment, and ensure that the mission is accomplished—no matter what! Do not let the members of your Tasking Committee pick some politically acceptable model officer or the latest cult hero!"

"You have my assurance we will select the best officer available," Pavlovskiy answered. He knew too well that these committees frequently turned into popularity contests with no regard for the final outcome.

"Tell me the truth, Sergey," the General asked, sitting back, meticulously inspecting a *zahuski*. "Will the Summer Harvest force be ready by mid-December?"

"Comrade General, we are ready now to begin training the attack force. They will have plenty of time for rehearsals and final coordination by December first. They *will* be ready.''

The General drained his glass and turned to his aide. "Major Tret'yak, will you please refill our glasses and leave us?''

Pavlovskiy was surprised by this unusual order. Tolubko's aide was always present, hovering about the General. Looking at his half-empty glass, he realized it was only his second and the General had finished his fourth. Downing the vodka, he offered his glass for refilling. He might need it!

Tolubko stared into his glass for a long moment after the major left. He suddenly presented his glass to Pavlovskiy. "To the Soviet Union!" They clinked glasses and both shot the vodka down in a single swallow.

"Sergey, you have been ordered to plan, organize, and prepare an assault force for a retaliatory action against an American military target, as a response to an expected American provocation. That, however is not the real reason for this—exercise. On December twenty-fifth, the armed forces of the Soviet Union will attack NATO's central front. Operation Summer Harvest will coincide with our offensive in Germany. Its goal is twofold, a diversionary attack to draw interest away from Europe, and the neutralization of one of the largest concentrations of armor in the West.''

Pavlovskiy reached over and refilled both glasses, suppressing a slight smile. He had suspected as much all along. It was the only explanation that made sense.

"You are not surprised, Sergey?''

"Not at all, Comrade General. The Americans have provoked us continuously since the Great Patriotic War, but they have never attacked our homeland, nor we theirs, and for the same reason; such an attack would mean war. We have always attacked their foreign bases in response to provocations, and always with surrogate forces.''

Tolubko smiled and shook his head. "I hope we can fool the Americans better than I have fooled you, my young friend.''

Pavlovskiy leaned forward. "Permit me two questions, General. How *will* we fool the Americans? Surely they will notice our preparations and be on guard for an attack such as Summer Harvest.''

Trust our masking and disinformation efforts, Sergey, both

political and military. We have already announced our annual Winter Shield training exercise for January in East Germany. Our buildup of equipment and our movement of combat units will appear to be for this exercise. We have already begun slowly adding to our war stockage. By December, we will have a sixty-day stock. What is your second question?''

"Can a handful of raiders neutralize an entire corps of armor?''

"That is for you to make certain, Sergey! You have studied Ft. Hood. You know the plan. You tell me.''

"I meant, sir, what about the pre-positioned equipment the Americans already have in Europe? The Americans need only to get the III Corps troops to Europe, draw this equipment, and deploy into battle.''

"This is true, my friend, but this equipment will be rendered useless by air attacks from the 16th Air Army, SS-22 missiles dumping persistent nerve agents, and *reydoviki*, raiders, of your GRU 5th Directorate. The attack on Ft. Hood will destroy much replacement equipment needed for a prolonged fight.''

"I see, Comrade General,'' Pavlovskiy said carefully. "Thank you for sharing the information with me. It will help me make the right selection for Summer Harvest's leader.''

"You will report back to me when the commander has been selected. I want very much to meet this young killer, Sergey.''

As his car left the Kremlin gates, Pavlovskiy thought of a film he had seen in the United States, a film about the Japanese attack on Pearl Harbor. A phrase used by the Japanese commander had stuck with him and now it had a more personal meaning: "We have raised a sleeping giant and filled him with a terrible resolve.'' The American giant was no longer even sleeping.

★3★

16 September

Jenkins! Get in here!

"K-Y time," Jinx said, smiling at Nancy, the boss's secretary. Jinx straightened his gig line, and opened the door to Col. Joseph A. B. (Jab) Donlon's office.

Donlon sat slumped at his desk, his face resting in his hands. Several newspapers from Central America and the U.S. were spread out in front of him. Each had a story and photos of a burned school bus and the bodies of little dead girls.

"This is charming, Jenkins, just fuckin' charming," Donlon began, the sarcasm in his voice too thick to cut. "Please don't try to tell me what it's about, 'cause I don't really care. What matters is that the Goddamn Sandinistas are having a field day in the press showing dead schoolgirls and pinning it on your merry band of Indians."

"Now, of course, I'm getting phone calls from the Agency, the DIA, the State Department, the White House, and," Donlon added, his voice rising in both pitch and volume, "from a whole bunch of foreign people I haven't ever even heard of!"

Donlon was on his feet now, and once again, Jinx was struck by how much the man looked like a Maytag washer with a head on it. Although only five feet five inches tall, Jab Donlon was an imposing character. Angry and red-faced like this, he looked like a nuclear reactor about to melt down.

Donlon swore loudly and often that he would trade his

eagles to quit this assignment and return to his first love,
Armor. His office decor looked like a museum at Ft. Knox.
Tank rounds of polished oak flanked his desk. His paper-
weight was a metal model of an M1A1 Abrams tank. Smiling
tankers behind turret-mounted .50s looked down from a dozen
photos on the paneled wall behind the desk. You could almost
smell diesel fumes in the room. Donlon hated the shadow
world of unconventional warfare, and mistrusted the people
in it.

"So, having had the entire ass burned out of my Nomex
underwear, I'm now going to clog-dance on you. What in the
name of God *happened* out there? Where were *you*? What
are you doing to *do* about it?

Donlon perched on the corner of his desk, playing with
the metal tank model. Jinx knew that the only way to handle
the old man when he was like this was bend over and take it
like a man.

"Sir, to answer your questions in order: a trap; right there
where it happened; and get the East German bastard who set
up those poor little girls."

"That's it? Pay back some fucking Kraut? Captain, do I
need to send you over to the medics so they can install a glass
navel in you, so you can see out with your head so far up
your ass? Jesus, man, you were in 'Nam. Didn't you learn
anything there?"

Learn anything in 'Nam? Jinx thought. Oh, yes, he had
learned a lot in 'Nam. Things this miniature martinet would
never understand.

"Jenkins, no one expects this type of war to be pretty, but
do you remember when those four nuns got killed in Salvador
a few years ago? All hell broke loose over that, and compared
to the coverage these schoolgirls are getting, those nuns look
like mercy killings! I swear," he went on, picking up a paper
as he walked back around his desk, "these journalist types
who come down here from the States are just like hemor-
rhoids; when they come down and go back up, its irritating
enough, but when they come down and stay down, they're a
real pain in the ass!"

Donlon dropped into his chair and began unwrapping a
small, ugly black cigar.

"Sir, I—"

"Jinx, ordinarily I would have your ass on the first thing smoking north this afternoon. I need this kind of trouble like Custer needed more Indians. Unfortunately, I need your services with the Misura a little longer," Donlon went on, as he patiently lit the cigar and puffed at it until the tip glowed.

"It wasn't the Misura's fault, sir—"

"Spare me, Jinx, I've read your report. If I could ship you out of here tonight, I would, but I need somebody who knows those Indians for a special little job."

The words "special little job" gave Jinx a queasy feeling in the pit of his stomach. When Jab Donlon referred to something as special or fun or easy, it meant you could count on heavy losses, extreme discomfort, or a body bag.

"For the last two months," Donlon began, his color returning to normal, "we have been getting satellite pictures of a camp under construction in your area of operations. Human resource reports indicate the camp is to be used for some special training, not for Sandinista troops, but for foreigners. Security for the camp is in place, and it's all Soviet. That camp is your road to atonement, soldier. If you can find out what they are doing in there, it might make up for this schoolgirl business."

"When does the operation kick off, sir?"

"When the spooks learn a little more about the place; a couple of weeks, maybe."

"What should I do until then?"

"Go back to your Misura camp, keep a low profile, and stay away from TV cameras."

"With all due respect, sir, what are you going to do about this propaganda mess?"

"Just what the paramilitary section motto says: *'Admit Nothing, Deny Everything, and Make Counteraccusations.'* "

★4★

17 September

The hunter crept. As silently as a gray wolf, he slid across the stones. Tentacles of mist writhed around his legs. His gray clothing, like the wolf's coat, faded from sight as the night fog swirled around him.

Minutes passed before he reappeared in the distance. He crouched in the misty darkness and beckoned with his arm. Others of his kind flowed down the sides of the ravine before disappearing into the gloom on the far side.

The watcher of these eerie movements rose from the ground and motioned his followers forward. The ambush site had been selected at dusk. Every *ikhotniki*, hunter, of Group 24, 2nd Company, 38th Independent Spetsnaz Brigade, had been thoroughly briefed and rehearsed. They knew where to be and what to do.

Maj. Aleksei Bodnya, commander of the brigade's 1st Battalion, led his small support *podrazdeleniye* (subunit) across the ravine and into position. Silently placing the RPG-16 rocket launcher and the RPO-A flame thrower teams, he watched the new group commander, Lieutenant Kuznetsov, moving along the positions. Only two weeks in Afghanistan, and fresh out of the Carpathian Military District's Spetsnaz training program, he was already gaining acceptance from the cynical veterans of Group 24. The men had even given him a nickname, a good sign. They called the young lieutenant *Kuznyets*—(Blacksmith)—a takeoff on his name and a fair description of his size and manner. The hunters of Group 24

26

liked a strong leader. The Blacksmith's predecessor, *Kroko-dil*, had been very strong, often as brutal to his own men as to the bandits in these mountains. The Blacksmith was easier on the men; tonight Bodnya would see if he was any easier on the Basmachi vermin.

Aleksei Bodnya was there tonight to watch the Blacksmith and Group 24 in action. Every man in the unit knew it, and none was more nervous than the Blacksmith himself.

Let him squirm, thought Bodnya. This operation certainly places him under pressure, but that won't hurt. We must see how he performs on the hunt. Bodnya had suggested that he command the support subunit so he would not just be extra baggage. He already felt the cold through the grip of his AKSU submachine gun.

Bodnya's mind wandered aimlessly as the night dragged on. He was jolted back to the present by every shiver that shook his body.

At least none of the men will doze off, he thought. Lying on these frozen stones will prevent that. In milder weather, it was always a problem. He shivered again.

Maybe it hadn't been such a good idea to come on this particular operation. His deputy could have done it just as well. Nonsense, he thought, I am a Spetsnaz commander. I expect my men to do this often. I must set an example and suffer their hardships with them. Another shiver rattled his teeth.

On the other hand, I have fought alongside these men in these same mountain passes during our sweeps and raids. They have seen my valor. The deputy could have done an excellent job of checking out the new lieutenant. Another shiver.

Hell, he thought finally, I'm here now and I must stick it out. These young hunters are certainly quiet. Maybe they can sleep under these conditions. A glance at his East German watch showed that only eight minutes had passed since he had last checked it. It seemed like hours.

An icy dagger drove through Bodnya's spine and he was instantly awake. Bone shaking shivers racked him. Will I ever stop shaking? he wondered. Will I ever be warm again?

I should have observed the Blacksmith on a more active

operation. Most ambushes only result in a miserable night and nothing more. The shivering continued.

Another icy dagger drove in him, this time through his heart. A small clicking of pebbles came from the far right. Another small shower of pebbles followed, then a faint crunch of stones. His heart pounded, the cold forgotten. No matter how often he did this, it was always the same. A rush of adrenaline and a pounding in the ears.

More soft crunching of stones and the rustle of clothing. A muffled cough. A brief clatter of stones that sounded as if someone had stumbled. The stumbling sound seemed a signal for the hunters to pounce. Almost as one, two dozen automatic weapons spewed yellow-white flames. Scores of red tracers streamed into the ravine, ricocheting in all directions. The blaze of continuous muzzle flashes illuminated a scene of jumbled, crisscrossing shadows. White-sparking flashes from RGO and BG-15 fragmentation grenades cracked, sending their splinters whining through the ravine. Totally blinded by muzzle and grenade flashes, no one could see anything. They fired until their weapons emptied, reloaded, and kept firing.

Shots!

Raz froze in his tracks, afraid to even breathe. In the cold night air, the gunfire echoed across the ridgeline, sounding much closer than it was. Around him, the older Mujhadeen silently spread out along the ridge to determine the source of the shots. Behind him, his old friend Hamed leaned forward to whisper.

"Ambush, probably one of their hunter teams of black soldiers—commandos."

"Who could have known?"

"They don't know," Hamed whispered, "they simply hunt for Mujhadeen in the mountain passes the way wolves hunt for rabbits."

"What will we do now?" Raz asked softly.

"Now we hunt for them the way the men of Faizabad have always hunted for wolves!"

Raz couldn't imagine how they could hunt for anything in the pitch black night, much less for the hated Russians.

"How can we hunt them? They always come in tanks or in the tank-that-flies."

"The black soldiers move as we do, with only rifles and grenades. They can be killed," Hamad hissed. "Damn their infidel hides."

A motion from ahead signaled that the way was clear, and the Mujhadeen column once again made its way silently down the tiny trail. Hamad lifted the heavy American-made anti-aircraft missile onto his shoulder as if it were a feather. "Stinger" they had called it at the base in Pakistan, like the stinger in a scorpion's tail. The men who had trained Raz and Hamad had been Afghans, but their strange accents had sounded more like white men than true believers. For all that, the missile was a gift from Allah. Raz hoped the two of them would soon get to use the missile to send some of the accursed Russians to the hell that awaited infidel scum.

It was over in less than twenty seconds. The RPKS-74 machine gunners on the flanks hammered their last rounds into the ravine. More grenades were hurled in, their sharp cracks the last sounds of combat. The clatter of magazines being changed, coughs, and a few muttered words, then all was silence again. There was some muffled scuffling as the Blacksmith shifted some of the killer subunit to protect the group's flanks, in case there were more bandits. There was no sweep of the kill zone, and no hasty withdrawal. The chances of another bandit gang braving a fire fight in the darkness were slim. It was possible to bag a few more of the pests if they attempted to pull their dead and wounded out of the ravine. Bodnya knew the hunters were scanning the kill zone with NSP-2 infrared sights, and PNY-57 night vision binoculars. One of their rifles cracked, doubtless dispatching some wounded Afghan. Bodnya and the rest of the support subunit resettled themselves to await dawn and a detailed search of the kill zone. The Blacksmith had maintained control, and everything had gone as planned. Daylight would show how well the young leader handled the results of his night's work, and would provide the answers for which Bodnya had suffered through a long, freezing night.

Dawn comes late in the mountains. The pale, washed-out sun reflected off the gray overcast. The weak rays of sunlight held no warmth. The gray peaks, gray clouds, gray rocks and gray mist made this the most depressing place on earth for Aleksei Bodnya. No sunlight fell yet on the deep shadows in their little mountain pass. The kill zone was silent. No sound had emerged since the ambush. Now, Blacksmith, thought Bodnya, we shall see how black your heart really is.

Through bleary eyes, Bodnya watched the lean form of Ensign Kovpak move from his boulder pile toward the Blacksmith. Reluctantly, Bodnya forced himself to his feet with aching joints and a passing wave of nausea, the result of an empty stomach and a cold night. Nodding toward a senior private rifleman, he muttered, "Take command of this subunit, *ikhotniki.*"

"It is done, Comrade Major."

Ensign Kovpak was standing to the rear of the command position, as the Blacksmith went from man to man, designating the ones to take part in the sweep. The small Ukrainian flashed a small grin from under his large, bushy mustache. "How do we feel this fine morning, Comrade Major?"

"Like a bucket of shit thrown on a turnip patch."

"Ahhh," smiled the little Ukrainian, "has the leader of the pack lost his enthusiasm for the hunt?"

"Answer this question," Kovpak said, starting their old game. "What two things do you desire most at this moment?"

Rubbing the stubble on his chin, Bodnya absently replied, "A hot glass of tea and a toothbrush."

"No, Comrade Major, no!" It should have been a bottle of vodka and a woman! You disgrace the Spetsnaz, Comrade Major."

"How about just the vodka and a toothbrush?"

"In view of your advanced age, Comrade Major, it is well enough! Today, I can agree with you. I myself do not feel as elite as I once did."

Kovpak had started the "what two things do you desire most" game when they had served together in the Democratic Republic of Germany and later in the Belorussian Military District. Those days seemed a lifetime ago.

"Maybe you have been out here with the young wolves too long yourself, Pavel," Bodnya said as a group of hunters moved forward from their positions toward the still-silent kill zone. "You know that I am slated to become brigade chief of staff next month when old 'Blockhouse' returns to the *Rodina*. I will need a new chief of operations for the 1st staff section. You are well suited for the job."

"I am honored by your trust in my ability, Comrade Major, but I must weigh the advantages of my own advancement with the needs of the 2nd Company," Kovpak responded with the standard Soviet Army reply. His tone made it clear that he would accept.

"Very well, Ensign, I am pleased to accept you as my new chief of operations."

"How soon may I pack, Comrade Major?"

"The instant my 'orderly' finishes packing my bags, I will send him for yours. I thought you might have had enough of fighting these Basmachi. Two tours are enough for anyone. Let the young wolves have the hunts, you and I will plan them. Here comes Kuznetsov, let us see how he handles the realities of Soviet aid to Afghanistan's revolutionary government."

Lieutenant Kuznetsov lumbered up to the two men. A huge man, his AKSU submachine gun looked like a child's toy in his hands. His simple peasant face belied his intelligence. For a junior officer, he was extremely well read.

"Comrade Major, I have sent a detail to search the ravine, and covered the ends of it with machine guns. There appear to be fifteen bodies there. Do you wish to inspect it yourself?"

"Thank you for the invitation, Comrade Lieutenant, but the Ensign will accompany you. I will remain here by the radio in case another group calls for assistance."

"Very well, Comrade Major."

In reality, Bodnya had no desire this early in the morning to examine the contents of stomachs and the other gruesome wounds caused by 5.45mm bullets. The tiny slugs had an airspace at the tip backed by a lead plug and a steel core to improve penetration in hard targets. When it struck a soft target like flesh, the tip mushroomed sending the bullet on an erratic path that caused terrific damage. The resulting wounds looked like those produced by the soft-tipped hunting bullets prohibited by the Geneva Convention, but that prohibition was of little concern here in reporter-free Afghanistan.

The Blacksmith hesitated a moment.

The lad is probably hoping for a word of praise, thought Bodnya. A little at this point would not hurt. He deserved it and confidence building is good early in the hunt. Bodnya knew that there would be many opportunities for that confidence to be shaken in the future.

As the Blacksmith turned to leave, Bodnya said, "Lieutenant, I admired the ability of your group to maintain noise discipline and the simultaneous manner in which they opened fire on the bandit gang. I am certain that surprise was complete, and none of the bandits escaped. Give your hunters my congratulations. The efficient way you redeployed the men to protect your flanks after the ambush is to be commended as well."

"I serve the Soviet Union!"

Bodnya caught a quick wink from Kovpak as he turned to follow the group commander.

Minutes later, the riflemen began to drag the Basmachi bodies out of the ravine and place them faceup, head to toe on the rocky trail.

"Hunters displaying their kill," thought Bodnya, "and providing a warning to others of their kind."

Kovpak and Kuznetsov returned, the Lieutenant a little wide-eyed.

"Comrade Major, there are sixteen bodies, but they are not all bandits. There were only four fighters. The rest were civilians."

"How many civilians, Lieutenant Kuznetsov?" Bodnya asked idly. "What were their ages and sex? How many weapons were taken?"

"There were six women, four men and four youths—boys! The fighters, all young men, were armed with AK-47s, an SKS, and two bolt-action rifles, British, I believe. They had very little ammunition."

"The civilian men, were they old?"

"Yes, Comrade Major. I had no idea. The circumstances of this mistake will be in my report!"

"Did they have any documents, maps, anything of that nature?"

"No, Comrade Major. We went through all their clothing and belongings. There was nothing of military value. I feel badly about making such a mistake on my first operation! They must have been refugees trying to escape to Pakistan.''

"Kuznetsov, there are no refugees in this war. Only bandits and *Basmachi*. What did you expect, a uniformed platoon armed with modern weapons reinforcing those bandits harassing our belated return to this shit hole of a country? Those vermin you eliminated *are* the enemy. They resist the lawful government of this state and the aid offered by the Soviet Union. You have heard the stories of how they treat brave Soviet soldiers who have fallen into their hands. Remember those stories and you will find the right words for your report.''

For a moment, Kuznetsov looked confused, then a sudden look of comprehension came over him, a look of relief that his first mission would not end in failure.

The lieutenant stood up straight, squared his shoulders, and replied in a firm, strong voice. "Comrade Major, we have killed sixteen bandits and captured four weapons!''

"Very good, Lieutenant. Now I think the men would like a hot meal back at the base.''

"I will form them up immediately! Ensign Kovpak, bring in the sentries. We march for the helicopter pickup zone in five minutes!''

As the lieutenant began to assemble the subunits, Kovpak, before turning away, gave Bodnya another wink and a large grin. That was all he needed to know that the Blacksmith had conducted himself properly before the men in the ravine, and did not become too excited over the results of his workmanship. He had paid attention to the details, as well: age groups, sex, weapons, and so on. You may do all right, here, Lieutenant, Bodnya thought. Welcome to Afghanistan, and the Limited Contingent of Soviet Forces. In a couple of hours, I can have my toothbrush and hot tea. Screw the vodka.

As the hunters moved out to the pickup zone, Bodnya watched as the Blacksmith moved the men with confidence. The successful ambush had filled the man with self-confidence, and reassured his men as well.

You learned much from this first victory, young *ikhotniki*, Bodnya thought as he slung his AKSU, you will learn more from your first defeat—if the bandits permit you to survive it.

* * *

Raz's breath made large steam clouds in the weak morning sun.

I look just like Kasim's old horse when he used to pull the wagon into the village, he thought as he slumped against the cold rocks. He smiled as he remembered the huge old horse snorting huge blasts of steam as he trudged along the road that ran through Faizabad, and of the good times he had watching the men and women (especially the women!) haggle with the trader. The smile faded when he remembered the last time he had seen Kasim's wagon. He had hardly recognized it, so thoroughly had it been burned, with the trader inside and his old horse, still in the traces, lying scorched and dead next to it. Russian bastards!

The climb up the last ridge had been almost straight up through cracks that were barely large enough for a man to slip through. The way was hard, but it made it almost impossible for the enemy to see them moving up the ridge, even from the air. As Raz sat catching his breath, Hamed slowly climbed the rocks to look out over the ridge. He had hardly reached the top when he slid quickly back down, almost landing on Raz's upturned face.

"Come little one, Allah has sent us some Russians to kill!" Hamad said, laughing, as he grabbed up the missile and plowed his way up the trail.

The landing zone was a flat spot between two small ridges. The Blacksmith sent one subunit ahead to secure the ridge line before moving the rest of the group into the open area.

Once the entire group was in place, the lieutenant and Ensign Kovpak made contact with the helicopters circling high over a valley several kilometers away. In minutes, a huge Mi-24 Hind gunship, bristling with weapons, swept over the landing zone, followed by two Mi-8 Hip transport helicopters.

The sound of helicopters suddenly filled the air, and Raz's heart almost stopped until Hamad growled. "Come little warrior. Hurry."

Panting, Raz followed Hamad up the trail, then down another shallower crack in the rocks. The crack was only about a meter deep, and both Mujhadeen were soon crawling on hands and knees to keep below the edge. When they had gone about thirty meters, Hamad slowly laid the missile down and pulled Raz closer.

"Look! Three birds for the taking!" Hamad smiled wolfishly, "*Inshallah*, we will take one this morning!"

Raz eased his head up over the edge, fully expecting a bullet to take off the top of his head. Below the ridge, a large Russian helicopter was landing in a small flat area. Two more helicopters, one a gun ship, circled the ridge. Men were running toward the helicopter—the hunters from the night before! Raz quickly dropped behind the rocks. He could not understand how the Russians did not see him.

Here was their chance to shoot down a Russian helicopter, the chance he had dreamed of. Still, it seemed like he was watching two other people prepare the missile for firing. Hamad was praying as he worked, asking Allah to steady his hand and sharpen his eye that he might rid Afghanistan of more of the infidel invaders.

As the first transport flared out for a landing, one subunit ran for its clamshell doors, the others maintaining a watch for uninvited *Basmachi* guests. As the first Hip took off, the second came in to pick up the remaining Spetsnaz. The pickup had gone as smoothly as a training exercise.

As the second helicopter lifted off, Hamad made one more quick check and said, "Ready!"

The helicopters banked as they lifted off, heading directly toward Raz and Hamad, who crouched now, waiting for a target to come overhead. Suddenly, noise and a large shadow swept over them and Hamad was on his feet, sighting through the glass and shouting, "Die now!"

Bodnya moved forward through the crew door to speak to the pilots. As he entered the forward cabin, the helicopter pitched violently to the left, then to the right, dropping sharply.

Caught by surprise, Bodnya hit his head on the bulkhead as he fought for balance. The pilot was pointing at a ridge ahead to the right where tracers, both red and green, were arching toward the Mi-24 gun ship.

The Hind was already banking sharply to the right, its rotary gun raking the ridge, covering the transports.

As the first Hip cleared the ridge, a pair of bandits, apart from the others, stood up out of an almost invisible crack in the rocks. They hefted a long, thin tube onto one's shoulder. As the two square metal ears popped out on the front of the tube, Bodnya recognized the weapon—a Stinger missile!

When Hamad pulled the trigger, nothing happened and Raz's heart sank. A second later, the missile exploded out of the tube, just like it was supposed to. By the time the smoke and dust cleared enough to see, it was halfway to the first helicopter. The awkward-looking craft was turning and twisting, but the little missile was like a falcon after a pigeon. It struck the Russian bird, which exploded in a huge ball of fire.

"Allahu Akbar!" screamed Hamad, still holding the empty launcher on his shoulder. As Hamad screamed, so did Raz. Coming down the ridge was the tank-that-flies. There was no place to run. Already, the huge helicopter's gun was raking the rocks, looking for Mujhadeen.

Hamad saw the Hind, and with a look of hatred and triumph, shook the empty launcher at the infidel machine that would take his life and the life of the boy.

"Come, Raz," yelled Hamad as the green fireballs walked across the rocks toward them, "we go to join the holy martyrs! Allahu Akhbar! Allahu Akhbar!"

Raz joined in the chant: "Allahu Akhbar! Allahu Akhb—"

His helicopter was almost directly over the two bandits when the missile leaped out of its launch tube and streaked for the lead Hip. The Hip's pilot was diving into the next valley, twisting his ship as hard as it would go in an attempt to shake the missile.

It took seven endless seconds for the Stinger to catch the hapless Hip. The missile hit just below the right engine, over the fuel storage. The small puff of black smoke from the missile's warhead was followed a split second later by a huge fireball as the helicopter's kerosene fuel detonated.

Straining to keep sight of the falling Hip, Bodnya could not see the two bandits on the ridge, cheering as the missile went home. He did not see their look of triumph as they held the empty launcher over their heads and screamed their defiance at the gunship which swept down the ridge, tearing their bodies to bits with a dozen rounds from its 12.7mm rotary gun.

All he could see was half of Group 24 dying in a whirling, falling inferno. His ship flashed overhead as the dead Hip smashed into the rocks below. "Damn the bandits," Bodnya cursed as he craned his head to watch the downed Hip, "and Damn the American gangsters who gave them the missiles!"

There would be no survivors. Even if someone lived through the crash, the *Basmachi* did not take Spetsnaz prisoners.

★5★

18 September

Aleksei Bodnya slowly made his way across Kandahar's muddy parade field toward the headquarters of the 38th Spetsnaz Brigade. "No sense rushing to your doom," he reasoned.

He passed a row of T-55 tanks belonging to the Afghan Army's 7th Armored Brigade. A young Soviet lieutenant was loudly haranguing an Afghan *Dreyom Baridman*—a junior lieutenant. The Pashto-speaking Pathan probably could not understand a word the Soviet lieutenant was saying.

The Afghan Army was almost a joke. On the eve of the 1979 Soviet intervention, the DRA Army's effective strength was about eighty thousand. A year later, casualties and desertions had cut it to twenty thousand. Some said the desertion rate was ten thousand per year. Total strength was now about thirty five thousand, but most units were just shells. The 7th Armored Brigade was in reality a large battalion, and the 15th DRA Infantry Division, also at Kandahar, numbered only two thousand men. A Soviet division had over thirteen thousand men.

The Soviets used the DRA troops to bear the brunt of the fighting while Soviet units held overwatch or blocking positions to prevent desertions and minimize their own casualties. This sorry Afghan officer was probably one of the many illiterate *badmashes*—punks—attracted by the relatively high pay.

Bodnya approached the grubby concrete building housing the 38th Spetsnaz headquarters with a deep sense of gloom. At the entrance, the *yefretor*—senior private guard from the 70th Independent Motorized Rifle Brigade snapped to attention. Most of the motorized Riflemen were nothing more than cannon fodder, known in the Soviet Army as *churka* (worthless woodchips), but at least this one looked well turned out. As he entered, Bodnya managed a smart return salute; one never knew who might be looking out the window.

"Maj. Aleksei Bodnya reporting to the Brigade Commander as ordered," Bodnya said as he stepped up to the duty officer's desk.

"The Commander is expecting you, Major," replied Captain Altunin, one of the brigade staff officers. Lowering his voice, Altunin asked softly, "What the hell happened out there? The Commander is chewing dirt!"

"I lost a bird to some Basmachi this morning, Genka, no survivors. Half of one of my groups, including Kuznetsov, was killed by two *chernozhoph* (black asses) and a damned American rocket."

"I'm sorry, Aleksei. No wonder the Elephant is trumpeting so loud this morning. Good luck, my friend."

"If he's not bellowing my name in the same sentence with 'firing squad,' maybe I'll live!"

To be standing before Col. G. K. Zinchenko's desk was not an enviable position. The office itself was forbidding enough. The ill-lit room was more of a cell. The gray-white walls were unadorned, except for an issue graphic of V. I. Lenin. The desk was almost bare. On it an ancient green-shaded lamp cast a pale yellow glow on the papers Zinchenko held in his large hands. Also on the desk were an old-style pen holder, a leather-bound notebook, and an American M6 bayonet letter opener, the latter item from the Colonel's days as an advisor to the People's Republic of Vietnam. It was the only memento of his career. The office was devoid of anything that even hinted of careerism or personality.

For a routine visit, the Elephant was quick to offer even a subordinate a chair. For more serious discussions, the victim remained standing. He kept Bodnya at attention as he studied the papers, but finally looked up and rumbled, "Sit down, Major. Make yourself comfortable." The straight-backed wooden chair made any comfort seem unlikely.

"What happened, Major?"

Bodnya quickly related the events leading up to the loss of

the helicopter, with special detail given to the *Basmachi* attack and the Stinger missile.

"I was afraid of that," replied the Colonel, "the shitballs get better every day with their advanced weapons. The loss of sixteen good *ikhotniki* is unfortunate. This brigade has not suffered such a loss in over a year. The loss of young Kuznetsov is unfortunate, too. How was he looking?"

"He had the makings of a good Spetsnaz officer, Comrade Colonel. He performed well and the men seemed to take to him."

"Maybe I'm getting old and hard to please, Bodnya, but it seems that good junior officers are getting scarce. Most of these young hunters seem to be here only to get their three-for-one service credit."

Bodnya was confused at the Colonel's cordiality and lack of apparent anger, but was in no mood to rock the boat.

"The Colonel must remember it has been a long struggle," replied Bodnya. "Twelve years is a long time to subdue counterrevolutionaries. Since we can kill them faster than they can grow them, our success is assured, but it has been a long struggle. Also, with the *Rodina* so near, the contrast is difficult for any young soldier."

"Perhaps you are right, Bodnya," sighed the Colonel, "How many times have you served here?"

"I have served the *Rodina* on three tours, Comrade Colonel."

"And I have served on five. I hope the end is in sight. We have learned much and perfected our special skills, but we have other enemies with which to concern ourselves. I am convinced that even in these days of computers, electronic combat, and weapons of mass destruction, that our special skills will be crucial to the future success of our armies."

"Exactly so, Comrade Colonel," Bodnya replied formally, his anxiety growing as he waited for the Colonel to get to the point. "I hope to be in the forefront of any such action."

"I am certain you will, Bodnya. The reason I called you here is to inform you that you have been ordered to report to 40th Army Main Headquarters immediately. It appears that your special skills are needed elsewhere. I personally regret this reassignment, as I had some plans for you myself. Report to the Personnel Section for your orders. I wish you the best of luck, Major. It has been an honor to serve with you."

Bodnya stood and saluted. "I serve the Soviet Union!"

* * *

An even more confused Bodnya made his way across the parade field. Three months yet to go on this tour and he was being reassigned. Most unusual! At least he had not gotten the reaming he had expected. The Colonel had been quite complimentary. Very unusual, indeed!

The reassignment obviously had nothing to do with the morning's disaster. The orders had been waiting for him. What else? He searched his mind for any error or indiscretion on his part. He knew well that officers were often dismissed by the *zampol-its*—political officers—or by the KGB officers of the Brigade's Special Section for reasons based only on hearsay, speculation, or jealousy. It could even be trouble with a family member. Possibly his asshole brother. He frequently was in trouble with the Militia since he had managed to wrangle a Moscow resident card. Probably selling Soviet Army belt buckles to western tourists again! That kind of family nonsense could land you an assignment staring at *kosoglazyi*—slant-eyes—across the Chinese border. He waited for the T-55s to pass, eager to get back to his quarters so he could read the orders. He had not looked at them when they were presented. It never paid to appear anxious. He had been told to pack with haste; he was to take the afternoon flight to Kabul.

Ensign Kovpak was walking down the hall of the officers' quarters, a remarkable coincidence, when Bodnya entered. He asked no questions, but his querying expression was enough.

"I have been reassigned, my friend," Bodnya said quietly. "I have orders to report to 40th Army Main Headquarters. I report this afternoon."

"Because some *Basmachi* shit used a rocket on one of our ships?" replied Kovpak, clearly agitated. "This cannot be, Major, there was no way for you to prevent it!"

"I am not worried," Bodnya lied, "The Elephant was not even angry. He merely said I was needed elsewhere. He did not say it was not about this morning, but I doubt it. I will write you from my new assignment, and if possible, get you out of this shithole. Right now I must pack and be on my way."

★6★

11 October

Well, there was a God after all. A week after the massacre, a fortuitous Washington scandal involving a prospective congressional candidate from Utah, two showgirls, some cocaine, and a playroom done up in early leather had focused attention away from Central America. Photos of the two showgirls, nicknamed The Grand Tetons, had replaced the photos of schoolgirls in the newspapers. With the heat off, Jinx could get back to work.

He needed to do two things. He needed to dig out his spy and he needed to get his troops in the field again and win one. The Indians were still depressed about the ambush and it was all Jinx and the Indian commanders could do to keep morale up. They needed another mission, something to think about. There was no point in planning anything until he flushed the spy, though. They had barely escaped a trap last time. This time they might not be so lucky.

Sitting on the bank of the creek that formed one side of the camp, Jinx began a list of suspects. His reverie was broken by a shout. It was Pablo calling from the perimeter wire.

"Radio message, señor. Mocoron calling."

In the radio shack, Louisa, the radio operator, handed Jinx the handset from the large military radio.

"Jenkins here, over."

"Jinx, Donlon here, I need you and your number two here tomorrow morning, 0930. Over."

"Roger that, sir, 0930. What's up? Over"

42

"You'll find out at 0930. Understood? Donlon out."

The connection went dead. What the hell, Jinx thought as he handed the handset back to Louisa and left the commo shack, we need some action to liven up this place anyway.

"Pablo, we're going visiting mañana, to Mocoron."

Mocoron, 12 October

Mocoron, the home of the Honduran 6th Infantry Battalion, was three hours down a ruined dirt road that ran along the southern Honduran border. Along the way, there were dozens of bunkers, concealed fighting positions, and command posts, all facing Nicaragua. Not all the positions were manned, but all were kept up and ready to use if the Nicaraguans made another of their frequent border incursions.

The Pumas of the 6th Battalion were the Honduran Rangers—elite, high-spirited troops stationed far from the bulk of the Honduran Army, far from the political intrigue of the capital, and far from any reinforcements if the shit hit the fan.

Their base was all modern prefab concrete buildings. The streets were paved and well kept. The troops ran in formation wherever they went and their military courtesy was excellent. Jinx always felt like a poor relation when he went to the base, and his own camp always looked like a pigsty when he returned.

The Honduran gate guard was expecting them, and ten minutes later, he and Pablo were seated in the briefing room of the Puma's military intelligence section.

Already seated were Lieutenant Colonel Gravas, head of the Honduran MI section, Colonel Aguirre, the base commander, Jab Donlon, and two other Americans.

One of the Americans was Pete Jackson, an old Agency hand that Jinx had known for years. The other was a stranger.

"Take your seats, gentlemen. I am Mr. Russell," the stranger began, "and this is Mr. Jackson. We're here to show you some pictures."

Russell untied a large folder on the desk and removed sixteen-by-twenty-inch black-and-white photographs, each covered with a red-bordered SECRET cover.

44   James B. Adair and Gordon Rottman

Folding back the cover sheets, Russell lined the photos up on the chalk tray of the blackboard that covered one wall of the briefing room. Jackson took five file folders from his briefcase and gave one to each person.

"For several weeks, we have been observing the construction of a camp in Zelaya Province," Russell continued, taking a telescoping pointer from his shirt pocket and extending it full length. "We became interested in this camp when it did not conform to standard Nicaraguan or Warsaw Pact layout, and especially interested when the tarps appeared."

Russell snapped the pointer on the first photo, which showed the camp in its beginning, mostly scraped-off roads and tents. The second photo showed the camp more complete, with no tents, several wooden structures, and large areas covered by canvas tarps. Russell snapped the pointer on each one for emphasis.

"Obviously, the tarps are to keep us from taking satellite and aerial photos during the day," Pete Jackson took up the briefing, "so we have stepped up our night observation by infrared. These infrared shots show shapes beneath the canvas, but we cannot identify the shapes. We can identify an increase in human activity around these shapes at night."

The infrared photos looked like Rorschach tests to Jinx; he couldn't make anything out of them. God knew what they looked like to Pablo.

"It is our supposition that the people working around these areas at night are not out during the day. The daylight photos show minimal activity in the camp," Russell went on, snapping the pointer around each photo and making Jinx wish the man had his pointer somewhere the sun couldn't shine on it.

"About all we can see during the day are perimeter guards, and they appear to be Soviets, not Nicaraguans."

"So much for the Monroe Doctrine," remarked Jinx. This was rewarded by a glare from just about every other American in the room.

"Obviously, we can't draw any conclusions from the information we have. That's where you come in, Mr. Jenkins. We want your native troops to scope out this place, see what they are up to, and if possible, put them out of business."

"Let's not be so formal, gentlemen," Jinx said, bristling. "You can call me Jinx. You can call *Teniente* Lockwood here

Pablo, and if you promise not to call his Misuras 'native troops' again, he won't call you assholes!''

"Jinx!" Donlon snapped before Jinx could put his foot in it any farther.

"Sorry, sir," Jinx said in a humble tone that belied the angry look on his face. "I just don't like the term 'native troops,' especially when someone wants them to do the dirty work."

"Your objection is well taken, Jinx," Jackson said, smiling. "The last thing we want to do is offend the Misura freedom fighters. I'm sure Mr. Russell was only speaking in the generic sense. He hasn't been down here long enough to appreciate the Misura's sacrifices and courage." Jackson ended with a look of warning to Russell.

"Yes, well, where were we?" Russell went on, slightly flushed. "What we have in mind is a raid on this camp to identify the nature of the covered objects, and to disrupt or destroy the activity there."

"That's where the Misura come in," Jackson said. "They can run combat operations in the area without arousing the press or the overwatch committees."

"Likewise, if they die, no one in the U.S. will get too excited," Jinx couldn't help but interject.

"Exactly!" Russell agreed, missing the sarcasm and apparently delighted that Jinx seemed to grasp the concept.

This man is Zen-like in the purity of his obnoxiousness, Jinx thought as the two Agency men rambled on about the nuts and bolts of the raid. It was hard enough to handle a guy like Donlon, much less an Ivy League dickhead like Russell. He forced himself to pay attention, since they were talking to him.

"Can your people handle a raid of this importance, Mr. Jenkins?" Russell was asking.

"Not as well as a SEAL team," Jinx said as casually as he could. "Why don't you let the pros from Coronado handle it? You could even go to Sears and get them some of these snappy suits like the Misura wear."

"You know that is not a viable option, Mr. Jenkins," Russell snapped, the sarcasm lost on him again.

"Just a thought."

If looks could kill, the one Jinx was getting from Donlon would have sent him home in a baggie.

Pablo, long silent, finally spoke up. "How many enemy are there, and how many of them are Nicaraguan?"

Finally, Jinx thought, a simple, pertinent question.

"We aren't sure," Jackson said, taking over from Russell to prevent any more friction. "The night photos show a lot of activity, but they cannot provide precise numbers, let alone nationalities. We believe there are one hundred to two hundred personnel, but the numbers could be half that or double."

"So what you want us to do is attack a camp of people, you don't know how many, or what weapons they have, figure out what they are doing in that place, then mess it up. Is that what you want?" Pablo asked, unbelieving.

"Exactly!"

"Bese me cojones," Pablo muttered under his breath, as Jinx chuckled.

"Mr. Jenkins, I see nothing to snicker about."

"Then I guess you'd better send us on our Milky Way," Jinx responded.

"God damn it, Jenkins!" Jab Donlon exploded.

"Sorry, sir, it won't happen again," Jinx lied.

"Before this gets out of hand, can we get back to the purpose here?" Jackson asked, frustration in his voice.

"I believe, Mr. Jenkins, that the Misura have a forward base in this area, is that right?" Russell again used the pointer to indicate an area along the Rio Coco, Nicaragua's northern border.

"It is true," Pablo answered, "but there are no troops there now."

"Excellent, then it will be a perfect training base to prepare for this raid."

"How soon are we talking about doing this raid, Russell?" Donlon asked, suddenly more interested in the conversation.

This is the part ol' Jab likes, Jinx thought; the part where you get to shoot some folks.

"We want to watch the place for a little while longer to see if they bring in any hardware we can identify or more personnel," Jackson explained. "I forsee this happening in a month, maybe six weeks, unless something unusual happens first.''

"Of course, the need for secrecy between now and then should be apparent,'' Russell added. "God save you if they know you're coming.''

"God save us anyway, I think,'' Jinx said. "You want us to go in against Soviet troops, search and destroy the camp, then get out with information and intact skins.''

"Precisely.''

"What do we do until then?'' Pablo asked.

"Pick your people, train in basic skills, and wait till you hear from us again.''

"Don't call us, we'll call you, eh?''

"That's right,'' Russell said as he gathered up his photos and notebooks.

"*Señor*, my men need new uniforms, boots, combat gear, spare parts, and food,'' Pablo injected. "We could hardly undertake such a mission until such humanitarian supplies were available.''

"Of course, all those things will be provided,'' Jackson assured the Indian, "the way we have provided them for years.''

There was something in Jackson's voice, but Jinx let it go. He knew that it was easy to get tired of people begging, even if they were doing a job you couldn't or wouldn't do yourself.

The meeting broke up with assurances that Russell and Jackson would be in touch if anything changed.

As the Americans and the Misura officer walked out, the two Hondurans, who had not spoken throughout the meeting, turned to each other.

"Well, Gravas, what do you think?'' Colonel Aguirre asked as he lit a tremendous cigar.

"If these people are our allies,'' Gravas answered quietly, "I think we need to pray for the safety of our country and drill our troops night and day.''

Trying to laugh with a mouthful of cigar smoke, Aguirre's coughing fit could be heard all the way out in the street.

★7★

It was dark when Jinx and Pablo got back to the *Tropos Especiales Atlantio* (TEA) base. Jinx pulled the flaps down over his windows and turned on the bare forty-watt bulb that hung over his makeshift desk. Hopefully the generator would run for a while tonight. He lay back on his cot and tried to pick up where he had left off earlier. Who was their spy?

The only people who had access to the bus ambush plan had been Pablo and the three senior NCOs, but there was always the possibility of accidental leaks. Boasting, pillow talk, even Catholic confession could let a secret slip. Quite possibly, the Sandinistas had a network of agents in their camp, and had pieced the information together; but this time, Jinx suspected a single source.

All of them had been on the mission, except Pecos Bill. Had one of them talked in bed? Two of the NCOs were married, Pablo and Pecos Bill were both single. Of the two single men, Pecos Bill was renowned as a cocksman with the Indian girls, but he was also a ruthless killer who had a ten-year reputation as a Sandinista hunter. That left Pablo, but Jinx couldn't see him as a spy. Of course, maybe that's what made a good spy. Anyone else?

Of course. Torres.

Joachim Torres had been assigned as a liaison man to the Indians from *Union Nicaraguense Opositoro* (UNO), the main Contra command. Torres had served with the Democratic Revolutionary Alliance (ARDE) under Eden Pastor Gomez before coming here. He never went on missions, but was always in attendance at planning sessions. The men liked him because he always had a joke or a good story to tell, but Pecos Bill hated him, called him a phony.

Now, how to flush the rat? Start by putting out some cheese and seeing who ran first. When he narrowed the field, then the hunt would start.

Jinx spent the next week cautiously watching each of the men on his list. None of them did anything suspicious. Pablo and the NCOs worked like they always did, and Torres just loafed around like he always did.

Late one afternoon, Jinx got lucky. Torres was playing a game with some of the kids from the village, something he frequently did. When the kids all ran off, one little girl stayed behind, talking to Torres. If he hadn't been watching for it, Jinx would have missed seeing Torres give her the small note. The little girl kissed Torres on the cheek, and ran off after her small friends. Jinx quietly strolled off toward the village. The little girl had gone straight home with the note. A few minutes later, her mother, Juanita, came out with a basket of wash and started for the river. Juanita said she was a widow, the wife of a schoolteacher killed by the Sandinistas.

Jinx followed her toward the river, keeping her in sight all the way to the bank of the Rio Coco. She set the basket down on the rocks, wet a few pieces and wrung them out, then looked carefully back up the trail and down the riverbanks. Certain she was alone, she went to a large pointed rock halfway up the bank and took a metal ration can from beneath it. She pulled Torres's note from her dress, and slipped it into the can. After replacing the can under the rock, she set a flat, white, river rock in a niche next to the large rock.

A classic drop, Jinx thought as he watched the woman pick up her basket and start back up the trail.

Now he knew the rat. Next, the trap.

Three days later, Jinx called Pablo and the NCOs for a raid planning mission.

Everyone attended, including Torres.

"I feel that we need to get the men back into the field for another mission to keep them from feeling bad about the bus incident," Jinx led off.

"I agree," Pecos Bill said. "They are looking like whipped dogs, whining and feeling sorry for themselves!"

"Perhaps they are feeling sorry for the little girls and the nun," Pablo answered quietly.

"We all feel sorry for the nun and the girls," Jinx injected, trying to head off any argument, "but regardless of who they are feeling sorry for, we need to get a victory under their belts to keep them going."

Heads nodded in agreement all around.

"What I propose is a simple ambush on the road to Waspam," Jinx continued. "It will be easy to get to, and easy to make sure who we hit."

Waspam was a small Nicaraguan border town about twenty-five miles away, just across the river from Honduras. The Sandinista garrison there patrolled the riverbanks looking for, but rarely finding, Contra infiltrators. A two-day wait on any road in the area would turn up a patrol or convoy.

"Why Waspam?" Torres asked absently, cleaning his fingernails with a demo knife. "Why not Bilwaskarma or one of the other garrisons?"

"Waspam is closer," Jinx answered, "and I think we ought to keep up more pressure on it, anyway."

"Sounds good to me," Pecos Bill grinned. If Jinx wanted to invade Managua with BB guns, it would sound good to Pecos Bill. All he wanted was as many opportunities as possible to kill Sandinistas.

The others nodded.

"OK, suggestions?"

Everyone had an idea, and most of them were good. The men spent three hours going over a variety of plans until they found one that seemed easy and as near foolproof as possible. As the meeting broke up, Jinx called Pecos Bill aside.

"I agree with you about the men, *señor*—"

"That's only part of the reason, Bill," Jinx interrupted, closing the door to the hut. "We also have a traitor we need to deal with."

Pecos Bill's face clouded up like a thunderstorm.

"You know who it is?"

"I think so, but I want you to help me prove it."

Jinx explained his discovery of Torres, and his plan. When he finished, Pecos Bill stood and unsheathed his buck knife.

"Let's just kill him now and be done with it," Pecos Bill said calmly. The thought of killing any Sandinista made him happy, but killing a traitor would be a real treat.

"I'd rather do this right, Bill," Jinx chided. "If we do it right, we'll get him and a whole bunch of Piris, too. Will you help me?"

"*Con mucho gusto, señor!*" Pecos Bill said slyly, putting away his knife. His face was split by a smile that gave Jinx the creeps.

"If you see any of the village kids in camp, let me know."

Two hours later, Bill stuck his head in Jinx's hut.

"*Señor*, our friend is playing with his little playmates."

"Good, Bill, let's go for a walk."

It was nearly dark when the woman came down to the river with her basket. Again, she followed her ritual with the wash, then placed the message in the hidden can. When she was out of sight, Bill retrieved the message from the can. In it were the plans they had made that morning. The rat had taken the bait.

They moved the signal rock and took the message with them. The Sandinistas would get no warning this time.

★8★

Two days later, forty Indians crossed into Nicaragua ten kilometers west of Waspam. They traveled southeast toward the road that ran north from Cocoland to Waspam.

Torres was with them, much to his displeasure. He had come at the insistence of the Indians after Pecos Bill had criticized his reluctance to fight. His machismo would not let him stand accused of cowardice, but the farther into Nicaragua the patrol went, the more apprehensive Torres got. Each time they crossed an open area or other danger zone, he could be found at the rear of the column. He claimed he was picking up stragglers.

When they finally reached the road, Torres was clearly confused, though he put up a front of nonchalance.

"I'm surprised we did not run into any *Piri* patrols on the way," Torres said as he dropped his pack and reached for his canteen.

I'll bet you are, thought Jinx, glancing over at Pecos Bill. Bill was wiping off his M16, forcing back another wolfish grin.

"Maybe we'll get lucky this time," Jinx replied. "No reason not to, is there?"

"Of course not," Torres answered back.

At 0630, the first sounds rattled down the tubes of the Indians' 82mm mortar. The huge mortar was rarely used, since it and the ammunition for it were heavy and cumbersome. After sunset, the huge tube and its baseplate had been floated on rafts across the river into Nicaragua. It would have been easy to shoot across the river from Honduras, but the Honduran Army was careful about preserving the illusion that they were not at war with their communist neighbors.

Twelve seconds later, the first round hit the Sandinista garrison at Waspam. Papillion aimed for the side of the camp farthest from the village, walking the rounds back on the camp itself. Civilian casualties were not the goal here, only panic.

Closer to the enemy camp, another three-man mortar team set up their small 60mm mortar. It lacked the power of the 82mm, but it was light and the team could carry twelve or more rounds of ammunition each. They, along with the machine guns, would keep up the pressure on Waspam. The two M60s were firing from their maximum effective range, nearly a thousand meters. The ten men in the fire support teams would give the impression that the camp was under attack by a sizeable force.

In the Sandinista base, Manuel Rios was just getting to the good part of a splendid wet dream when the first mortar round hit, tossing him from his cot in the radio room. It took him a second to get his bearings, then he flew to the transmitter.

"Cocoland, this is Waspam! We are under attack!"

When the muffled thumps of the mortars started, a ripple of noise and excitement went through the Indians lined up along the road eight kilometers south of Waspam. Reinforcements from Cocoland would have to come down this road to reach Waspam. The main Indian force was waiting for the reinforcements. It was an old Viet Cong trick; attack an outpost, then ambush the reinforcements. It worked well enough on the U.S. Army and ARVNs in Vietnam and it worked just as well against he Sandinista Popular Army of Nicaragua.

"OK, Bill, deploy your teams," Jinx said softly.

Bill smiled, his eyes dilating with excitement.

He loves this, Jinx thought, truly loves combat. Well, what the hell, I must, too. I'm here.

Bill was moving down the line, checking each fire team, making little changes here and there. Mostly, he was pep-

talking each little group, making them feel like the fate of
Nicaragua and the lives of their friends depended on each
round they fired.

While Bill rallied the troops, Jinx moved down out of the
tree line to make one last check of his Claymores. There were
two rows of the deadly devices, one ten meters off the road
on the ambush side, and another twenty meters on the other
side of the road. The Claymores were all linked by detonating
cord. When the first mine was triggered, each one down the
line would follow. The detonating cord exploded at the rate
of twenty-three thousand feet per second, making the blasts
seem instantaneous. The mines on the near side would be
detonated as soon as the column stopped. Packed into the
open trucks, the Sandinistas would be riddled by the first row
of mines. The Claymores on the far side of the road were
tied in the trees, aimed down into the ditch that ran beside
the road. If any of the reinforcements took cover in the ditch,
the second row of mines would catch them from behind. Jinx
ran the wires to make sure there were no breaks, then plugged
the leads into the plastic detonators, called clackers.

It was a very simple plan. When the lead vehicle passed
over the charge set in the road, it would be blown. The column would then have to stop, or at least slow down. When
that happened, the first Claymores would be blown and the
troops would open up. Each soldier would fire two magazines
full auto into the trucks. The four M79 gunners would fire at
each truck, aiming for their fuel tanks. The two M60s would
rake the column. When the riflemen had finished their two
magazines, they would pull back, using the M79s and M60s
for cover. The second set of Claymores would be blown and
everyone would go home. This ambush style was adopted
from the OSS, who had used it against the Japanese in Burma.
A fast ambush with lots of firepower and a quick retreat. It
inflicted the maximum punishment on the enemy with the
least danger to the friendlies.

Satisfied with his Claymores, Jinx returned to camouflag-
ing his position. Bill came back, with Torres in tow.

"*Señor*, I think Torres and I should set up an observation
post up the road," Bill said, hardly able to keep from looking
at Torres, "to warn of the enemy's approach."

"Good idea, Bill," Jinx replied. "Be careful and take care of Torres, OK?"

Torres was pale and sweating, even though a cool breeze was blowing the morning mist off.

"*Capitán*, I think—"

Jinx cut him off. "I know you'd rather be here in the kill zone, Torres, but we need a couple of good men on that OP, men who won't blow the ambush."

"But—"

"I'm sorry," Jinx said flatly. "Now, move out."

As the two turned to head up the road, Bill turned and winked quickly. Torres would soon take his place in the hall of martyrs.

"*Madre de Dios*, where are they?" Manuel screamed as another explosion shook the camp. Mortar rounds were falling slowly, but continuously. One had hit the dining hall, setting it on fire. Another had hit a few meters from the radio room. The radio set was all that saved Manuel from the shrapnel. The radio had been demolished.

He had escaped to a shallow trench that drained the center of camp. It was full of slimy mud, but it offered some protection from the machine guns sweeping the camp. The camp's forty Popular Army defenders were putting up good return fire, but it was hard to find targets through the mist. The camp mortars were firing blind. At least the attackers seemed in no hurry to assault the camp. Perhaps help would come in time.

"Here, Torres, you work the radio," Bill said softly, as the two men slipped into a small depression behind a fallen pine tree. The hole was a natural fighting position, deep enough to hide in, but shallow enough to see and shoot from.

"Surely we do not need to be so far from the main body," Torres protested, watching Bill's every move for a chance to overpower him. He couldn't believe his luck when the norte had sent them out here. Now he could warn the relief column and be "captured." A few weeks in Managua would be nice. He would make his superiors a present of this celebrated Contra murderer.

Bill took out a pair of binoculars and searched the road to

Cocoland. Torres moved around behind him, quietly slipping a full Uzi magazine out of its pouch. The loaded magazine weighed about a kilo. It made an excellent short club.

Pecos Bill heard the snap open on the ammo pouch and looked over at Torres.

"This is a good spot. We can see straight down the road, and there is good cover." Pecos Bill kicked the log several times, then put the radio up against it. "Sit down, amigo, we have some time to wait."

Torres made a show of examining the magazine in his hand, then put it away.

"You really think they'll come?"

"Oh, yes. They won't abandon an outpost under attack. If they did, the people would think they were afraid of us."

"How big a force do you think they will they send?"

"Probably a company, they don't have that many combat troops to spare at Cocoland," Bill said as he slipped off his pack and pushed it up against the log. He sat down and leaned back on the pack, lacing his fingers behind his head. "Might as well relax." He pushed his floppy hat forward to shade his eyes.

Torres sat quietly, watching Bill's face. He would have to strike before the trucks came by. If they saw movement in the brush, they would open fire. He must make his move soon.

Bill let his body relax, and slid his hand under the loose top flap of his pack. He shifted his body a little to cover the movement. The little pistol was still there on top. Bill pulled it a little to free it up in the pack. He held the grip gently, waiting.

Torres watched as Bill's head nodded forward. Soon, he thought, soon he will doze off, then I'll get him. He eased the knife out of its sheath. Slowly, silently. Torres moved his foot back and leaned forward, shifting his weight, poised to strike. He brought the knife back just past his ear, and slowly moved up into a crouch. He would stab Bill through the neck, side to side. Bill's M16 was beside him, but he would not be able to reach it with Torres on top of him. The wound would be almost instantly fatal, and no scream would be possible. He shifted his weight forward. Now.

Bill felt, rather than heard the man move. He had been

waiting for this movement. He wrapped his hand around the pistol. Come on, *comunista*, do it.

Torres took a deep breath, then jumped forward toward the sleeping figure. In that extended moment, Bill's hand snapped down from behind his head, a small pistol in his hand. The thick black barrel made five sounds like matches striking, and Torres could feel the .22 bullets walking up his chest. He opened his mouth to scream, but only a wet choking noise came out.

Surprised, and mortally wounded, Torres landed on Bill's pack, his knife stabbing into the left shoulder strap. Bill was on his feet now, his rifle in his hands. He dropped to one knee, watching Torres flounder in the dirt. The man was still alive, but not for long. Hollow-point bullets had traced a line from his heart to his larynx. The traitor rolled over on his back, gasping.

Bill sat back on his heels. "So, *amigo*, you wanted to give me a shave, eh?"

Torres, his eyes wide with fear and surprise, tried to speak.

"How?" he gasped, then coughed, blood splattering out of his mouth.

"How? My friend, you should never send women or children to do your work." Bill pulled a half-smoked cigarette from his rolled-up sleeve. He lit it and took a long drag, then held it out to the dying Torres. "Smoke?"

Torres did not answer. His eyes were rolled back, his breathing wet and shallow. The blood in his chest left little room for air.

"No," Bill said. "Well, OK, I didn't think so."

He pinched the fire off the end of the cigarette and rolled the rest back up in his sleeve.

"You know, my friend, killing is like sex," he laughed, talking to the dying man lying on his pack. "A cigarette always tastes so good afterward."

Torres's chest had stopped moving.

Bill used the barrel of his rifle to flip the knife from Torres's hand, then picked it up, never taking his eyes off the man. He looked dead, but Bill knew better than to take a chance. He pulled his pack from under the dead traitor. The man had not bled on it much, anyway. Bill pulled the little pistol out of his belt to put it away, then stopped. He checked the chamber for a round, then placed the muzzle between Torres's eyes. The little pistol spat once more. A tiny, neat hole appeared in the hollow just above the nose.

"Le coup de grâce, Monsieur Sandinista."

Bill pressed down the bolt hold-open, letting the slide return. He slipped in another magazine and put the tiny pistol away. As he tightened the pack straps, he heard the sound of trucks.

The radio clicked three times, then three times again. They were coming.

Jinx passed the word up and down the line: get ready!

A moment later, they heard the trucks rumbling up the road. Jinx pressed himself into the ground next to the clump of grass. The first truck came into view, churning dust behind it. There were two men in the cab. Above it, a People's Army soldier held a PK machine gun on some sandbags, searching the roadside for trouble. There were more troops in the truck, facing outward, guns at the ready. The trucks were moving fast, closing on the kill zone. Jinx slipped the safety wires off both clackers. He looked at Pablo, who held the ten-cap blaster poised, waiting for Jinx's signal.

The lead truck was twenty meters from the buried charge, a V-shaped linear charge three feet long. Ten meters—Jinx nodded to Pablo. Pablo twisted the blaster handle once, then again.

The truck almost cleared the charge before it went off under its bed, cutting the drive shaft, and incinerating four SPA soldiers with its focused line of flame. The blast lifted the truck's rear wheels two meters off the ground, where they hung suspended for a second as the truck rolled forward a few meters, then fell. The driver of the second truck ran up under the first truck as it crashed back down. The soldier with the PK was thrown over the top of the cab and landed in front of it, his machine gun falling with him.

Jinx waited a heartbeat, then squeezed the clacker in his left hand. The line of Claymores erupted in an ear-shattering roar. All four trucks were caught in the fan of steel. The soldiers on the right side of the trucks were either killed outright or wounded. The others were pitched forward when the trucks slid to a stop in a cloud of smoke and dust.

The roar of the Claymores signaled the rising crescendo of rifle and machine gun fire. M79s added their soft clumping noise, the grenades bursting against the trucks, igniting the spilled fuel. Long bursts from the M60s raked the sides of the trucks, ripping into the soldiers trying to escape and tearing pieces out of the ones already dead.

The Sandinistas were quick to exit their stricken vehicles. To stay in them was suicide. They clambered over the left side rails and sprinted for the relative safety of the ditch. As in every firefight, there was one enemy who seemed to be bulletproof. After the third truck stopped, a lone Sandinista soldier turned his AKM on the attackers. He fired a whole magazine, changed it, dived for the rear of the truck as the gas tank caught fire, rolled out, fired again at the ambushers, then ran backward, firing as he went, toward the ditch. Unscathed, he rolled backward out of sight. Jinx laughed out loud. There was always someone the bullets seemed to go around.

The others who made it the few meters to the ditch were returning fire as best they could through the smoke and fire from the burning trucks.

Jinx quickly scanned the trucks. He could see no one left moving in them. He squeezed the clacker in his right hand, firing the second string of Claymores. Thirty-five hundred quarter-inch steel balls slammed into the ditch. Those who had escaped the slaughterhouse of the trucks were riddled in the metalstorm of the narrow ditch.

In the fifteen seconds since the ambush began, most of the Indians had fired their two magazines and were pulling back. In the kill zone, there was little movement, only the screams and moans of the wounded. Jinx pulled the pocket-sized H&K flare gun from his fatigues and fired the tiny red flare over the road. He then pulled the two clackers loose from their firing wires and scuttled backward into the brush.

Bill heard the explosions and firing of the ambush. He took Torres's pack and personal effects, and left the body behind the log. He used the dead man's knife to dig up the earth at the edge of the depression, and scooped the dirt out with his hands to cover the body along with some rotten limbs kicked over the mound. He waited until the firing had subsided, held his M16 up and fired an entire magazine into the air. Later he would say he and Torres had engaged a truck that was lagging behind the others and that Torres had died like a patriot.

The trip back was fast and uneventful. The teams harassing Waspam had broken off their attack when they saw the red flare. They pulled back to the river to act as a covering force for the ambushers. The entire force crossed the river back into their sanctuary without incident. The three beat-up Toyota trucks were, for once, all running at the same time. Five and a half hours later, they drove through the gates of TEA base.

Back at the base, Jinx was anxious to question the woman, Torres's partner. She was not in the village. The Indians would say only that she had gone. They did not know when or where. The little girl had gone with her. Jinx did not press the issue. It was better not to know. When he returned from the village, a message was waiting. Come to Mocoron ASAP.

★9★

Bodnya sat rigidly on a varnished, red-cushioned wood chair in a small waiting room in the Kremlin. His trip to this place had been a disorienting whirlwind.

Maybe that is what they want, Bodnya reflected, a little test before the interview.

The An-12 flight from Kabul to Termez, Uzbek Soviet Socialist Republic, along with tank engines returning for overhaul at 40th Army's huge maintenance depot, had taken only a brief half hour. There he had received one more surprise on this day of many. He reported to the one-story stone building bearing a sign announcing it as the "Signal Coordination Office." It actually housed the 3rd Group of the 2nd Department of the Army Staff, the Spetsnaz group of the intelligence department. Here he learned he was to depart for Moscow immediately.

The three and a half hour leg to Moscow was made in a more comfortable Aeroflot IL-86 airliner. Bodnya, who had never smoked, was reminded of Aeroflot's irritating practice of seating smokers on the left side and nonsmokers on the right.

A much too young and far too highly-shined *desantniki* (paratrooper) captain had met him after only a brief wait at the Sheremetyevo Airport, with a car and driver no less! Formal and correct to distraction, the captain had obviously never served the Motherland in 'Stan.

We cannot all be state heroes, mused Bodnya.

61

Once in the black Volga M-124 sedan, the captain seemed to relax. A light snow dusted the recently swept streets. The young sergeant driving seemed oblivious to any conversation in the back, a developed and encouraged trait. The night masked Moscow's shabbiness, something Bodnya appreciated. Even though not a Moscovite, it was still the Soviet Union's capital, the capital of world communism, and its dreary appearance was enough to secretly sadden the heart of every true Russian, though not always the hearts of the state's many other ethnic citizens.

"Is the war against the *Basmachi* progressing to your satisfaction, Comrade Major?" the captain asked. Bodnya never did catch his name.

"As well as can be expected since we have had to reestablish our domination over areas we evacuated in 1988 and '89. Our reentry into those sections of the country was costly. But we were forced to do it in order to save a friendly government. The American puppet *Basmachi* did not keep to the terms of the agreements. As we withdrew, they increased their pressure on the legal Socialist government. Even though the bandits continued to fight among themselves, the government was in danger of falling when we reentered. If we had let the Kabul government fail, what would that have shown our friends, that we are no more trustworthy than the Americans are with their propped up puppet governments? It would have shown that we do not possess the strength and will to support those who have joined the revolution. That we are as helpless and indecisive as the Americans."

Bodnya took a deep breath. He had never been so outspoken. Maybe the strain of combat was beginning to take its toll. "I apologize for boring you with my prattling verbosity, comrade."

"There is nothing to apologize for, Comrade Major. It is a pleasure to hear such words from a recently returned veteran. Most do nothing but complain of the hardships. I myself have a posting to the 103rd Guards Airborne Division in Afghanistan. I leave at the end of the month and am looking forward to the opportunity to serve international socialism."

"I wish you luck, comrade." And Bodnya did; he would need it. Time to change the subject.

"What have our new leaders accomplished to combat street

crime? I was approached by a prostitute in the airport. She walked right up to me and opened her palm. Fifteen rubles was marked in lipstick on it.''

"I beg your pardon, Comrade Major," the captain said in an affronted tone, "there are no prostitutes in the Soviet Union—there are only whores!''

This received a subdued chuckle from the driver, who in turn got a stern look from the captain by way of his rearview mirror.

"Yes, some things never change. Some things always change. How are our citizens accepting the 'reachievement of seeking Socialism's true goals'?''

"I can answer that with a story. President Gortov went to the All-Union Institute of Computer Sciences and ordered the staff to construct an all-powerful computer able to forecast the future. All available information was to be put into its memory banks to form its database; the contents of every newspaper, magazine, book, and government document. He authorized them all the resources they needed and the best that stolen western technology had to offer. He then gave them two years to complete the project.

"Upon his return to the institute two years later, he ordered the staff to demonstrate the computer. The chief scientist asked him to ask it a question. Comrade Gortov asked, 'How far are we from achieving true Communism?' The question was put to the computer and its program began to run. After a brief time the printer began to clatter and the answer was printed out. Gortov eagerly ripped the sheet from the printer and read, 'SEVENTEEN KILOMETERS.'

" 'What is the meaning of this?' he screamed at the scientists. The chief scientist said, 'but Comrade President, you gave us the data on which the computer based its findings, in a speech you made last year.'

" 'And what is that?'

" 'You said that with the completion of every successful five year plan we come one step closer to achieving true Communism!' ''

Both Bodnya and the driver had laughed, the captain sparing the latter a hard look this time.

* * *

Now, uncomfortable in his new surroundings, he sought to calm his rushing mind. There was a mirror hung on one of the hand-rubbed wood paneled walls. He stood to inspect his uniform; the purpose, no doubt, for which the mirror was provided. His Air Force blue full dress uniform still fit as well as it had the last time he had worn it, almost a year ago. He had barely had time to replace his faded and dusty sky-blue paratrooper's beret at the Moscow Officers' Club during his all too brief rest there.

He quickly checked the alignment of the orders and badges on his right chest; two Orders of the Red Star, 1st Class Order of Service to the Motherland in the USSR Armed Forces, two 1st Class Military Service Merit medals, Expert Parachutist, Ryazan Higher Airborne Command School, and Guards' badges.

He reflected on the references in the Western press that Spetsnaz could be identified by the fact that they did not wear the Guards badge, but the airborne divisions did. The Spetsnaz brigades did not since they had not existed to be awarded the honor title during the Great Patriotic War.

Now we all wear the Guards badge as part of our *maskirovka*, our masking efforts, he thought.

Pinned under the lower edge of his left lapel were the 1st Class Merit in Military Service, 2nd Class Irreproachable Service, Afghanistan Defense, and Afghanistan Brotherhood Aid medals. His boots were polished to a reflective gloss. He would pass any inspection.

"Major Bodnya, your presence is ordered." A lieutenant colonel of motorized rifles, his sea-green uniform bedecked with a weighty array of badges, orders and medals, stood in the open conference room door. Stepping through the heavy wooden door he was confronted by a long conference table, so highly polished that it looked glass-topped. Though well lighted with crystal chandeliers, the room still had a somber appearance. The walls were covered in dark wood paneling. Heavily embroidered burgundy drapes hung from the ceiling to the matching carpet.

Bodnya had been to more than one of these selection boards, but the rank of the seated officers startled him. A colonel general of tank troops resided at the head of the table. To his right were a signals and an air force lieutenant general.

On his left were two ground forces major generals. Two official looking civilians also sat at the table. The other five officers seated were colonels from various combat branches.

He stared at them; they stared back. He saluted.

"Major Aleksei Bodnya reporting as ordered," he said in what he hoped was a steady voice.

The lieutenant colonel stood slightly to his right holding an officer's record folder: his. Most of those seated at the table were looking down at similar folders. He could see more folders on a small table against the room's left wall; other candidates for the board.

The lieutenant colonel began to read from a typed sheet clipped to the folder's cover. "Major Aleksei Bodnya; born 30 May 1950 in Safonovo, Russian Soviet Federated Socialist Republic. Noted for actively participating in the Volunteer Society for Assistance to the Army, Aviation and Fleet premilitary training programs in school. Completed secondary school education in Safonovo and attended the Ryazan Higher Airborne Command School from 1969 to 1974. Cadet Bodnya graduated with superior marks and was certified as an automotive mechanical engineer. His language speciality was German. His political steadfastness and involvement in the school's Komsomol was demonstrated repeatedly and he was accepted into the Communist Party of the Soviet Union. Cadet Bodny's performance at Ryazan was noted, leading to his promotion to lieutenant and immediate assignment to the Reconnaissance Faculty of the Kiev Higher Arms School."

This last statement came as a mild surprise to some of the panel members. The special faculty at Kiev was the Spetsnaz officers' school. Bodnya had been sent there without the usual probationary period in an airborne division.

"The lieutenant was then assigned to Department 660, Belorussian Military District." This was the *maskirovka* designation of the district's Spetsnaz brigade.

"Following this assignment, Lieutenant Bodnya was assigned to the Group of Soviet Forces Germany Airborne Regiment." Another Spetsnaz brigade *maskirovka* designation. "Here he completed English language instruction and was involved in the cross-border observer-driver program using East German International Transport Agreement trucks. Promoted to senior lieutenant, he was assigned as a liaison officer to the Soviet Military Liaison Mission in Frankfurt, West Germany. Here he had direct contact with American military personnel while conducting collection operations. He was never compromised on any of these assignments. Promoted to captain, he was assigned as the 1st Staff Officer, 4th Battalion, Group of Soviet Forces Germany Airborne Regiment.''

"Because of his effectiveness as the battalion operations officer, his past performance, his demonstrated commitment to the goals of communism, and his English proficiency, Captain Bodnya was assigned as an observer officer to the United Nations Soviet Element, UN Truce Supervision Organization, Observation Group Sinai in Cairo, Egypt from 1977 to 1979. This provided him with additional opportunities for contact with Americans. He successfully completed his assigned collection tasks. This assignment was followed by the attendance of the War Dog Course at the KGB Higher Border Troops Command School, Alma-Ata as part of a study in countering tracker dogs. The study group to which he was assigned developed an effective training program for our special source troops.''

Special source troops was yet another deceptive term for Spetsnaz, thought Bodnya. We live in a world of shadows and delusion.

"Again assigned to Department 660, Belorussian MD, as the unit's 1st Staff Officer, Captain Bodnya was instrumental in implementing the counter-tracking training program as well as preparing troops for service in Afghanistan.''

"Captain Bodnya served as the 1st Staff Officer of Department 770 with the Limited Contingent of Soviet Forces in Afghanistan where he was wounded in direct combat. He was assigned as a liaison officer to the East German Ministry for State Security while recuperating. During this period, he was detached for a special training mission in Northern Ireland.''

It was actually only a minor leg wound, Bodnya remembered, but in 'Stan that limited one's usefulness.

"He was again assigned to Afghanistan as a battalion 1st Staff Officer, promoted to major, and given command of a Department 780 battalion. His combat record in the fight for international socialism is beyond reproach and the effectiveness of his unit's operations have done much to eliminate the counterrevolutionary elements in our brother socialist state. His decorations include—"

"Thank you Colonel Yakir," rumbled a deep voice near the head of the table, "we can see the major's kickshaws." The signals lieutenant general rose from his chair. "No offense, Comrade Major, but our time is limited. You may be seated."

Bodnya relaxed from the position of attention he had held during the mildly embarrassing introduction and took the offered chair set two meters from the table's end. Now for the questioning. This was no easy task. He did not have an inkling what they were looking for. Again, this was intentional, a common practice for such boards.

The lieutenant general stood behind his chair. It appeared he wanted to dominate the board. The board's chairman, the colonel general, seemed more interested in watching Bodnya.

"Major, did you ever have any unofficial conversations with Americans, perhaps where you discussed their careers and political beliefs—or yours?"

"Yes, Comrade General. That was part of my duties; to collect information on specific officers."

"Yes, yes, I realize this, but I mean *unofficial* conversations. Talks where the two of you came to some gentlemen's agreement to pull the stops and compare your ideologies."

"I attempted to give that impression, on occasion," Bodnya answered calmly, "if I felt it would obtain more information. But I never let myself go. I always maintained control."

"Not even during a heavy drinking bout?"

"Major Bodnya has proven himself to be a moderate drinker, Comrade General," said a tough-looking tank troops major general sitting across from him. Bodnya thought it unusual that he wore an expert parachutist badge and even more unusual that he had spoken up for a candidate.

The lieutenant general ignored this, and went on to another subject. "What are your thoughts on the effectiveness of the American Army officer corps, since you have personally dealt with them?" There seemed to be a tone of disdain in the question. He must be careful with his answer.

"The American officer corps is professional, for the most part. They know their jobs, but often fail to see much beyond them, or below them, for that matter. When they move to a higher level, though, they immediately adapt to the larger picture, but just as quickly forget the problems and lessons learned at the lower level. They seem to prefer to respond to the actions of others, rather than to initiate actions themselves; much like their national policies as a whole. I also find their concept of initiative to be intriguing. With us, initiative is the measure taken by commanders to insure that the mission is accomplished within the guidelines of the higher headquarter's operation plan. The Americans emphasize the use of a 'non-stereotyped' approach for combat actions, defining this as initiative. This must make coordination of their combat operations extremely difficult.''

The tanker major general smiled at this answer and immediately shot in his question. ''Describe the planning procedures and execution of the raid you commanded,'' he requested, glancing at a notepad, ''in April of this year.''

This was one of Bodnya's most successful operations. The tanker general appeared to be striving to put him in a good light while the colonel general seemed resentful of his presence. He first described the situation, went through the planning sequence and pre-operation training to the devastating conclusion of the air assault on the bandit base camp.

The other board members asked simpler questions, usually dealing with planning and troop control procedures plus occasional ones obviously aimed at getting an insight on his politically reliability. Most of these he answered with the accepted ''exactly so'' and ''in no way.''

He was thanked for his cooperation and told to relax, to see the sights of Moscow for a few days. He would soon receive orders for his next assignment. All he wanted now was a good night's sleep. Tomorrow, maybe, he would look up his brother. Bodnya was not enthusiastic about that.

Maj. Aleksei Bodnya was exactly what Maj. Gen. Sergey Pavlovskiy had expected when he first reviewed the officer's records. Keeping in mind what Col. General Tolubko had requested, ''no politically-acceptable officers, or the latest cult hero,'' he had searched for a half dozen good candidates with both proven combat records and the requisite skills developed in peacetime training exercises, in which the Soviets placed almost as much faith as they did in combat experience. Previous service in America or direct experience in dealing with American officers was also required. Luckily, there were more opportunities to acquire this foreign experience than many realized.

The cult heroes being produced in Afghanistan were becoming a real problem within the officer corps. An official party effort was under way to glorify combat service in Afghanistan. As a result, many officers went out of their way to receive whatever honors and small benefits could be gained by such recognition, even at the expense of their units. Recognition for faithful adherence to the party's myths was to be expected in a military, and indeed, a society that officially decried individuality.

Lieutenant General Yurasov was of a different mind. "No doubt this Bodnya has had a great deal of experience, but he seems to me too lighthearted to be given the responsibility of leading a mission of such importance as Summer Harvest."

Pavlovskiy quickly responded. "He has demonstrated throughout his career that he has an analytical mind in formulating operational plans and conducting effective unit training programs. His soldiers have always achieved higher than expected training norms."

"Lieutenant Colonel Lavrov has been a longtime and effective instructor at the Kiev Higher Arms School, plus has a more suitable rank!" Yurasov shot back.

"I am certain that the rest of the Tasking Committee will agree from their own experiences that a teaching bench at a service school, even one as demanding as Kiev, does not compare with the actual experience to be gained leading special source troops," responded Pavlovskiy. "As for the matter of Major Bodnya's rank, he is due to be promoted shortly. He would have been so sooner, but he repeatedly sought the position of 1st Staff Officer in an effort to gain the operations and training expertise so necessary to command a special source unit effectively."

The other committee members had for the most part stayed out of the conflict between the two GRU generals. The president of the board, Col. Gen. N. I. Butakov, stayed out of it too, choosing to let Pavlovskiy and Yurasov fight it out between themselves. Besides, he found these little dramas mildly amusing. Little else in life was for him now.

"I feel that Larov's degree of demonstrated valor on his one tour in Afghanistan, a tour that earned him more recognition than your Bodnya by the way, is sufficient to earn him the command of a mission of such importance to the *Rodina*," Yurasov countered.

That is the problem, thought Pavlovskiy, the recognition. "This may be true, Comrade Yarasov, but I also feel that Major Bodnya's firsthand experience with Americans on two tours, a total of almost three years direct contact, is another principal qualification."

"This is important comrades," Colonel Artuzov, the committee's American expert, hazarded to inject, "and he does appear to have a realistic grasp of the mind of American military specialists."

Yarasov did not wait a moment for his reply. "Lieutenant Colonel Larov actually operated in the American Southwest as a collection officer."

"For two years at the Soviet Consulate in Nogales, Mexico, listening in on officers' wives telephone gossip at Ft. Huachuca, Arizona," Pavlovskiy shot back.

This drew some light laughter from the other committee members. Nogales was a small border town, probably the world's smallest boasting a Soviet consulate. The sole purpose of the consulate was to monitor activities at the U.S. Army's Intelligence Center and School at Ft. Huachuca.

"He crossed the border on numerous occasions on collection missions." Yarasov replied indignantly.

Time to finish this argument off, thought Pavlovskiy. "But, does he have the wolf's killer instinct? Does he have the motivation, the will to enter the enemy's homeland, to drive his men to accomplish impossible tasks? To commit acts of violence on unarmed civilians if necessary? I think not!"

Yarasov started to open his mouth.

Now to close in for the kill. "The day before yesterday, Major Bodnya lost part of his unit in a helicopter crash," Pavlovskiy went on. "He has taken it hard and no doubt wants revenge."

"I do not see what that—" Yarasov quipped.

"It was shot down by an *American-supplied* Stinger mis-

sile!'' Pavlovskiy pounced. "That is what it has to do with
this committee, Comrade General.''

A deep voice rose from beside the two glaring generals, a
voice as deep as the rumble of T-62s crossing a stone bridge
in Prague, the route by which General Butakov had led his
tank regiment into the Czechoslovakia capitol in 1969. "Let
me see Major Bodnya's record. I think we have our *ikhotniki*.''

Bodnya had originally been told that Summer Harvest was
a contingency plan to be put into action as a reprisal for
continuing American provocations in Europe. He had not
been told that it would take place in America itself. When
the time came for this, he was only told that it was merely a
"worst case eventuality.'' He was not told that it was to coincide with the general offensive into Western Europe.

Little was actually required of Bodnya and his small planning staff as far as the overall operation was concerned. This
was taken care of by the Tasking Committee's own planning
staff. He did not question this lack of participation, as this
was the standard practice with Soviet operational, or in this
case, strategic planning. The special airlift requirements,
training areas, even the method of training, quarters, supplies, weapons and equipment, contact with frozen agents,
coordination with Nicaraguan and Cuban authorities, this was
all done for Bodnya's small new "special source" unit.

Its *maskarovka* designation was the 800th Construction
Training Company. Col. Gen. N. I. Butakov's wry sense of
humor had been apparent in the selection this designation,
one previously used by fledgling German commandos before
to the Great Patriotic War. *Bau-Lehr-Kompanie 800* were the
original Brandenburgers. Its only official designation was
simply Unit 3816, no more than a field post number.

Summer Harvest's ninety hand-picked *ikhotniki*, drawn
from Spetsnaz units in the western Soviet Union, had suddenly found themselves thrust together in an isolated Caucasus Mountains camp near the Caspian Sea. Each of them had
at least one tour in 'Stan. All spoke German or English, a
few both. They were politically reliable, emotionally stable,
and flexible in their outlook.

The Summer Harvest force was composed of a small headquarters and four attack groups, each with a specific target. Although they did not yet know their actual group assignments, every man was assigned to a subunit of two to six men, even the company's commander. The headquarters consisted of Bodnya, Ensign Kovpak, and Senior Sergeant Malinkov. Bodnya, along with the group commanders, planned the mission's on-the-ground execution details. Bodnya was given considerable latitude in this aspect of the mission.

Also part of the headquarters was the *Osobye Otdely* (Special Section) consisting of two Spetsnaz-trained KGB officers charged with counterintelligence functions to preserve the mission's secrecy and, though not discussed, to serve as watchdogs. A one-man *Seketno Otdely* (Secret Section), was responsible for the safekeeping, accountability and issue of classified documents and maps; and a *zampolit*, or political officer, made up the special officers assigned to the mission.

This latter individual, the *zampolit* was no longer the overzealous guardian of communist ideology from the days of the Commissars, but served more as an advisor to the commander on political education, character guidance, troop welfare, and organization of recreational programs.

That is not to say that the often boring political education classes were a thing of the past. These consisted principally of current news events, slanted to demonstrate that the Party's way was right for the world.

Another man assigned to the headquarters was the *feldsher*, or physician's assistant. Besides looking after the men's health he was responsible for training the *sanitary instruktor*, who were the *ikhotniki* medics.

★10★

15 November

For the most part, the training had gone well. The subunits were working well together. Only the change in climate had affected performance. To protect security, none of the men knew the exact nature of the mission, nor the target. As a result, rumors were rife. The practice sessions on the tank and armored personnel carrier mock-ups identified a mechanized unit, not an unusual target for the Spetsnaz. Most of the speculation centered around whose tanks and when.

Targets from England to Afghanistan were postulated. Bodnya ignored the rumors; it gave the men something to think about. Only the *zampolit* and KGB watchdogs worried about rumors and speculation. The most fanciful rumor identified the target as the tank units stationed in the Azerbaidzhan Soviet Socialist Republic, and the mission to quell a bid by that republic to secede from the Soviet Union. Others thought this was absurd since they were in Central America. Maybe the target was Nicaraguan or even Cuban, for the same reasons. Captain Belousav, the *zampolit*, had been very concerned at that mention of dissent, and began conducting twice the usual number of political lectures. These lectures took valuable time away from training, but, as Kovpak pointed out, it gave the men a chance to catch up on their sleep.

All training was done at night. Not only did it duplicate the mission, but it kept observation to a minimum. The American's satellites and reconnaissance aircraft passed over Nicaragua, and everything possible was done to thwart them.

Nicaraguan personnel in the camp were kept to a few cooks and drivers.

The terrain around the camp reminded Bodnya and Kovpak of their days in the Belorussian Military District. The rolling hills and tall, thin pine trees could be a dozen places in Western Russia or Poland. The temperature was wrong, though. It was never this warm in Russia in late November.

After their initial training in the Caucasus Mountains in October, they had boarded the plane for Cuba in the first week of November wearing parkas and insulated boots. It was seventy-five degrees at night here, in the eighties during the day. It rarely got that warm this time of year in the Caucasus Mountains.

Only two mock compounds had been constructed. Training was done on a rotating basis, since there were not enough mock-ups for the entire group. When a subunit was not practicing on the mock-ups, they did foreign weapons familiarization, practiced close combat skills such as *sambo* and attended language classes. Spanish, English, and German were taught.

In this camp, one could practice all three languages. The Cubans spoke Spanish, as did the Nicaraguans, who also spoke English. The East Germans spoke German and some English.

Lucky we don't have any PLO here, Bodnya thought, we'd have to take Arabic lessons, as well. Bodnya had trained some PLO members before. They were stubborn, ignorant brutes who firmly believed they had a mandate from Allah to kill Israelis and Americans. He knew that they were essential in keeping the Western powers distracted and divided, but personally, he detested them. Besides, they smelled bad. He wondered if he had taken out his dislike for those Palestinians on their Moslem brothers, the Afghans.

I hope so, he thought cheerfully.

Another week here and they would be off to Punte Huerte, the departure airfield. Before he left for America, Bodnya would brief the troops on the actual mission and target. They would, of course, be kept in isolation to prevent any leaks or defections. The *zampolit* and KGB officers always worried that soldiers would try to run away from battle. That irritated Bodnya. Spetsnaz soldiers never ran from anything! Many of their missions were suicide, but they not only went, they came back alive and victorious.

The damn *zampolit* and KGB *Chekists* project their own fear onto my men, he thought, men whose boots they are not fit to polish.

Bodnya banished these thoughts as another pair of subunits formed up to practice. He could see Captain Karmasov speaking to them. Bodnya smiled. Karmasov had that gift for making even reluctant soldiers want to do well, a gift he had made the most of in Afghanistan. Bodnya couldn't hear the words but the *ikhotniki* suddenly shouted "Da!" in unison. Karmasov looked pleased.

Two subunits loaded onto the waiting Zil lorry. The big truck drove out the front gate and down past the end of the camp perimeter. There it turned slowly onto a parallel road farther from the fence. As the truck came even with the first of the two compounds, three figures dropped from its rear, executing perfect parachute landing falls. They rolled to their feet and sprinted into the brush between the roads. Nearing the second compound another trio dropped from the truck. It continued on past the camp after the last threesome had slipped off the back.

The road was empty, silent, after the passage of the truck. The two trios rose and slowly walked across the road and up to a Spetsnaz soldier acting as a gate sentry for their particular compound. A brief conversation took place with the sentry who wore a helmet, backpack and carried a one-meter stick. Suddenly, the sentry staggered as one of the group caught him from behind. With the aid of another, they dragged him into the small sentry hut while the third recovered the stick and pulled off the helmet. The first two then walked to the gate, never hurrying. They cut the gate's padlocked chain with a bolt cutter, opening one section of the double gate just wide enough to slip in. The third man, wearing the helmet and pack, and armed with the stick, emerged from the sentry hut and closed the gate after them. Now the scene sped up. One *reydoviki* mounted the dark shapes under the canvas canopies. The other positioned himself behind them. From packs on their shoulders, each man began placing small blocks at specific spots on the mock-ups, the one on top of the structure stepping from one mock-up to the next, smoothly moving along each row. The other moved to the canvas-muzzled pipes projecting to the rear, slashed at the cap with a knife, and slapped a block into the pipe.

When they were through with the last of three rows of mock-ups, they met and sprinted for the gate. Small fires flared from the blocks placed on the first row. Meanwhile, the "sentry" returned the helmet, pack and stick to their previous owner in the hut. Before opening the gate he bent over the pack and simulated firing his pistol.

As the men walked back across the road, blocks flared on the last mock-ups. Each simulated device had a ninety-second fuse. The *reydoviki* were out of the two compounds before the devices on the last row went off. Even if they were discovered, they could hold off any defenders until all the devices had ignited. Once ignited, the thermite blocks were impossible to extinguish. The truck came slowly back down the road and the two trios boarded it as it passed.

Ensign Kovpak stepped out from behind one of the mock-ups and blew his whistle. The lights under the canvas came on, and the *reydoviki* leaped from the truck and ran to him.

Almost like puppies expecting a reward, Bodnya reflected. Kovpak formed them up and took the group over to the headquarters building for a critique of the practice exercise. Although it had gone well, Kovpak would not be pleased and the subunits would come back tomorrow night to try again to perform satisfactorily. Two more subunits boarded the truck while Captain Karmasov moved into Kovpak's observation position.

In a week, they would be able to run the course, not by rote memory, but by instinct. Then they would be ready to learn their destination.

★11★

28 November

"So, Pete, where's your friend, Mister Personality?"

"Lighten up, Jinx. I know the guy's an asshole, but he's the son of some congressman, so I'm stuck with him."

"OK, OK, what have you got for me?"

"Here's the most recent air recce photos of the camp. The daylight shots show only the tarps and the vague outlines underneath, but the night shots tell another story." Jackson said, pulling a set of large, dark photos out of his safe.

"These are infrared shots of the same spot," Jackson pointed to an area of red shapes in the center of the photos. "The tarps have been removed, and the shapes are clearer, now. These look like some type of small buildings, and we're not sure what these stripes are, trenches maybe."

To Jinx, the shapes were just that: shapes without meaning. "What are these little yellow dots everywhere?"

"People. Warm bodies show up hotter. There's obviously a lot of people working around those structures, but at what, we don't know."

"How about your agents in the area, what do they say?"

"No good. They clear the camp of all Nicaraguan personnel every afternoon," Jackson shrugged. "It's all Cuban and Soviet at night.

"Here's the kicker." Jackson turned on the TV next to his desk, and inserted a cassette in the recorder. After the obligatory SECRET NOFORN warnings, a title page with date-time group, latitude-longitude, mission number, identity code

77

of the camp, and lots of other incomprehensible letters and numbers; the tape then began a sequence of infrared video, with a changing date-time group bar in the bottom right corner.

"This sequence was made in one night," Jackson explained, running the tape in fast-scan to speed up the real-time action. "There is almost no activity until 2300 hours, then the place comes alive for twenty minutes, then completely vacates."

On fast-scan, the images looked like fireflies swarming around a red neon.

"What took these?" Jinx asked.

"MAJOR GAZE aircraft. Don't ask what it is, okay? Thirty minutes later a handful of people are back, then the whole process repeats itself."

"Might be training of some sort, Pete," Jinx said, rewinding the tape and running it forward to the point where the activity started. "Let me watch this part at normal speed."

On the screen, the red shapes glowed darkly. The warm yellow glow of a vehicle floated across an edge of the screen. Abruptly, two small clusters of pale yellow dots appeared at the top of the screen. There were three dots in each cluster. The clusters stopped, waited a moment, then moved rapidly down to the red shapes. It was hard to keep oriented because the picture's angle kept changing as the aircraft flew a race-track course.

"Assault teams?"

"Maybe."

Each clump broke into pairs that went down the rows of structures. Two of the yellow dots seemed to float through each red shape.

"What's this?" Jinx asked, stopping the tape, and circling one of the red shapes with a finger.

"Hard to say. The analysts think that the structures either have no roof, or these guys are on top of them."

The dots made their way down the length of the red shapes, regrouped at the far end, and moved to the next row together.

"Watch this." said Jackson. A series of small white flares appeared down the length of rows as the yellow dots departed.

"I dunno, Pete, this looks like a classic sweep through a target to me. Maybe they're using flares to simulate grenades."

"That's what we think, too. The question is, what is the target?" Jackson said, standing. "That's where you and your men come in. We want you to recon that camp and, if possible, attack and destroy it."

"Why attack? If you want a recon, what's the point of attacking? You only tip your hand and let them know you're interested."

"Ordinarily, yes, but this time we don't want to let Ivan think he can run his special ops training in our backyard. We had enough of that crap from the Cubans playing Spetsnaz in Panama back in '88. The Marines had to kill a couple of them to cut that shit out."

"And using the Misura keeps Uncle's skirts clean in the bargain."

"Exactly. It looks like Nicaraguans cleaning their own house, not U.S. aggression."

"When do you want it done?"

"As soon as you can get ready."

"Two weeks minimum, more if you drag your feet getting the Misura's grocery list filled," Jinx said, standing and stretching.

The grocery list was the supplies the Misura wanted before they would participate in any operation. It was always a sore point between the Indians and their American suppliers.

"All right, OK," Jackson said tiredly, as he locked the photos and the videotape in a safe. "I'll get the stuff rounded up myself, but, Jinx, make sure they know we expect results from all this largesse."

"All this largesse would seem pretty pitiful to even an American sharecropper," Jinx shot back. "We aren't doing these folks any great favor, Pete, and don't think they don't know how we treated the 'Yards, Cambodes and the Hmong. Our track record stinks in this area, so try not to act too put upon."

"You're right, Jinx, I'm sorry—no offense."

"None taken, Pete, just treat these guys right, OK?"

"Will do."

Largesse, my ass, Jinx thought as he walked out of the

briefing room. How can they even think like that? We use
these people like toilet paper, then complain about the cost.
If it were little American boys getting killed in this armpit,
it sure as hell wouldn't be largesse!

Unable to shake the bad mood, Jinx spent the whole trip
back to TEA base thinking about the Montagnards he had
fought with, the look of disbelief and despair on their faces
as his subunit had pulled out for the last time, leaving them
to the tender mercies of the Vietnamese. It hardly mattered
whether the North or the South won, the 'Yards would have
to fight for their lives anyway. Those faces haunted him now.
The 'Yards had gotten off easier than the poor Hmong,
though. For a decade, the Meos and other hill tribes had
fought the Pathet Lao in a secret little war in Laos. After the
Agency and the Special Forces left, the Pathet Lao had been
all too happy to let the Soviets use the Hmong as human
guinea pigs for testing their chemical and bacterial weapons.
No one in the U.S. seemed to give a damn, either. Jinx shook
his head remembering the American professor who claimed
the yellow rain reported by survivors was really just bee poop.
The genocide of an entire people reduced to bee poop! Christ!

Would the next set of faces be Indian? Better to not think
about that now; down that road, madness waited.

★ 12 ★

5 December

"Well, my pretties, are you ready?" Captain Karmasov asked. Each man smiled and nodded. "I hope so. The Ensign said you looked like crippled old women last night!"

At this, the smiling stopped. Pleasing the Ensign seemed impossible. Each time they ran this course, they did it the same way, and each time, he found something else to criticize. The first night, they had been too slow, the next, their movements were uncoordinated. Every night it was something.

"Tonight, my little wolf cubs," Karmasov went on, "you had better improve. Subunit Six can already taste that rum."

To keep motivation high, Karmasov had traded three Spetsnaz camouflage jackets for a case of good Cuban rum, a prize for the best subunit. Nothing spurred training like competition, and rum was a prize all could share. The Cuban flight crew had been happy to swap the rum for the uniforms.

"So, tonight you need to be faster, quieter, more agile, and proficient. Just because you have done it within the time limits twice does not mean you can do so every time! Can you do it?"

"YES!" the subunit shouted in English.

"Good, then show me what Spetsnaz troops look like."

Karmasov boarded the truck first as he too was a subunit leader, in addition to being Group 1's commander. The others boarded in reverse order. When they were all in, Karmasov banged on the cab and the truck lurched forward out the gate.

81

At the end of the road, the truck turned on to the other, and the men all crouched on the steel floor. As the fence came in sight, the first trio hopped off the tailgate, rolling with the impact. They ran for the brush as the second threesome moved to take their place on the tailgate. Then only Karmasov and his partners were left. They slid out on the metal shelf, got their balance, and hopped off. They hit the packed dirt surface, rolled up onto their feet and ran for the brush. Once there, Karmasov waited a moment, checked his watch, and signaled forward with his hand. It was important that all of the subunits approach their targets within seconds of each other. Both three-man subunits crossed the strip between the roads and ambled up to their "sentry."

"Got a light buddy?" Karmasov asked in English. The night before he had been instructed to ask it in German.

As the sentry reached into his pocket, Senior Private Zalmanson's hand appeared with a P-6 silenced pistol, which he rammed into the sentry's chest, precisely over the heart. They had even practiced that move for hours. The sentry, looking suitably startled, began to fall to the ground, "shot." Senior Private Dymshitz caught him under the arms. Karmasov grabbed his legs and they dragged the "body" into the sentry hut. Zalmanson recovered the fallen riot club and pulled off the guard's helmet. Inside the hut he struggled to remove the pack filled with fifteen kilos of sand, the "dead" sentry offering no assistance. Hefting the pack onto his back, which he was told would actually contain a radio, he emerged to see his comrades cut the gate's chain with a small bolt cutter and enter the compound. The cutters had at first been a problem because the cutting edge of the Soviet-made ones were too soft and dulled after repeated use. Bodnya promptly procured West German-made cutters. The *zampolit* had not liked this, as he wanted this to be an all-Soviet mission, but it was rumored that the major had squelched this protest by saying that he would rather lead a "true internationalist" success rather than an all-Soviet failure.

Closing the gate, he began a sentry's leisurely pace down the compound's fence. He had been instructed to observe the road and pay no attention to what went on in the compounds.

Karmasov went first, covered by Dymshitz. When both were through, they moved forward to the target mock-ups.

Karmasov climbed up on the back of the plywood box. Dymshitz was on the ground behind the box. Some nights they switched positions. A path had been beaten in the hard soil behind the boxes from frequent practice. On each mock-up there was a small white square where the charge was to be placed.

Over a tank's engine compartment, thought Karmasov. Dymshitz slashed an X with his razor knife in a canvas cap over the "muzzle" of a pipe which simulated a tank's main gun with the turret turned to the rear. The other compound's mock-ups did not have the pipes, but rather a small box on top. On these, both subunit members would place their charges on white squares atop the mock-up's right front and on top of the box. They were, no doubt, armored personnel carrier mock-ups. As each man placed his charges, he pulled the fuse igniter that lit a ninety-second burning fuse. There were fourteen mock-ups in each of the three rows, spaced less than a meter apart. The rows were about twenty meters apart. The subunits had to place their charges on each row and be off the mock-ups before the first charge on that row ignited.

As he jumped from one box to another Karmasov noted that he was the slow man tonight. The subunit in the neighboring compound was nearly finished. They would be well off the mock-ups when the fuses ran out. It was a pleasure to soldier with such good men.

He and Dymshitz emerged through the gate as Zalmanson "shot" the radio. Major Bodnya wanted to do as much damage as possible to the enemy, whoever they might be. They were crouched in the brush, watching, when the last row's igniters flared. A pleased murmur came from his subunit. Karmasov shushed them sternly, forcing down the grin.

This subunit wants to win, he thought, but they want to beat Subunit 6 as much as they want the rum.

Karmasov saw Ensign Kovpak step out and blow his whistle. They had dispensed with the truck pickup tonight as that no longer required practice.

When the lights in the compound came on, the subunits double-timed to Kovpak and formed up into a loose rank.

"Comrade Captain, please move your men into the classroom," Kovpak said as Karmasov turned to him.

"It is done, Comrade Ensign!" Karmasov answered, giving a mock salute. Kovpak winked back.

As the troops double-timed to the building, Kovpak joined Bodnya.

"They look better every night, Major."

"Do you think they will be ready in a week, Ensign?"

"Without question!"

"*Prevoskhodnyy* my friend, excellent."

★ 13 ★

11 December

It had taken four days to reach the camp. The Indians were eager to shoot some Russians, and they kept the pace up all the way. Jinx worried that they would be intercepted, as the Indians preferred to use dirt roads rather than move cross-country, but as usual, there were no Sandinista patrols. The frequent road ambushes that Jinx encouraged had dampened the Popular Army's enthusiasm for road trips. They mostly moved in convoys now, frequently supported by armored personnel carriers.

During a break on the first day Pablo had sat down beside Jinx. "I have found something you might like, *amigo*."

He reached up and pulled off Jinx's bush hat and pinned a badge on it. Handing it back, Jinx was surprized to see a scratched peace symbol.

"Maybe one of these days this may come true, you think?"

"Let's hope so, *amigo*. We're both getting too old for this shit."

On the night of the fourteenth, Jinx was filling his canteen from the Sisin River, four kilometers from the Soviet camp. The camp itself was bordered by the river, which curved around two sides of it. Recce photos showed it to be a big place with two large training compounds, a headquarters, and barrack areas. It was too big to secure all of its perimeter with the number of people apparently on hand.

Every place has it weak spots, thought Jinx. Let's just hope we find the right one.

* * *

Out-fucking-standing! Jinx mused to himself. It was one of those rare tropical nights that was totally silent. The light breeze had died with the sunset. Now there was not a breath of air to stir the trees. The sluggish river was mute. Even the insect noises had stopped. Where were all the goddamned *cooty-whoos* like in the movies?

Jinx shifted his position to bring the big binoculars back to his eyes. Even the rustling of his dirty fatigues was too loud. There was a lot of movement about the camp, but its pattern did not look like the video tape's. Something else was going on. Several trucks were backed up to the headquarters building and barracks. No one was in the training compounds.

Here we go, thought Jinx. Two trucks rumbled to life and started in the compounds' direction. Their low engine noises and grinding of gears were a welcome sound. One pulled up to each compound and a man jumped out to *open the gates*! Leaving them open, they followed the trucks inside.

Triple shit! What's going on? Jinx looked at his watch: 2336 hours.

Men jumped out of the backs of the trucks. Even though it was dark, the binoculars gathered enough light that Jinx could see into shadows to some degree. He saw a fuel drum in the back of one of the trucks. The men were filling buckets from it. The same thing was going on at the other truck. The men trotted over to the square structures and began throwing the cans' contents on them and returned to the truck for more.

"Christ," Jinx said softly to himself, "They're pulling out!

Turning to Pablo he whispered, "They're going to burn the place, *amigo*! Is everyone in place? We've got to hit them now!"

"I think so, but why you attack if they going to destroy it for us?" As usual, Pablo asked the reasonable question.

"It's the principle!" Jinx exclaimed, "Get on the radio and alert everyone; we go at 2350. And make sure the mortars are ready!"

Captain Karmasov was still trying to adjust to the sudden change in the situation. They had been told to prepare for another night's training. Tonight, his subunits were to practice grenade throwing from within buildings. They had just moved their bunks into the barrack's center when Ensign Kovpak came in and told them they were all leaving at 0100 hours. The soldiers began packing their rucksacks and bulky clothing bags while the officers and sergeants were assigned details to destroy the entire camp.

Now, already smelling of petrol, Karmasov counted out the remaining practice charges they had used in training, placing them in rucksacks. His men doused the mock-ups with paint cans of petrol, the same cans that had been used to paint them.

"Stay well back when you throw the charge on the mock-ups," he told Dymshitz as he handed him a pack. "We need no singed wolf pups!"

KA-BLAM! A yellow-white flash lit the barracks area followed by another, even louder. A shower of glowing orange sparks burst from the training area, the burning particles falling all over the camp.

"Attack!" he screamed needlessly. His men were already on the ground looking up at him. We are leaving, he thought, and we are destroying the mock-ups so the enemy cannot find what we are up to. We must finish the job!

"Place the charges and fire them! NOW! Then move back to the headquarters. Do not take the truck, it is too dangerous!"

No sense in leaving it. Grabbing one of the charges, he stepped well back from the tailgate. Looking around the truck to make certain his men were clear, he pulled the fuse lighter pin and tossed it in among the petrol drums, several filled paint cans, and remaining charges. As he ran from the truck, machine gun tracers were lacing down the rows of mock-ups.

"Hot damn!" Jinx exclaimed. A big red and orange fireball mushroomed into the night sky. Maybe they'll think we're using nukes! Just like an A-camp getting overrun in 'Nam, except we're the fucking VC! Plus, both sides used red tracers now.

Followed by a Misura squad, Jinx and Pablo ran for the main gate. It was wide open. A crumpled figure lay on the road, framed by the gate posts. Jinx crouched by the body momentarily. A Cuban, with the upper left part of his head missing. He had been popped by a Misura, Louis Fischer, with a Soviet SVD sniper rifle, a trophy from an earlier operation. Pecos Bill's squad raced past them on their way to the training compounds.

He could hear truck engines revving up on the other side of the barracks. Several men ran out of the headquarters' front door. Two Misura fired at them from the hip, but no one fell.

"*Teniente!* Let's go for the headquarters, we can check out the compounds later!"

It looked like everyone had left the building. Pablo picked two men and told the squad leader to secure the building's front, fire at anyone in the nearby barracks area, and to cover the headquarters' windows, in case someone popped up.

The first Misura started through the front door and was immediately hurled down the three steps into Pablo, knocking him to the ground.

Jinx emptied half his K sub gun's magazine through the door and the wooden wall to its left. The other Misura rifleman, known as Cot-head, did the same, with his G3, through the right wall.

Lockwood, though down, wasted no time. Shouting "*Grenada!*" he flung the M67 frag through the door and rolled over facedown. The blast shook the flimsy wood structure and fragments shredded the clear plastic sheeting covering the windows.

As Pablo checked the dead trooper, Jinx and the remaining Misura bounded up the steps. A sandy-haired body lay to the door's right, riddled with holes. He wore a Cuban camouflage uniform, an AKM still clutched in one hand.

Has to be an East German, thought Jinx. The room, filled with a light haze of smoke and dust shaken loose from the rafters, was bare except for a battered kitchenette table and several mismatched chairs. Newspapers littered the floor.

No sense in taking time to look at them; we want official-looking stuff.

Pablo, gasping for breath, edged up to him.

"You okay, *amigo*?" Jinx asked.

"*Bien, bien.*"

Pablo moved toward the door on the right that led to another darkened room. Sheetrock chunks began to fly from the riddled interior wall. Jinx instinctively stepped back, firing, and tripped over a metal chair. Most of his 9mm rounds clanged through the corrugated tin roof.

Jinx took the fall on his hips and shoulders, but his head banged the floor, dazing him slightly. On the floor, Cot-head emptied the rest of his magazine through the wall and door. Jinx heard retreating footsteps in the adjoining room and the rattle of the Misura changing magazines.

Jinx rolled to his side and popped a fresh magazine in his K. He sat up and looked down into Pablo's staring eyes. The left half of the neck and throat were gone.

"Fuck me! Fuck me! Fuck you, Kraut!" Jinx screamed. He dug in the extra ammo pouch on his belt and found the single M67 he carried. *"Grenada!"*

He hurled the frag through the door, giving the Misura barely enough time to hit the floor again before the deafening bang.

He racked the K gun from left to right, firing through the wall, then burst, through the door, the Misura on his heels. Nothing. Plank work counters attached to the side walls, folding metal chairs stacked against the shot-up wall, used by the Kraut as cover, more newspapers. The air smelled of burnt powder and gasoline. A flickering orange glow lit the next room.

They've torched the place and run, Jinx thought. Should we get out or go on with the search? That's what we're here for. That's what Pablo died for!

Jinx stepped into the large flame-lit room. A too-big shadow moved to his left. A blow like a well-aimed swing with a baseball bat hit a homerun on his chest. He bounced into the right door frame and rebounded into the left, knocking the Misura back into the other room, then crumbled to the threshold. He thought he had heard a shot.

"Amerikanisch hundscheisse!" rasped a blond German captain. He was raising his PM pistol to put a 9mm bullet into the American's head.

Some twenty 9mm rounds streamed into the German's chest and face from six feet, turning his head into an exploding shower of bone fragments, tissue, blood, and gray matter.

Jinx struggled to his feet bracing his back against the door frame for support. *"Deutsche hundscheisse."* Got to get some documents—something. What else did Pablo die for? Not those bastards in Mocoron!

Flames from the burning trash can had spread to the particle board nailed to the wall. The map on it was burning. A broom handle, used to stir the burning papers, protruded from the miniature firestorm within the can. Vaporous flames were spreading across parts of the dirt-tracked plywood floor as spilled gasoline ignited.

The Misura grabbed him by the shoulder. *"Vamanose, mi Capitán!"*

Jinx shook the pleading hand away and darted into the room. He could not help thinking, "Into the jaws of Hell!" Grabbing the map sheet's corner he pulled. He saw the crisscross of military grid lines and *English* words.

Bodnya grabbed Lieutenant Plaski by the arm. "Drive the trucks through the fence. Get everyone out of here!"

Let the *Chekist* earn his officer's stars now! he thought. Fortunate indeed that everything was loaded! But there were still documents and maps to be destroyed in the headquarters' secure room.

He ran to the truck. Soldiers were pulling their comrades into the back. Bodnya grasped the fat, tubular RPO-A launcher and its canvas backpack, and rushed back to the headquarters. The sound of automatic weapons fire seemed to come from all directions. From the pack he pulled an eleven-kilo canister and shoved it into the breech of the launch tube. Shouldering the RPO-A recoilless flamethrower, he squeezed the trigger, making contact with the electrical firing system. The napalm-filled rocket projectile exploded from the tube and streaked toward the already burning building. Though the weapon was recoilless, the sudden departure of twenty-four pounds from a five-pound tube on his shoulder made Bodnya stagger back. The rocket's napalm warhead hit the left side of the wall, blowing a two-foot hole and splattering the burning liquid the length of the wall.

Kovpak yelled as the incendiary rocket impacted. "Aleksei! We must go!" He surprised himself that he actually called out his friend's first name. Maybe he will not remember. Worse yet, I hope none of the men heard!

* * *

The map was still stuck to the particle board when the world caught fire. The blast, off to his right, split the map board, and hurled Jinx backward. As he reeled from the blast, his foot kicked over the burning trash can. The gasoline in the can flowed like a burning river back toward the door. Jinx batted out the two burning globs on his clothes, then searched through the smoke for the map. It was still hanging by a corner, burning. Jinx grabbed the only corner not burning and jerked the map off the wall. He stomped out the flames. Only a fragment of the map remained, but it was all he could find. The fire was burning briskly, now. Time to get out, but where? The rocket hole in the wall was the best option.

As the two Russians watched, a figure hurtled through the building's burning wall. Wreathed in smoke, silhouetted against a wall of flame, the demon-man-creature smoothly rolled to its feet and pointed a submachine gun directly at Bodnya's face, less than ten meters away. Bodnya slowly lowered the launch tube to his side as he stared at the glowing eyes set in a blackened face. Kovpak was so stunned, even with all his combat experience, he was unable to raise his AKSU.

The smoldering creature pulled the trigger—and nothing happened! The submachine gun went down and the creature glanced at it. "Fucking shit!" It looked up at Kovpak and back to Bodnya. "Next time, comrade!" Then the smoking apparition disappeared into the shadows on the building's far side.

Jinx stumbled out the gate with Cot-head's aid. Two men from Pecos Bill's squad also lent a hand as they returned from the compounds. Of all the stinking luck! He had a Russkie dead to rights and the fucking K gun was empty. They had stared right into each others' eyes from thirty feet. He had to be a Soviet officer! And the other guy just stood there with a weapon in his hands! It was pure luck. Luck, too, that he was able to dive straight out the hole when the whole wall went up in flames. What the hell did that Russkie shoot anyway? he wondered, wiping soot off his face.

Standing in the edge of the woods, Jinx and his Misura watched the camp burn. The headquarters was now totally consumed by flames. He looked at the crumbled and charred corner of a map sheet clutched in his fist. As he dropped it into a zip-lock plastic bag, he noticed for the first time the long wood sliver in his shoulder. Where the hell did he pick *that* up? Cot-head helped Jinx out of his web gear and shirt. Jinx took a deep breath and nodded. Cot-head pulled the sliver out and pushed a field dressing against the hole to staunch the blood. It hurt, but not too badly. Jinx pulled his hat off and removed the small peace badge. He pinned it over the Misura's left pocket.

"You deserve a medal, *amigo*."

The small brown warrior reflected on how strange the *gringos* were as they moved off into the trees.

★14★

13 December

"Be seated Comrade Major."

Bodnya inspected the GRU colonel seated behind a battered wooden desk. The desk was battered like everything else in this poor excuse for a Socialist state, but the items displayed on it were meticulously arranged, using some unfathomable formula to place every object just so.

"Thank you, Comrade Colonel." The man had not yet introduced himself.

"Major, I represent the Summer Harvest Tasking Committee. There has been some concern expressed that the action the night before last at the Sisin Camp may have compromised your operation." Bodnya noted that it was suddenly "his" operation.

"Explain to me why you feel that the operation should still be executed—if necessary."

"Comrade Colonel, we were in the process of destroying the camp when the counterrevolutionaries struck. All of the mock-ups were burned, as was the headquarters building. Everything of intelligence value had been moved out or burned. I personally set the headquarters building on fire."

"Was any essential equipment lost?"

"No, Comrade Colonel." Bodnya responded patiently. "It had already been loaded on trucks."

The colonel glanced at some papers. "Your force sustained a number of casualties. Were any of the wounded men critical to the success of the operation?"

"In no way. One of the KGB Special Section officers suffered a leg wound from a bursting mortar shell, but his loss will not affect the mission's success." The colonel was nodding in agreement. No GRU officer would feel that the loss of a KGB officer on a mission would affect its success. In fact, it might increase its chances of succeeding.

"Two soldiers and a sergeant were wounded. One of the soldiers is in critical condition," Bodnya continued. "Another severely twisted his ankle while boarding a truck and will not be able to take part. Several of the East German and Cuban support personnel were also killed and wounded."

"Where are our wounded now?"

"In a military hospital in Managua. They are in a closed ward with GRU sentries. The man with the ankle injury and one slightly wounded soldier are already in the Soviet embassy. I understand that all will be returned to the *Rodina* very soon."

"Yes, Major, that is correct. You still have enough personnel to complete the mission?"

"Yes, Comrade Colonel. We were assigned six standby personnel to serve as replacements in the event we suffered training injuries or illness. They had been taking part in the training and have already been assigned to subunits and briefed on their duties."

The colonel looked thoughtfully at the wall behind Bodnya's head. "So you feel that there was no compromise?"

"In no way, Comrade Colonel."

"And you feel that your force can successfully accomplish the mission in light of the casualties?"

"Exactly so, Comrade Colonel!"

Giving Bodnya a stern schoolmaster's look, "Let us hope so, Comrade Major, for the sake of the *Rodina* and for your sake."

Bodnya returned the colonel's hard look. "You have my utmost assurances that this mission will be a success, Comrade Colonel."

The colonel stared back into those unblinking, pale blue eyes. Bodnya's frank expression was unsettling, almost an affront to the colonel's rank and authority, but at the same time he realized that if anyone could complete this mission, this prime example of New Soviet Man could.

"Exactly so, Comrade Major! We are all counting on you. Now, perhaps you might like to learn more about your target?"

"Indeed, Comrade Colonel." Bodnya's training map had no name or location markings, nothing to give away the real target.

The colonel reached into the top drawer of the desk, and produced a thick folder. He spread on the desktop a U.S. military map.

"Your target is the U.S. Army base at Ft. Hood, in the state of Texas, United States of America."

Ft. Hood, a sprawling military complex in central Texas, was thought to be the largest concentration of armor in the free world. Over thirty-eight thousand troops and fifty-six hundred civilian employees were stationed there. Bodnya's ninety *ikhotniki* were to take on an entire armored corps.

The force would consist of four groups. Each of the four groups was organized with a different number of two- to six-man subunits, depending on the specific target. Group 1 was targeted at the 1st Cavalry Division's armored cavalry squadron, and its four tank, two mechanized infantry, two self-propelled artillery, and one air defense artillery battalion's motor pools, one three-man subunit per motor pool. Group 2 was similarly organized, but intended for the 2d Armored Division's area on the east side of the post.

Both armored divisions had only two brigades, the 1st Cavalry's third brigade was provided by the 155th Armored Brigade of the Mississippi Army National Guard. The 2d Armored Division's third brigade was based on West Germany's northern plains. The "Cav" or "First Team," as the 1st Cavalry was known to its troops, had been at Ft. Hood since 1971 when it returned from Vietnam. There it served as one of the Army's most effective divisions using the airmobile concept. On its return, it had tested a combined armored/mechanized/helicopter concept, but was converted to an armored division in 1974. The 2d "Hell on Wheels" Division had been at Ft. Hood since 1957 and had not seen combat since World War II, though its battalion-sized armored cavalry squadron had served in Vietnam.

Ft. Hood was also the home of III Corps, the self-styled

"Mobile Armored Corps." This was NATO's reinforcement corps, the "cavalry" that would rush to Europe by air and sea if the Warsaw Pact chose to invade Western Europe. Their combat vehicles and other heavy equipment would be left behind. They would draw vehicles and equipment already pre-positioned in Europe. The "Phantom Corps," as the Germans had called it in World War II due to its habit of appearing at the most inopportune times, was a key element in America's plans to reinforce its NATO allies. Major efforts had been made to prepare for this eventuality. In the early 1980s the airfield at West Ft. Hood had been extended to handle any transport in the Air Force's inventory and a large departure terminal with cargo handling facilities had been built. Heavy equipment would be sent by ship from the Texas ports of Houston, Galveston, and Beaumont, to replace battle losses.

Also stationed at Ft. Hood were the corps' 13th Support Command providing logistical and maintenance services, 3d Signal, 6th Air Cavalry, 75th Field Artillery, 89th Military Police, and 504th Military Intelligence Brigades, and the Apache Training Brigade which trained and equipped new attack helicopter battalions.

Other corps units were stationed elsewhere in the country: 3rd Armored Cavalry Regiment and 11th Air Defense Artillery Brigade were at Ft. Bliss, Texas. The Corps Artillery's 212th and 214th Field Artillery Brigades were at Ft. Sill, Oklahoma. Other units included the Army Reserve's Texas-based 420th Engineer and 807th Medical Brigades, and the Oklahoma Army National Guard's 45th Infantry Brigade. Three mechanized infantry divisions were also allotted to III Corps: the 1st at Ft. Riley, Kansas, 4th at Ft. Carson, Colorado, and 5th at Ft. Polk, Louisiana. These units were beyond the interests of Summer Harvest.

Group 3, led by Bodnya, had a mixed bag of tasks. Target 3-1 was the fuel storage depot. The attack on it would signal all other subunits to initiate theirs. Target 3-2 was the III Corps Headquarters, a large, modern glass and steel building built in 1989. Bodnya's own subunit would handle this purely psychological target. Target 3-3 was subdivided into several individual targets, the homes of the two division commanders, the corps commander, and his deputy. One assassin would be dropped off at each of their government houses in Wainwright Heights. When the attack began, these commanders would be called by duty officers, if not alerted by the action itself. They were to be executed as they rushed out their back doors to their cars. No one was irreplaceable, but this would be another psychological victory.

The 6th Air Cavalry Brigade's AH-64 Apache and AH-1S Cobra attack helicopters at Ft. Hood Army Airfield were not forgotten. Designated Target 3-4, the six-man subunit slated for it was to destroy as many of the advanced tank-killing gunships as possible. If time and ordnance remained, they were to destroy UH-60 Blackhawks, twin-rotored CH-47D Chinooks, OH-54C Kiowa scouts, and UH-1H Hueys in that order of priority.

Almost as an afterthought, someone on the Tasking Committee had remembered the Texas National Guard's 49th Armored Division. Stationed in dozens of armories throughout the state, it was the principal Guard unit aligned to III Corps. Some of its combat vehicles were kept at unit armories, but most were located at the Mobilization and Training Equipment Site at North Ft. Hood, a secluded sub-post some twenty-five kilometers north of the main post. Here too were vehicles belonging to the Guard's 36th Armored Brigade. Formed in 1988, it was the third brigade of the New Jersey Guard's 50th Armored Division. The planners reluctantly added another fourteen Spetsnaz to the Summer Harvest force and allotted resources to get this fourth group to North Fort Hood.

Bodnya left the briefing room stunned and impressed. The mission was far more ambitious than he had dreamed. That he had been picked to lead it flattered him immensely.

14 December

The hangar was small by Soviet standards, but better than most in Central America. The old hangar had been destroyed by the earthquake in 1972. Cuban combat engineers had scraped off the jumbled ruins, poured some extra concrete on the sides, and put a prefabricated metal building up on the old foundation. The building would not accommodate an entire An-12, so the tail stuck out through openings in the two hangar doors.

The tail was not important. What was vital was the cosmetic work on the nose of the transport. The sharp nose of the An-12 was being reshaped to resemble the rounder, dolphin nose of a U.S. C-130 Hercules. The rest of the Russian plane bore enough resemblance to the Hercules to pass. The rearward thrust of the wings was the most noticeable difference, but few casual observers would notice that unless the planes were parked next to each other. With its new nose and painted with the U.S. night camouflage pattern and markings, it would easily pass for a C-130 visually and on radar.

Walking around the huge plane, Lt. Col. Ivan Vasilich Scheverard wondered what the Soviet Air Force would do if Lockheed ever quit designing aircraft. Both the An-12 and the Ilyushin IL-76, the workhorses of the Soviet air transport fleet, were close copies of American designs. Changes were made only in those areas where Russian technology could not duplicate the American construction. The Soviet Army's equipment was all original designs, but the Air Force relied on the West for inspiration. Scheverard voiced none of this, of course. Such comments were anti-Soviet in nature.

Inside, the plane was unchanged. The nylon seats and twin static line cables were identical to the American aircraft. Scheverard was inspecting the cables when one of the painters called from outside.

"Colonel, are you in there? You have guests."

As he stepped down from the plane, Scheverard looked over his visitors. The two Spetsnaz stood out from the rest. They were thinner; hard and professional looking. The taller of the two, the major, looked like a recruiting poster. His rugged good looks and bearing were the model of the New Soviet Man. His companion looked like a reeducated street criminal by comparison. Shorter by a head, he had a look that made Scheverard want to keep an eye on the man, to make sure he didn't steal the plane while no one was looking. They were a strange pair, certainly.

"Good morning, Colonel," the taller one said, stepping forward and extending a hand. "I am Major Bodnya. This is my aide, Ensign Kovpak."

"Good morning, Comrades," Scheverard replied. "I heard that you had some excitement the other day."

Bodnya and Kovpak exchanged looks. News traveled fast here, even classified news.

"A little." Bodnya answered. "We didn't think it was common knowledge."

"In such a small country everything is common knowledge."

"Then perhaps we need to get out of this small country as soon as possible," Kovpak said, walking up and patting the side of the An-12.

"Indeed."

"Colonel Scheverard, will these modifications really disguise the airplane enough to pass for an American C-130?" Bodnya asked as he walked slowly around the front of the huge plane.

"Not to one of the builders, certainly, but it will pass a casual inspection, especially at night."

Bodnya stepped back to watch the painters at work. Using huge templates, they were painting the plane in a pattern of dark green and black. The pattern was the current one used by the U.S. Air Force special operations squadrons.

"What about your tail guns?" Bodnya asked. "The Americans do not arm their transports."

"Those will remain," Scheverard replied. "The tail has been reshaped, too, but the 23s stay."

Bodnya nodded, and continued his walk-around inspection. The plane was ready, save for the paint. This plane was the part he worried about. The men would do their job. He knew them, lived with them, fought with them. They would do what they were told. This machine was the unknown. So much Soviet equipment didn't work, either from poor construction or haphazard maintenance. If this plane failed, the mission failed.

"Colonel Scheverard, our entire operation revolves around this aircraft. It must be in perfect order."

Scheverard was stung by the remark, but kept his composure. "I assure you, Major Bodnya, this An-12 is in perfect condition. I have supervised every step of its modification and preparation. The engines are new, just arrived from Havana. I have experience in covert flight operations and Spetsnaz insertion."

"Tell me about your crew, Colonel."

"My copilot is Maj. Aleksei Sukhoverko. He has flown with me for two years," Scheverard answered. "Our navigator is Maj. Andre Dorroffeyev, from Aeroflot. He is an experienced navigator, familiar with U.S. air traffic control procedures, and an excellent English speaker. Maj. Nikolai Ershov is our Radio-ECM operator. We will have four enlisted crewmen, a load master, two assistant loadmasters, and a gunner for the 23mms."

"All of these men have flown in Afghanistan in support of remote outposts and ground operations," Scheverard went on, happy to get the chance to brag of his crew. "They have flown many missions in the Panjshir Valley. It took steady nerves and a sure hand to drop supplies through a curtain of 14.5mm fire. They are no strangers to combat. They will complete this mission. My aircraft and crew will not fail you."

"I hope so, Colonel. The *Rodina* is counting on us." He was impressed with the ranks of the flight deck crew. The Air Force had sent some of its best.

Bodnya and the ensign shook Scheverard's hand and walked toward their waiting vehicle.

"Oh, Major," Scheverard called after them, "I believe we have worked together before."

Bodnya stopped and turned back toward the pilot.

"Is that so?" he asked. "When was that?"

"In Winter Shield '86. I flew your team on the insertion at Eisleben."

Bodnya smiled. That flight had been the most frightening ride of his life. Thunderstorms had kicked the plane around like a toy, and when they finally entered the valley around Eisleben, a snowstorm had virtually blinded them. He and his troops had jumped blind, certain that they would never find their dropping zone, much less the target. They had landed perfectly, right where they needed to be. The snowstorm had covered their movement and they had placed their charges on the opposing force's communications complex and escaped undetected. Their mission had been hailed as outstanding.

He had never known the pilot of that flight, but had blessed him.

"You should have said that immediately," he smiled at Scheverard. "I could have saved you that little speech."

Scheverard returned the smile and saluted.

As Bodnya turned back for the door, he put his arm around Kovpak's shoulders and said loudly, "Did I ever tell you about Eisleben? Now that was a mission!"

Scheverard laughed quietly as he climbed the steps into the An-12. He wanted to check the instruments once more before lunch. He would have the copilot check them again later.

★15★

16 December

The after-action debriefing had been in Mocoron. Pete Jackson had been there, and Jinx smelled trouble the minute he saw Jackson's face. Russell had been there, too, smug and bloodthirsty. Jab Donlon had come in looking like a guy whose vasectomy was still sore, and was reluctant to even look at Jinx.

"Shall we begin?" Russell led off, his voice almost trilling.

The tape recorder was turned on and Pete Jackson made the introduction.

"After-action review, Sisin Camp raid, 10 December."

After each of the participants had introduced themselves for the recording, Russell began.

"Captain Jenkins, will you read us your mission summary?"

"On 15 November, a force of fifty Misura soldiers from the *Tropos Especiales Atlantico* attacked the camp ten kilometers from Sisin, Nicaragua. I acted as an advisor to the unit, and was present for the attack. Our mission was to gain as much information as possible concerning the activities and purpose of the camp, and to destroy it."

"Was the camp intact when the attack began?" Russell interrupted.

"Well, yes and no," Jinx replied.

"Which? Yes or no?"

"The camp was intact, but there were people at work in the training area—"

"Doing what?"

"Why don't you let Captain Jenkins finish his summary?" Jab Donlon snapped at Russell. "Don't be in such a rush."

"Certainly."

"Our force moved into position two hours after sunset, and took up positions to the west of the camp and across the Sisin River. The element across the river were to give fire support to the assault force. The attack was scheduled for 0300 hours, when it was assumed that the camp personnel would be involved in whatever training was being conducted. We hoped to cover our initial approach with the firing, if any, from the training, penetrate the camp, and to hopefully acquire some human assets for intelligence gathering."

"You mean you planned to *kidnap* Soviet military personnel?" Russell cloyed, stressing the word kidnap.

Jinx paused, looking up. Pete Jackson was studying a fly on the wall, Jab Donlon looked like his nuts were hurting, and Russell looked like a cat target-locked on a canary.

"No, I mean the Misura intended to take some foreign mercenaries, in this case, Soviet mercenaries, as prisoners of war, for the purpose of interviewing them prior to returning them to the Soviet Embassy in Tegu," Jinx replied, deftly evading the trap Russell was obviously setting.

What's this little bastard up to? Jinx thought. He must think I've never done this shit before.

"Go on, Captain."

"As we observed the camp, we could see activity in the training area. There were troops moving around the buildings and the square shapes."

"Jinx, Captain Jenkins, tell us more about the square structures," Jackson injected.

"Sure. In one compound each structure was approximately twenty-five feet long, ten feet wide, and five feet high. On top of each structure there was a pipe approximately eight feet long. The other structures were about seven feet high with a small box on top, no pipe. There were no markings on the structures and no apparent openings. They appeared to be made of painted wood. We really couldn't make out—"

"Did you get any photographs of the structures, Captain?" Russell snapped.

"Unfortunately, no—"

"Were you equipped with a camera for this mission?"

"Yes. Mr. Jackson brought me one, a Canon 35mm."

"They why didn't you get any photographs?" Russell practically sneered.

"I'm coming to that—"

"Russell, let the man give his report!" Donlon barked, color rising in his face. "Go on Captain."

The look that passed between Donlon and Russell was a warning flag to Jinx that he was entering a minefield.

"Well, we watched this activity for a while and, when we saw no evidence of training going on, we—*Teniente* Lockwood and myself—decided to move up the attack time."

"Why?" again from Donlon.

"We observed the people in the training area filling up buckets from fuel drums, and we were afraid that they were going to burn the camp before we could get a better look at it. At any rate, our fire support was in place and ready, so we kicked off the attack right then."

"What time was that?" Jackson asked quietly.

"2350 hours."

Jackson nodded, "OK, go on."

"We entered the camp through the main gate, under covering fire from two M60s and a 60mm mortar. The assault force split into two groups. Lieutenant Lockwood, myself, and a Misura rifle squad made for the headquarters building. The headquarters area was defended by some Cubans and approximately ten or twelve other personnel."

"What kind of other personnel?" Jackson asked, for the recording.

"East German and Soviet."

"You're sure about the Germans?"

"Very. I killed one of them no farther away than you are," Jinx said softly, looking directly at Russell. Jinx's stare implied that he would be happy to demonstrate how.

"At any rate, we surprised the defenders and made our way into their headquarters building itself."

"Who was with you at that time?"

"Lieutenant Lockwood and two Misura soldiers."

"OK, what happened inside the building?"

"We gained entry, and started to search the rooms. We lost one of the Misura troopers to a German when we entered the building, but we neutralized him. As we prepared to enter the second room a German shot Lieutenant Lockwood, and I shot him. He had been burning papers in a trash can."

"Were you able to recover any of those papers?"

"Unfortunately, no."

"Why not?"

"I'm coming to that, Russell, keep your shirt on," Jinx snapped, leaning toward the microphone, so the comment would be clear on the tape.

"Russ, let the man tell his story, all right?" Pete Jackson said sotto voce, covering the microphone with his hand. "You can ask questions when he's finished."

"Go on, Captain," Donlon said.

"After neutralizing the German, I observed a map on the wall behind the burning trash can, and started for it, when the wall blew in," Jinx went on. "The blast knocked me down, but I made it over to the wall, or what was left of it, and secured a portion of the map. The rest of the map was destroyed by the blast, as well as the material in the can."

"You were wounded at that time, am I correct?" Jab Donlon interrupted.

"That's correct, but it was just a scratch," Jinx replied in his best Chuck Yeager voice, red-lining the humble meter.

"What else did you observe in the room?" Jackson asked.

"Nothing really. By that time, the room was on fire, and I took what I could find and left."

"What about those structures, Captain?" Russell asked softly. "Did you get a look at them?"

"Yes. They looked the same up close as they did at a distance. They were hollow, but there were no doors on them. There were boot scuff marks up the sides of the end ones in each row, as if someone had climbed on top, but no other markings."

"Why didn't you get photos of them, Captain?"

"Well, Mr. Russell, the camera was hit by a bullet when we assaulted the headquarters building," Jinx drawled, reaching into the bag under his chair.

He pulled out a wrecked Canon F-1 camera. The camera

was dirty, its lens shattered and bent to one side, the back twisted and bulged out.

"It was hanging around my neck at the time," Jinx said lightly. "I hope I can get a report of survey on it."

Everyone was looking at Russell, who looked like he smelled something rotten.

"Don't worry about it, Captain," Pete Jackson chuckled. "We can get another one. Finish your report."

"By the time Cot-head, uh, Trooper Cunningham, and I got out of the headquarters, the return fire from the Cubans and Soviets was slacking off, and we made our way out of the camp. It appeared that most of the enemy had withdrawn from the camp. I suppose they didn't want to fight too hard for something they were going to burn anyway. Most of the box structures were on fire, but some of the men were able to get close to a few of them for a closer look. In fact, they used them to cover our withdrawal. We had a smooth exfiltration, total casualties were two killed, four wounded, including myself."

"So basically you got some men killed and collected no information of any use," Russell sneered. "Is that about right?"

Here it comes, Jinx thought, the chance this little paper-pusher has been waiting for.

"We destroyed the camp."

"Just ahead of the Soviets, from what you said."

"There is the map fragment, too."

"A needle in a haystack, I'm afraid, Jinx," Pete Jackson said, picking up the burnt paper in its baggie. He dropped it back on the table as though it were a dead mouse.

Russell stood and walked over to the window.

"Captain Jenkins, your record has been a disaster from start to finish. I'm recommending that you be reassigned to a post that better fits your capabilities."

"What a surprise," Jinx laughed. "I'm *so* shocked!"

Russell turned to face Jinx.

"This is not funny, Jenkins," Russell snapped. "Your attitude is a big part of what's happening to you."

"What is happening to me, Russell?" Jinx crooned in mock distress, leaning back in his chair. "You gonna to bend my dog tags and send me to Vietnam? Oh please, B'rer Fox, don't throw me in dat briar patch!''

Donlon had been sitting staring at his fingertips.

"Damn it Jenkins, can't you be serious for a minute?"

"Get real, sir," Jinx said, standing so abruptly that his chair fell over backward. "I've spent months in this rat hole trying to make soldiers out of a bunch of farmers while guys like Russell here sat under their air conditioner and played with themselves. Now this little weasel, who's never heard a shot fired in anger, tells me I'm not good enough to stay here. Great! Out-fucking-standing! Send me home today, right now. I'm ready. Send Russell back to Rus Rus to take my place. He needs to see how the other half lives. Now, if you don't need me—"

Jinx turned and walked toward the door.

"Jenkins, you're through!" Russell shouted.

"Let me guess," Jinx said over his shoulder. "I'll never work in this town again, right?"

Jinx walked rapidly from the briefing room, down the corridor, and out the front door, making a beeline for the BOQ so no one would see the huge grin beginning to spread across his face.

Free at last, free at last, great God a'mighty, we free at last, he thought.

When he opened the door to his room, the phone was already ringing.

"Crisis Hotline," Jinx answered, deadpan.

"Jinx, it's Pete. Sorry I didn't get to warn you. Russell's been head-hunting you for weeks. I don't know what his problem is."

"He's an asshole bureaucrat, Pete," Jinx laughed, "but I couldn't be happier. This whole now-we're-in-it, now-we're-not war is a pain in the butt. I'm tired of trying to not win, you know? I'm ready to go home."

"Come by later, I've got your travel orders and ticket."

"First class, I assume?"

"Coach, and lucky to get it."

"Bye, Pete."

So, that's it, Jinx thought as he stuffed his shaving kit into his aviator's kit bag; sent home in disgrace. Fuck it, I've been thrown out of better places than this.

Going home didn't bother him. Hell, that was the good news. What wouldn't leave him alone was the Indians. Oh sure, someone would replace him in a few days, but how long would he stay? Would he be able to do anything while he was there? It was too frustrating, and he was getting too old. His arm started to throb, reminding him. He hadn't even noticed it during the debriefing. Now it was just another ache. At least it would heal quickly. The ache in his guts and in his heart would hurt a lot longer.

He pulled the map fragment in its plastic bag from his trousers cargo pocket and placed it between the pages of a news magazine. This went into the kit bag as well.

"Good morning, Major, I am Capt. Feodor T'sinko," the officer barked. His hand shot up in a perfect salute. "Please come in."

"Good morning, Captain," Bodnya replied casually, returning the officer's salute. "This is Ensign Kovpak, my aide."

Kovpak nodded.

"Why don't you begin, Captain." Bodnya suggested. Kovpak closed the door to T'sinko's small office and took the remaining chair. The room was windowless, the only light coming from the bare bulb that hung from the ceiling. A large map of Nicaragua dominated one wall. An equally large map of Mexico and the southern U.S. faced it on the opposite wall. T'sinko's desk and the three rickety wooden folding chairs were the only furniture in the room.

"Yes, Comrade Major. There will be four of us on the initial party. You and Ensign Kovpak, a Sr. Sgt. Sergei Malinkov, and myself. I understand that Sgt. Malinkov was your choice. May I ask why?"

"Malinkov is a good soldier, steady and unquestioning. When he has a task to complete, I never have to wonder if it will be done. He speaks English fairly well, too."

Beside Bodnya, Kovpak smiled slightly. "Not to mention that he is the best silent killer in the Spetsnaz."

T'sinko looked a bit startled, but recovered. "Yes, well that's excellent. Where was I?"

T'sinko had been trained as a parachutist and in Spetsnaz skills at Ryazan Higher Airborne School for just such an eventuality as this, but that had been over four years ago. He had almost forgotten what these men were like.

T'sinko took a rolled-up overlay from his desk and stepped over to the map on the U.S. on the wall. He pinned up the overlay and used a pencil from his pocket to point to the spot on the Texas coast where the freighter would drop them off.

"The four of us will be inserted into the United States by water at a point south of Corpus Christi, Texas on the night of 22 December. We will make our way to shore by inflatable boat. On shore we will be met by one of my agents and a group of American partisans."

"How far offshore will we be when we are dropped off?" Kovpak asked.

"Four to six miles. We will then accompany the partisans by automobile to Austin, Texas. Here."

He pointed to the city in the center of the state.

"The trip should take four hours. The partisans maintain a safe house there, and it will be our operational base for the mission. From this base, we will conduct a reconnaissance of Ft. Hood the following day and meet with my frozen agents in place there. After this reconnaissance, we will return to Austin for the night. The following afternoon, 24 December, we will return to Ft. Hood to prepare the dropping zone for your troops. My agents will provide transportation for the different target groups and a command vehicle for yourself. Do you have any questions so far?"

"Yes, Comrade Captain, I do," Bodnya said. "Tell me more about these partisans. I do not like trusting any part of a mission to troops not under my control—or yours."

"Major, these partisans are members of a group called the Concerned Citizens for Latin American People, CCLAP, as they call themselves. They are patriots who despise the American government's racist oppression of the peoples of Central America. They work to defeat these policies by bringing across the border people fleeing the repression of the puppet governments run by the American CIA. They have smuggled at least one hundred twenty-five Polish and East German aliens, those who have deserted their homeland, into the U.S. They have also smuggled in two of my agents in the same fashion. They are dedicated to their cause."

"Are they Communists?" Bodnya interrupted.

"Well, not as such, but they serve our needs in the area. They are what we call useful fools."

"I see, so what you are telling me is that we are entrusting our mission to a handful of Americans who are not Communists, but only seek to bring foreign people into the United States and evade the American border police."

T'sinko looked uneasy. "Well, yes, but do not be mistaken, Major. These are good people, led by one of my own."

"As you say. Tell me then about the two agents at Ft. Hood."

"These two men have worked for me for the last three years. One is an American defector, the other a Russian raised in the U.S. by a GRU family. They were infiltrated into America from Mexico City. Both have been excellent in obtaining information of all kinds for me."

"What type of information have they provided?"

The young captain looked very uncomfortable discussing his agents. This was understandable. In peacetime, the network of agents in America was a precious and fragile resource. Agent runners like T'sinko were very jealous of their agents. The agents had to be courted, seduced, and often bought. Like a lover, agent runners were jealous.

This, however was not peacetime, not for the Spetsnaz. They were at war already. Only their enemies had not been informed.

"Well," T'sinko went on, "a variety. One of them works in the base printing shop. He provides all orders and other publications printed there. The other, the defector, works for the telephone company on base. He installs telephone systems for the Army. His information comes from monitoring devices he installs with the telephones. He has been invaluable at acquiring computer and signal intelligence."

"Will these agents participate in the actual raid?"

"Yes comrade, they will be driving the vehicles, due to their familiarity with them and with the different target areas."

Bodnya studied the GRU officer for a moment, making him uncomfortable. Like many intelligence officers, T'sinko was uncomfortable around combat troops. The world of intelligence was all shadow and whisper; that of the soldier fire and steel. Each was essential to the other, but they did not mix well.

"Make no mistake, Captain. I am concerned about these men. One double agent would not only cause the mission to fail, but could compromise the war effort itself. I do not trust men who have two faces."

"These men have worked diligently for me in the very heart of the enemy camp. They have not been turned, I assure you. They will give their all for the *Rodina* when the time comes."

"Very well. Continue."

"We have rented trucks for each of your teams," T'sinko went on. "They are common rental trucks, and will attract no suspicion. After the mission, these trucks will be abandoned. For the escape phase, a larger truck has been procured, with a series of cargo boxes in it to hide the troops in case it is searched. It is located in a warehouse near the base."

"How will we get from the targets to the warehouse?" Bodnya asked.

"The original trucks will pick up troops and take them to the warehouse. If some troops miss the pickup, they will be on their own. We cannot wait for them."

"Have you no provision for stragglers?"

"The agent's carryall will be available, as will a van, but someone else will have to drive. After the attack, it may be difficult to pick up stragglers at all."

"You expect a strong response to the attack?"

"No, but I expect a great deal of confusion. The men in the residential area will be the hardest to pick up. They must know that we will not wait for them."

"They know."

"Major, why not establish a rally point for any troops not picked up?" Kovpak asked. He pointed to a complex on the base map. "Captain, what is this building?"

"It is the base gymnasium."

"Would it work for a rally point?"

"Yes, it is centrally located and would be easily found by anyone who misses his pickup. A civilian vehicle in the parking lot would not attract any attention. Who will be there to pick up stragglers?"

"I will," Bodnya answered, "and you will."

The Captain looked strained at this idea, but did not flinch. "Of course."

For the better part of an hour, the three men went over the attack plans, looking for flaws, choreographing the dance of death. Finally, Bodnya stood and stretched.

"Thank you for the briefing, Captain. We will go over the details again when we are away from here."

T'sinko snapped to attention and saluted again. Bodnya returned it, staring into the GRU captain's eyes.

★16★

17 December

"Beth, who's that character in 12C?"

"Beats me, but he's drinking up the whole liquor cabinet," Beth Conners answered, stretching up for the last tray of tiny liquor bottles in the cabinet. "He's had about four straight bourbons, and is asking for more."

"I hope he's not going to be a mean drunk like that guy last week," Alicia said. "I thought that flight would never end."

"No, I think this one will be okay, he seems to be in another world," Beth said, straightening her uniform skirt. "I just hope he doesn't pass out."

"Assholes," Jinx said to himself for the thousandth time. "What a bunch of assholes."

He'd had just enough alcohol to adjust his attitude, and the green hills of Honduras had disappeared behind him. The ocean thousands of feet below looked blue as lapis, and the clouds were bright white.

Amazing how clean everything looks up here, Jinx mused. The world looks OK and everything seems possible, somehow. No wonder pilots seemed like they were from another world—they were.

I'm going to find another line of work, I swear, Jinx thought to himself. Something normal. Well, not too normal, but not as weird as this. Security work, maybe.

He knew a guy in Houston who had a company, doing

security consulting for multinational corporations. That would be a snap after what he had been doing lately, and corporate bigwigs couldn't be any bigger assholes than guys like Russell.

Maybe I'll write this stuff up and sell it to the movies, Jinx thought, settling into a warm alcohol glow. It'd make a better story than most of the crap on TV! Hollywood Jenkins—it had a nice ring. When he got settled, he'd buy a typewriter, some Hawaiian shirts and gold chains. Yeah, why not?

Settled where? He needed to find a place, but somehow the thought of finding and moving into an apartment didn't sound too appealing. He wanted to unwind a little first, clear his head, and relax. He also wanted to ask Mr. Benjamin Joseph Kirkley about the map fragment. If anyone could make something out of it, BJ was the guy to do it. Come to think of it, BJ was probably what he needed right now. After the Indians and those uptight assholes at Mocoron, he could use some intelligent conversation—and some serious partying.

"Hi, guy."

"AAIIIIEEEEHHH!" Kirkley screamed, jumping back and making a cross with his fingers toward Jinx, his usual form of greeting.

"It's nice to see you, too." Jinx replied, laughing.

"I don't believe it!" Kirkley yelled, grabbing Jinx in a bear hug and pounding his back. "Spooks from Hell, right here in my humble dwelling."

"Humble is right," said Jinx, stepping into Kirkley's small apartment. "This place looks like a paper recycling dump."

Kirkley's apartment was filled with stacks of magazines, boxes of books, and mounds of newspapers. Along one wall, a row of dusty file cabinets lay buried under several hundred manuals, both U.S. and foreign. All of it dealt with military units, equipment, or combat. Like Benjamin Joseph Kirkley himself, the place was a storehouse of military facts. At twenty-eight, Kirkley was an expert on soldiering; rarely wrong, never ignorant. He had spent two hitches in the Special Forces, but got bored with the routine and the ever-diminishing role of that unit. His job as an NCO with G Company, 143d Infantry, Texas Army National Guard, one of the Army's five long-range reconnaissance companies, kept him on the edge of the power curve and he was frequently consulted by both the private sector and the U.S. military for information or confirmation. Even though he was only an NCO in a National Guard unit, he ran with the big dogs in the military. In civilian life, he sold scuba gear and taught diving, a job that kept him in groceries, allowed him to attend the various seminars and schools offered by the Army, kept his six-foot frame tanned and lean, and his sandy brown hair sun-bleached.

It was almost impossible to walk through his accumulated literature. There were discrete trails that led to the bedroom, bathroom, and kitchen.

"I'm shocked that you can cast aspersions on this library of lethal lore," Kirkley shot back, feigning distress. "You of all people should appreciate the depth of my research and study."

"I of all people can appreciate living in a pigsty."

"Indeed," BJ agreed, heading for the kitchen. "So what brings you back from the Fourth World?"

"Bad conduct."

"You scamp. What was it this time, female trouble?"

"No, this time it was Princeton problems."

Kirkley laughed. It was a standing joke that the CIA recruited a large number of its case officers from Ivy League schools. Princeton traditionally furnished more than most. Many in the Agency who were not Ivy Leaguers called themselves "land grant scum" to irritate their Ivy colleagues.

"I know, it's so hard to remember which fork to use when you're eating with a c-rat spoon."

"You know, BJ, sometimes I think those prissy bastards believe guerrilla war is some type of squash game. Win a point here, lose a point there. They don't care a thing about people dying, as long as they look good in the final report."

"It was ever thus, old son," BJ answered from the kitchen.

"I know, I know, but it just burns my ass—"

"Like a three foot flame," BJ finished the phrase. "Want a beer?"

"You bet."

BJ brought two cold Negro Modelos from the tiny kitchen and plopped down on the couch.

"Want to talk about it?"

"Not really, its just the same bullshit as always. What's the old saying? SOSDD, same old shit, different day?"

"That's it," BJ said, sucking back half the bottle of dark brown brew. "Sounds like you need to get away from it all and clear your mind."

"Get away from it all? Hell, I went down there to get away from it all here, remember? I just got back."

"Not to the boons, babycakes," BJ said as he dove off the couch into a pile of brochures under the small coffee table. "What you need is the beach! I have a pre-Christmas dive trip going to Cozumel tomorrow. Why don't you come along? It's just a four-dayer."

"You know how long its been since I went diving?"

"Who cares? It'll come back to you," BJ replied, sifting the brightly colored brochures, "like riding a bicycle."

"I dunno, man—" Jinx hedged.

"Got other plans? Come on, man, you need to decompress. It'll be blonds, beaches, and bikinis!"

"What are blonds? I've forgotten."

BJ surfaced from the pile, coming up with a brochure.

"Here it is," he said, handing Jinx the flyer. "What say, eh?"

"Hmm, what the hell, OK. But I want to go to Austin when we get back, and I want you to come with me."

"Great, Austin's an outstanding party town too! I've got plenty of scuba gear you can use. Got a swimsuit?"

"Sure."

"Then we're all set," BJ beamed. "It'll be great. Trust me."

Jinx laughed. The phrase "trust me" usually meant a fucking of some sort, maybe this time it would be the good kind. He had come here to unwind. Why not do it in some tropical paradise? A different kind of tropical paradise this time. Blonds, eh?

★17★

18 December

I swear, I feel like I'm in a revolving door or a repeating dream, Jinx thought, looking out the window at the bluer than blue water below, I just did this trip in the other direction.

Jinx hardly had time to wash his clothes before the dive trip. The flight would be a short one—two hours to Cozumel. Leaning back in his seat, it was impossible not to think of the last time, fourteen months ago, when he had flown south to get away; from his wife, from his life. Thinking of her now brought a lump to his throat, and a clutch to his heart. Her leaving had hurt so badly, he'd felt like the donor in a heart transplant. He didn't miss the pain, but he still missed her.

"You OK, buddy?" BJ asked softly, breaking Jinx's reverie.

"Yeah, just thinking about ol' Connie," Jinx answered, happy for the distraction.

"Can't do that on this trip," BJ said as he turned over the paperback book he was reading and stretched. "Only thoughts of scuba diving and irresponsible behavior allowed on this trip."

"Got it. By the way, where are we staying?"

"The rich folks are at the El Presidente, you and I are at the Sol Caribe. I thought we'd get you in the pool this afternoon and do a quick scuba refresher before you hit the ocean."

"Good idea."

BJ went back to his book, read a moment, then laughed.

"Listen to this, Jinx, this is great," BJ said, reading aloud from the thin adventure novel. " 'Struck by the powerful 12.7mm bullet, Elmo's head became a wet pink mist slowly drifting on the warm summer breeze.' Ha! God, I love this stuff!"

Jinx looked at his young friend blankly.

"What is that you're reading?"

"Death Commandoes #29—Beirut Bloodhunt."

"BJ, aside from having no taste in literature, you are a deeply disturbed human being."

"Thanks, buddy," BJ beamed.

The low, emerald-green island of Cozumel spread across the airliner's path and they began to descend toward the V-shaped runway.

Three hours later, Jinx was splashing around the deep end of the hotel pool in his borrowed scuba rig. Everything worked OK. Sitting on the bottom of the pool, Jinx felt the dirt and the frustration of the last eighteen months flow out of him like Lipton's out of a tea bag. The sensation was so real, Jinx turned his palms up and began a slow "OOOOOOMMMMMMMMMMM" through his mouthpiece. Underwater meditation, what a concept!

Half an hour later, he was still down there, playing with a hair clip he found next to the drain, when BJ swam down and hauled him to the surface.

"Whatsamatter with you; you got rapture of the pool?" BJ asked as they broke the surface.

"No, guy, I just forgot how well the other half lives," Jinx answered, as they swam to the edge. "This was a great idea, thanks."

"Swimming in the pool?"

"No, coming down here."

Jinx packed the scuba gear in a large mesh bag as BJ ordered a couple of cold Coronas with limes. When they came, BJ held the bottle up for a toast.

"Vive l'amor, vive la guerre, vive le sacré mercenaire!" BJ intoned in his worst French accent.

"Tu madre!"

They clinked bottles and Jinx had a mouthful of beer when BJ shook up his bottle and sprayed him with the icy brew. In seconds, Jinx and BJ were both covered in beer, as were two schoolteachers from Oklahoma who had the misfortune to be at the next table.

★18★

19 December

The next morning, the Caribbean was like a lake. Only the few low, rolling swells reminded you it was the ocean. Susan Elliot had seen enough brochures to know that Palancar Reef was one of the most beautiful in the world, but the reality of it was even better than the ads. She had dived in Texas lakes, on the Gulf's oil rigs and small reefs, had been to the Florida Keys a couple of times, but she had looked forward to this trip to the Mexican Caribbean for weeks. The excitement, the anxiety and the anticipation of the last two months had been so great, she needed this time to relax and get herself centered. She also wanted to get some sun on her pale white skin. She had collapsed right after checking in the day before and now she couldn't wait to get underwater. When the dive boat finally stopped, she took her time getting in. The last thing she wanted now was to be part of a herd. She wanted to see the sights at her own pace. When she stepped off the boat only a tall, skinny guy with strange tan lines and cuts and bruises on his chest was left on deck, struggling into his gear.

God, this is so incredible, Susan thought as she glided down the reef wall. The colors jumped out like neon and the fish were everywhere. The white sandy bottom was only at sixty feet, but when she swam over the mighty Palancar's wall, she almost wished for something to grab on to! It was a six thousand foot near vertical drop-off. With two hundred feet of crystal clear visibility she looked down into the changing shades of blue filled with a rainbow of fish. Turning right and stabilizing her buoyancy compensator at eighty feet, she began to drift effortlessly along the coral wall with the gentle two-knot current. No wonder they called it a drift dive! She could easily see the other divers and the Mexican divemaster ahead of her. Every few yards she stopped to study some wonderful new plant or animal.

One fish, a bright blue one, swam past her and dipped into a channel through the reef. On impulse, Susan followed it, swimming easily through the bright coral fans lining the channel. The little fish swam slowly, unafraid of its human pursuer. Ahead, the channel became a tunnel and light streamed through a hole in the reef.

Oh, this is fun, Susan thought, I wish I had borrowed a camera!

The little blue fish swam through the hole ahead of Susan and turned right with the current. Watching it, Susan swam through the hole herself, her arms back at her sides. She gave an extra hard kick to keep up with her little fish and—stuck! She was halfway through the hole, her arms pinned at her sides. Her chest had squeezed through the hole, but the hose on her buoyancy compensator was wedged in the coral and she could not get any leverage to pull it free. The more she twisted, the more the coral bit into her arms through the thin dive suit.

Shit! Maybe I can pull back out of here, she thought as she felt for a handhold on the back side of the hole. Nothing. Concerned now, she twisted her body to try to dislodge it. As she twisted to the left, the power inflator button of her buoyancy compensator, connected to her air tank, pressed up against a lump of coral and filled her BC with air, wedging her even more tightly in the hole. The buoyancy compensator, essentially an adjustable life preserver, allowed divers to rise, sink, or hover at will by adding or releasing air. Now it was like a vice holding her in the reef. The inflator button was being held down by the inflated compensator, making an open, free-flowing channel into it from her air tank. In seconds, the pressure in the BC reached its maximum and the relief valve by Susan's left ear blew open to relieve the over-pressure. Now she was stuck tight and the air in her tank was being quickly bled out by her own buoyancy compensator.

Oh God, oh no! she thought, panic rising in her. Help me, for God's sake somebody. Her thrashing made her mask slip and water began to trickle in.

The air from the relief valve was a steady column of bubbles as the inflator and relief valves equalized. At this rate her tank would be drained and she would quickly be out of air.

Panic washed over her, blotting out all her training. She screamed, almost losing her mouthpiece. "Help me, help me, help me, oh God, help me!"

Jinx had a little trouble getting into the borrowed gear, but when he stepped off the boat, the warm water felt great and sure enough, his scuba memory came right back to him. The others were all in the water. Jinx was the last to go in. He pressed the deflator button on his compensator and began to slowly sink toward the reef sixty feet below.

The thought that she really might die here seized her like a fist and she began to hyperventilate, using even more of her precious air. The little blue fish swam slowly by and turned to peer at her.

He's come back to watch me die, she thought as her vision closed down to a dark, narrow, tunnel with the blue fish at the end of it. The world that had been so beautiful moments before closed in on her, killing her.

Jinx made his way slowly down the reef letting the current carry him along. The rest of the group was much farther down the reef, their bubbles barely visible in the distance.

This is great, he thought, I really needed this.

As he drifted by a deep channel in the reef, Jinx noticed a steady column of bubbles streaming up from the reef. Kicking over to check it out, he heard a high-pitched sound of some sort and stuck his head over the edge of the coral head for a look.

Down about fifteen feet was half a girl sticking out of the reef! Her BC was bulged out over the edge of the hole she was stuck in, and bubbles were pouring from it. She was thrashing her head around and howling through her regulator.

What the hell, thought Jinx, how did she get in there?

He rolled over the edge of the reef and kicked quickly down to her.

"Nonononono," Susan screamed. "Please, God, don't let me die, pleasepleasepleaseplease!"

The tunnel of her vision was getting smaller, with hyperventilation and panic drawing the circle tighter. She twisted and writhed, her hands clutching and grasping at her sides, trying to get a hold on something, anything. The coral bit into her arms, but she was past feeling pain.

Jinx couldn't tell for sure what had happened, but it was obvious that her BC was jammed in the hole and pouring air out the relief valve. As he reached her from above, Jinx looked for the inflator button. It was down inside the hole, but not very far. He could probably get it out, but not with the BC inflated. The girl looked panicked, but with her hands pinned, she couldn't get hold of him to try to drown them both. God knew how much air she had left, probably not much if that valve had been open long. Dropping down in front of her, Jinx held her face in his right hand so she would see him and turned off her tank valve with his left hand.

Her eyes were wild anyway, and when she took that last breath from her closed tank, they practically popped through her half filled mask!

Jinx pulled the emergency regulator, the "octopus," from its BC pocket and took her regulator in his left hand. In one motion, he pulled her mouthpiece out of her mouth and stuffed the new one in, holding the purge button to keep air flowing as she inhaled. She tried to scream again, choked once through the octopus, and caught her breath.

Her compensator was still stuck in the reef. It wasn't blowing out any more air through the relief valve, but the pressure was still holding it firm against the reef. Jinx pulled the cord on the relief valve to dump the remaining air in the BC. The girl's thrashing pushed out more air and, though she was still stuck, she wasn't wedged in anymore.

She felt like she was being squeezed to death. The BC was squeezing her so tight, it was all she could do to breathe. She was still frantically squirming to try to free herself, but it only seemed to wedge her tighter. She was making noises, although she could not hear them.

Try, TRY! she thought as she closed her eyes and twisted as hard as she could. Nothing.

When she opened her eyes, there he was! Relief and joy washed over her! Thank God! But joy turned to fear when the stranger reached up and turned off her tank. What the hell was he doing? "NO!" She screamed at him. He just reached down and pulled the regulator out of her mouth! As it came out, another mouthpiece came in; the air from it making her choke on a mouthful of salt water. She felt like gagging, but fought it down. What the hell was he doing? Then she figured it out. The BC! He was deflating the damn BC.

Pulling on her inflator hose brought the jammed inflator button out of the hole and stopped the vicious cycle. For good measure, Jinx pulled the power inflator hose to the tank off the oral inflator hose. With this accomplished, Jinx turned her tank valve back on.

Here comes the tricky part, he thought as he got her regulator back in his hand, getting her to switch back to her air for a minute. Sure enough, when he held her regulator in front of her, she shook her head back and forth. When he tried to pull his regulator out of her mouth, she bit down on it like a pit bull and wouldn't give it up.

OK, sweetheart, calm down, Jinx thought, hovering in front of the girl. Calm down a little and we'll get you right out of there.

In a minute, she seemed better, and Jinx again held her own regulator up in front of her and purged some air from it. This time she nodded yes and Jinx pulled out his regulator and shoved hers back into her mouth.

As he pulled the relief valve, it felt like she was released from a vice. Able to inhale again, she pulled long breaths from his regulator until she got dizzy.

Then, he reached for her regulator again and scared her for the second time. When he blew air out of her mouthpiece, she figured out what was going on, and took her own regulator back. She couldn't see him, but she could hear him digging on the coral above her.

* * *

Now the hard part. He could easily push her back through the way she came, but he wasn't sure she could get turned around and come back out, especially as excited as she was. If she got in trouble inside the tunnel, he wouldn't be able to get to her. That left one alternative, and Jinx reached down for the knife on his right leg.

He kicked up above her and stuck the flat knife point into the coral about eight inches above her tank. Hitting it with the heel of his hand, he managed to sink the knife a couple of inches into the coral. Working the knife back and forth, Jinx broke off a chunk of the bright coral.

I hate like hell to kill this coral, he thought as he jammed the knife in again, but better that than kill this girl.

Putting a fin against the coral on either side of her, Jinx reached down and got a tight grip on the tank valve. He pulled hard, and the tank moved forward a little.

I need to get on with this, or she will suck all the air out of her tank, Jinx thought as he got another firm grip and pulled the tank upward, pushing with his feet against the coral.

This time, a large piece of coral broke off just above the tank, and the panicky girl floated up out of the hole into Jinx's arms.

When he put a foot on either side of her and squatted down over her head, she wondered again what he was up to. It hurt when he pulled on her tank, but then she was free and he was holding her in his arms!

With her arms suddenly free, she grabbed at Jinx, who turned her sideways, made a thumbs-up sign and started kicking slowly for the surface. She nodded yes, and seemed to relax a bit. Jinx took his time, rising slowly through the bright water. Her tank pressure gauge showed about 100PSI, not much, but plenty of air for the sixty-foot trip to the surface. She wanted to swim up as fast as she could, but Jinx held on to her and kept the ascent slow to prevent the bends.

Not a bad rescue, my man, he thought immodestly, as they made their way upward, not bad at all!

As they broke the surface, she spit her regulator out and sucked the fresh air deeply into her lungs.

"Easy, easy," Jinx said, inflating his own BC all the way to keep them both on the surface, "don't hyperventilate. I don't have any paper bags with me."

She nodded, the fear slowly leaving her face. Suddenly she grabbed Jinx and kissed him, their masks clashing together.

"Thank you," she gasped. "I don't know who you are, but you saved my life. Thank you, thank you."

"No problem," Jinx said. "Here, let's get your BC inflated again."

Jinx took her inflator hose and blew into the mouthpiece, filling the BC with air again.

"There, now you'll float for a while."

The girl nodded, still trying to get her breathing under control.

Jinx did a slow circle in the water, looking for the pickup boat. The dive boat had drifted past them on the current, following the rest of the divers. It was two hundred yards away and there was no one on the boat looking in their direction.

"We need to get their attention, somehow," he said, knowing how hard it was to spot someone in the water even if you were looking for them.

"Here, use this," Susan gasped, pawing at the front of her BC. "Whistle."

Jinx found the orange plastic whistle clipped on the chest strap of her BC.

"OK, here goes," Jinx said, blowing the water out of the whistle, "Hold your ears."

He took a deep breath and blew as hard as he could on the plastic whistle. It made a high pitched whistle that nearly split his ears.

If they don't hear this, they're deaf, he thought, taking another breath, and we're fucked.

The second blast brought a crewman around to look for the source of the noise. Jinx waved furiously at him and after a second, he waved back. Turning toward the wheelhouse, the dive attendant yelled at the boat captain and pointed back at the pair in the water.

Jinx was relieved to see them wheel the boat around and head back in their direction. The captain kept looking back to keep track of the other divers' bubbles. He turned to the girl.

"I'm Richard Jenkins, and you are?"

"Happy to be alive!" Susan yelled.

"Nice to meet you, Happy," Jinx laughed. "Howd'd you get stuck like that?"

"It wasn't easy—no, it was real easy," she replied, still short of breath. "I'm Susan Elliot. Nice to meet you—real nice."

The boat was now on its way toward them, closing the distance as fast as its aging engine would go.

Back on Cozumel's ferry dock, BJ insisted that Susan see a doctor. As BJ collected her gear, she pulled off her dive suit. Under the stretch Lycra dive suit, she wore an old Texas Diver bikini. The navy-blue top was barely able to control her large breasts as she pulled the red bottoms with the white diver stripe up over her hipbones.

"Christ," Jinx said softly to himself. He looked over at BJ who just laughed and whispered, *"Torpedos los!"* His German accent was even worse than his French.

"I feel fine, really, BJ," Susan called out as she struggled into a pair of tight cutoffs, "I just need to get a band-aid for my arm."

She came toward them, showing a cut about three inches long on her left arm. The other arm was badly scratched, but not cut. "No way, sweetie," BJ answered. "On my trips if you get hurt at all, you go to the doctor."

"Well OK," she said. Turning to Jinx, "Mr. Jenkins, I want to take you to dinner tonight. It's the least I can do."

"OK, I'll let you," Jinx answered. "When and where?"

"The bar in the El Presidente, about eightish?" she suggested as they walked up the pier.

"Great!"

"See you then," she smiled as she and BJ got into a cab to go to the clinic.

Jinx could hear BJ quietly admonishing Susan about the wisdom of staying with a dive partner. It was a role he would be quite willing to undertake.

★19★

Jinx was waiting in the big hotel's bar when Susan came in. She had traded her bikini for a white cotton sundress. Several acres of cleavage showed above the bodice. On her arm, a square of gauze covered the coral cut. Except for those two features, Jinx would hardly have recognized her. Her dark, curly hair, pulled back with a rubber band this morning, now framed her face like a shimmering cloud, accentuating her pale skin. Bright red lipstick defined a very sensuous mouth and her eyes now looked large and beguiling, not pale and terrified.

"Hi," she said as she slipped up on a bar stool next to him. "Am I late?"

"Right on time," Jinx answered. "I see you got treated for your wound."

"Complete with tetanus shot," she said, rubbing her shoulder.

"You look a lot different than the last time I saw you."

"Amazing what a little makeup can do, eh? Lets take a cab to the Costa Brava."

The restaurant was at the south end of the island, just across the street from the Naval District headquarters. The front was open. Cane mats covered the walls. The floor was concrete. Although the place had a funky look to it, the food was reputed to be excellent.

128

"So, what do you do in the world?" Jinx asked, as they sat down. "I mean, for a living."

"I'm in school at the University of Texas," she answered as she stirred her slushy frozen margarita with a straw, scanning the menu.

"Yeah—studying?"

"Sociology with a minor in psych."

Oh God, Jinx thought, it couldn't have been something simple like nursing or nuclear physics.

"Really."

"How 'bout you, what do you do when you're not saving girls' lives?"

"Corrupting their morals, usually," Jinx laughed as she raised her eyebrows. "No, actually, I'm a consultant."

"On what?"

"Oh, technical advice, mostly," he said. "I'm sort of a troubleshooter."

"Well, lucky for me!" she said as she killed the last of her margarita.

The rest of dinner was spent in small talk, mostly scuba stories. Jinx was reluctant to discuss his recent employment, so he kept the conversation light. For her part, Susan was drinking a lot to put the trauma of the day behind her.

After the meal, they moved out to a table on the large patio for another margarita. Their table was next to the rail around the edge of the large, tiled patio. The breeze from the water was warm, and the moon looked like a big spotlight in the dark sky, its beam washing clean everything it touched. A nearby lighthouse winked its own reflection across the still water.

"You know, the only thing I don't like about this place is that it's in Mexico," Susan said, leaning back on the railing.

"What do you mean?"

"I mean, I love to dive and it's beautiful here, but I hate coming down here with a bunch of Americans waving our money in these peoples' faces."

"I suspect they would like it a lot less if we didn't bring our money down here," Jinx answered, remembering BJ describing how the sleepy fishing town had prospered and bettered itself over the years, by exploiting willing tourists' dollars, still managing to keep its easy lifestyle.

"I know that. I just hate the exploitation of this place and these people."

Oh, God, here it comes, he thought. The woman is turning into everyone I hate at a cocktail party. Why does there have to be such a bleeding heart under those fabulous boobs?

"I mean, we just do this to people all the time," she went on. "We use their countries like playgrounds and the people like servants."

And worse, Jinx thought, if you only knew.

"Could be worse," Jinx answered. "They could have some ruthless totalitarian government like Nicaragua to ruin the economy and spend all the money on weapons they don't need."

Susan gave him a strange look. "Or like El Salvador, to ruthlessly suppress the will of the people with death squads," she shot back.

"Or like Cuba, which uses its army as mercenaries to pay off its debts to the Soviet Union," Jinx said, wishing they hadn't started this. Susan moved to the table and stood with her knuckles on the glass tabletop.

"Or—" she started, her voice rising.

Jinx raised his hand lightly. "But we just came here for dinner, didn't we, not to solve the world's problems?" Jinx interrupted, hoping to defuse the forthcoming battle.

She stared at him for a second, then her shoulders slumped a little.

"That's right," she said softly, her eyes wandering the room, "and we've had dinner, so let's call it a night, OK?"

"Fine, I need to meet BJ anyway."

As they got to the street, she turned to Jinx and shook his hand.

"Thanks again for the help this morning."

"Any time."

"I hope there won't be another time," she laughed.

Jinx put her in one of the exploited's cabs and started off on foot for the Sol Caribe.

As Jinx walked back to his hotel, he thought of a song by Steely Dan called "Hey, Nineteen." It said: "Hey, Nineteen, we've got nothing in common, we can't talk at all." Indeed.

BJ was just coming out of the lobby of the hotel as Jinx walked up.

"There you are, patron." He grabbed Jinx's shoulder. "Come with me."

"Where are we going?"

BJ smiled. "Remember those teachers from Tahlequah we hosed down with beer? They want to give us a chance to apologize."

Jinx brightened. "Is that right?"

Since it was only a few blocks to the teachers' hotel, they walked.

"I take it you didn't hit if off with Susan."

"Too right," Jinx said slowly. "She's a little to the left of Lenin."

"Yep."

"I thought all that campus activism was over and now everybody in school just wanted to get rich."

"Well, Susan has a history. Her parents were big antiwar protestors back East. She was brought up to blame America first, last, and always. Sort of a second-generation asshole. I taught her scuba one summer when she was taking a class at Rice."

"The '60s will never die, I guess. So what do her peace-loving folks do now?"

"Real estate, I think."

"Figures. BJ, why is it that those old protesters never look back to see what their higher morals wrought, huh? Millions of people died so they could feel righteous in their indignation, and they won't even acknowledge it."

"I think it's TV, Jinx. Plus the media is always at war with the President, no matter who he is. Whatever the U.S. does is wrong, regardless."

"It sucks, man."

As they passed an open alley, three men lurched out, one of them slamming into Jinx and spinning him around.

"Jeez, guys, you want to watch where you're going," BJ said, catching Jinx to keep him from falling.

"Why don't you watch where we're goin', punk?" the largest of the three replied.

By their accents and their relentlessly floral attire, Jinx figured them for New Yorkers on vacation. They each had at least one beer in their hands and were three sheets to the wind, weaving and swaying.

Mean drunks, Jinx thought, how charming.

BJ, unfortunately, was rising to the bait. "Somebody should, asshole. You sure can't see shit," he snarled.

"Let it go, BJ," Jinx said sharply. "Let's go."

"Listen to your friend, Dipwad," one of the other two drunks chimed in, gesturing with his Corona bottle. "Hit the road before youse get hurt."

His two buddies began a chorus of low-level abuse, the sort of taunting that has launched a million bar fights.

BJ looked at Jinx, who could already see where this was headed. It was stupid to waste time and energy fighting that could better be used entertaining the ladies. Sometimes events just took control of reason. This looked like one of those times.

"Is that right, Pond Scum?" BJ said quietly, folding his shades and carefully placing them in his shirt pocket. "Perhaps you'd like to make me."

The largest of the drunks, a florid, barrel-chested ox of a guy, stopped laughing and looked intently at Kirkley. His two cronies suddenly got real serious as well, looking back and forth at Jinx and BJ. It was one of those seconds that seems to last a lot longer. Jinx surveyed their adversaries. Besides the big one, there was one guy who was short and slight, with a nasty, weasel face, and a tall skinny one with long blond hair. The skinny one looked mean.

"Uh-huh, I would," the largest one said, draining his beer and turning the bottle around in his hand.

"Shove that Corona up his ass, Pat," the weasel said. "Get'm!"

BJ was waiting, already up on the balls of his feet, his hands down at his sides. The big man took a step toward BJ, who lunged forward and snap-kicked the bottle out of the man's hand. When the big drunk looked to see where the bottle went, he got another snap-kick in the balls. That got his attention, and he bent forward, howling. BJ danced backward a few steps, waiting. Big Pat looked up at BJ, his howl of pain becoming one of rage. He ducked his head and charged BJ like the bull he was. BJ stepped forward and spun around on his left foot, cocking his right foot for a kick. His foot lashed out just in time to connect with the charging drunk's face. There was the ugly sound of cartilage ripping and Pat cried out in pain.

This time BJ did not wait. He swept his foot around the big man's leg, jerking him off his feet. Pat hit hard on his chest, but tried to roll up on one arm. BJ's roundhouse kick caught him in the belly, and what little wind was left in him whooshed out. He fell over on his back, making little gurgling noises.

His two friends had not been idle. After BJ kicked the big man, both of them turned their attention to Jinx. Weasel-face rushed him, throwing a wild punch. Jinx grabbed the man's arm as it passed and threw him with an easy judo hip throw. Using the drunk for a support, Jinx kicked backward in time to catch the skinny one in the stomach. Jinx let the weasel have a pair of kicks in the ribs for good measure. As he stepped back, the skinny one, still on his feet, stumbled back against the wall of the alley. Jinx hoped the fight was out of both of them, but the skinny one caught his breath and broke his beer bottle on the wall.

"Drop it, man," Jinx yelled at him, but the drunk was past any rational thought. He stepped forward toward Jinx, holding his bottle in front of him and flicking it back and forth.

Jinx waited for him to make his move. Finally the man lunged, grabbing for Jinx with his free hand and slashing upward with the bottle. Jinx feinted to the right, then stepped to the left and caught the hand with the bottle, twisting it outward and down. His left arm shot forward, striking the man's elbow. The man yelled in surprise and pain, dropping the bottle. Jinx then threaded his left arm under the man's arm and grabbed him by his long blond hair. Using the arm as a lever, Jinx spun the man around and smacked his head into the wall with all the force he could muster. The drunk collapsed like a poleaxed steer.

The fight had taken maybe thirty seconds. All three of the drunks were on the ground, holding various anatomical parts and moaning in harmony.

As they backed away down the street, Jinx looked over at BJ, whose smile wrapped around his whole face.

"Come on, man," BJ said, his voice cracking with the

adrenaline still rushing inside him. "We have ladies waiting."

It had taken a dozen piña coladas, followed by two bottles of champagne, followed by several hours of the most exhausting apologizing Jinx had ever done to atone for their sins. The teachers, Leslie and Melissa, had come to Cozumel to do those things forbidden to them as small town schoolteachers.

Apparently, everything was forbidden in Tahlequah, Oklahoma. As he stood out on the balcony, Jinx could hear BJ snoring. BJ was wrapped around Leslie on one bed, Melissa was on the other. All three of them were dead to the world.

Kids, Jinx thought, they just don't have any staying power.

What a bizarre day! So far, he had saved a woman's life, then found out he couldn't stand her. He'd been in a real good fight and then had his brains screwed out by two ladies he had met while spraying beer on them. Is this a great vacation, or what?

For the second time that night, it struck Jinx just how out of touch he was with the people of his own country.

I've been an American for forty years, he thought, but I seem like an alien. He thought about the Russian who had nearly killed him with that rocket. I have more in common with that guy than I do with the people in this hotel room, Jinx thought, I wonder where that Russian is tonight?

★20★

How hard to remember it was December, Bodnya thought as the old green Chrysler staff car entered the Punta Huerte airfield. Newly extended, it boasted the longest runway in Central America. The breeze off Lake Nicaragua was cool, but not cold. By morning, there would be mist in the low spots and clouds covering the top of Masayan Volcano to the south. The stars were brilliant, so close you could bump your head on them.

The base was well secured. A detachment of soldiers had arrived from the Soviet motorized rifle brigade in Cuba and they secured the small cluster of buildings allotted to the Summer Harvest force. Sent to Cuba in the early 1980s, the brigade had always been a major annoyance to the American government. The Soviets had agreed to withdraw it if the U.S. would simply withdraw its troops stationed in Turkey. The U.S. troops, principally Air Force radar and electronic intelligence personnel, were still in Turkey, and the brigade was still in Cuba. The base's outer perimeter was secured by the Nicaraguan Interior Ministry's *Tropas Pablo Ubeda*.

Their car was a holdover from Somoza's days, a '79 model. There had been no more American autos after the revolution, but it was in good shape, and the driver, a Cuban, was proud of it. Now he pulled up in front of the large brick building, stopped, and leaped out to open Bodnya's door.

"Here you are, Major," the Cuban said brightly. "I will be waiting whenever you are ready!"

As Kovpak preceded him through the glass double doors, Bodnya saw in the reflection the Cuban wiping down the Chrysler with a rag.

The building had once been the base movie theater when the airbase had belonged to Somoza's *Guardia Nacional*. Inside, the ninety Soviet soldiers sat quietly in the plush folding seats, talking among themselves.

Kovpak entered the theater and shouted, "ATTENTION!"

Immediately, ninety men came to their feet and froze, rigid as dogma. Bodnya and Kovpak walked the length of the center aisle and mounted the small steps to the stage. The stage was bare except for a small table, stage right. Bodnya crossed to the center of the stage and faced his troops. He left them at attention for a minute as he scanned their faces. They were young, terribly young, but their faces were not those of boys, but men. Hard men, ruthless men, the pride of the Soviet Army. When he looked at them, Bodnya felt a thrill. It was pride, yes, but more than that, it was power. These men were his instruments, his weapons. Everyone else read history; these men made history.

"Be seated!"

As one, the ninety soldiers dropped into their seats.

"You have heard, for the last month, rumors and speculation about the training you have done. I am here today to put those rumors to rest."

Bodnya paused. There was no sound in the room except the tired creaking of the ceiling fans turning slowly above them. What there was in the room was electricity. It steadily increased the intensity, making hair stand on end and skin prickle. Bodnya let it rise, welcomed it.

"You are NOT going to attack anything in the following countries: Pakistan, Afghanistan, Iran, Germany, the People's Republic of China, Cuba, Nicaragua, or the Azerbaidzhan Soviet Socialist Republic."

Quiet laughter rippled through the ranks. Bodnya smiled. Now he had their attention, certainly. They leaned forward now to discover the real mission. Bodnya put on a worried face.

"Our comrades in the Committee for State Security have discovered and confirmed a plan by the NATO alliance to exploit the current economic situation in the U.S.S.R. and to bring the *Rodina* to her knees! We will not let this plan succeed. As our fathers gave their lives to stop the Fascist invaders in the Great Patriotic War, so will we too stop these invaders! You have been chosen to strike at the heart of these invaders, to take the fight to them before they can wreak havoc on our sacred *Rodina*."

Tension was high; he had their undivided attention. The Soviets have always placed great emphasis on learning from history. History is also used as a political/motivational tool. One's will, one's desire to succeed against insurmountable odds, is in direct proportion to one's faith in the Party and its leaders.

"Comrades, our mission will put us against a powerful enemy and overwhelming odds. It will demand that you draw from reservoirs of courage you never knew you had in the past. It will demand a sacrifice from which you can hold nothing back!" Lowering his voice, "we will succeed. The *Rodina* is depending on us."

Not a man moved, not a sound was made. "In the autumn of 1942, our forces were reeling before the invading Fascist armies. Our fathers gave their blood freely for every meter of the *Rodina* before relinquishing it to be defiled by the invaders. Though our resistance was stubborn, we were forced to fall back to the Don River. Many major battles were fought at that time, but there is one small operation that should be of special interest to us, one from which we can learn."

Bodnya paused for effect. "In the town of Maikop near the Caucasus Mountains, the Fascists had established an airfield one hundred kilometers from the Black Sea. From here they raided our shipping and attacked our forces holding the Caucasus Mountains. Forty fleet parachutists of the Red Navy were hand-picked to raid this airfield and destroy its fifty-four aircraft. They undertook intensive training, studied aerial photographs of the airfield, learned about aircraft basing patterns, and planned the most effective way to destroy the aircraft. They were organized into control, covering, and sabotage groups." The men were beginning to see the parallel.

They were parachuted directly onto the objective on an October night. Two partisan guides jumped in with them. On the ground, they destroyed twenty-two aircraft and damaged twenty more, killing many of the invaders while suffering only light casualties." He did not mention that the raiders on the obscure Maikop operation had lost fourteen men.

"The victorious force linked up with local partisans and were exfiltrated to friendly lines."

Bodnya signaled to Malinkov in the projection booth. The lights in the theater dimmed and an image appeared on the screen around Bodnya. The image was a map of the United States. When the soldiers realized what they were looking at, a sound, a visceral noise rose in the theater. Without knowing where or what, they knew that this was the realization of their dream—to fight the dark forces of the United States.

"Your target is here," Bodnya said as he stepped back to the screen and pointed to the red circle near the center of a state's outline familiar even to the Soviets; it was marked TEXAC. "You will attack and destroy the tank and mechanized formations stationed at Ft. Hood, Texas."

"This attack will prevent these forces from grinding the *Rodina* beneath their treads," Bodnya went on, his voice rising to a shout, each word a rifle shot. "You will break the backbone of the American reinforcement forces, help secure the victory over the forces of darkness, and secure for yourselves and the Spetsnaz a place in the history of the Soviet Union!"

The ninety Spetsnaz leaped to their feet and roared. Bodnya stood and let the sound wash over him, through him, exalted.

When they had reluctantly resumed their seats, Bodnya went on. "You have been training as subunits, now each of those subunits will be designated as part of a group. Here are your target assignments." He signaled to Malinkov. The map of the U.S. was replaced by a map of Ft. Hood. An overlay of differently colored routes and areas marked each group's target area.

"Subunits 1 through 10, you are now part of Group 1. You will attack the motor pools of the 1st Cavalry Division. These consist of four tank, two mechanized infantry, one armored cavalry, two field artillery and one air defense artillery battalions."

"Subunits 11 through 20, you now belong to Group 2. Your target is the 2d Armored Division. It has the same numbers and types of motor pools as the 1st Cavalry's."

Subunits 25 through 30, you are now part of Group 4. Your

target is the equipment storage facility for the 49th Armored Division, and 36th Armored Brigade with part of the equipment for eight tank, four mechanized infantry, one armored cavalry, and four field artillery battalions.''

"Subunits 21 through 24, you have been training for different missions. As Group 3, you will attack the main fuel depot, III Corps Headquarters, the helicopters at the army airfield, and the residences of selected individuals.''

Bodnya signaled again to Malinkov. The map of Ft. Hood was replaced by an enlarged detail map.

"You will parachute onto the fort here, using two dropping zones known by the Americans as Antelope and Ft. Hood Drop Zones, northwest of the main cantonment area,'' Bodnya explained. "From there you will be transported by truck to your targets. You will attack them in just the manner you have practiced for the last few weeks. Our goal is to delay the departure of III Corps for at least twenty-four hours, destroy as many combat vehicles as possible to prevent their future use, sow confusion, shatter the enemy's morale, and shake the confidence of the American people in their government!''

"Tonight and tomorrow each group will be given further briefings on their respective targets by their group commanders. You are to discuss nothing further about the mission between groups. In the meantime you will be undertaking additional weapons and hand-to-hand combat training. You will also receive instruction on survival in America: rules of conduct, currency, how to use the telephone, emergency contact telephone numbers and how to buy bus tickets. You will be issued identity papers. And, foremost, you will study maps. Prior to infiltration you will be briefed on pickup procedures and exfiltration. An advance element, including myself, will infiltrate early to meet you on the ground. Captain Karmasov will be in command in my absence. As of this moment, you are under quarantine until completion of the mission.''

The background sound in the room rose again. There was no trace of fear or misgiving in it, only excitement, anticipation. Bodnya looked out again over the faces of his soldiers.

These are the dogs of war, he thought, straining at the leash.

★21★

20 December

The flight from Managua was brief but very comfortable. The Tan Sahsa 727 was plush and the three Mexican stewardesses stunning. This was a stark contrast to the military transport in which Bodnya and his men had flown to Nicaragua. This plane was plush compared even to Aeroflot.

Kovpak stared at the stewardess, Lucia, and whispered to Malinkov. His gestures made it clear that Lucia was the topic. Malinkov was smiling and nodding in agreement. Only T'sinko did not appear to be having a good time.

I need to watch those two, Bodnya thought, as Kovpak held his cupped hands in front of his chest. God knows when they last had a woman. Then Bodnya remembered that T'sinko was here to watch them. He was watching all of them. As bad as damned security officers!

They changed flights in Mexico City, continued on to Monterrey, and were met at the airport by a car from the Soviet Consulate. The driver was resident GRU, but said nothing to them on the short trip. Rather than be seen at the consulate, the men were taken to a safe house in the suburbs, away from prying eyes. The consulate here was under constant surveillance by the Americans, as was the embassy in Mexico City.

The hacienda was completely surrounded by huge trees that hid it from the blistering sun as well as from any watchers. It did not seem possible that the house had once belonged to a single Mexican family. In the Soviet Union, only members of the higher *nomenklatura*—the *nachalstvo*, the elite party bosses—lived this way.

At the front door, a tall, stylish young woman met them. "Good morning, comrades," she said extending her hand. "I am Sr. Lt. Anna Bonderchuk, your liaison officer. Welcome to Mexico." She shook hands with each man. Her handshake was warm and firm. She led them from the foyer into the spacious living room. The size and opulent decor surprised the soldiers.

"Today and tomorrow I will brief you on your infiltration plan," she explained. "You will also be issued your equipment for the mission. When you finish here, you will be transported to your departure point for the target infiltration."

No one ever mentions the United States, Bodnya thought as the lovely lieutenant went on, it's as if they do not wish to invoke the name of some evil spirit.

"We have lunch prepared for you," the svelte lieutenant continued as they entered a long room dominated by a heavy, dark wood dining table, "after which we will issue you your new identities for the infiltration. Please sit down."

The visitors seated themselves at one end of the table, where four covered dishes waited. The food was spicy, but very, very good. The coffee was dark and rich. The contrast to their duty in Afghanistan was striking. The food there had frequently been inedible, the living conditions primitive. Their Afghan allies had been the dregs of Afghan society, criminals and misfits who worked for the Soviets because they could work nowhere else. By comparison, this mission was luxury. It lacked the sharp edge of real combat. Bodnya hoped that his men were not forgetting the reason they were being treated so well. This was the feast of the gladiators. The arena was waiting.

Lieutenant Bonderchuk stood, breaking Bodnya out of his reverie.

"Now, you will all please go to your rooms and change out of the clothes you are wearing. Put on the clothes contained in the bag which bears your new name. Your new identities are: Alex Brenner, Paul Kuschow, Stefan Mayer, and Fredrick Talki." She handed each man an East German passport bearing his new name.

"Major, you and Ensign Kovpak are in the room on the left, Lt. T'sinko and Sgt. Malinkov in the one on the right. If you'll follow me—"

She pointed them down the short hall. The large room he shared with Kovpak had two massive beds, dressers, a closet as large as an apartment in Moscow, and more of the huge, dark furniture found everywhere in the house. One wall consisted of three huge windows that opened onto a courtyard. Bodnya stepped over and opened the center window. A warm breeze blew through the room. Kovpak was sitting on his bed, bouncing.

"Major, can you see that we always have such accommodations on our missions?" he asked.

"Perhaps all this luxury is to reward us now for being heros, since we may not be alive to do it later."

Kovpak stopped bouncing, and began to go through his bag.

Bodnya opened the zippered nylon bag with the name Alex Brenner. The clothes were all of American manufacture. They were not new, but they were clean and well pressed. The shoes were nylon and leather, the type used for running. There was one pair of khaki pants and a yellow pullover shirt to go with it. Underneath them was a pair of the denim pants Americans called blue jeans, the type so coveted in the Soviet Union. With them was a gray cotton T-shirt. At the bottom of the bag was a navy blue hooded sweatshirt.

"It is winter, do we get no heavy coat?" Kovpak asked as he emptied the bag labeled Paul Kuschow.

"The temperature has been above seventy degrees in the daytime and only down in the forties at night, Ensign," Lieutenant Bonderchuk replied softly from the doorway. "Surely a Spetsnaz can withstand such mild conditions for a few hours."

"Ah, but I frequently need something warm to wrap up in," Kovpak said. "Something soft and furry."

Bodnya fought to keep from laughing out loud. He had heard this particular line at least a dozen times in three different languages.

"Perhaps we can accommodate your special needs," Bonderchuk purred. "Check with me later this evening. Now I must check on the others. When you have changed, please come back to the dining room.''

After she left the room, Bodnya sat on his bed and looked at his friend.

''You have a single thought, Paul, and that thought is women.''

''Not true, Major; I frequently think about the Army and our sacred mission. Besides, does not every condemned man get one final meal?'' Kovpak asked as he stripped off his clothing and dressed in the cotton shirt and canvas pants he pulled from the bag.

''Not such as you have planned.''

''I am a gourmet,'' he said, smiling wolfishly at the Major. ''Hurry, Comrade, we will be late for the briefing.''

Bodnya elected to wear the blue jeans and the pullover shirt. Kovpak was already out the door by the time Bodnya tied his running shoes and followed him down the hall.

In the dining room, the others were waiting.

When Bodnya entered, the woman lieutenant closed the doors and opened a folder on the table.

''You will leave here at 1400 hours tomorrow and fly to the town of Tampico. There you will board the Russian freighter *Sergei Lermontov*, and set sail for the United States.'' She traced the route on a map of south Texas and the Gulf of Mexico.

''The ship will continue up the coast to a point south of Corpus Christi. You will disembark at 2130 hours and proceed to the shore by rubber boat, cross a barrier island with the boat and proceed to a pickup point in Baffin Bay. There you will be met by a reception party made up of American resistance fighters accompanied by a Soviet adviser named Brian Hollis, who works for Comrade T'sinko. He will coordinate your movements to the state capital at Austin where you will stay in a safe house in preparation for your mission.''

She turned to T'sinko.

''In Austin, Captain T'sinko, you will contact your people at the target. Hollis will ensure that you make contact with them.''

T'sinko nodded. His expression was odd, cold and distasteful. Bodnya wondered if he disliked getting his orders from a subordinate rank or if he just didn't like taking orders from a woman.

"Before we go into the specifics of the insertion, do you have any questions?"

"Where are our weapons and combat equipment?" Malinkov asked.

"You will be issued your equipment at the safe house," Bonderchuk answered. "If you are apprehended before that, you must not be caught with any weapons or equipment. We do not wish to alert the Americans to our larger plans."

Malinkov scowled.

"Don't worry, Sergeant," she added, seeing his expression, "there are plenty of weapons waiting in America for you. There is no need to—how do the Americans say it?—to take a sandwich to a banquet!"

"I'm sure there are American weapons waiting for us," Malinkov added. "That is why I would like one also."

Everyone laughed, but Malinkov still looked uneasy.

Bodnya had his own concerns on this matter, but Bonderchuk assured him that the Americans had nothing equivalent to the KGB's Border Troops. The Custom Service's Border Patrol was more of a police organization mainly concerned with apprehending illegal Mexican and Central American immigrants attempting to find work. Even in this they were ineffective, as thousands slipped through each month.

Later that afternoon, the four men practiced using the inflatable Zodiac boat that would carry them from the freighter to the beach. As the three Spetsnaz had experience with amphibious operations, they spent their time teaching T'sinko the finer points of small boat handling. He was a timid pupil, but after an hour of motoring up and down the tree lined stream that ran next to the GRU hacienda, T'sinko became more confident. If the weather wasn't bad he would be OK.

Throughout the evening meal, Kovpak traded innuendos with their hostess, and it came as no surprise later that night when Kovpak quietly opened the window to the courtyard and slipped out. He returned three hours later, and slipped into his own bed, humming a Ukrainian folk tune.

★22★

21 December

"So, Tiger, How's the boy this morning?"

The question was largely rhetorical. BJ's eyes were very red, in contrast to his face which was pale gray. He leaned against the door frame for support.

They had spent another warm Cozumel night with the two tempestous teachers, after a day of diving on Santa Rosa Wall and Paradise Reef. Hot Mexican food and cold beer, lots of cold beer, had given them this morning's hangover.

"I feel like I got ate by a wolf and shit over a cliff," he said bleakly.

"What a coincidence," Jinx grimaced painfully. "That's just how you look."

"Please, show a little respect for the dead, OK?" BJ muttered as he made his way from the door to the edge of the dresser.

"What, did something get you down last night?" Jinx laughed.

"Got me down, got down on me, got me off, just plain got me, man. The Blister Sisters rode me like Trigger."

"Please, I hate to hear a grown man whine," Jinx chuckled then grasped his head to still the pain brought on by the sudden movement. He zipped his nylon suitcase shut. "C'mon, get your gear packed, we've got to be at the airport in an hour."

BJ fell face first on the nearest bed.

"Just send me back air freight."

145

"Whiiiinnnneeeee, whiiiinnnneeee," Jinx taunted.

"OK, OK, but first, I really think I'd like to invoke the name of the porcelain god."

BJ rolled off the bed and crawled on all fours into the tiny bathroom.

"Don't try to shave, BJ," Jinx called after him. "You would never survive the attempt."

The flight back to the U.S. was uneventful. BJ had a screwdriver for a little hair of the dog, but if anything it made his raging hangover worse. He slept fitfully most of the way to Houston. Susan Elliot was on the same plane, but she barely acknowledged Jinx and BJ. When the plane landed in Houston, she disappeared. That was fine by Jinx.

After a superficial customs inspection, they headed back to BJ's apartment near Rice University. When they arrived, BJ was in bed before Jinx got his jacket off.

"BJ," Jinx said, "I need to take care of some things and see my mom. When you're alive again, I want you to look at a piece of a map."

"If I'm alive when you get back, I will," BJ replied. "Now please leave me in my bed of pain."

Since BJ wasn't going to be any fun, Jinx put his coat back on and went out to BJ's Camaro. The cold air was a real shock after Cozumel, but it felt good. It was nice to experience real winter again. In Central America, winter and summer just meant wet and dry. In the window of an appliance store across the street, twenty TVs said there was a chance of snow in north Texas by Christmas.

Jeez, a white Christmas, Jinx thought. When was the last time?

He wanted to see his mother, but he dreaded talking to his ex. The thought dragged his spirits even lower.

As he drove past the mall, there were eight choices of movies, most involving screaming teenage girls being killed by some faceless terror.

The image of a burning bus shouldered its way to the front of his thoughts. I've already been to that movie, Jinx thought.

As he turned BJ's car into the subdivision five miles west of Fulshur, Jinx felt his old calm returning. The late after-

noon sky had turned a bright neon orange, common here in
fall and early winter. The colored sky gave the winter countryside a postcard quality for an hour or so before turning
abruptly black, with just a thin line of dark orange on the
horizon to mark the onset of night. The air was crisp, what
his mom called sweater weather.

He always felt better at his parent's house. It always seemed
serene, somehow detached from worry and strife. The subdivision had originally been built as a commuter haven, but
it was too far from Houston to succeed in that and it had
become a retirement community of large rambling homes
surrounded by pecan trees. His mother had stayed in the place
after his father died in '84.

His folk's rambling ranch house had been painted since he
last saw it and the big Chinese tallow tree that had stood next
to the carport was down, a victim of lightning. As he pulled
into the long, curved gravel driveway, he saw his mother
working in the kitchen. She looked up and waved, wiping her
hands as she started for the front door.

"Hi, Ma." He smiled.

"Rich, honey! Come in, Come in," she said, pushing the
screen door open.

They hugged, then she held him at arm's length to look
him over. "You look like hell, son, don't they feed you down
there?"

"Not like you do." He winked.

"Come on in, I was just putting dinner on the table."

Dinner was chicken-fried steak and mashed potatoes with
white cream gravy. After a year and a half of beans and rice,
it was ambrosia. Jinx nearly cried when he saw her simple
country food.

"How long are you home for?" She gave him a quizzical
look. He had never discussed his job with her, but she was
no fool.

"Until further notice, Ma. I'm on an extended leave."

"You'll be here for Christmas, won't you?"

He nodded. "Sure, but I need to go back into Houston
tomorrow for a couple of days."

They ate in silence for a moment.

"I saw Molly the other day." His mother just sort of
slipped it in. Molly was Jinx's ex-mother-in-law. A short con-

versation with her usually took half an hour and involved news of everyone she knew.

He cocked his head, a bite of food halfway to his mouth. "Yeah, Ma, what did she have to say?"

"Not much. Have you heard anything from Connie?"

He shrugged. "Just the divorce papers a year ago."

After ten stormy years, his marriage to Connie had finally fallen apart. At the end, there had been little overt hostility; their lives had just gone in different directions. Jinx lived in a world of constant conflict, Connie lived in a world of comfort and consumption. She had never been happy with his work. Although they had traveled the world from one posting to another, they were never part of the in-crowd. The other wives always seemed to know who Jinx really worked for, whatever his cover job, and Connie always felt like an outsider. The money had never suited her, either. She came from the upper middle class and expected to live in a certain style. It was hard to get a Neiman Marcus credit card when your husband's employer wouldn't admit to his existence, much less verify his salary. She had a degree from U.T., and had worked at several editing jobs over the years, but the money she made was always hers, never theirs.

He had taken the job in Central America to get away after their breakup. He was living in a tent on the Coco River when his divorce papers came. He hadn't heard from her since. Thinking about her always made his throat tight, and brought back that old ache deep down inside. Jinx was surprised how much it still hurt after such a long time.

"You know, Ma, I still don't know what happened to Connie and me," Jinx said. "Everything just seemed to fall apart. I guess I wasn't much of a husband."

"Well, honey, I'm not sure how much of it was your fault. I mean, your job would run off a lot of women, but I don't think that was all of it. Since you left, Connie's had a whole bunch of boyfriends, but none of them seemed to last too long. I'm not sure Connie knows what she wants, for sure." She laughed softly. "Her mother is a little worried about her reputation."

"Is she still around here?" he inquired softly.

"Yeah, she lives over off Kirby somewhere, in an apart-

ment. Molly says the place isn't big enough to cuss a cat in."
His mother held a coffee mug in both hands.

"I guess I need to call her and see where my stuff ended
up. It's probably in the dumpster."

She cocked an eye at him. "Molly gave me her number."

After they had cleared the table and put the dishes in the
dishwasher, Jinx went into the back bedroom and dialed Connie's apartment.

"Hello?" The voice was soft, quizzical, but he felt a familiar tug he thought he had forgotten.

"Connie? It's Jinx."

"Oh—"

"Listen, I just called to find out if I have anything left
after you moved." He knew he was speaking a little too fast.

"Yes, Jinx," she spoke with just a touch of condescension.
He had failed her. "It's in a storage space over on Bisson-
nette. There's a bed and a couch and some other furniture.
Your clothes are there, too."

"Connie—"

"Don't start, Jinx, there's no point. You have your life and
I have mine. Let's just let it go at that."

"It's hard to let ten years go like that." At that moment
he hated himself for his weakness.

"Jinx, I need a man who's here with me, not off somewhere sneaking around in the shadows." Connie answered,
irritation rising in her voice. "Besides, I don't like lying about
my husband's job. I like to eat out somewhere better than
Burger King and to have something decent to wear, too."

"I don't think we were ever poor." Stop it, you fool, his
inner voice said.

"We weren't. That's not really the point."

"What is the point?"

"The point is that I need stability and security in my life,
and that's just not your long suit, is it?"

"I had the same job for ten years. That was stable."

"This conversation is pointless, Jinx."

"I guess so, babe," Jinx said, suddenly angry. "So tell
me, have you found someone to make you happy?"

"Good-bye, Jinx. I'll send the key to your mom's."

The click of the telephone was the saddest sound Jinx had
ever heard, like a door shutting forever.

Later that night, in bed, Jinx remembered a song he had heard on the car radio. The singer asked, "If somebody loves you, won't they always love you?" It don't look like it, Jinx, sure don't look like it. Well, Connie, be happy, if you can.

The dull throbbing of his healing shoulder wound paled in contrast to the sharp aching in his guts and the tightness in his throat. The wound would heal, the wounded heart would not. An old mercenary friend, Doyle Michaels, had once explained why men went off to the Foreign Legion after a broken heart.

In his atrocious Australian accent, he had said, "Hell, the enemy just wants to kill you, mate, not break your heart." It was the only profound thing Jinx had ever heard the man say.

Tomorrow I'll get started on that map piece, Jinx thought, trying to force down the sadness. The stuff in storage would still be there when he had time to get to it.

22 December

Jinx walked into BJ's apartment at 10:30 the next morning. BJ was slumped over a coffee cup at the tiny kitchen table.

"So, it lives."

"Very funny. Want some coffee? I'll pour you a cup." BJ answered as Jinx dropped his bag on the sofa.

"Don't bring it. The last time I saw your hands, they couldn't be trusted with hot coffee. I'll come get it."

As Jinx poured his coffee, BJ turned a chair around and straddled it. "So what is this cryptic map piece you've got?"

"It's all that's left of a map that was on the wall in a Spetsnaz training camp in Nicaragua. I would have gotten the rest, but it burned up."

"Say what?" BJ blurted as his chin went down and his eyebrows shot up.

Jinx smiled. "Yes, Virginia, there is Sandinista Clause."

"Holy shit, what are you doing here with it? It should be at Langley!"

"They don't seem to want to see it. Their man down south is the one who sent me home."

"Well, goddam, if they don't want to see it, I sure do."

"It's in my ditty bag. Get me another cup will ya?" Jinx

pulled the round nylon bag out from under the couch and took the plastic zip-lock bag from it.

"What happened to the rest of it?"

"This Russian had some kind of rocket launcher. Looked like a German Armbrust, but when it hit the wall it blew up in flames, kind of like our old M202 Flash launcher. I was in the room, and the whole wall caught fire at once. This was the biggest chunk I could find, in fact, the only one."

"You're lucky you didn't get your ass burned off. Sounds like an RPO-A rifleman's recoilless flamethrower."

"Indeed? Must be something new." Jinx looked up.

"It is. Spetsnaz, in Nicaragua. They must be playing for keeps, man. You certain?"

"Yeah, that's what they looked like. And you know they always play for keeps."

BJ took the paper and held it first one way then another. He held it up to the morning sunlight streaming in through the window. "You've got no idea what this is?"

"None. The whole map was about five feet by four. Standard U.S. five-color military map. You could see the grid system, one to fifty thousand scale. It was dark when I went into the room, then the whole thing went up."

"Can I ask what the Soviets were doing there, or is that a secret?"

"It's a secret. OK, we never figured out what they were up to. The whole camp went up before we got much of a look at it. That's what pissed off the Agency so bad. They wanted us to bring home the TO&E, unit roster, and the commander's ID card, and all they got was that burnt piece of map. That piece is all there was."

BJ squinted at the fragment. "It looks like a military post. Any idea which one?"

Jinx shrugged. "Nope."

"Well, I suggest we look over the maps I've got and see if we can find anything like this. These shapes look like some kind of buildings. Maybe we can find a match."

BJ made a path to one of his file cabinets, and pulled out the bottom drawer, removing it from the cabinet. The entire drawer was filled with neatly folded maps. Most of them were standard military maps, but there were maps of every other sort there, too. Road maps, National Geographic maps, even a tourist map of Grenada, the one the Rangers used when they invaded. There were maps of Europe, Russia, East Germany, Poland, Czechoslovakia, all the Warsaw Pact nations.

"When we finish these, I have two more drawers full."

Jinx and BJ spent the next seven hours comparing the map fragment to every map BJ had.

"I'm getting cross-eyed," Jinx finally said. "All these maps are looking just alike." He stood up and stretched, rubbing his eyes with his fists.

"Me, too, man, my ass is asleep," BJ agreed. "Let's take a break and come back to it. I don't think this place is in Europe. Maybe it's—"

The weight of what he was saying suddenly hit them both. It had never occurred to Jinx that the map he had seen on the wall could be of a U.S. installation. It was absurd.

"Do you realize what we're saying?" Jinx said. "U.S. base maps, for Christ's sake! The Russians would never hit anything in America, it would cause a war."

"They might put a group of terrorists up to it. Things have been heating up down south, and in Mexico too."

"Jesus."

"Let's go over to the unit," BJ suggested. "We have some more maps there."

The Houston Light Guard Armory was just south of the main downtown area. Built in 1924, it was the oldest state armory still in use. Its castle-like architecture was quaint when contrasted with Houston's skyscraping glass and steel temples to the great god Oil.

BJ was a recon. team leader, a staff sergeant, in Company G (Long Range Surveillance), 143d Infantry. Jinx was familiar with the unit through BJ. G Company was rapidly re-achieving its former reputation as one of the National Guard's model units. Formed in 1980 when the old 36th Airborne Brigade was disbanded, Company G had been a showpiece unit until 1987. The Army's new tactical doctrine, the Air-Land Battle, had all but forgotten the Long Range Reconnaissance Patrol (LRRP) concept. G Company's efforts to integrate itself into this doctrine were instrumental in the development of the new Long Range Surveillance Units, LRSU, pronounced "larsue."

Company G had participated in extensive joint training exercises with NATO LRRP units, far beyond the one weekend a month and two weeks in the summer typical of most Guard units. Its Stateside training was demanding and challenging with the unit maintaining high selection standards.

This training was expensive, though, and the bureaucracy was unwilling to support it. No one really understood why, but official reasons included too much time in the field, too high operating costs, demanding too much support from state resources.

Admittedly the unit's paperwork standards sometimes suffered because of field training, but pencil-pushers from state headquarters, whom BJ called empty uniforms, used this as an excuse to withhold support from an excellent unit rather than assist in corrective action.

In the past year, though, things had begun to change. New leadership took command at the state level. G Company got a new company commander. There was a turnover in the unit members. The unit began to reachive its old standards and reputation.

There were two other LRSCs in the National Guard; one in Michigan and one in Georgia, and two Active Army companies in West Germany. All were assigned to different corps' military intelligence brigades. Company G was III Corps' LRSC.

Parking on the wrong side of the street in front of the armory, BJ and Jinx bounded up the front steps.

"Some building you've got here, BJ."

"Yeah, that's another battle we've been fighting with the state. They want to tear it down, been letting it deteriorate for years."

"It must be as old as the unit."

"Not hardly, Jinx!" responded BJ. "The unit was formed in 1873. That's why we're also called the Houston Light Guard, back then they didn't bother numbering units."

The full-time company clerk, Sgt. Bill LeMoyne, was typing busily on a form of some sort, cursing with every other keystroke.

"Fukin' lousy typewriter," he yelled. "Everybody else in the world has a computer, but I got to use this old Selectric."

"Hi, LeMoyne," BJ said cheerfully. "Problems?"

"Just the usual, filling out a thousand unnecessary forms on a worn out, sorry typewriter. What are you doing here?"

"Looking for a couple of maps. This is my friend, Richard Jenkins, Jinx to his friends."

"Glad to meet ya," LeMoyne said, not looking up from his machine. "You know where the maps are?"

"Sure do, thanks," BJ answered as he led Jinx to a large back office on the second floor. "Where is Hagger?"

In a metal map cabinet in the closet, there were hundreds of maps stacked in the shallow drawers.

"Where do we start?" Jinx asked, looking with dismay into the stuffed drawer.

BJ gazed into the drawer like a soothsayer examining a crystal ball. "How about the big bases in the south, and the Air Force bases?"

"Sounds good."

BJ groped familiarly into the pile.

The two each took a box and began rifling through it.

"Ok, I've got San Diego, Ft. Ord, Ft. Sill, Tinker AFB, Ft. Sam Houston, Ft. Bliss and NASA," said BJ.

"I've got Ft. Hood, Travis AFB, Ft. Gordon, Ft. Jackson, Ft. Stewart, Pensacola NAS, Eglin AFB, and Amarillo."

"That ought to keep us busy for a while."

A hulking figure in camouflaged BDUs came through the door. "Do I hear rats in my house?" His nametag read, "Hagger."

"Hey, Kurt, what's up?"

"Same ol' shit!" The sergeant first class threw his maroon beret on his cluttered desk top. "The OMS is dragging their feet mounting those new receivers in the commo vans. What you guys rootin' around for?" Hagger made an instinctive scan of his bookshelves making sure that BJ hadn't borrowed something again.

"We're looking for some maps. Just want to look at some training areas for Jenkins's Reserve unit," BJ lied.

"Captain Jenkins, 304th MI Battalion." Jinx quickly offered his hand. It was the first Houston area Reserve unit he could think of.

"Kurt Hagger. Find what you need, sir? We're always glad to help out the have-nots!" The training NCO alluded to the fact that many Reserve units were short on field training time.

"Yeah, we found 'em," BJ said. "These guys are interested in some rear area security stuff. You still got that canned briefing on the Spetsnaz?"

"Sure."

"How 'bout giving the captain here a quick run-through, if you got a few minutes?"

"Well, its about an hour-long briefing, but I guess I can give you a quick look. Meet me down in the classroom. I'll get the carousel."

Jinx and BJ went down several flights of stairs into the musty classroom. "You up on these guys, the Spetsnaz, Jinx?"

Jinx shook his head. "To be honest, no. Most of my experience is in Latin America and Southeast Asia. I know they're the Soviet equivalent of the Special Forces, like our Green Berets."

"Well, not really equivalent. They're different, but some bad mothers! And don't call me a Green Beret. I don't do that stuff anymore, I'm a LRRP now!"

"Hey, if you're a sneaky peek you obviously blow up bridges and cut throats."

"Yea, that's the problem with the Army, the conventional types can't tell the difference between the different special ops units. All we do is go in, get the info, get the heck out of Dodge, and never let anyone know we were there. Someone else can kill 'em."

Hagger came in and took a vehicle recognition carousel off the slide projector. "I'll blast through these just for dramatic effect." He laughed. "If you see any that interest you, just holler, sir."

The first slides were the typical introductory graphic visuals. As Hagger spoke, scenes of camouflage-uniformed troops wearing blue berets and blue-and-white striped undershirts flashed on the screen.

"The Spetsnaz, so often compared with the U.S. Special Forces and British SAS is a far different organization. In fact it's not even an organization in the sense of the SF or SAS. Spetsnaz is simply the Russian acronym for *Spetsial'noye Naznachenie*, Special Purpose, a generic term for specialized units tasked with special operations missions. Some units are

organized with specific wartime missions in mind, others for
general employment as needed.''

More Soviet soldiers appeared on the screen, running
across an open field, rifles at the ready.

''Their internal organization and training is different. Some
are readied for direct action missions: raids in the enemy's
tactical defensive rear areas to destroy, command, and control; field and air defense artillery systems; and support units.
Others are intended for deeper DA missions to interdict reinforcements moving to the front, or to attack major headquarters, communications networks, and missile sites. Some
are trained for diversionary missions, small skilled teams that
will assassinate or kidnap government officials and senior officers, sabotage public utilities, interfere with civil communications networks, and interrupt transportation nets:
highways, railways, airports, river and canal traffic. They may
be required to work jointly with agents or terrorist groups.''

Now the slides showed men in camouflage suits hunkered
down in bushes, looking through binoculars. Hagger went
on.

''Still other units conduct operational and strategic reconnaissance, like we do. Small teams skilled at passive intelligence collection by surveillance and close-in recon. Avoiding
contact with enemy forces and civilians, they'll hit high-value
targets of opportunity if the payoff warrants loosing their value
as intel collectors. This is especially true if a nuclear delivery
system is located. It's a standing order for any Spetsnaz unit
to immediately destroy nuke missile launch sites, even at the
risk of compromising the primary mission or assuring its own
destruction.''

One slide of particular interest, copied from a Soviet magazine, showed a paratrooper firing at a Scud missile. It had
been touched up to give the appearance of the missile exploding.

''Recon subunits will also kidnap PWs, field interrogate
them, and most certainly eliminate them, to gain intel info.
Collected intel is transmitted by high-speed burst transmission AM radios to base stations in their rear areas.

''Regardless of their mission, the Spetsnaz soldiers are
tough, dedicated opponents. They do not volunteer for Spetsnaz duty, but are selected after intensive screening. Most are

chosen from the Guards airborne divisions and the air assault brigades and independent air assault battalions, all of which are already parachute qualified. They are all airborne volunteers.''

Now the slides showed soldiers running through burning buildings, working out on exercise fields, skiing, climbing, swimming, and firing various weapons.

''Physically fit, highly motivated, proficient, emotionally stable, politically reliable, and of an acceptable ethnic group; no Western Ukrainians, Baltic state citizens, Georgians, Central Asians with Moslem backgrounds, or Jews. There are exceptions if certain races need to be exploited. Those accepted are given a rudimentary psychological screening. Training is physically intensive. High demands are placed on individual skills including weapons, land navigation, sabotage and demolitions, hand-to-hand combat, swimming, fieldcraft, surveillance, and survival. Athletic competition, endurance marches, confidence and obstacle courses, and physical and mental toughening by exposure to the elements take up a great deal of training time. Most training is conducted by the units themselves, not in special training units or schools, except in the case of officers.

''Selected individuals are further trained as radio operators and linguists for their target areas. All are cross-trained in their subunit's duty positions. Those in units assigned specific missions are taught the target country's customs, daily routine, geography, and about the armed forces. Depending on the mission's requirements, they may wear their own uniforms, those of the enemy, or civilian clothing.

''Other specialized training is undertaken depending on their area of operations: skiing, mountain climbing, scuba, small boat, desert. They are, however, not as versatile as their Western counterparts who are generally trained in a broader spectrum of individual and environmental skills. The Spetsnaz are trained for specific missions and AOs.''

Unit organization charts, looking like wiring diagrams, appeared on the screen.

''These guys are under the GRU, the Chief Intelligence Directorate of the General Staff. Most are formed into brigades stationed in each of the Soviet Union's sixteen military districts. In wartime they will be assigned to Fronts, roughly the size of our army groups. They consist of up to four battalions, eight in the case of Group Soviet Forces Germany's brigade. Battalions have three or four companies. Company strength varies depending on its assigned tasks, but about eighty seems common. These may be organized into groups of about fourteen or into subunits of five for recon missions, but this, too, varies as needed. There is also a long-range communications company to maintain radio contact and a small service support element. Each Soviet combined arms and tank army has a Spetsnaz long-range patrol company that operates similar to ours.''

Shots of various infiltration means followed. Different airplanes, helicopters, jumpers in free-fall, and rubber boats flashed by, followed by all sorts of Soviet weapons; some common, some not so.

''I'll skip over how they break in and the weapons stuff,'' said Hagger. ''Most of these troops do not even realize they're Spetsnaz. They're paratroopers in independent units, most bearing the honorifics of World War II parachute units. This they're aware of. The Soviet soldier, while usually none too pleased with military service, is proud of his unit's past history and accomplishments. However, they may not even know, in the case of the Spetsnaz, its actual designation, knowing it only by a cover name or simply by its field post number. They also know little or nothing of other such units. Career officers are familiar with the overall Spetsnaz organization though.''

Tables appeared listing vulnerability factors and protective measures.

Hagger put his pointer down. ''That's it, gentlemen, you too, BJ. The quick and the dirty.''

''I really appreciate that, sergeant,'' Jinx said rising. ''Interesting indeed.''

''If you want to borrow it and the full script for your unit, just give me a shout, sir.'' He took the carousel off the projector.

''You bet.'' Jinx and BJ headed for the door. On the way out, LeMoyne was still struggling with his typewriter.

''See you later, LeMoyne,'' BJ said as they hurried out. ''Don't let it get you down.''

As he shut the door, he could hear LeMoyne inside. "Fuckin' shit-lectric!"

What a bizarre trip, Susan thought to herself. I went down there to relax and center myself, and ended up nearly drowning and being rescued by a Fascist! Bizarre!

She'd changed her dive boat reservations to avoid diving with Jenkins again. She had seen him on the plane back home, but had not spoken. After all, she had thanked him. What more was she supposed to do? Besides, the guy gave her the creeps. He was worse than BJ, and BJ was a war-monger deluxe. Being around those people convinced her even more that what she and her friends at CCLAP were doing was right. The world had to be protected from people like Jenkins and BJ.

The thought of the operation tomorrow night gave her goose bumps. This would be her first time to really do something instead of just talk and argue. The thought that it was illegal made it that much more attractive. A thinking person had an obligation to break unjust laws! Anyway, she needed to get herself together for this trip to Corpus. She had a lot to do and only a day to do it. On the way home from the airport, she would stop at Banana Republic and get some nice hiking pants and a khaki shirt for the trip. Oh, and some Deep Woods Off!, too. The mosquitos down there were terrible! What else? Hiking shoes; they might have to walk to the rendezvous and her Reeboks would be ruined—

★ 23 ★

Luckily, the water was calm. Bodnya had done amphibious operations like this when the sea had been angry, and they were not pleasant memories. This was like rafting on a lake. It took just minutes to get the four of them and their small bags into the inflatable raft. As soon as they were clear of the freighter, Kovpak took a compass heading and, starting the electric motor, steered the small boat toward shore. The beach was a pale white line on the horizon. This deserted stretch was devoid of any light. Behind them, the *Sergei Lermontov* disappeared into the darkness. After leaving the freighter, T'sinko became very nervous. He had never been to sea in a small boat before, much less at night, and he was scared. Too, his GRU paranoia filled the night with enemies. He was certain that there was an American Army patrol on the beach, waiting to cut them down as they set foot on American soil.

An hour later, the long, white sand beach of Padre Island stretched before them. This part of Padre Island was called the Riviera of Texas; miles and miles of beautiful clean sand, much of it a state park. Its length and inaccessibility made it almost impossible to patrol. Running almost the entire length of the south Texas coast, there were few cuts through the several hundred meter wide barrier island. The Border Patrol had all it could do to watch the land border with Mexico, so the beach was virtually ignored. Only the Drug Enforcement Agency patrolled it, looking for smugglers, and they were usually looking for planes, not people.

160

The surf was light, causing little trouble as they made their run to shore. Cutting the engine to near idle, they slipped silently onto the beach, aided by the gentle waves. Kovpak flipped the motor into the up position. They quickly piled out, grabbed the rope fixed to the boat's gunwales, and struggled across the firm sand. The sand got softer as they approached the vegetation line, but their pace remained steady. Dropping the boat among the spiny brush and salt grass, everyone flopped down to catch their breath and to listen. There were no unusual sounds. Only the light chilly breeze, the surf's rush, the mewing of some disturbed sea bird.

"Let us go, we must cover over two hundred meters," said Bodnya. He kept an eye on T'sinko, who was still looking about for imagined enemies.

The going was difficult. Loose sand had drifted in soft piles around the tough, grabbing brush. T'sinko kept slipping and falling to his knees, dragging the others down with him. Kovpak and Malinkov gritted their teeth and cursed the officer under their breath. Bodnya realized that he was, too. The brush thinned, and suddenly they faced another empty beach, the beach of Laguna Madre, the narrow waterway which stretched 158 miles from Corpus Christi to Brownsville. With Padre Island to stop the waves, Laguna Madre was as smooth as a pond. They stumbled across the flat beach and shoved the boat into the dark water. Behind the boat, the tiny propeller left a thin phosphorescent wake.

Once inside the long, narrow lagoon, Kovpak directed them north-northwest to the entrance of Baffin Bay. They hugged the bay's northern shore, looking in the darkness for the point of land where they would meet their shore party. Finally, the shoreline turned sharply to the right.

"This is it," T'sinko blurted. He had been silent ever since they passed over the island. Kovpak steered right, making the turn around the shore's bend.

As they neared the beach, Kovpak suddenly grabbed Bodnya's arm and whispered, "Major! There!"

Just in front of them, off the beach, was a figure. He stood knee deep in the water, his arm arcing back and forth.

How did we miss him? The shadows on the dunes behind him must have hidden him, Bodnya thought feeling T'sinko tense. Here was his imagined enemy, after all!

"Quickly," Bodnya hissed, pushing Malinkov and T'sinko off both sides of the boat. Both men pushed away, staying in the water while the boat made its way to the beach.

As the small motor pushed their boat past the figure, Bodnya could see the man's long fishing rod in his hand.

"Whoa, you guys scared the hell outta me!" the stranger yelled, his voice booming in the night air. "Where the hell did you come from?"

As Bodnya and Kovpak pulled the boat up on the beach, the stranger waddled back out of the water, his long rubber waders squeaking on his plump thighs.

"You guys been out in the bay?"

"Yes."

"Really. That's a nifty little boat you got. What is it, an Avon?" the man said as he set down his fishing rod and ambled over toward the boat.

"I'm surprised I didn't see you go out. I've been here since about eleven."

"I think we drifted some way," Bodnya replied, trying to keep the curious stranger away from the boat. "It is a pretty night, yes?"

"You bet it is, I hoped they'd be running tonight, but I guess they stayed out in the deep water."

The fisherman took off his slouch hat revealing a nearly bald head with a fringe of wispy, gray hair. Bodnya figured the man was in his mid-sixties.

"Too bad."

As he nattered on about night fishing, the two men left in the water silently came up behind the old fisherman, Malinkov leading.

The old man must have sensed something behind him. He started to turn, but Bodnya grabbed his mesh fishing vest, pulling the man around, accidentally sinking a fishhook deep in his own forefinger.

"What the hell—"

Malinkov jumped, his right arm wrapping around the old fisherman's neck, his left arm completing the circle behind it. Malinkov kicked his own feet out behind him, pulling the old man over backward. As they hit the sand together, the snap of the old man's neck sounded like a small stick breaking.

"Put him out in the water," Bodnya said softly, sucking on the cut the fishhook had made in his finger. "The current will take him out."

Malinkov shouldered the limp form and waded out in the water till he was chest deep. He shrugged off the corpse and held it under to fill the lungs with water. With luck, the body wouldn't float for a day or so. By then, they would be far away. The packed wet sand showed little sign of a scuffle. They would leave the man's tackle box and folding chair in place. Perhaps it would look like he had drowned while wade fishing, until someone discovered the broken neck.

"Sergeant Malinkov forgot this fishing rod," T'sinko said as he walked up from the waterline.

"Indeed," Kovpak said, taking the rod from T'sinko and flicking it back and forth, "I will take care of it right now."

Kovpak quickly took the light graphite rod apart and tucked it into his luggage. Bodnya shook his head. Pavel was such a hoarder! Probably his distant Tartar heritage.

The reception party was not due for another hour. The team moved up off the beach into the dunes and found a place in the pampas grass that hid them from the road, but gave them a good view of the beach. T'sinko and Malinkov changed out of their wet clothing, rolling the wet things in the towel each carried in his bag.

"Well, we have completed the first phase of our operation," Bodnya whispered. "Hopefully, the rest will go as easily."

Kovpak stifled a laugh in his hand and Malinkov smiled. T'sinko looked confused. He hadn't been on a mission before. Getting in was always easy. Getting out was another thing.

The road stopped three hundred yards from the beach, and Susan was glad she had taken the time to get some good hiking boots. They had been expensive, but worth it. She still didn't see why they couldn't use flashlights. There obviously wasn't anyone around for miles. She had nearly fallen when she stepped in a hole, but Hollis was in charge of this pickup and he had done this before, so they did it his way.

The beach was a white, winding strip that stretched out of sight in both directions. This spot was far enough south of the resort area at the north end of Padre Island to escape any notice, but near enough to the highway to make the escape easy. They had parked the cars, Hollis's Suburban and the old Cadillac that CCLAP owned, just off the road on a stretch of hard surface. She hated the huge Cadillac, it was like a bus compared to her Volvo, but it would hold more people and luggage, plus it was not as memorable as a red Volvo. Hollis called it a better covert car.

The beach was deserted, so Susan and the other two sanctuary volunteers sat down on a driftwood log, concealed by brush, to wait for their guests. Hollis walked down to the water and scanned the horizon with his binoculars.

She had no idea how long they would have to wait, but it didn't matter. It was so exciting to actually do something to help people! All of the conferences and rallies and workshops in the world were useless if no one did anything.

Tonight, she thought, I stop being a pacifist and start being an activist! That thought thrilled her. Things would never be the same after tonight!

They heard the cars stop and instinctively burrowed deeper into their hiding place in the brush. If it was the American Border Patrol, their tracks in the sand would lead right to them, but Bodnya doubted that the Border Patrol would come in cars.

A few minutes later, the figures emerged from the tall clumps of grass onto the beach. They stood looking around for a minute, then sat down.

"Come, Comrades, our new friends are here," Bodnya said quietly, shouldering his bag.

The four men dusted themselves off. Malinkov and T'sinko stowed the wet items in their bags, and the advance party of Operation Summer Harvest casually walked down to the group of Americans huddled on the beach.

Susan didn't see the four men until they were almost standing next to her. It was as if they just appeared out of the dark. She gasped, and the tallest of the group chuckled.

"I am sorry. Did we startle you?"

"God, yes. Where did you come from?"

"Germany."

"No. I mean just now. We weren't expecting you so soon."

Hollis came up and greeted the men.

"Good evening," Hollis said, extending his hand. "I'm Brian Hollis. This is Gary Grant, Susan Elliot, and Mary Gerland."

"Hello, good to meet you," Bodnya responded. "I am Alex Brenner. This is Paul Kuschow, Stefan Mayer, and Fredrick Talki. We are so very glad to be here and thank you deeply for your help."

T'sinko stepped forward and shook Hollis's hand. "Our friend Luis says to you, 'Feliz Navidad.' "

"I hope he is feeling better," Hollis answered.

This password and countersign was unnoticed by the other Americans.

"Two of you can come with me in the Suburban, and two can ride with Susan in her car," Hollis went on, "but let's get off this beach and on our way."

"Is it wise to split our party?" T'sinko asked. "What about the American Border Patrol?"

"Don't worry about them," Hollis answered. "We are too far north to have any trouble with them."

"Are there many checkpoints?" Bodnya asked.

"None."

"None at all?" T'sinko asked, astonished. The idea that you could travel 240 kilometers without crossing a checkpoint was unbelievable.

"None. The only one I know of is way south of here near Raymondville. Welcome to America!"

They split up, Kovpak and T'sinko in the large enclosed truck, Bodnya and Malinkov in the sedan. Hollis got behind the wheel of the truck, one of the women drove the sedan.

"This automobile has as much room in it as my mother's apartment in Moscow," Malinkov whispered in Russian as they pulled onto the road.

"Everything is bigger in America, Comrade," Bodnya replied softly.

"Like the chest on our driver?"

"Especially," Bodnya answered, chuckling.

"So, did you have much trouble getting this far?" asked the young man in the front seat.

"Some, yes, but not too much," Bodnya answered. "Your people in Mexico were very helpful."

"That's great."

"How did you get here from Mexico?" Susan asked, looking in the rearview mirror.

Bodnya paused before answering. "We were instructed to not talk about that part of the trip," he said, "so better not to put our friends in Mexico in danger."

"Oh, oh sure," Susan answered, flustered. "OK, sure."

An easy evasion, easily bought, thought Bodnya, these Americans are as gullible as we were told.

The drive to Austin was long, but uneventful. Once they hit State Highway 37, Malinkov dropped off to sleep with the easy ability all soldiers seem to possess.

How simple to travel here, Bodnya thought. His own military papers enabled him to pass through any traffic control point in the Soviet Union, but travel was restricted for civilians. Here, there seemed to be no restrictions of any sort. Not only that, there were dozens of radio stations on all night, all playing different music. The two American dupes chattered like mad. This was their first mission. Bodnya smiled, remembering his excitement after his own first mission. The danger here was nothing compared to that, but the process was the same. The euphoria, the rush of adrenaline.

This is so exciting, Susan thought, to actually do something. The two men in the back seat were not exactly what she had expected, but what had she expected? They didn't have the cowed, fearful look that the Mexicans and Central Americans always had, but so what? These men were Europeans, and professional men. Or was it union men? Something, dissidents, anyway. They were mysterious and exotic, and they spoke English! Susan's Spanish was OK, but she spoke no German at all. Besides, the tall one was interesting. A couple of times, when they had gone through towns, she had gotten a glimpse of his face. She liked what she saw. He might be a refugee, but he was a hunk refugee. Brian had taken the other two. They hadn't said a word on the beach. She would let Gary take the shorter one. He looked like kind of a jerk. She would take the big one home with her.

★24★

In Austin, each car went to a different house. They would not meet at the sanctuary house until tomorrow, in case the house was watched.

The Soviets marveled at all the bright lights, the confusing mazes of freeways, and the many stores. Everywhere there were stores with the windows brightly lighted even at this late hour. All the windows were filled with riots of colorful goods. Even Bodnya, who had experienced similar wonders in Frankfurt, was beguiled.

Susan dropped Gary and Malinkov off at Gary's room. At her apartment, she went up first, then motioned for Bodnya to follow.

Cat and mouse games, Bodnya thought. These children are playing a game, and think that they are soldiers. If their soldiers could just be this stupid—

In her apartment, Susan called the other sanctuary members to report their safe arrival. They would meet tomorrow at the house on Brazos Street.

As she phoned, Bodnya walked to her bookshelf and scanned the titles. There were many books on social and psychological topics, as well as many about class struggle, especially the racist exploitation of black people. There was even a small copy of the *Mini-manual of the Urban Guerilla* by the Brazilian, Carlos Marighella. Next to the bookcase was a stereo unit better than any Bodnya had ever seen. There were records, cassette tapes, and a stack of small silver disks

167

of a type Bodnya was unfamiliar with. The equipment would have cost a year's wages in Moscow, if it could be found at all.

"Would you like some coffee?" Susan asked from the tiny kitchen.

"Oh, yes, please."

Bodnya was surprised to see her pour coffee beans in an electric grinder.

How odd, he thought, that she should have to grind her own coffee. Even in the Soviet Union, the coffee was already ground. As water heated on the stove, she placed a glass funnel with a wooden handguard on top of the pot. When the water was hot she poured it into the funnel to make the coffee. Very odd. She has an expensive stereo and a TV, but cannot afford a percolator for coffee?

"This is Jamaican Blue Mountain coffee," she said as the wonderful coffee smell filled the room. "Have you ever had it?"

"I am more a tea drinker myself," Bodnya answered, "but I remember seeing that name in the store when the Jamaicans were trading with Germany a few years ago. I could never afford it though."

"It's expensive here, too," she laughed. "About twenty dollars a pound, but it's worth it."

Twenty dollars a pound for coffee! I thought it was expensive in Moscow, but not like this! This woman was a sea of contradiction, poor and rich at one time.

They settled on her couch to drink their coffee.

She hadn't gotten a real look at him before, but now she could see that this man was really something. Tall, trim, and the palest blue eyes she had ever seen.

"Where in Germany are you from?" she asked, settling into the couch.

"Rostock. You know where that is?" He twisted to face her, his arm on the back of the couch.

"Oh, yes," she answered brightly. "Where the shipyards are." Rostock, Leipzig, and Berlin were the only cities she knew in East Germany. She only knew about Rostock because of the riots there. East German shipyard workers had followed the example of the Polish Solidarity movement in Gdansk.

"What did you do there?" She leaned forward and sipped her coffee.

"I was an engineer," Bodnya said, trotting out his cover story.

Susan was quiet for a minute, drinking her coffee. "Are you married?" she asked.

"I was. My wife died in a riot outside the shipyard last year." He looked mournful, and endearing.

"Oh no, that's awful."

"She was a member of—how do you say it?—the Worker's United Front. She fell and hit her head, an accident."

"I'm so sorry," Susan said sympathetically, although in truth, she was more relieved than sorry.

He nodded. "It happens, sometimes."

"Is that why you decided to come to this country?"

"No," Bodnya replied, acting his part to the hilt. "I was being pushed to do work on warships. I would not do that, more especially since Tatia died."

"Oh, no. I'm not surprised you wanted out."

Those eyes! she thought, studying his face. I've never seen such sexy eyes before. She found herself thinking about sleeping with this stranger.

Crazy! she thought; on the other hand, he's cute and it's been a long time.

As he sipped the hot coffee, she noticed the deep cut on his forefinger. "Oh, God, how did you do that to your finger?"

He had forgotten the fishhook wound. "A careless accident, I had forgotten it."

"Let me get a band-aid for it," she said, starting for the bathroom.

"It's nothing. Do not concern yourself."

"No, it could get infected," she insisted, returning from the bathroom with a small adhesive bandage, a washcloth, and a tube of disinfectant cream.

She sat on the couch next to him and washed the cut with the hot, wet cloth. Her hand was warm as she held his and ministered to the small cut. She made a production of applying the cream and wrapping the bandage around the tiny cut.

"There," she said brightly, "all better."

"Too much treatment for such a small injury."

"Maybe I should have just kissed it to make it better," she said, her eyes taking on a dreamy, distant look.

Bodnya had seen that look before. Regardless of their nationality, all women looked the same when they wanted you to kiss them. This one had that look all over her, and Bodnya wondered if he was falling for an American "honey trap." He had aided in setting the same trap himself when he was stationed in Berlin with the German Ministry for State Security, their targets the lonely secretaries in the American and British intelligence offices in West Berlin. He had been very successful.

I don't think this woman is an agent, he thought, if only because she is so artless.

She set her coffee cup on the table and turned toward him. Bodnya leaned forward, his face close to hers. He paused for just a second. When she didn't pull back, he kissed her. She kissed him back with fervor, her mouth opening, her tongue teasing his.

"Oh, God," she said, suddenly pulling away. "I really can't do this. I have a real problem getting sex confused with love sometimes and—"

Bodnya didn't let her finish. He ran his hand up over her shoulder and gently, steadily, pulled her face down to him, kissing her softly. She murmured a weak protest, then suddenly pushed against him, her mouth hungry. The murmured protests turned to anxious animal sounds. Her hands gripped him, pulling him tight against her breasts. Bodnya's hands slid up inside her shirt again, this time finding the wide, tight strap of her bra. He felt for the hooks, but there were none there.

How does she get this on if there are no hooks? he thought, confused. He ran his hands back and forth across her back, looking in vain for a way to remove the bra.

She pulled her face away, smiling, and laughed.

"Looking for this?" she said, pulling her shirt open and reaching between her breasts for the plastic clasp buried there. She pinched the clasp and the bra sprang apart. Bodnya slid his hands under the flimsy lace, cupping her breasts in his hands. He buried his face between them and squeezed them gently. Susan made a moaning sound and held his head against her.

Pulling his head back, Bodnya sucked greedily on first one nipple, then the other.

"Oh God," Susan moaned, "I like that. More—harder—"

Bodnya pulled both her breasts together and sucked both nipples at once.

"Oh!" she gasped. "My breasts get so sensitive, I almost think I could come from getting them sucked!"

Come? Where was she going to come from? Bodnya ran his hand down her back, reaching inside her slacks.

"Not here, come on."

She slipped off the couch and stood up, pulling Bodnya up. She led him into her bedroom and pulled the floral print comforter off the bed.

"I can't believe I'm doing this," she said as she slipped out of her slacks and panties. "This is crazy."

"I know it is."

She crawled into the middle of the bed like a cat, still wearing the shirt and the unbuttoned bra.

As Bodnya joined her on the bed, she pushed him down on his back and straddled him. As her tongue probed his mouth, she rubbed her crotch back and forth on him, feeling him getting hard beneath her.

Bodnya pulled her up on him and once more sucked greedily on her big breasts. She gasped and began to rub against him even harder.

In a moment, she sat up and smiled at him, slowly pulling the shirt away from her breasts, finally letting the shirt slide down her arms behind her. Bodnya caught her arms behind her and pulled her forward, licking first one nipple then the other.

"Oh Alex," she moaned, "yes!"

She rolled off him and sat next to him, stroking her fingers down his body to the bulge in his pants.

"Umm, what's this?"

She slid his zipper down and slipped her fingers inside his pants. His penis sprang out at her. She stroked his shaft for a moment then slowly bent down and kissed up and down the length of it, her tongue tracing its way back to the tip. She kissed the tip gently, then ran her lips down over it, taking nearly the whole length into her mouth.

"Boizshe moi!" Bodnya exclaimed, then was suddenly terrified that his Russian had given him away.

Susan seemed not to hear him, concentrating on her oral ministrations. She sucked rapidly and forcefully on him, making him hard as blue steel.

She rolled over on her back and pushed her breasts together, making a deep valley between them.

"Here, put it between my boobs. I really like it that way."

Bodnya stripped off his pants and straddled her chest. She

reached into the drawer of her bedstand an brought out a small bottle of baby oil. She put a few drops on one breast and rubbed them together to spread the oil. Bodnya pushed forward and slipped his organ between the freshly oiled orbs. Susan pushed on both sides of her breasts, forming a tunnel for him in between them.

"Oh yeah, sweetheart, that feels good. Go ahead, you won't hurt me."

Perhaps, perhaps not, thought Bodnya as he stroked back and forth in the slippery channel between her big boobs, We'll see. "Oh Susan, your breasts feel wonderful!" Bodnya said. "Squeeze them tight."

As she held them tightly together, Bodnya reached down and pinched her nipples, tugging and twisting them. She bent forward, her chin on her chest. As his organ emerged from her cleavage with each stroke, she kissed and bit at the tip of it. Bodnya gasped and went at it with a will, pounding against her breasts.

Just as he thought he could hold back no longer she suddenly released her breasts and caught his slippery tool in her hand.

"Come here, I want you inside me."

She pushed him over on his back, straddling him again, and slowly slid him deep up inside her.

"Oh, Alex."

Again she rocked back and forth, pushing him further up inside her. Her breathing became more ragged as she picked up the rhythm. Bodnya pulled and sucked on her nipples, and she moaned louder. She reached behind his head and pulled him tight against her straining breasts. In moments, her body was wet with sweat.

"Now, oh God, now!" she gasped and suddenly stiffened. She arched her back and clutched at him, then gasped and began spasming as her orgasm built. As she came, she made an odd, birdlike cry, its volume rising as she shook and strained for nearly half a minute.

Suddenly, she collapsed on his chest and gasped for breath. Before she could catch her breath, Bodnya slipped out from under her and got up on his knees behind her.

"Now we will do like we do in—" Bodnya almost said "in Russia" but caught himself, and said, "back home."

He pulled her hips up off the bed, and entered her from behind.

"Alex, I really don't like it this way," she complained as she tried to pull away. "Let's do it some other way."

Her protests were lost on Bodnya. He pushed her shoulders down on the bed, putting her in the "crawfish" position, the most popular Russian sexual position. She continued to protest as he pumped harder and harder from behind, but her protests turned quickly into cries of passion. He held her hips and pounded her as hard as he could from behind. In moments, he cried out, seized by his own wracking orgasm, and filled her with his sperm.

They collapsed on her bed, she on her stomach and he on his back. They both lay panting, straining to catch their breath.

"Oh Alex, that was something! You're really great."

"As are you, I think."

They lay there for a few moments, and Bodnya was almost asleep when her fingers again grasped his manhood. He smiled and simply rolled over on top of her. He slid back inside her and she wrapped her legs around the small of his back, her arms encircling his neck. She was thrusting her hips up to him, matching his rhythm.

"This is what you call the missionary position?" He asked.

"It sure is."

"Is surprising there are not more missionaries," he said, both of them laughing.

They rocked on like that for a few minutes, then Bodnya took Susan's ankles and put one on each of his shoulders, her legs stretched out on his chest. He began making long, increasingly rapid strokes in her. She held her own ankles and made little noises. Finally, she turned loose her ankles and dropped them down on the bed.

"Oww! That was great, but my legs gave out," she said, breathless. "Let's try this."

She slid both legs together underneath Bodnya, still inside her. She reached around him and grasped his buttocks, pulling him deeper into her. She squeezed her legs together, increasing the pressure on him. This was a new sensation for Bodnya, and in minutes, he could feel another orgasm building. He squeezed her breasts, and was just about to come again when she stiffened under him. She came again, making that odd sound, and he came with her, both of them only taking, not giving.

"That was incredible," Susan said, catching her breath.

"It has been a very long time since I last had sex, and your body is the most beautiful I have ever seen," Bodnya replied, telling the truth for the first time all evening.

After a moment's pillow talk, she fell into a deep slumber. Next to her, about to drop off himself, Bodnya wondered when he would get another woman. After this mission, the world would not be the same again. If he survived, it might be months before he was with another woman. He promised himself to have this woman again in the morning. What a strange mission!

The next morning, he was ready for a rematch, but Susan was like a dead thing. He kissed her neck and ran his hands around under her warm, heavy breasts, but she pushed him away with her elbow and made noises like a hibernating bear disturbed before spring. He persisted and she rolled over, half asleep and pushing him away. Her morning face was quite a surprise. Her pale face was puffy, and her eyes looked like two holes burned into a blanket. Was this she-bear the same siren who had so aroused him a few hours ago? Hard to believe!

The phone rang, startling Bodnya, but not even registering on Susan. He let it ring again, then an answering machine came on, playing her brief message. After the beep, there was a long pause before Kovpak's voice came on the line.

"Alex, are you there?" Kovpak asked, cautiously, his use of Bodnya's given name sounding strange and too familiar. Bodnya picked the receiver up.

"Yes, Paul."

"We will be coming over in some minutes to pick up you and go to the safe house, OK?"

Kovpak's English was better than that, so Bodnya knew he was playing his role as a German refugee.

"Fine, Paul, see you then."

Bodnya went to the kitchen and reheated the coffee in the glass carafe.

When Hollis's Suburban came by twenty minutes later, Susan was still dead to the world. Bodnya let himself out.

★25★

23 December

The sanctuary house was an old two-story wood frame house on Brazos Street, almost in sight of the state capitol building. It needed paint, and the yard wasn't kept up. It was a very low-profile place, just what the members of CCLAP were looking for to house those immigrants they helped avoid the Immigration and Naturalization Service. On the second floor there was a large common room and two bedrooms. From them they could see both front and back yards.

Hollis pulled around behind the house and parked next to the back door. He removed a black nylon carrying bag from the back of the Suburban. Bodnya waited next to the door, and the two entered together.

The sound of a car slowing outside caught their attention. Kovpak moved quickly to the curtained windows and cautiously moved the curtain away.

"It's Malinkov and the major."

As Kovpak continued to watch the street, T'sinko relaxed. A moment later, they heard the three men on the stairs.

"Anybody home?" Hollis asked lightly.

Kovpak greeted them at the head of the stairs.

"Good morning, Major," Kovpak replied, ignoring Hollis and Malinkov. Kovpak was eager to hear of Bodnya's night at the busty American's apartment.

"So, Comrade Major, was there a successful infiltration over those mountains we saw last night?"

175

Bodnya shrugged.

"Infiltration, why, most certainly there was a deep penetration in the valley below the mountains!" Malinkov said, smiling.

"Indeed," Kovpak went on, warming to the conversation. "Once again, the Spetsnaz has penetrated deeply in the enemy's rear!"

All stood looking at Bodnya, waiting for his reaction.

"I serve the Soviet Union," he said, saluting. Hollis and the three soldiers laughed. Only T'sinko stood frowning.

Our agent master must not like girls, Bodnya thought.

"First things first," Hollis said, after the laughter subsided. "I brought you some presents."

He opened the black bag and began removing weapons. There were three Beretta 9mm pistols, a MAC-10 submachine gun with silencer, and six American M-67 hand grenades. Malinkov took the MAC-10 and three grenades. The others each took a grenade and a pistol. None of the equipment could be linked to the Soviet Union.

From his briefcase, Hollis took a map and an envelope of photographs. The map was a U.S. Army map of Ft. Hood. The photographs were of tanks and armored personnel carriers parked in their motor pools. Some of the photos were night shots, taken with infrared film. They showed sentries walking their posts at these motor pools. Other photos showed small military houses with signs out front identifying the officer who lived there. At the bottom of each photo was a neatly typed stick-on label with the time, date, and a description of each photo.

"Here are your targets. Look them over briefly, now. We'll go over them again when we return from Ft. Hood."

"When are we leaving for Ft. Hood?" asked T'sinko. "I wish to establish contact with my agents as quickly as possible."

"Immediately," answered Hollis. "They are expecting us."

The five loaded into Hollis's Suburban and made the hour and a half trip to Killeen and Ft. Hood. The flat land reminded Bodnya of the Russian Steppes. When he mentioned this, Hollis laughed.

"You aren't the first person to notice. There is a city a couple of hundred miles west of here named Odessa."

As they drove through Killeen, the Christmas decorations were very different than in Austin. Here one sign had Santa Claus and his reindeer atop an M-1 tank. Another had helicopter gunships flanking Santa's sleigh.

"See, Major," Kovpak said, pointing, "here is truth of America, capitalist greed backed up by an imperialist war machine."

"Indeed," Bodnya laughed. "At least here they tell the truth."

"Is that not always the way with soldiers?" Malinkov asked quietly.

Both Bodnya and Kovpak turned to look at the huge soldier. He spoke so seldom, it always surprised them. Bodnya smiled. T'sinko, seeing the opportunity for a lecture, jumped in.

"It is always the case with soldiers of the revolution, Comrade," he began, "Only by—"

"Later, T'sinko, we are here," Bodnya cut the officer off as they pulled into the driveway of a small house.

Hollis reached in his jacket and pulled out a small plastic box. When he pushed the large button in the center of it, the door to the garage opened. Bodnya and the others grasped their weapons. If this was a trap, they would not be taken alive. Hollis, chuckling, slowly pulled into the garage, shut the garage door behind them, and shut off the engine. In the garage there was another vehicle, a yellow-and-white telephone company panel van. The Soviets sprang from their truck and took up firing positions around it.

Hollis slowly walked to the door of the house and pressed the bell in a series of long and short rings. An electronic lock opened and Hollis opened the door, motioning the others to follow.

As the Soviets entered, the two men standing in the kitchen stepped forward, their hands extended.

"Good morning," said the shorter of the two. "I'm Doyle Montgomery—Whisper, and this is Art Pugh—Cowboy."

"Hoddy," said Pugh.

T'sinko stepped forward.

"I am Falconer." he said giving the code name by which

he had communicated with the two men for the last two years. "It is a pleasure to finally meet."

What a strange pair, Bodnya thought, as he shook their hands. The one called Cowboy looked the part. Tall and thin, he wore a snap front shirt, jeans, sharp-pointed cowboy boots, a carved belt with a huge oval buckle, and a large straw hat bent up on the sides and down at the front and back. He was darkly tanned from the Texas sun, and held a toothpick loosely in the corner of his mouth. Kovpak stared open-mouthed at seeing his first real cowboy.

The other man, Whisper, was short, slight, and had the owlish look of a librarian. He wore wire-rimmed glasses and had a thin blond mustache that was almost invisible. His white pullover sweater had a small horse embroidered on the breast. There was an identical horse on his navy slacks. He wore white leather shoes that had Reebok written down the sides.

"Won't you sit down?" Whisper asked. "Can I get something to drink?"

"Nothing, thank you," Bodnya replied. "May we get started?"

"Of course, step over here to the table."

Whisper walked into the dining room where a large map and several photos littered the large table.

As everyone found a spot around the table, he began.

"This is the base, of course. We are located about a mile off post here," he said, pointing to their location. "The main gate is here, just off the highway. Here is a photo of the main gate."

This is an impressive display, Bodnya thought as the little man described the huge American base. Each area of interest had one or more photos to illustrate it, and the different areas of the map were color coded for their particular activity. What was most impressive was the array of armored might present there. In the photos, the sinister M-1 main battle tanks were lined up row after row, and where there were no tanks, there were M2 Bradley infantry fighting vehicles and their reconnaissance counterpart, the M3, each a tank killer as well as a troop transport. There were also rows of big CM109A3 155mm self-propelled howitzers. In the airfield pictures, there were dozens of AH-64 Apache attack helicopters. This was the most potent weapon on the base. Its Hellfire missiles

could be fired from behind cover and still home in on their
targets, guided by a laser beam aimed by a hidden soldier or
another helicopter. Its 30mm cannon could pierce the thin
armor on top of Russian tanks and personnel carriers.

In Europe, this combined arms counter-attack force could
blunt the Soviet attack, and kill thousands of Soviet soldiers.
It must never leave Ft. Hood.

"OK, that's a quick once-over," Montgomery concluded.
"I thought we would take a spin around the base, and then
come back here and go over it again."

"Excellent, Comra—er—Whisper," T'sinko stammered.
"How shall we do this?"

"Cowboy will take you."

Cowboy, who had been leaning against the wall, took the
toothpick from his mouth, and started for the garage.

"C'mon boys," he drawled. "Let's get in my van here and
we'll see the sights."

"We are just going to drive in?" asked Bodnya.

"Yup, partner, just like that." Cowboy replied, snapping
his fingers.

Cowboy's panel van was packed with telephone equipment. He folded down small seats in the rear for the men to
sit on.

"It's a bit cramped, but it's invisible."

Once everyone was in, Cowboy raised the door, and drove
quickly to the highway leading to the base.

As they turned onto the highway, T'sinko leaned forward.
"What do mean, it's invisible?"

"I mean that most people don't even see vans like this;
phone company, light company, vending machines, UPS.
They're so commonplace, people don't notice or remember
them. Sometimes that's real handy."

T'sinko looked puzzled but sat back down.

Three minutes later, Cowboy took the exit marked Main Gate.
As they turned off the highway through the Main Gate of Ft.
Hood, the Soviets tensed, but Cowboy assured them there would
be no trouble entering the base and there wasn't. The bored
MPs hardly looked at the van as it sped through the entrance,
noting only the base sticker on the front bumper. The Soviet
soldiers looked at each other in stunned amazement. Nowhere

in the world had they encountered such laxity at a military installation, particularly a headquarters complex.

"See, guys, what did I tell you?" Cowboy drawled.

"Almost too easy," Bodnya replied. "In such ways are traps sprung."

"Not here, buddy, at least, not today. Let's take a look at the drop zones first."

Antelope and Ft. Hood Drop Zones were gently rolling fields, seven kilometers from the main base. Both covered about four square kilometers and were separated by more than a kilometer of spare scrub oak. This would pose no obstacle to Soviet paratroopers. Nor Americans for that matter, Bodnya recalled, having watched one of their Ranger Battalions jump onto a dense brush-covered drop zone in West Germany, during one of the annual Reforger Exercises. The unit had deployed nonstop all the way from the U.S. A most impressive feat by anyone's standard.

Bodnya and Kovpak got out briefly to check the assembly point, a packed dirt airstrip, marked on the map as Landing Strip 12 on the northeast corner of Ft. Hood Drop Zone, and to get their bearings toward the targets.

Next on the tour was the 2d Armored Division. As they slowly drove down North Avenue, Bodnya was awed by the sight. Photos of American tanks were one thing, the reality, another. The mock-ups in Nicaragua were nothing by comparison. The sleek, green, black, and brown camouflaged killing machines, the pride of American technology, sat row upon row. They seemed to have a sinister quality about them that the less sophisticated Soviet tanks lacked. They passed a motor pool filled with ADATS air defense missile launchers. This successor to the ill-fated Sgt. York gun was a potent antiaircraft system. As the van passed compound after compound, a seemingly unending chain of motor pools filled with combat vehicles and equipment, Bodnya thrilled at the sight of them.

As they continued down North Avenue, his awe changed to excitement and a feeling of intense power. Tomorrow night, he and his hunters would turn these metal monsters into melted hulks; impotent steel slugs that would never shed Soviet blood. That thought warmed him. He and his Spetsnaz would protect the *Rodina* from these horrors, even at the cost of their lives. For a Soviet soldier, there could be no higher calling.

Through the dark, tinted side window, Kovpak and the others made mental notes of the location and layout of their various targets. They were obviously as impressed as Bodnya. Exclamations of *"boishe moi"* and *"vot kok"* marked each new area.

The 1st Cavalry Division's area offered more of the same. Bodnya noticed that even the streets had warlike names: Tank Destroyer Boulevard, Battalion Avenue. On Soviet installations the streets were named after past unit heros.

Turning south on Clear Creek Road, they passed two huge one-story buildings. Cowboy turned into one of the parking lots. The lot was crowded with vehicles, almost all civilian. It seemed that everyone, even low-ranking soldiers, owned a car. Uniformed soldiers, off-duty soldiers, and dependents in civilian clothes streamed in and out of the structure.

"And here, of course, is the main center of attraction."

T'sinko jumped forward, eager to see this important sight. "What is it, the communications center?"

"Naw," replied the American slowly, "it's the PX."

Bodnya laughed out loud at the look of total confusion on T'sinko's face.

"But—"

"Any of you boys need anything from the PX?" Cowboy asked as he got out of the van.

"What is a PX?" asked Kovpak.

"It is like a Voyentorg Army-Navy Store." replied Bodnya.

"Major, I would like to accompany him," Kovpak asked, turning suddenly to Bodnya.

"Under no circumstances!" T'sinko blurted. "There is to be no—"

"Go ahead, my friend, but be careful," Bodnya said, cutting off the GRU officer again.

As the two men walked away from the van, T'sinko was fuming.

"As security officer, I must warn you that this is a serious breach of security."

"And as commanding officer of this detachment, I must warn you to calm down before you have a stroke. There is no danger of Ensign Kovpak defecting, and he is an experienced combat officer," Bodnya added, referring to the GRU officer's lack of combat experience. "He will be fine."

T'sinko was not happy, but he sat down and looked out the window sullenly.

The truth was that Bodnya didn't like the idea much, either, but he would not back up the security officer against one of his own. He would discuss the matter with Kovpak another time. He would have liked to go in himself. When he was a member of the Soviet Military Liaison Mission, he had been entitled to use American PXs. He recalled with amusement the startled reactions he and his fellow officers received from newly assigned Americans when a group of Soviet officers in full uniform stomped into the Frankfurt Military Community's main PX.

Fifteen minutes later, the two men were back. Cowboy had a large sack with two six-packs of Coors beer, and Kovpak had a set of small earphones on his head and a tiny cassette recorder in his hand. T'sinko was instantly agitated.

"What is that, Ensign, where did you get it?" he asked angrily when the two men were back in the van.

"It is called a Walkman," Kovpak answered, removing the headphones, "My friend Cowboy purchased it for me in the PX."

Cowboy looked around and smiled as he put the van in gear and eased it out of the crowded parking lot.

"Are you insane?" the security officer shouted.

"No more than usual," Bodnya laughed. "Kovpak, where did you get the money for that device? I trust you have not been spending your emergency funds."

"From that fisherman on the beach," Kovpak replied, playing with the controls on his new toy. "He was quite rich."

"What if you had been detected by the Americans?" T'sinko fretted, a vein standing out on his forehead. "We could have been compromised, we—"

"Aw, man, there wasn't nothin' to it," Cowboy interrupted. "He just showed me which one he wanted, slipped me the money, and I paid for it. That black chick at the register was working so fast, she didn't look twice at either of us."

He held up a forged, pink plastic-covered card. "All I had to do was show her my Army Reserve ID card. Relax."

T'sinko did not relax, but he sat down and shut up.

"Anyway," Cowboy went on, "if you want to get excited about something, look between the PX and the Commissary. See that little building behind the schoolhouse, the one with the fence around it? That's the Nuclear Weapons Maintenance Shop. It's where they keep the tactical nuc's workin' right."

T'sinko's eyes bulged from their sockets. "Impossible. Out in the open like that, with no troops surrounding it? You are mistaken."

"That's it, bud. I just thought I'd mention it."

T'sinko's mind whirled. Any nuclear target took precedence over all others. "We—it—" he stammered.

"Don't worry, we will give it the attention it deserves," Bodnya reassured him. "Perhaps you can destroy it yourself. Would you like that?"

T'sinko was practically twitching with excitement.

This man acts like an old grandmother, Bodnya thought as they rode in silence to observe Group 3's targets. He wondered how the GRU officer would hold up under the strain of combat. Security officers had a bad reputation for using dogma and regulations instead of common sense in battle. He would have to watch this T'sinko closely when the action came. Maybe the Americans would do him a favor and shoot the little fool.

★26★

The voice on the line said, "Captain Peterson speaking, sir."

BJ winked at Jinx.

"Petey, this is BJ Kirkley. How you doin', lady?"

"Hey, BJ, I'm good. How're you?"

He leaned back on his couch, one foot propped on the middle cushion. "Fine, babe. Listen, a friend of mine is here and he has a story you need to hear. Are you going to be in all day?"

"Sure, BJ, I'm practically the only one here. What's the story about?"

"We'd rather tell you that when we get there, Pat. It'll take us about four hours, so we'll see you around noon."

"Why don't we just have lunch?"

"Great. See you then."

Kirkley hung up the phone and looked at Jinx. "OK, you're on for noon."

He nodded. "Let's do it."

Kirkley drove. He knew the way to the 163d Military Intelligence Battalion at West Ft. Hood so well, he could drive it in his sleep. An MI Tactical Exploitation Battalion, it was Company G's parent unit for wartime employment, and part of III Corps' 504th MI Brigade. He either called there or drove up at least once a week to trade bits of information, to pick someone's brain, or have his picked.

The drive was monotonous. The scenery was flat, with-ered, and abandoned, save for the occasional gas station along Highway 36. The highway was named for the Texas National Guard's old 36th Infantry Division. Jinx stared out the window of Kirkley's old Camaro, lost in a mental gumbo. Thoughts of Susan, Nicaragua, Russell, and the Russian all swirled and folded through his mind. It was an Andy Worhol movie called *Failure*.

If my life were a movie, he thought, Siskel and Ebert would give it two thumbs down.

"This road is boring me to death, BJ. Tell me a joke or something," Jinx said, wanting to shake off the descending gloom.

"I know a good Russian joke."

"OK, let's hear it."

"Well," he began in a Russian accent as wretched as his French accent, "it seems that Gortov was riding in his limo one day, and told the driver that he wanted to go faster. The driver said that he was going as fast as he could, that he could not go any faster, so Gorty told him to pull over. 'I'm President of the Soviet Union, General Secretary of the Communist party. I can drive as fast as I want,' he told the hapless driver. So Gorty took the wheel and the Zil shot down the freeway.

"It passed a Militia car with a sergeant and a militiaman in it. The sergeant said, 'I want to see how you handle a traffic stop of a party official, so pull that Zil over and give the driver a ticket.'

"The militiaman chased down the Zil and pulled it over. He got out and walked up to the the driver's door. Suddenly he snapped to attention, saluted, and came back to the patrol car.

"The sergeant threw a fit. 'Why did you not give him a ticket?' he asked the militiaman.

" 'I could not. He was far too important,' the militiaman answered.

" 'No one is so important that they can ignore the law. Who was he?'

"The militiaman looked at him and said, 'I do not know. I did not recognize him, but Comrade Gortov was driving him!' "

It was the first time Jinx had laughed all day.

* * *

Captain Patricia Peterson met them at the door of the MI battalion headquarters. The one-story building was surrounded by a chain link fence, but the gate was open.

"Beej, what it is, bro."

"What it was, mama," BJ answered, giving Peterson the old dap handshake.

"What it will be. Is this your friend?" Peterson asked. She extended her hand. Jinx took it. The grip was strong.

"I'm Richard Jenkins, Captain."

"Glad to meet you. Any friend of BJ's," she said, rolling her eyes toward BJ, "is hurting for friends."

"Yo' mama!" BJ punched the tall black woman on the shoulder. "Watch yourself, Jinx, this gal is a C-I spook!"

"I'll try not to hold that against her."

"Which, being counter-intelligence, or a spook? Come on back to my office," Peterson laughed. "Let's hear this exciting story."

They followed the tall, slim black woman through a rabbit warren of hallways to her office.

Peterson's office was small and bare, except for the huge map of West and East Germany on the wall opposite her desk. The front of the gray metal army desk sported a bumper sticker that read "Communism Sucks." A small bookcase against the wall held Peterson's personal library of Communist lore, most of it about the KGB.

Peterson leaned back in her chair and propped her feet on the desk, crossing one slack-clad leg over the other. "I'm all ears."

"Two weeks ago, I led a small group of Nicaraguan Contras in a raid on a camp in Zelaya Province in northeastern Nicaragua. In the course of that raid, I observed a Russian officer, probably Spetsnaz. That Russian and his buddies were there practicing for some type of mission, using mock-ups. Their dimensions were about the same as tanks and APCs. I managed to salvage a portion of a map there and brought that fragment out with me. BJ believes the area in that fragment is part of Ft. Hood."

Peterson's tiny spit shined boots hit the floor. She was suddenly very interested. She leaned forward on her desk, tenting her fingers under her chin.

"Let me back up for a minute," the MI officer interrupted. "Tell me some more about why you ran this raid."

"Air recce identified some shapes and activities at the site that the higher-ups decided needed to be eyeballed. Word from our agents there was that the camp was all Soviet. The plan was to find out what they were doing and twist Ivan's tail at the same time. By the time we went in, the Soviets were about to pull out and burn the camp. We sort of helped them. The map fragment was all that was left of their HQ after the Russian officer I mentioned put an RPO-A rocket through the wall."

Peterson whistled through her teeth. "Who were you working for down there, Mr. Jenkins, if you don't mind my asking?"

"I was with the Agency's PM Section in Honduras. I worked for Jab Donlon."

"J.A.B. Donlon?" Peterson asked.

Jinx nodded.

"I know him," Peterson said, "He was here for years, you know. Is he still doing his George Patton imitation?"

"Has him down cold."

Peterson laughed out loud. "OK, so why are you back here talking to me?"

"The Agency hotshot in Tegucigalpa has a hard-on—I beg your pardon, a dislike—for me and shipped me out right after the raid. Said the information was useless. That's why I came to see BJ."

"Have you got the fragment with you?" Peterson asked.

"Sure," BJ answered. "Take a look." He opened the envelope and took out the map of Ft. Hood and the fragment.

"Put it there," Peterson said. She pointed to a small light table against the wall.

BJ laid the fragment on the map above the 1st Cavalry motor pool area. He stepped back so Peterson could see.

Switching on the table's light, Peterson spent several minutes matching the fragment to the map, trying it against different areas. Light showed through the map and the charred fragment. The symbols on the two could be clearly seen and aligned. She whistled through her teeth as she studied.

"Did you see the entire map?" Peterson asked over her shoulder.

"Sort of. I was in the room with it, but it was so dark, I couldn't tell anything about it. Then the rocket hit."

She looked up.

"Um-hum. What size did you say the mock-ups were?"

He shrugged. "Twenty-five by ten by eight feet. About the same size as an Abrams."

"Uhmm."

Peterson stood up and faced the two visitors. "Well, this looks like it could be our friends at the 1st of the 7th Cav."

"The 7th Cavalry?" Jinx raised an eyebrow. "Custer's old outfit?"

"Uh, yes," Peterson replied. "OK, so what exactly do you want me to do?"

Jinx and BJ looked at each other.

"I don't exactly know," BJ answered. "We just wanted to warn you that you might be getting a visit from some really bad motherfuckers."

"You don't have any more information than this?"

"No."

"Gentlemen, this is interesting as hell, but I don't know what to tell you," Peterson said as she folded up the map. "I'll make a report of our conversation and pass it along. I'm sure that we will want to talk to you again, but for now that's about all I can do."

"That's it?"

"For now, yes," Peterson said. She held up the fragment. "I would like to make a copy of this, if I may."

"Sure," Jinx said as Peterson walked next door to the copy room.

"I would show this to the C.O., but he's on leave," Peterson said from the next room. "Nearly everyone here is on leave for Christmas."

Peterson came back in with her copy. "Anyway, until the old man gets back, I can't do much with this."

Jinx's face showed his frustration.

"Don't get me wrong," Peterson went on. "I think you have something here, I just don't know what. The Russkies are not usually that transparent."

"Pat, do you have anything that might indicate Ivan's intentions?" BJ interrupted. "They went to a lot of trouble to do all this."

"They have gone to a lot of trouble on a red herring before, not to make a pun. This could be part of some elaborate maskirovka plan, or simply a training exercise. There's a lot of stuff going on in Europe, what with their big exercise coming up and the changes in their leadership. It could be anything. It's not likely to happen soon, though, Ivan hates to start something in the winter."

"So that's it?"

"For now, yes. You guys want some lunch?"

"Captain, I don't believe this is a trick. I believe that it indicates a Soviet plan for an attack of some sort on this installation. As far as what the Soviets do in winter, you might keep in mind that they invaded Afghanistan on Christmas eve, 1979. Please don't just shitcan this information!"

"I won't, Mr. Jenkins, I assure you. Now, do you guys want to get a burger?"

"Sure, you buy," BJ said brightly, his eyes conveying a message to Jinx. The message was, Drop it.

They went to the small West Ft. Hood Officer's Club for a hamburger. Peterson and Kirkley had an animated conversation about the reorganization of Soviet artillery brigades, but Jinx paid little attention. The frustration was back, the door to depression opening wide.

They dropped Peterson off at her office. As the Captain walked away, Jinx called after her, "Captain!"

Peterson turned at the gate.

Jinx just smiled at her and said, "Remember Pearl Harbor."

As they left the East Gate, BJ glanced over at Jinx. "What did you think of Pat?"

"Well, she was not what I expected. I'm not used to female officers yet."

"You haven't spent much time around the New Action Army, have you? Don't let that black rap fool you, she's sharp as a tack. Baylor grad. One of the few Poli-Sci majors I've met who sees the world right."

Jinx just nodded his reply.

He rode to Austin in a deep funk. BJ knew him well enough not to intrude.

★27★

At the safe house, Whisper was waiting.

"Was your tour satisfactory?" he asked as the team filed in. "I took the liberty of getting us all some lunch."

The kitchen table was piled with white sacks, each with a yellow M on the side.

"Have you eaten any American fast food, yet?" the young American went on. "This is from McDonald's. There are hamburgers, french fries, and Cokes. Help yourselves."

Malinkov and T'sinko emptied the sacks and unwrapped each burger for inspection. Malinkov looked very skeptical at the two-layered burger dripping sauce, but T'sinko immediately took a huge bite of his and beamed.

"Horosho," he said, grease and special sauce running down his chin, "I have always wanted to try a McDonald's Big Mac."

Like most Soviets, T'sinko was intensely curious about America, even though his job was to help undermine and destroy it. He did not see the dichotomy. Few Soviets did. They prized blue jeans and cassette tapes made by the capitalist society they condemned.

"I have already had McDonald food," Bodnya said. "I spent some time in West Germany. There were many Mc-Donalds there."

He watched the others devour the food with considerable gusto. Malinkov seemed particularly amused by the ketchup pouches. He tore the top open, then squeezed the entire contents into his mouth.

"Come Major," Kovpak said over his shoulder. "There is plenty."

"I like Burger King better, myself," Cowboy said from the living room. "I ain't been able to eat a McDonald's since that business about there being ground up worms in their meat."

All chewing stopped instantly. Malinkov and T'sinko looked at each other and almost simultaneously spat the food out. Malinkov spat his on the floor next to the table. T'sinko spat into the open sack in front of him. Both men took long drinks from their Cokes, rinsed their mouths and spat the contents out. Only Kovpak continued to eat with gusto.

Whisper's eyebrows shot up in surprise and embarrassment. "There aren't any worms in there!" he shouted. "Damn it, Cowboy, why did you say that?"

" 'Cause that's what I heard," Cowboy replied. He sat down on the couch and put his feet on the coffee table. "Burger King only uses one hundred percent beef."

"How can you eat that?" T'sinko asked Kovpak. "Didn't you hear Cowboy say there were worms in it?"

"I don't see any worms," Kovpak replied, grabbing a handful of french fries. "Besides, that sounds like dezinformatsiya to me. This is good. If you do not want it, I will eat it."

He beamed at the other two. Bodnya laughed out loud. Whisper went over and angrily picked up a burger. He made a production of eating it, never taking his eyes off Cowboy.

There is real animosity in his expression, Bodnya noted. The remark about the worms was meant to demean Whisper in our eyes. Bodnya suspected that these two worked together only out of necessity. There was obviously little love lost between them.

"Since no one seems to have an appetite, Whisper," Bodnya said, "let us go over the plans for your part of the operation."

Thankful for the chance to forget the lunch gaffe, Whisper stood and walked back to the table where he had conducted the morning's briefing.

The others followed. Kovpak was still eating the remains

of Malinkov's hamburger. *Oui vybrasyvayut chtoto khoro-shoye*. (They throw out something good!) These men obviously had not been really hungry before, as he had!

Once again the star, Whisper immediately went into his presentation. He produced another set of photos from his case. Pictured in the photos were trucks. One truck was a box-type lorry, the other a tractor-trailer. The lorry was bright yellow with the word Ryder painted on the side. The tractor-trailer was silver, emblazoned with the Safeway logo.

"We have already rented the three lorries and a large cargo van. Right now, the van is parked in a garage nearby. The trucks we will pick up tomorrow morning. Each truck is enclosed, twenty-two feet long, with a roll-up door. I will drive one, Cowboy will drive another, and Hollis will drive the third. Major, you will take the Suburban. Do you have someone to drive the van?"

Bodnya nodded. "Sgt. Malinkov can drive it. He is an excellent driver." He noted that the little man seemed to glow as he ticked off the details of his part of the raid. Obviously, Whisper had lived for this moment for years. Bodnya hoped that when the actual fight came, the spy would have the courage to carry through. The other man, Cowboy, leaned against the door frame, as unconcerned as ever. Not inattentive, just unconcerned. This one I am not worried about, Bodnya thought. He will do his job.

"The escape truck is in the warehouse, ready to go, if needed. I hope we will not have to use it. It is a long drive to the border and the authorities will have been alerted. Hopefully, they will not know exactly what they are looking for, or where to look, but—"

Whisper took yet another map from his case. "This is the route for the escape truck. It ends here at Piedras Negras, in Mexico, across from Eagle Pass. Once there, Comrade T'sinko's people will have to provide transportation." T'sinko looked unconcerned, as if such contingency plans were unnecessary.

"Our An-12 will be waiting for us, Comrade," T'sinko said quietly, "to take us home."

"Fine then. Hollis will drive you back here tomorrow. All will be ready."

"You have done your work well, Whisper," Bodnya answered; "both of you."

Whisper came to attention. His face was damp with a sheen of perspiration, not from exertion, but excitement. His eyes were shining.

"I serve the Soviet Union!" he replied proudly.

By the door, Cowboy grinned and nodded.

"So you going to mope forever?" BJ asked from the bathroom. They had checked into a cheap hotel just off the Interstate in Austin.

"Yes." Jinx lay on the bed, staring at the ceiling.

"You want me to go down to the drug store and pick up a package of razor blades for you?"

"Too messy; maybe just some Jonestown Kool-Aid."

"You like loud music?"

"Right now, I don't like anything."

"And you feel like a fire hydrant in a world full of dogs," BJ crooned in a singsong voice. "Let's go get some grease and then I'll show you greater downtown Sixth Street. It won't be as lively as usual, since the college kids are all gone for Christmas, but it'll take our minds of this stuff for a while."

★28★

The Suburban had barely pulled into the driveway when Susan's red car pulled in behind them. Bodnya and Kovpak went back to talk to her and keep her away from the others.

"Good evening, Susan," Bodnya said, taking both her hands in his. "I didn't expect to see you here."

"I know," she answered. "I just thought that you might want to get out tonight and see something of Austin."

"We have seen much of Texas today," Kovpak said, intruding on the conversation. "Brian took us sightseeing."

"Really, Paul," Susan asked. "What did you see?"

"The Alamo in San Antonio," Bodnya said quickly, seizing the conversation and giving Kovpak a look. "It is very famous in Germany. We have seen the film with John Wayne."

"Oh, God," Susan laughed. "John Wayne— Anyway, I wanted to see if you were in the mood—to go out, that is."

"Oh, I should not," Bodnya started to say. "I really should stay here with the others tonight."

"No, no Maj— my friend," Kovpak caught himself before he addressed Bodnya. "Go on, we will be fine here."

His lewd smile infuriated Bodnya, but there really was nothing else to do that evening.

"Oh, all right, I would love to," he said, bringing a smile to her face.

* * *

"BJ, do you really like this stuff?" Jinx screamed over the din of the screeching music.

"Sure," BJ screamed back. "You don't like it?"

Jinx opened his mouth wide and poked a finger toward it. "AAAAAAGGGGGHHH!"

"OK, OK, come on," BJ said, looking disgusted. "Let's see if we can find you some elevator music."

Out on the street, Jinx zipped his jacket against the cold. "God, I'm having a hard time getting used to the cold again. A year or so down south makes your blood thinner."

BJ shrugged. "I think you've lost contact with the American scene altogether. You can't even tell good music any more."

"If the noise in that place was music, then you're right. That sounded like a long, amplified train wreck."

"You know what they say. If it's too loud, you're too old!"

"Fuck you, bubblegummer!" Jinx sneered.

They passed another club where a group of young kids stood around the front door. The girls were dressed like their current rock idol, and the boys sported hair shaved close on one side with a long straight mop on the other.

Jinx tried unsuccessfully, not to stare.

"I'll tell you, BJ, these kids look strange. Those boys look like alien visitors, and the girls look like brain-dead sluts."

BJ laughed. "You know what they say the difference is between Austin and yogurt?"

"What?"

"Yogurt has an active, living culture."

At the corner, they paused for the light, then started across the street, headed for the bar on the corner of Sixth and Brazos. Jinx was in the middle of the crosswalk when he saw the Russian. He was wearing a black leather jacket and tan slacks, but it was him. Jinx stood rooted to the spot, staring. The Russian was with a woman, but Jinx could not see her face. He didn't care about her, just about the Russian.

The loud blast of the car horn scared Jinx, making him jump. "Out of the street, asshole!" the driver screamed through the windshield. Jinx ran the few steps to where BJ waited on the curb in front of the hotel bar.

"You OK?" BJ asked. "You look like like you saw a ghost."

"Look! It's him!" Jinx yelled, grabbing BJ's coat and pointing across the street. "There, with that woman!"

"Who, where?"

The Russian and the woman with him were gone. For a second, Jinx wondered if he had really seem them.

"I just saw the Russian who blew out that wall and burned up the map in that camp in Nicaragua!"

BJ just stood and looked at his friend. His expression was concern mixed with caution. "Here in Austin, Texas, USA, you saw a Russian from Nicaragua."

"I'm telling you," Jinx said, searching the street for another glimpse of the Russian.

"You don't have, like malaria or some fever, do you?" BJ asked.

Jinx glanced back. "No, I'm fine. Why?"

BJ didn't reply, but stood looking at Jinx from under raised eyebrows.

Jinx glanced back again and saw BJ's expression. "What, you think I'm seeing things?"

"I think maybe you're tired."

Maybe he's right, Jinx thought, scanning the street again for the Russian and the woman, maybe I am seeing things.

"You could be right, amigo. Come on, buy me one more drink, and we'll call it a night." He turned and walked up the three steps into the bar, with BJ right behind.

Never have I seen such gaudiness, Bodnya thought, except maybe in Frankfurt. Walking down Sixth Street with Susan, he was amazed by the amount of Christmas decorations. Every window seemed to have the twinkling lights of a tree, or lights around the building itself. What a waste of electricity. Shoppers scurried with their packages. The annual orgy of greed was in full swing.

"What do you think?" Susan asked, as if reading his thoughts.

"Americans make a big show of Christmas." he said.

"That we do. There's no bigger holiday," she answered. "We spend the rest of the year paying for it and working up to the next one."

"Where are we going now?"

"There's a little club in here that plays excellent jazz. I

thought we might have something warm to drink. Have you ever had Irish coffee?''

"No," Bodnya lied. "What is it?"

"Coffee with Irish whiskey and cream. It's good."

Indeed it is, Bodnya thought, remembering the weeks he had spent in Armaugh with the Provos. He and Kovpak were in Ireland to teach the IRA how to use the weapons the Soviets had supplied them. Bodnya had developed a real taste for their whiskey, Kovpak for their red-haired colleens.

"Sounds interesting," Bodnya replied as Susan pulled him through the tall door. Inside, a saxophone was playing.

Two young scotches later, BJ and a much more mellow Jinx hit the pavement of Sixth Street. They were nearly back to the car when Jinx looked across the street and saw him again. Not watching where he was walking, Jinx slammed his head into a pole bearing a One Way sign. The impact jarred him, but when he looked back, the man and the woman were still there, walking along, chatting as if they hadn't a care in the world. Now Jinx could see the woman's face. The sight of Susan Elliot with the Russian jarred him even more than running into the pole.

"Christ, Jinx, are you OK?" BJ asked from a hundred miles away. "That hurt to listen to."

Jinx reached back and grabbed his friend, not wanting to take his eyes from the pair now directly across the street from them.

"There, across the street, do you see him?"

BJ looked across the street. "You mean that guy over there with the big knockered chick?" he asked, just as recognition struck. "Holy shit! That's Susan."

"And that's my boy!" Jinx said, his eyes never leaving the Russian. "BJ, get the car. I'm going to follow those two."

Susan and the Russian were just pulling away from the curb when BJ pulled up in the Camaro. The red Volvo was easy to follow even in the traffic, so they stayed a few car lengths behind, shadowing the couple.

When she pulled into the drive on Brazos Street, BJ just drove on by, as Jinx made a note of the address. The two men drove another block, then turned around and drove back, parking their car in the shadows, between a VW Vanagon and an old Buick station wagon. They sat there, watching the driveway for ten minutes, before Susan pulled out in her car. She was alone.

Damn it, she thought angrily, what was the matter? She had expected him to come back to her apartment with her, but he had refused. He needed to stay with the others tonight. For what? Damn! That awful feeling was coming back again. Every time she had sex with someone on their first date, they either pulled away or they never called.

When will I learn? she asked herself, I'm not a tramp. Why do I keep acting like one?

★29★

24 December

"Good morning, I'm Richard Jenkins, this is my friend BJ
Kirkley."

"Come in Mr. Jenkins, I'm Tom Harper and this is Special
Agent White."

Jinx and BJ took the two chairs facing the desk. The two
FBI agents were a classic Mutt and Jeff team. White was tall
and thin, Harper short and stocky. Agent Harper resumed his
seat behind the desk, and White stood behind and to one side,
leaning against the window frame. The morning sunlight
streamed in through the tiny office's single tall window, the
rush-hour traffic noise still audible outside.

"You said you had some information about a Soviet agent
in Austin?"

"That's right," Jinx began. "He is an officer in the Soviet
Army. I suspect he is either in the Spetsnaz or the GRU."

Jinx reached in his jacket pocket and pulled out his Agency
ID holder. The two FBI agents looked it over and returned it
without a word.

"How is it that you know this Soviet officer?"

Jinx outlined his job with the Contras, his encounter with
the Russian in the camp, and the Ft. Hood map fragment.
During this talk, White seemed unconcerned, even bored. He
stood looking out the tall window onto the street below. The
sunlight illuminated the smoke from the pipe which he held
in the corner of his mouth. Harper was all ears, and occa-
sionally stopped Jinx's narrative to ask questions.

"And you say you saw this man again here in Austin?"

"That's right, last night. He was with a woman down on Sixth Street, and then they went to a house on Brazos Street, where she dropped him off."

"Did you recognize the woman?"

Jinx looked at BJ, who just raised his eyebrows and shrugged.

"Yes. Her name is Susan Elliot. She is a student here at U.T."

At the mention of Susan Elliot's name, the two agents traded glances, careful not to let any emotion show.

"How do you know her?"

"I taught her to scuba dive," BJ broke in. "That's what I do for my honest money."

Agent Harper smiled. "I see."

Jinx didn't feel that he needed to add the part about saving her life in Mexico, so he let BJ's explanation stand.

White turned and sat back on the window ledge, chewing on his pipe.

"Let me see if I've got this right. You saw this Russian in Nicaragua at a camp you attacked. It was dark, and you had just been wounded. Now you think you have seen him again coming out of a club here in Austin with a woman you just happen to know. Mr. Jenkins, this is not some personal thing, is it?"

For a second, Jinx just sat and stared at the man.

"No, Mr. White, this is not personal. This is infiltration of the United States by a foreign military officer for the purpose of espionage, possibly sabotage," Jinx said, starting to get hot. "This is an elite Soviet soldier who is not here on a vacation. This is a man who was training on tank mock-ups two weeks ago! The man is not here on vacation."

The two agents just sat and looked at Jinx, waiting to see how emotional he was going to get over this. Jinx realized what they were doing and quickly composed himself.

"Have you contacted any military authorities about this man?" White asked.

Jinx looked over at BJ again. He was studying the fingernails on one hand.

"Yes, we talked yesterday with the Counter Intelligence detachment at Ft. Hood."

"What did they think of all this?"

"The officer we spoke with was skeptical," Jinx said. He almost added, "But she said she'd check it out!" but caught himself. That would have sounded too lame.

"Well, Mr. Jenkins, I'm afraid I share some of his skepticism," White said slowly, "but, you have posed some questions that need to be answered."

"About the Russian or about me?"

White's face remained placid, but Harper grinned slightly, glancing at his colleague.

"We will look into this, Mr. Jenkins, I assure you," Harper said, rising to his feet. "Thank you for coming in. We do need a phone and address where we can contact you."

At the door, Jinx turned back to the two agents.

"Don't blow this off," he said. "This is real."

"Yes, we understand," Harper said, the smile fixed on his face.

"Fucking cops!" Jinx exploded when they were back in Kirkley's Camaro. "They're all alike, the patronizing bastards."

BJ said nothing. He knew that Jinx was not looking for conversation, only venting frustration.

"You come to them with a real foreign agent, just the sort of guy they are supposed to be looking for, and what do they do?" Jinx ranted on. "They ask you if it's a lover's spat. Christ!"

BJ could feel the heat coming off Jinx, who sat in the passenger seat, arms tight across his chest, fuming.

"Maybe I should have said he was a coke dealer or something, maybe that would have got their attention."

BJ just smiled and said, "Listen. Why don't we chill out for a while? It's Christmas Eve and I haven't bought a single present. Why don't we go to the mall, do a little Christmas shopping, and then make a new plan?"

Jinx didn't answer. He just nodded, looking out the car window at the high clouds moving in slowly from the north.

"So what do you think?"

White relit his pipe. "I thought it was bullshit until he mentioned our girl Susie. Let me get her file."

Susan Elliot was a familiar name to both agents. She turned up for every rally or conference that had to do with U.S. Central American policy. Her main affiliation was with Concerned Citizens for Latin American Policy, but she turned up at functions sponsored by half a dozen other radical organizations. She was a tireless talker, but she had never shown any tendency toward direct action.

In a moment, White was back with two manila folders. The tab on one read, Elliot, Susan J., the other, CCLAP.

"What have we gotten lately about these folks?"

"Not much. After that big trial last summer, all the sanctuary groups have kept a low profile."

The previous summer, a nun and priest had been tried in Federal Court for aiding illegal aliens evade the INS. They had been found guilty, but sentenced to probation. The trial had brought the sanctuary movement a lot of media attention, but less public support than the movement's proponents had hoped. Public support in Austin had waned after the failed attempt by Austin's Mayor Frank Cooksey to get Austin declared a sanctuary city in 1986. Since then, the Bureau had monitored the groups, but had discontinued surveillance of them.

"That address on Brazos is CCLAP's safe house," White said, taking a photo from the folder and handing it to Harper. "If they really did see a Russian there, I guess we ought to check it out."

"Maybe, I want to see what we can find out about Jenkins and his buddy. Didn't you work with the MI people at Ft. Hood on some of this a while back?"

"Yeah, I'll give 'em a call. Why don't you ring up Martinez at INS and see what he's got. We can go over and check out the house later."

★ 30 ★

"There she goes."

Susan's red Volvo pulled out of the small parking lot and turned north on Seventh Street.

White and Harper were parked half a block away. They had confirmed Jinx's story with the duty officer at the MI, Capt. Peterson. Peterson had heaped praise on BJ Kirkley, but had little information on Jinx. INS had had nothing to offer, but was very curious. They had closed down the Polish Pipeline a few years earlier, stemming the flow of illegal aliens from Eastern Europe through Mexico. If someone was opening it back up, they wanted to know about it.

The brown Dodge Aries with the two FBI agents followed Susan's Volvo. The woman seemed oblivious to the tail. She drove straight to the CCLAP house on Brazos Street.

"Well, well, well," Harper said softly.

"Let's pay a visit. Maybe she'll invite us in," White replied.

As she walked to the front door of the house, Susan did not notice the sedan park behind her. Turning her key in the lock, she heard the car door shut. She turned and watched the two men walk up to the porch.

"Can I help you?"

"Susan Elliot?" Harper asked.

"Yes. Who are you?" Susan replied, suddenly very scared.

"I'm Special Agent Harper, this is Special Agent White,"

Harper said as he extended his hand. "We're from the FBI. We'd like to ask you some questions if you don't mind."

Susan backed into the doorway. Harper dropped his hand to his side.

"Am I under arrest?"

"Not at all," White said. "We just want to ask about someone you may know. May we come in?"

FBI! Susan thought. Oh God. She knew that they were here about Alex and the others. She had to warn them upstairs, but not let these two men in the house. How am I going to do that?

"Do you have any sort of warrant to come in here?" she said, loudly, as she stepped back into the foyer. "You can't search this place without a warrant."

As she stepped back into the entryway, the two agents followed through the front door.

"We didn't come here to search anything, miss," Harper said calmly, "We just want to ask you about someone."

"I don't think I want you to come in here," she said, her voice rising. "I don't think I have anything to say to the FBI!"

She's warning someone, Harper thought. He looked quickly around. The large living room was empty and looked unused. A large sectional couch dominated the center of the room. It was covered with sheets. Empty bookcases lined the far wall on either side of a fireplace filled with cobwebs.

At least this place is well provisioned, Malinkov thought as he finished the last spoonful of soup and stepped to the sink to wash the dish. To be so well fed and well looked after was rare on a combat mission, but then this was hardly an ordinary mission. He dried the bowl and returned it to the cupboard. When he shut the cupboard door, he heard the car drive up.

"Major, we have company!" Malinkov shouted up the stairs.

At Malinkov's shout, Bodnya stepped to the window, expecting to see Hollis in the truck. It was Susan.

What the hell is she doing here? Bodnya asked himself as she shut off the engine.

The driver's door of the red car opened, and the American woman got out. She was almost to the door when the other vehicle pulled up. When the brown sedan drove up, Bodnya released the curtain and stepped back, watching through the thin fabric. He knew at a glance that the car was official. Somehow, cars of all governments looked the same. Perhaps it was the lack of adornment, the drab, humorless quality. These were policemen of some sort. They left their car and started for the house.

"Police! You two stay here!" Bodnya barked at the two others as he picked up the M-10 on his way down the stairs.

T'sinko and Kovpak instantly dropped their gear, and grabbed their guns. Kovpak moved to the rear window and peered through the thin material. There was no sign of movement in the backyard. He checked the chamber of his automatic for a round, then crouched, watching the backyard for armed visitors.

Bodnya ran down the back stairs and handed Malinkov the heavy submachine gun.

"Behind the sofa, quickly. When you hear my voice, be ready to shoot."

Malinkov spun and disappeared behind the large L-shaped couch, crouching near the end, Bodnya heard him pull back the bolt knob on the M-10.

Bodnya went the other way, through the back of the house. A second later, the front door opened and the woman's voice pierced the quiet. She was shouting at the two strangers.

Trying to warn us, Bodnya thought.

Bodnya slipped his jacket over his arm, concealing the pistol in the pocket. He took a deep breath. The adrenaline rush was starting, making his body hum, his senses more alert. Now.

He walked casually back the way he had come. Susan and the two men were just inside the door. She seemed to be losing all composure. At the sight of Bodnya, terror crossed her face.

"Good afternoon, gentlemen. Can I be of some help?" he asked.

Behind the sofa, Malinkov eased one eye past the sheet covering the furniture. Both the men were looking at the major. Malinkov silently rose to his feet, and took a very slow step forward, his weapon trained on the man nearest him. The woman was between the two strangers, blocking a clear shot at both. The major would have to take one. Malinkov motioned with his gun toward the agent on the left. The major acknowledged with a tiny nod. He took another slow, silent step.

"I'm Agent Harper, this is Agent White. We're from the FBI. And you are?"

"I'm Alex Brenner. Is Susan in some kind of trouble?"

"No, I'm not. These two storm troopers barged in—" Susan butted in, the anger rising in her voice. She pushed her way between the two agents, her confidence returning with Bodnya's cool presence.

"We would like to ask her, and you, some questions," White went on.

"Are we under arrest?" Bodnya asked, feigning concern.

"No, we would just like to talk to you both."

As he spoke to the agents, Bodnya watched Malinkov silently rise from behind the couch. The man was catlike for all his bulk. Malinkov pointed to the one he would kill. Bodnya shifted his weight, watching the other. The woman was between the two agents. Bodnya hoped she would not get in the way and block their shots. She would die if she did. Malinkov took one more step.

"What would you like to talk to us about?" Bodnya asked. "Have we done something?"

"We have a report that someone in this house may be in this country illegally," White said calmly.

"You have no right to come here!" Susan shouted, turning to White, "You—" She stopped as she saw Malinkov standing by the couch.

White followed her eyes. As he saw the figure behind him, he reached for the Sig 226 nestled under his left arm.

"GUN!"

Malinkov had the Ingram trained on the agent. When the woman looked back at him, he thrust the weapon forward. The American policeman was turning, reaching for his weapon. Malinkov jerked the trigger, released, and jerked it again. The black gun's silencer coughed and stuttered, empty shell cases showered out of the ejection port. The first burst caught the American in the right arm and chest. The man continued to turn. Even shot, he was still drawing his pistol. The second burst slammed him against the wall, 9mm slugs shredding the fabric of his jacket. The American fired his pistol harmlessly into the hardwood floor.

When Susan looked back at Malinkov, Bodnya knew that it was time. As the agent named White looked around, Bodnya made a show of looking, too. The American in front of him, Harper, reflexively glanced back as he reached under his coat for his own gun. Bodnya thrust his hand into his jacket pocket. Without trying to remove the pistol, he fired once, then twice again. The roar of the pistol was only a vague background sound to Bodnya. His whole being was focused on the man in front of him. The two men were bound together by this most ancient act. The first round took the American in the upper chest, turning him back toward Bodnya. The next one went in his open mouth, and the third gouged through the man's right eye. He never even got to the Colt Python on his hip. Harper was dead on his feet.

The Americans seemed to move slowly, mimes in death. The woman's strangled scream was a distant sound, not connected to this dance, this awful, wonderful ballet.

The entire event took only three seconds. The two American policemen were on the floor, dead. The woman was silent, now. She stood against the wall, staring at the dead men with wild unseeing eyes. Her mouth was open, but she had to force out the words.

"You killed them! Why, who—"

Bodnya stepped forward and took Harper's gun from his belt. Malinkov retrieved the other agent's weapon, stuck the pistol in his pocket, then stepped over to the woman.

"I will take care of her, Comrade Major. I am sorry she has to die," Malinkov said. He pushed the woman toward the kitchen.

"No. We may have use for her before this is over. Bind and gag her." Bodnya turned and started up the stairs. "Kovpak, T'sinko, we are all right. Anyone else outside?"

Malinkov gave his superior a look, but said nothing. This was the first time he had seen the man show any compassion for an enemy, man or woman. Malinkov spun the bewildered woman around and pulled her half-zipped jacket down over her shoulders, pinning her arms to her side. She protested with small whining noises, but offered no resistance. The

reality of the violence she had just seen had stunned her. Her
weakness disgusted Malinkov.

Upstairs, Kovpak and T'sinko were at the windows.
"Nothing out front, sir."

"N-nothing behind!" T'sinko stammered.

He is shaking like a leaf, Bodnya noted as he entered the
room.

"Let us get our gear ready. Hollis should be here soon,
but we have have to move quickly if those shots were heard."

T'sinko seemed not to hear.

"Captain!"

"Yes!" the frightened officer snapped around, his eyes still
wide.

"Get your gear ready to go, Captain," Bodnya said slowly.
"Ignore your fear. It will get you killed."

"Yes, Major."

"Ensign, when you have your gear collected, go down and
help Malinkov with the bodies." Bodnya said. He knew that
the Ensign's gear was always ready. Kovpak shouldered his
bag and ran down the stairs.

Malinkov was dragging the agent he had killed toward the
kitchen. The other was already there. The woman was in a
chair, her hands and feet bound with a length of clothesline.
A piece of silver duct tape covered her mouth.

"Good work, my friend," Kovpak said. Malinkov looked
up, but did not respond. "Can I help?"

"Yes, Comrade Ensign," Malinkov replied. "You could
get some of those paper rags and clean the blood up in front
of the door."

"Da."

There was surprisingly little blood on the floor. The one
man's coat had soaked up most of the blood from his chest
wounds. Only the other man's head wound had bled much.
Kovpak mopped up the clotting blood with towels from the
roll.

Very tidy, he thought as he stood and looked for any tell-
tale spots. All evidence of the violence was hidden, save for
the acrid smell of blood and gunpowder that lingered in the
entryway.

Satisfied, he returned to the kitchen. Malinkov was stuffing the smaller of the two men into the cupboard under the large twin sink.

"You know, when he gets stiff, it will take a wrecking bar to get him out," Kovpak laughed.

Malinkov looked up, amused by the thought. "You have an odd way of looking at things, Ensign Kovpak."

Kovpak just chuckled. He walked over to the woman. Her eyes beseeched him. Tears had streaked her mascara down her face. She breathed in ragged, terrified gasps.

"Why so sad, my pretty?" he asked, cupping her chin in his hand. He slid his fingers down her throat into the open collar of her flannel shirt. He pulled back the fabric, exposing the top of her cleavage.

"This woman's chest reminds me of those two mountains north of Kandahar," Kovpak said in Russian. "You remember them?"

Malinkov snorted.

"Only they were not as soft as these, nor as warm."

"You were not there in the summer, Ensign," Malinkov said. "They were very warm in the summer."

Kovpak did not answer. He was much more interested in the deep valley hidden by the plaid shirt. As he slipped his hand down into the shirt, she squirmed in the chair, making strangled noises against the tape over her mouth. Kovpak slid his hand down inside her bra, squeezing the soft flesh, searching. When his fingers found the erect nipple, he pinched it hard.

Susan lunged against her bonds and tried to scream.

"A screamer. I like that in a woman," Kovpak said, smiling.

"Comrade, if you are not too busy, I could use some help with this one," Malinkov said quietly.

"You have no romance in you, Sergeant."

"Not today, Comrade Ensign."

As they began to lift the corpse, they heard the sound of another vehicle in the driveway. Dropping the body, both men sprang to the windows. Hollis was just emerging from his Suburban. Malinkov and Kovpak met him at the back door.

"Is that Susan's car in the driveway?" Hollis asked as he walked through the back door.

"It is, yes," Kovpak replied lightly. "She came with two visitors." He stepped back to reveal the woman tied to the chair and the dead agent on the floor.

"Jesus Christ," Hollis blurted, astonished. "What— Who?"

"Police, what do you call them, FBI. They are both dead," Kovpak said flatly. "The woman is our guest for the moment."

"FBI! Jesus Christ!" Hollis's eyes darted to Susan. Her eyes pleaded with him and she made small, pitiful noises behind the tape.

Hollis whistled softly through his teeth. "Let's get out of here, then. Are you all ready to go?"

"Yes. Sergeant, get the Major."

Malinkov nodded and went to fetch the others.

"Get me Susan's keys, I'll move her car behind the house."

"And the FBI car, too?" Kovpak asked.

"Fuck it, let's get out of here."

Hollis left to move her car, leaving Kovpak alone with the woman. He ran his hand along her cheek. She pulled her head away and glared at him. Kovpak grabbed a handful of the thick curly hair and bent down, pulling her face close to his. Terror replaced anger in her eyes.

"It is too bad," he whispered, "that we do not have more time. We could become great friends. Close friends." He smiled at her, then pulled her head back sharply and bit her lightly on the neck. She shook all over, making terrified little sounds in her throat. Smiling, Kovpak slid his tongue down her neck, into the warm groove between her breasts. When he heard the sound of steps on the stairs, he released her hair and stood up.

"Perhaps another time."

The pain had awakened him. He had hurt like this once before, long ago, in a valley called A Shau. For a second he thought he was back in the A Shau, but the voices were wrong, foreign. Then he remembered the huge man with the black gun. White opened one eye just a slit. A kitchen. A man whose face seemed familiar was going out the back door. Another, the man with the gun, was leaving the room the other way. The woman, Susan Elliot was tied to a chair and a stranger was kissing her neck while she struggled. Slumped against the wall, White could tell his automatic was gone. Slowly, he pulled his right foot back. It took all the strength he had. The stranger had not heard him, engrossed in the woman. White slid his fingers up the cowboy boot. The tiny Charter Arms .38 was still there in his boot top. White held the pistol and slid his leg back down to remove it from the boot. He tucked the pistol under his leg, too weak to lift it.

Bodnya, T'sinko, and Malinkov walked into the room just as Hollis reentered from the back.

"I moved Susan's car. Is everyone ready to go?" Hollis asked. He was still shaken, but the fear was gone from his voice.

"Yes. Help Sergeant Malinkov with the woman," Bodnya said. "We will bring the equipment."

Kovpak stepped over behind the chair and cut the cords holding her to the chair with the Gerber folding knife he had taken off the dead fisherman.

"Come on, Susan," Hollis urged as he and the burly sergeant hauled the struggling woman to her feet, "let's go."

She whimpered and twisted, looking at Hollis, her eyes wide with confusion and fear.

As they left the back door, T'sinko was staring at the agent crumpled against the wall.

"What about this body?" he asked, stepping closer to White. "Is he dead?" T'sinko took another step closer to the American. "I think he's still alive."

"He should be dead," Bodnya answered, "Kovpak, make sure."

Now, White thought, while you have the strength. As the man took another step toward him, White twisted the gun out from under his leg. He didn't have the strength to lift the gun. His arm felt like it weighed a ton. He pivoted the barrel of the gun up, twisting his wrist to point it at the man's chest. He pulled the trigger as hard as he could. The roar of the small pistol stunned everyone in the room. T'sinko sprang back. Kovpak grasped the blade of the Gerber and threw it as hard as he could at the suddenly lively corpse. Unbalanced, the knife turned over once in flight, the brass handle striking the riddled American in the forehead. The gun dropped to the floor.

"I, I—" T'sinko stammered, his eyes fixed on his chest. On his sweater, a hole gaped just below the hollow of his throat. A dark stain was already flowing down his chest, away from the hole. T'sinko turned to Bodnya, confusion in his eyes.

"I—" T'sinko's eyes rolled back in his head, showing only the whites. He crumpled to the floor like a rag doll.

Bodnya stepped quickly to the fallen officer. The bullet had entered through his breastbone, driving splinters into the lungs and aorta. T'sinko was not dead, but he soon would be, drowning in his own blood.

Kovpak sprang to the American agent. Pulling the trigger had been the last act of his life. His head hung to one side, a small cut just above his right eye where the knife had struck. There was no blood coming from the cut. His dead eyes stared at the tiny pistol still held in his hand.

"Come we must hide these two, then get away from here," Bodnya said. "Give me a hand."

They put both bodies in the large pantry. Malinkov and Kovpak dragged the American while Bodnya pulled T'sinko's body. Both corpses were still warm. Malinkov dropped the dead American right between T'sinko's spraddled legs.

"They look like lovers that way, Major," Kovpak snickered.

"I am sure that somewhere, Comrade T'sinko is happy," Bodnya answered. "Finally he is in the arms of another man."

The three men walked quickly out the door, laughing. Someone might find the bodies, but by then they would be far away, and the world would have more on its mind than two dead policemen.

In the trunk, Hollis asked, "What happened back there? Where is T'sinko?"

"He is dead," Kovpak answered. "A dead man killed him."

Hollis frowned in confusion, then backed the Suburban out of the driveway onto Brazos Street. The street was empty. No one had heard the shots. They were on their way. It was not an auspicious start. Someone had alerted the Americans. Bodnya wondered why only two men had come, not two companies of militia. The Americans must not know much, then. If they made it to Killeen, it would be a good sign.

★31★

"Damn it BJ, no one believes us!" Jinx exploded as he slammed the door of the Camaro.

BJ settled back in the driver's seat. "It's a pretty hard story to swallow, Jinx. If I didn't know you, I would have trouble with it, too. Plus, it's Christmas, and no one wants to think about anything else, especially Russians."

"Blind Fuckers!" Jinx raged.

"I know, guy, but there it is."

They drove the rest of the way back to the motel in silence. BJ picked up two cups of coffee from the coffee shop and brought them to the room.

"Maybe I'm nuts," Jinx said bitterly. "Maybe these folks are right and I'm seeing Communists under the bed. Maybe I need to go home and have a nice Christmas and let it go at that. Then I can check into the V.A. hospital and get my head shrunk for a while. Shit."

Was this how insanity worked? he wondered. Everyone else was out of step but you. Everyone was blind but you. You alone had that crystal vision of the future. Maybe so. If I'm not crazy now, Jinx thought, I will be if I keep thinking about this. I need to take Scarlett's advice, and think about this tomorrow.

Bleak, Bodnya thought, It was the only word that fit. The countryside was bleak, this trip was bleak, their chances were bleak.

213

The scenery on either side of the highway was flat and dead. The fields were brown, the trees mere sticks against the gray sky. No birds wheeled and sang. No farmer tilled the soil. There was no movement at all. Nothing lived.

After today, nothing will live, he thought. There was a time when I would be thrilled and eager to get on with this. A hero of the Soviet Union! A dead hero. The others are quiet, too. I wonder if they feel the same way? I cannot ask. I must shake this despair. He looked at Kovpak.

Kovpak was turned in his seat, watching out the back windows of the Suburban, and looking at the woman cowering in the back corner. Her jacket was still pulled down over her arms, which were securely tied behind her at the wrists and elbows. The position thrust her breasts out and gave Kovpak an occasional peek as he watched for any sign of pursuit.

What a shame to waste such a body on this American slut, Kovpak thought. Those bosoms make Anna's chest look like a small boy's. He smiled at the memory of his brief liaison. The smile faded as he wondered when he would get the opportunity again. The smile returned as he looked at the helpless woman. Who knows? Maybe—

"How did you come to be in the Spetsnaz, Ensign?" Malinkov asked.

The sergeant's question broke Kovpak's train of thought.

"I came from the 12th Guards Tank Army, originally, Comrade."

"Why did you leave it, if you don't mind my asking?"

Kovpak wondered why Malinkov had suddenly developed this personal interest. Spetsnaz seldom talked about themselves. He had once heard Bodnya tell another officer that there was no life outside the Spetsnaz. Why was Malinkov so curious now?

"Have you ever been in a tank unit?"

"No, I came from an airborne division."

"Tankers get the worst food, the worst billets, the least time off, and the most dangerous job in the Soviet Army. Plus there are mostly Uzbeks and other little foreign people in tanks. It's hard to have a conversation."

Malinkov laughed. Soviet tanks were so cramped inside, only short soldiers could fit in them. Slavic Russians were usually too tall, and the job of tanker usually fell to the conscripts from the Central Asian republics. A common joke was that if there were no more left-handed midgets, there would be no Soviet armor units. Kovpak's slight stature made him a natural tank commander.

"I just wondered." Malinkov shrugged.

Kovpak nodded. "That is not really true, Comrade. There was something else. It is a fascinating story, if you would like to hear it."

Malinkov grinned. "Yes, I think I would."

"I was a young Junior Lieutenant in the 12th Guards Tank, in Neuruppin. You have been to Neuruppin, haven't you? I thought so, since that is where the Spetsnaz brigade is based. A wonderful town. Especially for women."

"Why did I know this story would be about a woman?" Malinkov snorted.

Kovpak just smiled. "There was a lusty wench who worked in our headquarters named Ulle Meiner. Ulle was a clerk who supplemented her earnings with favors from a rich boyfriend. I did not care that she had another boyfriend. I was not looking for a wife, after all. At any rate, I persuaded her to share her abundant charms with me. For about three months, this was a very good arrangement. Then one week when I was supposed to be in the field on maneuvers, I barged into her flat and caught her performing a very deviant act with the colonel who commanded my very own regiment. He was the rich boyfriend. She was doing something with a summer sausage that I had not ever imagined before. I was shocked, as you might guess. More than that, I was disgusted. I would never have kissed those lips had I known where they had been before! I called her a few names. My colonel called me a few names, and before I knew it, I had orders to report to the Transbaykal Military District, the one farther *east* than the Siberian Military District.

"I went to the Colonel and suggested that if I were to discuss his sexual predilections with his uncle Vanya, the General who commanded the 20th Guards Army, he might take a dim view of them. I suggested that the Diversionary Troops might need my services, and here I am. He got me, though. When I reported, I found I had been reduced in rank to Ensign. I am probably the oldest Ensign in the Army."

"You are right, Ensign," Malinkov said. "That is a fascinating story. I am very sorry I asked."

Kovpak laughed out loud. Perhaps, he thought, I should leave out the part about Ulle and the colonel. Ulle failed to report for work one morning, and was not seen again. Only Kovpak knew where her body was now. He could still see it in his mind, the summer sausage stuffed in her mouth, emerging from the wide cut over her throat. The colonel had been mysteriously run over by a tank during night maneuvers two weeks after Kovpak's departure. The cost of that accident had been high, but it had been well worth it. Debts were debts and had to be paid in full.

"While we are speaking of women, Major," he asked, "what are your plans for the one with us?"

It was a question for which Bodnya had no answer. He had spared her life at the house because she was one of Hollis's people, but Hollis seemed not care about her at all.

"What would you do with her, Ensign?" Bodnya asked.

"Amuse myself first. I would surely like to reconnoiter the valley between those mountains."

"Is that right?" Bodnya chuckled. "She would like that, too, actually. She is quite fond of probes in that area."

Kovpak laughed lewdly, intrigued by this concept, then his eyes showed the sudden dawning of an idea.

"A martyr!" he said with admiration. "Every movement needs a martyr. This woman will be a hero after killing the two FBIs and dying gloriously in the attack on Ft. Hood."

"Exactly so, Ensign." Bodnya answered, happy that Kovpak had supplied him with a plan.

"Brilliant, my major," Kovpak fawned. Too bad there won't be any spare time, he thought, I have never fucked a martyr.

This was a dream, and awful dream, a nightmare. She had never known terror like this. The killings, the awful roar of the guns, the blood. It was too much to comprehend. Who are these men? Alex; who are you? What am I into? Where are we going?

Her arms hurt so bad. Pinned at her side, they were almost numb from the pain. The fear was returning, the fear she had felt in Mexico trapped in the reef, unable to catch her breath.

The tape and her coat pulled down across her chest kept her from breathing now. She had peed on herself a little when the shooting started. Now the wet crotch of her jeans chafed against her thighs. Panic and misery suffocated her. Tears ran down her face, pulling her mascara along with them. Her nose was running from the crying, making it harder to breathe. She wiped her nose on the carpet of the Suburban. Afraid to try to blow out the wet mucus, she sniffled it back down her throat and swallowed it. Its rheumy taste made her queasy.

Now and then, the little weasel one that Alex called Compact would turn and look at her. He winked and blew a kiss. Susan shut her eyes tight to block out the sight. The thought of his hand on her breasts made her skin crawl. Nausea washed over her, hot and insistent.

Oh God, please, no, she thought, fighting the rising gorge. If I puke, I'll drown. Please, please, no.

She slowed her breathing into long, deep breaths. The tape over her mouth made it hard, but not quite impossible. The nausea slowly subsided, but she was left still queasy and soaked with sweat. She shifted her position, tried to sit up a little. Her whole body ached from the cramped position. Her left foot was asleep. Soon the whole leg would be.

They won't let me go; they can't, she thought. They'll kill me. Compact was looking at her again. She turned her head away toward the Suburban's rear doors and wept again. Bodnya's remark came to her, something about a use for her. Maybe she could survive if they needed her for something. Some hope was better than nothing. At least she was still alive; those two FBI agents were dead.

Please, God, she asked as the tears came again, let this be over soon. And let me be alive.

★ 32 ★

Jinx drove his fist into his hand. "BJ, I can't just let this guy get away. I'm going over to that safe house and bag that red fucker."

BJ shook his head. "If that guy is really a Spetsnaz, barging in on him sounds like a great way to get your ass shot off to me, ace."

Jinx whirled on him. "What do mean, *if*? Don't you believe me either?"

"I didn't say that, I just mean that it's very unlikely he will be alone, if he's there."

"I know that. It's a chance I'll have to take. Why don't you give me an hour, then call the FBI switchboard and have them notify White or Harper."

"No way," BJ answered, folding his arm over his chest.

"You aren't going to help me at all?" Jinx said helplessly.

BJ smiled and uncoiled from the chair. "You don't really think I'm going to let you walk in on a bunch of Russian badasses and get your head blown off, do you?"

"I don't think you can stop me."

"I don't either, so I guess I'll just have to throw in with you." BJ walked outside to the car. He returned carrying a long aluminum case.

"This is my close encounter kit," he said, tossing it on the bed. "Come get what you need."

In the fitted foam bottom of the case were two rifles, an AR-15 and a Steyr AUG, magazines for both, a screw-on silencer, and four M67 grenades. The top of the case held nylon pouches for the magazines. Jinx picked up the AR-15 and checked the selector.

"Semis?"

"Yep, sorry."

Jinx just looked at his friend and smiled. He wanted to say thanks, thanks for believing, to say a lot of things, but it was not necessary. They were soldiers, professionals, bound by that strange psychic link, that shared experience that made them brothers, almost twins. Jinx punched BJ's shoulder gently.

"I appreciate it, man."

"Come on, let's go kill a Commie for Christ."

It was just after 1700 hours when the Suburban pulled into the warehouse in Killeen. Outside, the sun was a red ball just above the horizon that bisected the world into dark earth and light sky. A mass of high clouds was moving in, the radio spoke of snow for Christmas. Bodnya prayed that the snow would wait until after midnight. It would be his ally then.

The streets had been thronged with last-minute gift buyers. Bodnya had thrown a tarp over the woman to make sure she was not seen through the windows. She looked worse every time he looked at her. She had whined and cried at first, but after once choking herself with tears, she had calmed down.

Whisper was waiting for them at the door. As the Suburban drove in, he pulled down the overhead door behind them.

"Where is Comrade T'sinko?" Whisper asked as the four men got out of the Suburban.

"I am afraid he is dead," Bodnya answered dryly. "We had a visit from the FBI."

The agent blanched. "FBI? Where? When?" he asked. "Were you followed?" the little man's eyes kept darting toward the doors of the warehouse as if he expected them to be kicked in any second.

"Perhaps you know more about when and where than we do, Comrade," Bodnya said quietly. He stepped toward the agent to divert the man's attention from Malinkov, who was slowly circling around behind Whisper. "Where is your friend, Cowboy?" Bodnya asked.

"I'm right here, Major," the lanky voice answered from

behind the tractor-trailer. Cowboy stepped around from behind the big truck cab, an automatic shotgun cradled in his arms. He had the drop on them, and although they could overwhelm him if they chose, he would undoubtedly kill one or more of them.

Whisper finally grasped what the Russian was implying and started a flurry of denial.

"We don't know anything about it, Major. There hasn't been any leak here," Whisper looked a dagger at Hollis. "Perhaps it was someone at CCLAP, an informer. We thought you might have been detected. The base has tightened its security. They're checking everyone's ID at the gate."

"It would have been the INS who showed up if someone at CCLAP shot off their mouth, Hollis shot back angrily, "not the FBI."

No one spoke for a second, but the tension subsided. Whisper broke the silence. "So what happened to T'sinko?"

"Shot. We got the two FBI, though," Kovpak answered.

Malinkov shot a look at Kovpak, but said nothing.

"Jesus," Whisper said nervously, "you're sure you weren't followed?"

"I'm sure," Hollis replied emphatically. "I checked for a tail all the way here. There was none."

"So, Whisper, how will we gain entrance to the base now?" Bodnya asked.

Cowboy interrupted. "We can cut the lock on one of the gates out here on the west side of the post. They're not guarded at all, and they're closer, anyway."

"So. Are you ready to go, Whisper?"

"Yes, Major," the little man said with relief in his voice. "Ensign Kovpak will drive the Suburban, Cowboy will drive one of the Ryder trucks, Hollis one, and I will drive the third. Sgt. Malinkov will drive the van. We are ready to go whenever you wish."

"I want to make a final reconnaissance of the dropping zone just before it gets dark," Bodnya said. "Is there another vehicle besides the Suburban?"

"We got that van here," Cowboy hooked a finger over his shoulder. "We could take it. You can hide in the back again."

"Excellent," Bodnya said. "Cowboy, you will drive again. Whisper, you and Malinkov stay here."

"Major," Kovpak said quickly, "perhaps I should stay and coordinate the movements with Whisper in your absence?"

Bodnya looked at his number two, who had the guileless look of a cherub on his face. Bodnya knew the real reason he wanted to stay.

"All right, Ensign, but stay alert while you are coordinating."

"It is done, my Major!"

"Do not leave here before we come back," Bodnya admonished Whisper as Cowboy started the van.

"Of course not," Whisper replied, confused. "Why would we?"

Bodnya looked over at Kovpak, who was trying, and failing, to look innocent.

"Just remain here until we return," Bodnya said as he and Malinkov climbed in the van and shut the sliding door.

The man is incorrigible, he thought as as they pulled out through the warehouse door. Poor Susan. Maybe I should have done her a favor and shot her back in Austin.

The house on Brazos was dark. There was not a porch light, no glow from a TV, nothing. The air was chilly and dead calm as the two men crept from shadow to shadow.

"Think they are there?"

"I hope so."

Jinx and BJ had parked around the corner and approached up the alley, using a fence for cover. At the end of the fence, they could see the upper floor, and part of the ground floor. The garage blocked their view of the back door. Jinx lay down flat, and slithered forward, using the garage for concealment. When he reached the wall of the garage, he signaled BJ to follow.

"What do you think?" Jinx whispered.

"I think I'd like to drop onto that roof and work my way down from above," BJ answered, pointing to the side of the house nearest the garage.

Next to the big house, an old cottonwood tree stood, its branches reaching out over the roof. It would be possible to reach one of the second-floor windows, using a branch for support on the steep roof. There were no windows on the first floor on that side. The climber could only be seen from the second floor, where he would enter.

"OK, you go in from above, and I'll roll in the back door."

"Roger. On three?"

Jinx nodded.

"Wait one." Jinx slipped a thirty-round magazine out of his jacket pocket, snapped it into the AR-15, and pulled the charging handle. BJ did the same with the AUG.

"Ready? Go!"

BJ whipped around the corner of the garage, running low, making for the trunk of the huge old tree. There was no reaction in the house, no noise, no lights.

BJ slung the AUG behind him and began to scale the old tree. He climbed without effort, and was above one of the upstairs windows in less than a minute. When he was steady, he nodded to Jinx.

Jinx went around the back of the garage and slowly slid along to the corner. He risked a quick glimpse to get his bearings and then sprinted across the yard to the back door.

BJ gave him three seconds after he disappeared from sight, then counted loudly, "One, two, three!"

On three, BJ grasped the limb on which he was crouched, and swung out and down, like a gymnast on the uneven bars. He swung back in with both feet cocked, then kicked out in front of him, crashing through the old window sash into the dark room. He rolled to his right, using his momentum to carry him, and came up in a crouch next to a bed, the AUG in front of him. There was no movement, no sound in the room, except the crunch of broken glass under his feet.

Jinx was next to the back door when he heard "three." He pressed himself to the wall and thrust the rifle up toward the hinges on the far side of the door. He fired three rounds at each hinge, then spun around, smashing into the hinge side of the door with his shoulder. The damaged hinges gave in and the door, with Jinx on it, fell into the kitchen. Jinx rolled into the shadows at the base of the kitchen counter. There was only silence, the sound of his breathing loud in the darkness.

It only took moments for both of them to realize they were alone in the house.

BJ shouted from upstairs, "Jinx, don't shoot, I'm coming down."

"Come on, there's no one down here."

Jinx felt for the light switch and turned on the kitchen lights. BJ joined him in the empty kitchen.

"Anything upstairs?"

"No one and nothin'. The rooms looked like someone had slept there, but they're gone, and there was nothing left behind."

"Oh well, shit," Jinx said, plopping down in a chair at the small dinette. "They're gone."

BJ leaned back against the counter, then reached up and began looking through the cupboards that covered the wall above the sink.

"What are you looking for?"

"A glass. Forced entry always makes me thirsty."

BJ found a glass, and filled it from the faucet. He turned back to Jinx, who was sitting at the table, rubbing his forehead.

"You know what I think—" BJ began, then stopped midsentence. From this position, the overhead fixture cast a shiny glare across the pale linoleum. Two thin tracks ran through the glare into the closet across the room.

"What?" Jinx answered. When his friend didn't respond, Jinx looked up to see BJ staring at the closet door. Reflexively, Jinx rolled out of his chair and brought his weapon up, firing four round through the closet door before BJ yelled.

"Wait! Hold it."

BJ crossed to the door, stood to one side, and pulled it open. Inside, T'sinko and White were still locked in their embrace.

"Holy fuck!" BJ exclaimed.

Jinx got to his feet, never taking his eyes off the pair intertwined in the closet. "Who are they?"

"The one on the top is that FBI guy, White." BJ rolled the dead FBI agent to one side, got T'sinko by the feet and dragged him backward out of the pantry. "I don't know this one. Is this your Russian?"

Jinx looked down at T'sinko's staring face. "No. That's definitely not him. Let's look around a little better."

BJ found the other FBI man under the sink. "Here's what's-his-face, Harper. He's real dead, too."

"BJ, I think it's time to go to Ft. Hood."

"We ought to call the FBI."

"No, I don't want to spend all night answering questions. We'll call them from Hood. We need to call Peterson right now."

No one answered at the MI. When he called Peterson's number at the BOQ, BJ got her answering machine.

"Pat, this is BJ. We have two dead FBIs and a dead Russian here in Austin. There's gooks in the wire, baby. Jinx and I are on our way up there. See you in an hour."

★ 33 ★

She had, incredibly, almost dozed off before Alex threw that dirty tarp on her. The cramped position, the spent rush of fear and the droning of tires had lulled her. Now they were stopped. Where? She tried to sit up, but failed again. Both legs were asleep now, almost paralyzing her. Her arms ached, but even that pain was dulled now. Her fingers found a bit of tarp to grab, and she managed to pull it off her head, an inch at a time.

She could hear them talking outside the truck, anger in their voices. New voices were talking, too. She could not make out the words, but one of the new voices had a distinct Texas twang. She turned her head to hear better, and to try to see out of the truck. All she could make out from her position on the floor was a long fluorescent light fixture and a bit of ceiling. The door she had heard had been an overhead metal door like the one in the little U-Stor-It warehouses.

She rolled over on her back and pushed against the rear door with her unfeeling legs. She managed to push herself up a little against the seat back. The change in position brought back the circulation to her legs, and the pain of their reawakening brought tears to her eyes again. She could almost feel her feet again when she heard the door roll up again, and another exchange of voices. Then the door came down. For several minutes, no one spoke. Then she heard the one called Compact speaking. One of the new voices answered him and she heard footsteps echo in the warehouse.

She was still straining to hear when the smiling weasel face appeared in the rear window.

When the major left on his reconnaissance of the base, Kovpak knew he had the spare time he had wished for. He asked Whisper about the radio gear for the airplane signal and suggested that Whisper check it again. Whisper saw no need to recheck a radio he had checked only that morning, but at Kovpak's insistence, he walked over to the first Ryder truck, where the radio sat on the floor.

Happy to be off the hook about the FBI, Whisper did not feel like arguing. In fact, he was eager to get away from Kovpak. Malinkov was scary enough, but Whisper knew that the hulking sergeant only killed on Bodnya's orders. This one looked like he killed for pleasure.

"Hello, my pretty," Kovpak said as he opened one of the two rear doors.

The woman writhed against the bench seat of the Suburban, her eyes wide with fear and disgust.

"What? Not happy to see me?" he said, running his hands up her bound legs. "We have some unfinished business."

She tried to kick him, but he caught her ankles and deflected her feet to one side. He held her feet with his left hand as he slid his right hand up under her. Her writhing seemed to excite him and he grabbed her right buttock, squeezing. Abruptly, Susan stopped moving and forced her rear down on the truck floor, trying to dislodge his hand.

"You do have spirit!" his voice was oily with something worse than lust and the sound of it gave Susan chills. "Let us see what else you have."

He grabbed her ankles with both hands and pulled her halfway out the door of the truck. She clutched at the door frame to keep from falling out on her head.

Kovpak ran his hands between her legs, rubbing her crotch with his index finger. When he felt the moisture there, he smiled. "Wet already, eh? I am flattered."

Susan screamed, but the tape made it a high pitched whine. Kovpak jerked his hand out from between her legs.

"Shut up," he hissed, his face inches from hers. "We do not want to disturb Comrade Whisper, do we?"

He ran his hand down her front, kneading her breasts through the flannel shirt, then hooking his finger under the top button and ripping it out. He shoved his hand into her bra, roughly pawing her white flesh. She tried once more to scream. Irritated, he took her right nipple between his thumb and forefinger and pinched hard, twisting the soft tissue.

The pain was so sharp it took her breath away. The pain and the fear almost made her pass out.

"I told you to shut up," he said, "and I meant it. Are you going to be quiet, now?"

When she didn't answer, he applied more torque to her tortured nipple. This time her head nodded violently.

"That is better."

Discipline applied, Kovpac went back to exploring Susan's breasts, trying to pull the tight bra up off them. The tension on the bra straps, and the built-in underwire kept the bra in place, but hurt her in the process. She almost cried out, but remembered the lesson just administered.

Finally, he tired of playing with her chest and ran his hand down to the damp crotch of her Levis. He jerked the top button undone and pulled her zipper down slowly, smiling at her. With the pants undone, he reached under her, grabbed her belt loop and spun her over on her stomach. She dug her chin into the rough carpet to keep from falling as she tried to get a footing on the concrete.

Kovpak's hands were on her hips now, as he stood behind her. He grabbed a handful of denim on each side and pulled down as hard as he could, rolling the tight jeans off her hips down as far as the bonds around her knees would permit.

She twisted and bucked, but could not move away. When she felt the cold metal of the knife against the bare skin of her rear, she froze.

Kovpak slipped the blade of his recently acquired folding knife up under the thin lace of her panties. The sheer fabric parted instantly. One more cut, through the cotton panel, and she felt them pulled roughly from between her legs.

He leaned down on her back, his face over her shoulder, his breath hot on her face. She twisted her head to escape it. The cold metal of the knife was on the other side.

"Now my pretty, let us get acquainted."

He held the rope that bound her wrists, pulling it tight.

She felt his flesh against her leg and tried to pull away. His rigid cock explored her crack for a moment, the plunged deep into her. She screamed into the tape, and thrashed as hard as she could, not knowing that her struggling pleased Kovpak as much as the penetration.

He pounded into her, slamming her pelvis into the edge of the truck door. After a moment, he released her hand and took her by the shoulders, pulling her back to meet each thrust. The truck's carpet burned her face as she jerked back and forth.

It was over in a moment that lasted forever. She heard his breath catch in his throat, and felt his body stiffen and spasm.

"Ochen horosho," he murmured, *"ochen horosho."*

He stood behind her for a moment, catching his breath and rubbing his hand over her bare butt. Then he grabbed the rolled down jeans and pulled them back up over her hips. He ran his hands around under her and pulled the zipper up, leaving the button undone. Grabbing a handful of fabric on each side, Kovpak jerked Susan off her feet and threw her into the Suburban. She landed on her side, hitting her head on the bench seat again, the pain a distant distraction.

Kovpak leaned in and buttoned her jeans. "Thank you. That was enjoyable," he said, casually. "You are indeed a very useful fool."

Instinctively, she curled into a fetal position against the wall of the truck. She had kept her eyes shut tight during the assault. Now they were open and staring, unfocused. Kovpak shut the door of the Suburban, zipped his pants, and walked to the rental truck where Whisper stood staring at him. Whisper had not known there was anyone else in the truck. Watching Kovpak rape whoever that was had unnerved Whisper. He had never actually seen an act of violence before.

So, Whisper, how is the radio?" Kovpak asked as he strolled over to the Ryder truck.

"It—uh—it—" he stammered, "the—ah—equipment is in perfect condition."

"That it is, my friend," Kovpak laughed. "That it is!"

Whistling to himself, Kovpak opened the hood of each rental truck and calmly checked the oil, water, battery, and gasoline of each vehicle. He made no reference to the person in the Suburban. Whisper thought it prudent not to inquire.

★34★

They have finally settled down again, Captain Karmasov thought as he scanned the row of faces opposite. There is always the rush of excitement on takeoff, but it fades into boredom soon enough.

They had taken off from Punte Huerte, Nicaragua at 0100 hours for the two-hour flight to San Julian Airport in Pinar del Rio Province, Cuba. The An-12 had been rolled into a hangar there.

To pass the time, the men had slept, cleaned their weapons, and practiced their English, never leaving the building. Late in the afternoon, they reboarded the plane for the flight to America. At dusk, the An-12 was rolled out again for takeoff.

All air traffic in the area had been forbidden while they took off. There were no prying eyes to report the flight of an "American C-130" from a Cuban airfield. Heavy external fuel tanks extended the An-12's takeoff roll. Colonel Scheverard used the entire length of the runway to get the heavily laden turboprop into the air.

Their flight took them straight toward Monterrey along the regular commercial route. As they neared the coast, the An-12 gradually lost altitude until it disappeared into the ground clutter. Colonel Scheverard swung the big turboprop northwest along the Mexican coast for fifteen minutes, decreasing his altitude to sixty meters above the green water of the Gulf of Mexico. He then turned on a course of twenty degrees north-northeast, headed toward Houston. Over the Gulf, almost due south of Houston, they would correct course northwest to cross the coast and avoid the major airport radar service areas. Since English was the international language of aviation, they had an English speaker on board in the radio operator's seat. Andre Dorroffeyev was normally a pilot for Aeroflot. His English had so little accent that he was usually mistaken for a Canadian on the radio. He would handle any radio challenges that could not be ignored.

During their descent to sixty meters, the excitement again peaked, then faded. Some of the men had even fallen asleep, the true sign of veterans. The others were quietly singing or simply staring. The flight was half over; another two hours and they would be at their destination.

Across the aisle, Lieutenant Plaski fidgeted and looked very frightened. Karmasov smiled and reached across the aisle, poking Senior Private Toshkin's knee.

"Toshkin, did you hear that the Polish Communist Party has started using incentives to help recruit for the Party?" Karmasov said, cutting his eyes toward Plaski.

Toshkin knew what Karmasov thought of KGB Special Section Officers. He also knew that jokes about the Communist party in Poland were not treason. You could joke about the Warsaw Pact states, but not about the *Rodina* or the Communist party of the Soviet Union.

"No, what sort of incentives?" he answered quilelessly.

"If you recruit one new member for the Party, you do not have to pay your Party dues."

Toshkin nodded, "Yes?"

"Yes, and if you recruit two new members for the Party, you do not have to attend any Party meetings."

"Umm—"

"And," Karmasov wound up, glancing at Plaski, "if you recruit three new members for the Party, you get a letter stating that you were never even a member of the Polish Communist Party!"

Karmasov slapped Toshkin's knee and laughed loudly. Toshkin laughed, too. Only Lieutenant Plaski was not amused. He stared at the sergeant, then leaned forward.

"Captain, I am an officer of the Committee for State Security, the sword and shield of the Party, and I find no humor in jokes about any Communist party.''

''Oh, yes, Comrade,'' Karmasov purred. ''Please forgive me. I meant no offense against the State.'' He rolled his eyes toward Toshkin. ''I was just trying to break some of the tension with a little humor. Perhaps you have heard this one—''

''I do not wish to hear any more jokes, Comrade Captain!''

Toshkin arched an eyebrow toward Karmasov. This was pushing a little too far, but so what? They were already on a suicide mission.

Karmasov sat back, smiling. What an ass, he thought as he watched the young *Chekist* return to his fidgeting; what an incredible ass.

Flying at two thousand feet over the Gulf due south of Freeport, Dan Abernathy picked up the radar blip at maximum range.

''Bogie at two o'clock, right down on the deck.''

''How far, Dan?'' asked Bob Matthews, pilot of the Customs Service Beechcraft U-21.

''Twenty miles and closing fast. Let's check it out.''

''Roger dodger.''

Matthews kicked the right rudder, bringing the plane around to intercept the new target.

''So what have you got planned for the big day tomorrow?''

''No sleep, for sure. My kids will probably be up before I get home, ripping into the goodies. Then it's off to see the grandparents.''

''Ah, the blessings of bachelorhood,'' Bob laughed. ''I only need to be at Sweet Thing's house for Christmas dinner. After that, I'll get my present. And after that, we'll open the packages.''

''Spare me.''

Abernathy and Matthews had been on station since sunset. They flew every other night, looking for drug runners and other illegal border crossers. Their Beechcraft King Air was unarmed, but its electronics were state of the art, especially their look-down radar. This was the second contact of the evening. The first had been a private pilot asleep at the stick

of a Cessna 410 who had wandered out over the Gulf. When
Abernathy had shined the spotlight in his face to wake him
up, the old boy had nearly gone into a spin, thinking an
airliner was running over him. He had been very embar-
rassed, but happy to be sent on his way alive.

This blip was moving too fast to be a lost soul. Matthews
took up a heading for the target. Minutes later, a huge, dark
shape flashed underneath them.

"Geez, Bob, what was that?"

"Looks like a C-130. C'mon, let's get up close and personal."

Matthews put his throttles all the way up, and put the plane
into a shallow dive to pick up airspeed. Soon they came up
behind the huge transport. Matthews took up a position on
the aircraft's six o'clock position just above the whale-like
tail.

Lieutenant Colonel Scheverard scanned the instrument
panel for the thousandth time. It was habit, now, the constant
watch for any change, any abnormality. There was hardly any
need. The An-12 was the workhorse of the Soviet Air Force,
reliable and predictable. This one had been groomed for this
flight, checked and rechecked. It would not fail them. It was
flying now by computer, hugging the water and using satellite
navigation to plot its course, maintaining 322 degrees. The
pilots were only monitoring its progress. They would resume
control when they crossed the coast, and fly manually on the
way out, when reaction time would be more important.

Sheverard's thoughts turned to his father, Colonel Valeri
Scheverard, fighter ace and hero of the Soviet Union. The old
man had been disappointed when Ivan had been posted to
transports instead of combat aircraft.

He would be happy to see me on this flight, Ivan thought,
the first combat sortie against the Americans. To bad he didn't
live long enough to—

"Colonel, there is an aircraft right on top of us!" Sr. Sgt.
Paili Gregorian's shout cut short Scheverard's musing.

"Identify!"

"It is a small twin-engine propeller model. I cannot determine its weapons. It is moving to attack position behind."

* * *

"It is a 130, all right," Abernathy said, peering through his passive night vision goggles. "I wonder what it's doing out here?"

"From the looks of that green-and-black paint job, I'd say it was a Special Operations bird. They're probably on an exercise, out of Elgin."

"On Christmas eve?"

"Looks like it," Matthews shrugged.

"What are those things on the tail?"

"I dunno, antennas, maybe. They do some weird modifications to those birds."

"Think they'll answer if we call 'em?"

"Try it."

In the An-12, Paili Gregorian watched the plane through his gun sight and waited. The tiny plane had suddenly come up on his screen, too quickly for jamming. Now it was one hundred meters behind and above the transport in an attack position.

In the cockpit, Colonel Scheverard pondered his options. He could outrun the tiny interceptor, but not its radio. The coast of America was in sight.

Scheverard remembered his father's war stories about fighting Germans in the skies over Russia. His advice to young pilots was always the same. Fight, don't run!

"Scan for the American's frequency and jam it if they transmit," Scheverard said, looking over his shoulder at Dorroffeyev. "Captain, do not answer."

"Yes, Comrade Colonel."

"Sergeant Gregorian, if the Americans transmit, open fire. Do you understand?"

"I understand, Comrade Colonel."

Gregorian flipped the switch that armed the twin 23mm cannons in the aircraft's tail. On his optical gun sight screen, the targeting crosshairs appeared, white on the gray-green image.

"C-130, C-130 at Angels 200, this is U.S. Customs Service, do you copy? Please Identify. Over."

Gregorian moved the short grip that controlled the twin guns, placing the nose of the small aircraft on the first concentric ring of the sight. He pressed the red trigger and held it down. The 23mm guns spewed fire, empty shell cases tumbling from the ejection chute. At their cyclic rate of one thousand rounds per minute, the guns spit sixty-six rounds of high-explosive incendiary shells at the U-21 in just over two seconds.

Bob Matthews didn't even have time to react when the twin muzzles swiveled up and fired. The second round that hit the plane went through the nose and the windshield, detonating. The windshield shattered into a thousand shards that shredded the faces of the two pilots. Another round hit Matthew's head, exploding like a grenade. The back of his head came off, spraying the bulkhead with blood and brains. The impact knocked his body to the left, and his hands on the yoke moved with it, throwing the plane up on its side.

Two shells penetrated up through the instrument panel, one destroying the electronics, including the radio, and peppering both men with more bits of steel, aluminum, and plastic. Another round went off next to Abernathy's right leg, severing it below the knee. Both men died in an instant, chewed to pieces in their seats.

The Beech rolled over to the left onto its back, helpless. The crippled plane hit the water four seconds later, almost vertical. It disappeared in a tower of spray and a spreading pool of bubbles, two miles off the Texas coast.

In the cockpit of the An-12, it was strangely quiet. There was no cheering or congratulations. Everyone in the cockpit knew what had happened. They had drawn the first blood of the next war. There was no return now, as if there ever had been.

The lights of Brazoria flashed by the starboard windows. They would fly this course until they were over the town of Sealy, then turn slightly more north, heading for their Initial Point east of Ft. Hood. The IP, ironically, was over the town of Reagan. There they would turn due west for the run across Antelope Drop Zone.

In the cargo bay, the Spetsnaz heard and felt the 23mms go off. Plaski, instantly on his feet, scrambled to the cockpit.

"What has happened?" he cried, wild-eyed. "Are we under attack?"

"No, Lieutenant," Scheverard said calmly, "we were detected by one of their aircraft, a small twin engine, but we destroyed it. Tell your *reydoviki* that we have just crossed the frontier of the United States, and claim the first kill of this operation."

Plaski turned back to the anxious soldiers. He fought his own fear to put up a good front for the troops. He stepped up on the bench seat and shouted so all could hear him above the engines.

"Comrades, our valiant air crew has destroyed an American border police aircraft. We owe them our lives. We have just crossed the coast of the United States."

Plaski wondered if the other soldiers could see him trembling as he stood on the aircraft seat. He paused and scanned every face.

"Prepare yourselves to accomplish our mission. Remember, the *Rodina* expects each man to do his utmost, and to sacrifice his life if necessary, even as did those patriots who fought and died at Stalingrad to save Mother Russia from the Fascist invaders."

Oh, God, Karmasov thought as the KGB officer swung into his speech. Rising from the canvas seat, Karmasov made his way back toward the tail of the aircraft where the young gunner sat at his still cooling cannons. The young man's face was pale and his hands fidgeted over the gun controls.

"Good shooting, son," Karmasov said, taking a small metal hip flask from his leg pocket and offering Gregorian a drink of peppery vodka. Gregorian looked up at the captain. Ordinarily, he would have refused a drink from a soldier's bottle, but tonight he needed the vodka to calm him. As Gregorian tipped the flask up, Karmasov leaned closer.

"Congratulations," he said brightly. "You can tell your children that you fired the shots that started the Second Great Patriotic War!"

Karmasov would always remember the look of fear, pride, panic, and pleasure that crossed the young gunner's face.

As Lieutenant Plaski droned on, Mikhail Karmasov sat back down in his seat.

These bloody *Chekists*, he thought, all they can do is talk. They either bore you death with speeches, or cut your throat from behind. Karmasov hated the *Chekisty* and all other kinds

informers. His father had been one of them, a Party flunky
in their small town near Kiev. Young Mikhail was always
shocked by the glee his father took in ruining the lives of
others. No proof was ever necessary, just the accusation. It
sickened him. His older brother had followed in their father's
footsteps, becoming a militiaman. Mikhail had been happy
to start his DOSAAF training. He did well and was recom-
mended for an officer training course on conscription into the
Army. He was happy to leave for the Army. It got him out of
Vasil'kov and away from his family.

Life in the Soviet Union would be so much better, he
thought, but for the parasites, the political officers, the informers, and most of all, the *Chekists*.

He made the decision right then. This little bugger was not
going to make the trip. As he put together his plan, Captain
Karmasov fingered the Spetsnaz knife strapped to his jump
boot.

When Plaski looked over at him, Karmasov smiled and
winked. Plaski, mistaking the gesture for praise, prattled on
with vigor.

Soon, my little *Chekist*, he thought, soon you will get the
ride of your life. The idea warmed him.

The *Sergei Lermontov* had sailed on to Houston after dropping off Bodnya and his men. It entered the Houston Ship
Channel on the morning of the twenty-fourth. By 16:30 hours,
it was tied up at the main container unloading facility at Bar-
bours Cut. The huge overhead crane had removed most of
the twenty-foot shipping containers from the *Lermontov*'s deck
and central cargo hold. Two of the East German Gt containers
contained RDX explosive, the same explosive used to destroy
the Marine barracks in Beirut in 1983. In each of the two
containers was eleven thousand pounds of RDX. The containers were set to detonate on Christmas day. They would
damage the container facility, delaying even further the resupply of Europe. There was one more explosive container
on the *Lermontov*'s forward deck.

The huge time-bomb containers were not the *Lermontov*'s
only surprises. As it passed Corpus Christi after dropping off
Bodnya's party, it had dropped twenty-four acoustic mines.
Tuned to the specific frequencies generated by warships pass-

ing overhead, the mines were presents for the Surface Action
Group led by the battleship *Wisconsin*, home ported in Corpus Christi.

Victor Konstantin checked his watch, a prized Rolex. It
was 8:30 now. In two hours he would ease the *Lermontov* out
of its berth at the container facility and steer for the center
of the channel. When the *Lermontov* reached the Lynchburg
Crossing, it would stop, turn across the channel and open its
seacocks. Konstantin estimated it would take twenty-five
minutes to sink. When it finally rested on the bottom, it would
block the entire channel. The explosive container would be
activated by sea water. If anyone tried to raise the *Lermontov*,
a motion sensor would detonate the RDX. The explosive ex-
perts who had briefed Konstantin assured him that such an
explosion would capsize any ship in the area. The port of
Houston would be virtually useless for some time.

Konstantin's crew would escape in the cigarette boat that
was, by now, out of its slip at Watergate Yacht Center and
slowly making its way up the channel to rendezvous with the
Lermontov. The speedboat would take them into the Gulf.
With luck, a Cuban M-12 flying boat would pick them up the
next morning, two hundred miles offshore.

★ 35 ★

The night was cold, but very still. The wind had died after sunset, and now the air was still. Only the clouds threatened the operation, and they were still high, well above jump altitude.

Let it snow, then, Bodnya thought, looking up through the windshield of the van. Snow will drive their sentries under cover to stay warm. Snow will blur their vision and their radar. His hunters were used to the snow.

"What do you think, Ensign?" Bodnya said, turning around. "Will it snow for us tonight?"

"Perhaps, Major. Those clouds look right for it. Better snow than rain."

"Indeed."

Rain was the one thing Bodnya did not want. Rain would make the jump very dangerous. With the rain would be wind. It would help put out any fires his men started.

They had gained access to the base exactly as Cowboy had suggested. The huge base had many roads leading into it, some little more than trails. They had simply cut the chain, opened the gate, and driven through, closing the gate behind them.

As they turned right off Elijah Road onto Old Georgetown Road, Bodnya felt strangely content, his earlier pessimism vanished. This mission was the most daring, most dangerous, of his career, and yet, he felt an odd calm, almost joy. There was danger, yes, but not for him, not for his men. The Americans were the ones in danger. The wolves were among the sheep.

"Here we are," Whisper said, as he turned the Suburban off the road halfway across the drop zone. The headlights dimly lit a packed dirt runway just off the road. A line of scrub oaks screened them from the road. Hollis turned the Suburban around to face the road and turned off the lights. The four men got out, waiting in the darkness. The Ryder trucks appeared at five-minute intervals. At 11:10, the entire Dropping Zone party was assembled.

The cold night air felt good, invigorating Bodnya.

"Kovpak, take Hollis and Whisper," Bodnya said softly. "Set the strobe lights up, and leave Whisper there."

"Yes, Major!" Kovpak answered. He, too, was flushed by the excitement of the moment. Soon, very soon, they would engage the real enemy. This time it would be no unwashed tribesmen or backwater army. Tonight they would show the Americans what Soviet soldiers were made of.

"Come, Whisper," he called quietly as he shouldered the bag of strobes. The two men went fifty meters down the length of the DZ and pulled out the first infrared strobe. Made by Tekna, the strobe was the size of a large penlight. Two alkaline batteries would power it for hours. There were extra strobes in the bag to replace any that quit. Each strobe was attached to a short stake.

Fifty meters from the trucks, Kovpak pushed the first stake into the hard, rocky dirt so the strobe head was pointing straight up.

"Stand right here, Whisper."

Kovpak began pacing away, down the zone. Every twenty-five meters, he placed another strobe. Each time he set up one of the tiny lights, he tested it with infrared goggles. The goggles were of Israeli manufacture, purchased in October by Cowboy at a large gun show in Houston. When Kovpak had placed five of the small units in a straight line, he returned to Whisper. Making sure he was at a right angle to the line of strobes, he paced again and set three more strobes, forming an inverted L.

"Stay here, Whisper, and watch the trucks. When you see me flash this red light, turn on each strobe, then come back to the trucks. Understand?"

The young agent nodded. In a camouflage field jacket, he looked even smaller, and scared. As Kovpak turned to rejoin the others, he felt a cold touch on his face. Sleet? It did not matter.

"The dropping zone is marked, Major. Each unit was tested. Whisper is standing by for my signal."

While Kovpak and Whisper had been setting up the lights, Hollis had the transponder in the van set up. At 22:30, he would turn on the signal for the aircraft to home in on. When the plane locked in on the signal, the tone would change from short pulses to a continuous tone. An indicator light on the transponder would indicate a lock. The strobes would then be turned on to guide the pilot and jumpmaster.

The warning buzzer from the pilot cut short Plaski's speech. The soldiers immediately went about donning combat gear over their jump coveralls, and strapping on the heavy parachutes. Karmasov and Senior Private Toshkin went back to the tail ramp to check the four PDSB-1 weapons containers, in which were their extra incendiaries, RPG-16s RPG-22s, and the RPO-A flamethrower. They took the static lines from the containers and hooked them to the two thick cables overhead. The four containers would go first, then the troops would follow out the doors.

With the door bundles secure, Karmasov made his way back to his place at the front of the plane. His knife was now in his pocket, easily within reach.

The An-12 was going flat out now, as fast as its four engines would push it. The shorter the flight time to the target, the less opportunity for the Americans to intercept it.

Major Ershov touched his earphone. "Comrade Colonel, we have the tone."

"Send the confirmation and sound the warning."

It was difficult to believe that they could penetrate as easily as they had, Scheverard thought. The ring of Soviet air defenses would never have permitted a plane so deep into the Soviet Union. Well, except for that German boy in the Cessna. Heads had rolled at the PVO-Strany over that incident. Scheverard's friends in the Army joked that the Americans had deployed their child-mobile cruise missile. If the little plane had carried a nuclear weapon with a fanatic at the controls, well—

The red light on the radio startled Bodnya. The plane was locked on the signal! In minutes, he would welcome his *reydoviki* to America and together, they would change the course of history!

"Ensign, we have confirmation from the aircraft. Turn on the strobes and prepare the trucks. Malinkov, raise the truck doors and prepare to assemble groups."

As Malinkov mounted the first truck, Kovpak turned his flashlight toward Whisper and switched it on. The red light was not bright enough to see by, but easily seen by the little agent. Donning his infrared goggles again, Kovpak watched as one strobe after another blazed forth its invisible greetings and guidance to the night sky.

"The dropping zone is marked, Major!"

"Very well, Ensign, let us prepare to welcome our comrades." The excitement in Bodnya's voice spurred Kovpak as well. Even in the darkness, smiles lit their faces.

★36★

Jinx and BJ turned off Highway 190 at the Denny's, and drove north through a gauntlet of fast-food restaurants, pawn shops, video stores, and beer joints that cluster around the perimeter of every U.S. military base. Christmas was in the air.

BJ turned left through the East Gate. Oddly, an MP stopped the car and asked for IDs. BJ's Reserve ID and Jinx's Agency card got them through.

"That's odd," BJ said as he rolled up the car window, "they've never checked my ID before."

"I think it's a good sign," Jinx replied. "Maybe Peterson took us seriously after all."

They turned at the first right into Officer's Country. The row of two-story BOQs was on the right, just across from the sprawling Officer's Club. BJ parked in front of the third building, and led the way to Peterson's room.

They knocked on the door, then stood in the carpeted hallway, feeling like a couple of Jehovah's Witnesses coming for a convert. After a moment, BJ knocked again and shouted, "Hey, Pat!" through the door. Nothing.

The door to their right opened and a young officer, clad in a beige robe, with rollers in her auburn hair, stepped out.

"Can I help you?" she asked, eyeing the pair of civilians with some suspicion. "I'm Jane Taylor, Captain Peterson is my suite-mate."

"We need to see Captain Peterson, ASAP," Jinx answered. "Know where she is?"

"She's probably over at the O-Club party," Taylor said, jerking her head in the direction of the club.

"OK, thanks," Jinx said hurriedly, as he and BJ started back down the hallway.

"Can I tell her who was looking for her?" Taylor called after them.

"Tell her Cassandra came by," BJ grinned back.

"Unidentified aircraft, this is Grey Army Airfield Control," Spec. 4 Tommy Knot said, in the control tower on West Ft. Hood. "Please identify yourself and climb to one thousand feet. Over."

In the An-12, the transmission was clearly heard, but totally ignored.

Knot turned to Lieutenant Cranston. "Nothing, sir. Either they're not receiving or they can't talk."

Cranston watched the blip on the screen move closer. It was just northeast of Ft. Hood Army Airfield, heading due west.

"Try them again."

Knot repeated the message and got the same response as before—none.

"Tommy, watch this guy," Cranston said, irritation rising in his voice. "I'm going to call Range Control and see what the hell this is all about. I'm sick of us being the last ones to find out about everything."

Cranston stepped to the telephone and dialed Range Control, the office that coordinated all activity on Ft. Hood's gunnery ranges and the airstrips located in the training areas.

"Range Control, Sergeant Masterson, sir."

"Masterson, this is Lieutenant Cranston at Grey Control. What the hell do you guys have going on tonight?"

"Sir?"

"I have a plane on my scope crossing Ft. Hood east to west just north of your office. It won't respond and I don't have any NOTAMs for tonight. I want to know why we weren't notified."

"Lieutenant, I have no idea," Masterson answered quickly. "Let me check."

Masterson didn't have to check; there was no training activity on the ranges tonight. Didn't that moron lieutenant know it was Christmas Eve?

"Sir, I don't have anything on my schedule for tonight. Maybe it's that outfit from Abilene, again. I suggest we call the FAA tomorrow morning and raise hell with them."

There was a long pause on the other end. Cranston finally spoke. "OK, but I want you to make a note that we called and the time. I'm not going to let this ride, not on alert status. Do you understand me?"

"Yes, sir," Masterson answered apologetically. "I understand perfectly."

Cranston hung up the phone and went back to the screen. The plane was all the way across the base now, still flying east to west. Tomorrow he would get to the bottom of this SNAFU. He would personally call every C-130 wing in the state, and the one up in Little Rock, too. Heads would roll.

The jump warning sounded and all the troops began inspection of their equipment. Each man checked the one next to him. The tension in the plane increased geometrically as they neared their destination. This raid would make history, and they would be heroes, dead or alive.

Lieutenant Vorshaw, the jumpmaster, peered out the left door into the darkness. The base and Killeen itself were clearly visible, their Christmas decorations a fairyland of twinkling lights—so many lights!

Soon, he thought, there would be brighter lights, the light of burning tanks. The wind screamed louder as the tailgate went down.

He looked forward, toward the dropping zone. The icy blast pulled his cheeks back into a taut grimace, and tears streamed from his left eye. He leaned back in, wiped his eye and pulled his infrared goggles down, then leaned back out, pulled back in, and spoke into his microphone.

"Move to the door!" he screamed over the roar of the engines, his arms and hands pointing to the two gaping, dark holes in the aircraft's sides.

The two lines of paratroops moved like huge, disjointed centipedes, the lead men standing in each door, their hands on the outside skin of the plane. Tension, excitement, and fear hung in the air like incense, each man intoxicated by it.

The yellow light flashed green and the jumpmaster screamed, ''JUMP!''

The first two men tensed and threw themselves out into the cold blast. The two lines surged toward the door, each man chanting, ''JUMP, JUMP, JUMP!'' Their faces were masks, their eyes dilated and locked on the doors of the plane. There was little chance to stop them now. To interrupt this rush for the door, for the darkness and the sky, would require the jumpmasters to physically block them from the exits by violent force. Once the green light came on, they were mentally already out the door. Air Force sergeants shoved the two destruction-filled door bundles off the tailgate.

As his line surged forward, Karmasov slipped the knife out of its round metal sheath and held it against his leg. The young *Chekist's* eyes were locked on the door. He was shouting, ''JUMP, JUMP!'' As he passed the wheel well, Karmasov slipped the knife up through the loop in Plaski's static line. He pushed against the lieutenant, shouted ''JUMP,'' and pulled back. The razor-sharp blade cut easily through the cotton web strap. A second slash and the thin cable for the automatic opener was severed. The cuts were on the side away from the jumpmaster; he would notice nothing. Even if he did, it would be too late.

Quickly, Karmasov returned his knife to its sheath. In the dim red light, no one had seen him at work. All eyes had been on the doors and the lines of men moving, disappearing into the roaring darkness.

As they neared the jump door, Karmasov against pushed the *Chekist*, then intentionally stumbled. Plaski ran the last two steps and threw himself out the door, his loud cries of *''Adin, dvaw—''* trailing off in the distance. His static line drew taut, pulling free from the two elastic keepers. Plaski, his eyes closed tightly, as usual, was arched forward tightly, arms folded across his chest. There was one meter of static line left when the cut loop pulled free.

As Karmasov reached the door, the cut end of Plaski's static line whipped back through the door, just missing his head. He smiled as he threw himself into the blast. The little *Chekist* was halfway to the ground by now.

The ballistic parachutes did not require or permit the normal jump routine. When the static line activated the firing device, the parachute, in a rigid aluminum container, shot up from the backpack, deploying in less than a second. The rapid opening made it possible to jump from altitudes that precluded radar detection.

"Adin, dvaw—" Plaski counted out of habit. Impossible! There was no firing sequence, no parachute above him!

He broke his arch when he looked up and now the sky rotated as he tumbled over backward. Panicking, he clawed for the handle of the emergency chute strapped on his stomach, forgetting there was no emergency chute needed for such a low jump.

As he thrashed impotently, the rocky dirt of Antelope Drop Zone came up to meet him. Spinning, he was horizontal when he hit the ground like the snap on the end of a bullwhip. The main chute, still securely held on his back, broke his spine in three places. His black cloth jump helmet slammed into the sand, cracking his skull and snapping the vertebrae of his neck. His heels dug into the sand, leaving two grooves ten inches deep. The force of impact compressed both the main chute and Plaski's body, and the kinetic force then threw Plaski back up into the air. He bounced about a meter and came to rest in the crater he had just created.

Thirty-five meters above, Karmasov's chute had just opened when he saw the puff of dust from below.

"Good-bye, leech."

A good omen, Karmasov thought, as he drifted toward the flat Texas plain; not even on the ground, and already we are rid of a parasite. It was a good start! A strange thought struck him. Plaski was the first one on the ground! He would have been so proud! Karmasov laughed out loud.

On the ground, Bodnya watched the huge plane pass over them, dark figures streaming from both sides. It always thrilled him to watch a parachute jump. He, too, felt the adrenaline rush and the anticipation. The thrill was almost sexual, though strangely more satisfying. The light snowflakes on his face went unnoticed.

This jump, from only one hundred meters, was electrifying. The plane was so low it filled the sky, its engines roaring overhead. As each jumper's parachute deployed, it made a muffled, crackling sound like old canvas being torn. Deployed so low to the ground, each man was under his parachute canopy for only twenty-three seconds before landing. Some of the jumpers were already on the ground before the An-12 crossed the end of Antelope DZ.

As he watched the jumpers streaming from the plane, one figure detached itself from the column and fell faster and faster, tumbling toward the earth. The luckless jumper crashed into the ground one hundred meters from the collection point. Bodnya heard the impact over the sound of the plane's engines. The body bounced once, then lay still.

"God, which one?" Bodnya said softly. "Malinkov, come with me. Kovpak, see to the assembly of the groups."

"It is done, Major," Kovpak replied, his eyes on the shapeless mass lying in the dust.

The paratroopers were landing well away from the body, due to the angle of its fall, so Bodnya and Malinkov took the Suburban to retrieve it. When they reached the body, it was lying on its side. Bodnya shined his red flashlight into the dead face. It took a minute to recognize Plaski. His face was very broken and distorted by the impact, and one eye seemed to have burst out of its socket. Blood still ran from Plaski's nose and ears. His body was flaccid. Bodnya had seen death often enough, but this seemed very ugly.

"Well, Malinkov, I guess we will have to keep ourselves pure," Bodnya said softly as he looked at Plaski's ruined face. "We seem to be out of watchdogs."

"Good riddance, I say," Malinkov whispered. "If anyone had to go, those two were the best choices."

Malinkov leaned down and hooked his hands under Plaski's harness. He picked up the dead lieutenant like a rag doll and swung him onto his back like a rucksack. Plaski's legs dangled like ropes. There seemed to be no bone or joint intact. Malinkov opened the back door of the truck and threw the body in next to the woman. When she realized what it was, she recoiled and pulled away. Her scream was again stifled by the tape.

Malinkov drove back to the collection point in silence. Both men were relieved that no Spetsnaz, no real soldiers, had died. All of them were needed for the mission, the *Chekists* were always expendable. On the way back, they stopped to retrieve one of the PDSB-1 bundles.

At the assembly point, Kovpak was parceling the groups into their assigned trucks. They were stripping off their brown jump coveralls, revealing the camouflaged American BDUs. Those troops not present were in sight, running for the assembly point. The door bundles had been located. So far, the plan was running smoothly, but they had yet to meet any Americans. When that happened, the plan would change.

She thought she was beyond surprise, beyond horror, but she was wrong. Since the weasel had raped her, she had withdrawn into herself, blotting out the voices, the ride, the cold. She was vaguely aware that they had driven off the road, the rough surface had bounced her against the rear seat. Now they were stopped—the Russians were outside the truck.

Suddenly, the rear doors opened and a dark figure, Malinkov, by the size of him, threw a large bundle in next to her. It took a second for her to look over at it. Even in the darkness, she could see that it was a man, a dead man. His face looked like a Halloween mask. One eye seemed to be staring at her from where it rested on the carpet.

Panic caught her again and she strained against her bonds, screaming into the tape over her mouth. Like before, she choked, and had to fight to keep her breath. She pushed and clawed away from the lifeless form, wedging herself between the far wall and the rear seat. She wanted to pass out, to escape the horror, but she could not make it happen.

★37★

The Christmas party was a rarity at Ft. Hood. Most of the married officers preferred to be home with their families; but this year, a number of officers who were single parents had scheduled a party for their children. Single officers staying on post for the holiday were also invited. Santa Claus, in reality Master Sergeant Hal Musgrave, 3d Signal Brigade, had handed out presents beside the large Christmas tree.

At this late hour, most of the younger children and their parents had gone, but the older kids and the single officers were still celebrating.

BJ and Jinx found Peterson near the bar, laughing with two other young captains.

"Pat! We need to talk to you," BJ said, dragging Peterson away.

"Jesus, BJ, we're doin' Christmas here," Peterson protested.

"Captain Peterson, we just found two dead FBI agents in Austin," Jinx interrupted. "Something is about to happen here at Ft. Hood, and I, we think it could be tonight!"

Peterson stood looking at the pair. The chances of them being wrong were great, the chance of Soviets attacking here was tiny. She ought to send these two packing, but there was something about them that made her wonder. BJ Kirkley was one of the sharpest people alive when it came to the Soviets and their works. Jenkins was a cipher. Peterson had run a casual check through a friend at the Agency, and found that

249

Jinx was, indeed, one of theirs, but was on extended leave after a rocky time in Central America. She didn't trust Jinx's opinion, but BJ, though a bit strange sometimes, was seldom wrong.

"Come with me," Peterson said. She turned and left the O-Club, headed across the wide parking lot toward the BOQ.

"GO! GO!" shouted Bodnya at Cowboy. "You have the longest way to travel!" The yellow rented truck loaded with Group 4 bounced onto Old Georgetown Road with Cowboy double clutching the gears. They had little time to cover the twenty-two kilometers to the North Fort and the 49th Armored Division's equipment site.

He'd had to pull two men from Group 4 and switch them to Group 3. Cowboy had discovered at the last minute that a Christmas party was being held at the Officer's Club, something that was not normally done. He thought this an excellent chance to bag a batch of officers. Bodnya had agreed, but did not like a major change in plans on the eleventh hour. He briefed the two men himself to be sure they understood exactly what their task was and where to get picked up.

Next on its way was Group 3's white van driven by Sergeant Malinkov. Their route was probably the most time-consuming since they had to wind their way through the post, dropping off subunits at widely separated targets. Groups 2 and 1 followed with Hollis and Whisper driving the rented trucks.

Bodnya looked at Kovpak. "This has been the easiest infiltration we have ever accomplished, my friend. Let us hope it keeps going this way!"

"I have a feeling it will, Comrade Major! Tonight we will truly serve the Soviet Union!"

The two-man fuel depot attack subunit had finished loading their equipment into the back of the Suburban, ignoring the figure huddled in the back. Kovpak gunned the engine and searched for the gear shift lever by habit. He still was not used to an automatic transmission. The truck lurched onto the road as more snowflakes drifted to the ground.

Kovpak turned the Suburban onto deserted Turkey Run Road. The white van was already out of sight. He picked up speed. Peering at his strip map, he slowed for the Highway

190 turn-off. He kept his speed down as they rolled quietly past Comanche Village, the government housing area on the left. Crossing Copperas Cove Road, they soon crested the overpass over the railroad. An occasional car flashed by on Highway 190, eight hundred meters to the south.

Making a U-turn, Kovpak pulled the carry-all onto the north side of the overpass's downslope. The two Spetsnaz climbed out of the back, encumbered with their considerable load of weaponry.

Bodnya motioned for the sergeant. "I cannot stress the importance of your timing, Comrade! He said softly, Everyone is relying on you!"

"We will be to the second, Comrade Major! You just be on time to pick us up!"

"We are counting on each other then!" The two men disappeared over the railing and down the grassy slope as the Suburban headed back north.

They went straight to Peterson's room. Inside, she shut the door, turned the desk chair around, and sat down.

"OK, talk to me."

"We just an hour ago found two dead FBI agents, White and Harper were their names, and another stiff in the CCLAP safe house in Austin," BJ began. "We think the third one was another Russian. It looked like the FBI went there to check out our report and got zapped."

"Uh-huh. How did *you* happen to go to the safe house?" Peterson asked.

"Well, we didn't think anyone else was taking our story seriously," BJ said sheepishly, "so we sort of took matters into our own hands."

"I see," Peterson said, a grin spreading. "What else?"

"There's really nothing else to show and tell," BJ said. "It's just a gut feeling."

"But those two FBIs have another gut feeling," Jinx interjected. "Their guts are full of ball ammo; they were stuffed in a closet, dead. Freshly dead; they were still limp, no rigor mortis."

Peterson said nothing, staring at both of them.

"Plus, if they weren't in a hurry to get somewhere," Jinx went on, "they would have taken all three of those stiffs out and buried them. They wouldn't have left them there. That's why I think they are up to something tonight—here.''

This was one of those nightmare calls that all young career officers hate. If she ignored the warning and had another Pearl Harbor, her career was over. If she yelled, ''The Russians are coming, the Russians are coming,'' and they didn't, she was screwed, too. Mostly, it was a matter of trust. Did she trust BJ enough to believe him about this? BJ had to believe the other one, Jinx, or he wouldn't be here. BJ was no Chicken Little.

What it really came down to was, she was damned for doing, damned for not doing. The Captain of the *Stark* had been nailed for not doing, the Captain of the *Vincennes* had been nailed for doing wrong. Of the two, the latter had been treated better.

''OK, you two,'' Peterson finally said. ''I'm going to share something with you. As of this morning, we are on alert. The word I get is that the Joint Chiefs felt like the Soviets were a bit too active with their Winter Shield preparations, they had cancelled a disarmament talk, and there was a lot of extra chatter between their embassies and ships at sea. They tried to talk the President into calling a DEFCON 4, but he wouldn't do it. Afraid it would alarm the Soviets. Anyway, the Joint Chiefs sent out an order to maintain a higher standard of alertness until further notice. So, we're checking people at the gates, our guards are carrying M16s instead of nightsticks, and there are no leaves granted until further notice.

''Now, here you two come and tell me I'm the target for tonight, what am I gonna do? Well, I would rather get reamed for a false alarm than lose my ass, but if you two are wrong, you better book two tickets on the space shuttle.'' Then Peterson smiled. ''Better make that three tickets.''

Peterson picked up the phone and dialed the MP number.

''This is Captain Peterson, 163d MI. Let me talk to the duty officer.'' Peterson looked at the pair as she waited. ''Captain Dyer, this is Captain Peterson, 163d MI. I have reason to believe there may be an attack tonight by foreign nationals on the motor pools of this installation. I recommend that you put all MP patrols and Alert Forces available on combat status and get them out to those motor pool areas.

Please notify all unit duty officers and officers of the guard of this recommendation. This is no drill. I am on my way to your location to confirm this call. No, this is not a joke, Captain. Good-bye.''

Peterson looked at BJ and Jinx as she hung up the phone. She walked to her closet and took out a pressed pair of BDUs and her combat harness. She opened a drawer in the bottom of the closet and took out her personal Beretta 9mm pistol. After inserting a magazine in it, she holstered the pistol.

''Even if you guys are right, they're going to ream me for having a personal weapon in my room. Now, if you gentlemen will excuse me, I'll slip into something more comfortable.'' She disappeared into the bathroom.

''You know,'' she said through the door as she changed into the fatigues, ''the Chinese alphabet has a character that represents both crisis and opportunity. This better be both!''

Whisper watched Hollis's truck's taillights recede down South Range Road. Captain Karmasov sat beside him, a PB pistol in his hand.

''First drop-off.''

The truck's rear door was up, the lift gate providing an excellent jump-off platform. Karmasov banged his fist on the truck's side as Whisper slowed to a crawl. Subunit 1's three men spilled out the back and darted south into the roadside brush. A few seconds passed and Subunit 2 departed. He could hear a lieutenant in the back telling each subunit to stand by, and JUMP! They continued on down the road until all nine subunits were out. All that remained was Karmasov's own Subunit 10. Whisper brought the truck to a stop. Karmasov opened the door and stepped out. Turning, he looked back at the Russian-American.

''You have done well, Comrade. I will see you soon!''

''Victory, Comrade, victory!''

The door still open, the truck pulled into a range entrance road, turned around, and stopped with the lights off.

Subunit 10 trotted across the rocky ground toward the well-lighted motor pools. Karmasov thought they looked very far away. To their left were the lights of the Exclusion Area Facility, where they were told that TOW and Dragon missiles were stored for next day's use on the firing range. As this was a holiday, there were probably none in it. It had not been included as a target. There was little brush for concealment; he had expected more.

In the van, the twelve men of Group 3 were packed in the back with their weapons. On Malinkov's right was the PX they had visited the previous day. He paused at the traffic light at Clear Creek Road, even though no cars were in sight. As they drove through the maze of cream-colored warehouses and support buildings, the post was almost eerie; no traffic, no pedestrians. The bright yellow lights illuminating the building fronts cast a surreal glow. Falling snowflakes sparkled in the glare of their headlights. Tank Destroyer Road took them south of the Corps Headquarters building, the major's target. They turned left onto Twenty-fourth Street, passing the Officer's Club. Its parking lot was filled with cars, though some were leaving. Malinkov turned right at the corner, onto Wainwright Street.

He slowed just past the Officer's Club. "Subunit 3-3, go!"

Four men slipped out of the van's double back doors. They were unencumbered with any visible weapons.

"Three-five, go!"

Two more men, armed with AKS-74s, went out the right side doors. He had taken great care in loading the densely-packed men to ensure they could exit in the proper order. These were the two pulled from Group 4 to attack the Officer's Club.

Looking around for MP patrol cars, he drove on. Wainwright Street turned into Twentieth Street. Even though they had driven the route during their reconnaissance, that had been in daylight. Things looked much different at night. He relied on the strip map.

Off to his right front was the bowling alley. He turned right onto Central Drive. Winding slowly through the sleeping Walker Village housing area, the street curved to the north and became Martin Drive.

Looking to his left he was horrified to see a pale green MP car paralleling them on Redbud Drive. The two streets intersected ahead! He slowed a little. The MP car entered the intersection slightly ahead of him, turned left and suddenly sped up, heading back toward the main post area.

On the right were rows and rows of black-silhouetted helicopters, awaiting them! He felt a shiver of excitement! The six men in the back silently waited. Not too much longer now. And no one would be waiting.

★38★

When the last of the paratroops left the plane, Scheverard maintained his westward course. As the jumpmaster secured static lines and rolled the jump doors down, Scheverard put the throttles back and shut down the two outboard engines. The two AL-20K turboprops inboard had more than enough power to keep the empty aircraft aloft. Only the speed would be affected.

The jumpmaster reported that one of the static lines appeared to be cut, adding, "There is nothing we can do for that poor soul." Over Lampasas, he put the An-12 into a slow, banking turn to the left. This heading would take him southwest over San Saba County. There was an area between Lampasas and Brady that was sixty miles long and twenty miles wide. The An-12 would fly a racetrack course there until the Summer Harvest *reydoviki* signaled for their return. Even at sixty meters altitude, there were few obstacles, and those were clearly marked by order of the FAA.

If the signal did not come before the plane ran short of fuel, the Spetsnaz were on their own. When the signal came, they would return to Gray Army Airfield and land south to north.

The MP station was a one-story red brick building on the main drag. As the three drove up, MPs were filing out the front door, headed for their patrol cars and MP High Mobility Vehicles, nicknamed Hum-V's. Many of the MPs carried

M16s, a few 12ga. riot guns. All had 9mm pistols. Inside, Peterson walked up to the desk and asked for the duty officer.

A voice from behind them answered, "I'm Dyer. You Peterson?"

"That's right," Peterson replied, turning around to face the squat, nervous MP captain. "This is BJ Kirkley, he's with Company G, 143d Infantry; and Richard Jenkins of the CIA."

"What the hell is this all about, Captain?"

"These two gentlemen believe that a group of Soviet Spetsnaz are coming to Ft. Hood tonight to attack our motor pools. They have convinced me, and this alert is my responsibility."

The MP looked the two civilians up and down. "I hope you are right, Captain, I truly hope you are right. I took the liberty of calling the corps' duty officer. He wants to see you ASAP over at corps' headquarters."

"I hope we are wrong, Captain," Jinx shot back. "If we are right, there are going to be a lot of dead MPs tonight."

"Did you call the ODs and Officers of the Guard?" Peterson asked quickly, trying to change the subject.

"Yes, they're all notified," Dyer said, still looking at Jinx. "They had already issued the guards their weapons and ball ammo." He looked back at Peterson. "If they show up, we're ready for them."

Implied in his voice was the idea that if they didn't show up, Peterson was the one on the hook, not him.

"Come on, gentlemen," Pat said, starting for the door. "We can walk to the corps headquarters from here."

Outside, Jinx stopped the others and pointed at the car. "Let's drive, I don't want to be too far from the hardware."

They squeezed into the Camaro for the short drive.

As the threesome crowded into the Camaro, BJ suddenly stopped and looked at Jinx and Peterson.

"Look, you guys, I, uh, well—" He hesitated a moment. "Let me start over. I'm just one guy, this is only my opinion, but, you know—shit!"

"Go ahead, BJ, you're doin' fine," said Jinx, puzzled.

"Well, this is the way I see it. If there are really any Russians here," BJ quickly glanced at Jinx to see if he had angered him, "then we all got to pull together and try to stop 'em. I mean I'm just, you know, an NCO and you guys are officers and real spooks—no offense intended, Pat.''

"None taken, babe.''

"But we need to do somethin', like, like go out and kick their ass!'' He looked out the window.

Looking at Jenkins, Peterson said, "Well, with a speech like that to inspire us, I don't figure we have a snowball's chance in hell.''

Jinx, mournfully shook his head. "Yep, before I just *thought* we were in trouble, now I *know* we are!''

"Hey, fuck you guys!''

Sergeant Sokolov did not like the steep slope on the side of the railroad overpass. It was too hard to get a firm footing on the rocky surface. Senior Private Votrin was having trouble as well. They would have to move up to the road's shoulder when they initiated the attack on the fuel depot. This would also allow them to use the overpass's guardrail as a firing support. Both pulled off their heavy backpacks and placed them just below the lip of the overpass. Sokolov checked his watch again. Only minutes!

Most of the red-brick, two-story houses in Wainwright Heights were dark, except for front porch lights. A few had security lights in the back. Junior Sergeant Kapalkin looked both ways and walked down a *cul-de-sac* to one of the houses. He double-checked the address. A small plate next to the door proclaimed, MG HOLBERT. The commanding general of an armored division! thought Kapalkin. It almost scared him. Looking all about, he slowly walked into the backyard and positioned himself in the garage's shadows. He removed the glove from his right hand and rammed his hands under his armpits as he leaned against the wood structure.

The second hand swept around the watch's white face. As it passed twelve, Karmasov stood.

"We go now.''

Senior Privates Zalmanson and Dymshitz rose behind him and they began to walk across the rocky ground to their motor pool.

* * *

Lieutenant Pavlenko's Subunit 1 had been the first out of Whisper's truck. It was much farther across the strip to the second road than he had expected. There were several small ravines and ditches that made the going slow. After they attacked the motor pool, Subunit 11 was to take up a position near the intersections of North Avenue, Turkey Run, and West Range Roads. Captain Karmasov's subunit, the last one out, was to roll up the others and they were to assemble at Pavlenko's position where the truck would pick them up. He rushed his small command. The motor pools were so far away! Darting across Turkey Run Road they approached the motor pool's sentry from the west. The lieutenant was so concerned about making up the lost time that he forgot to time his approach.

Karmasov crouched behind a too-small bush. The area between the road where they were dropped off and the road fronting the motor pools was much wider than the one in Nicaragua. The area was almost devoid of brush as well! He hoped this would not confuse the other subunits or throw their timing off. Too late now to do anything about it.

He could see the motor pools well. Beyond the fences he could only see a jumbled mass of black. As the sentry passed a gap in the dark background, he would be silhouetted by the lights. Nothing seemed unusual. A light green car sped by. There was no other activity. He looked at his watch. Only minutes to go!

Sokolov touched Votrin's shoulder and they climbed over the guardrail. He took four magazines from his right pouch and laid them on the gravel road shoulder. Every other cartridge in each of the forty-round RPKS-74 magazines was a tracer.

Votrin pulled the two backpacks up, shoving one in front of Sokolov. From the other he pulled a slim 58mm rocket which he slid into the muzzle of his RPG-16D anti-tank rocket launcher. He extracted several more rockets, placing them on top of the pack.

The two men had been selected for this task because of their skill with their respective weapons. They had not taken much to each other at first but as rehearsals progressed and they began learning each other's tasks, each began to respect the other's expertise. They drilled each other on their respective weapons. They began looking forward to the mission for which they had practiced so long and hard!

Votrin leaned his AKSU-74 submachine gun against the guardrail. Sokolov adjusted the leaf sight on his RPKS for seven hundred meters. He checked his watch again.

"Prepare to fire," he muttered through a cloud of breath.

Votrin shouldered the heavy rocket launcher, making a minor sight adjustment.

The second hand seemed to not move at all. With agonizing slowness it finally edged its way up. Finally, all three hands stood straight up at twelve.

"Fire."

Sokolov hardly had the word out of his mouth when the RPG-16 rocket streaked toward the easternmost silver fuel storage tank.

The new Corps' headquarters was a three-story glass office building south of Battalion Ave. The duty officer would be in his office just off the lobby. BJ pulled up right in front of the double glass doors.

In the lobby, a young sergeant sat at the receptionist's desk. When Peterson entered the lobby, he rose.

"You Captain Peterson, ma'am? Major Stephenson is waiting for you."

A burly armor major sat propped up behind his desk, his fingers tented in front of him.

"Are you the person who has the MPs so excited on Christmas Eve?" he asked, not bothering to stand.

"Yes, sir, I am," Peterson replied. "I think we have reason to get excited."

"May I ask what those reasons are?"

She pointed at Jinx and BJ. "These two men are intelligence agents," she said, glossing over the details. "They believe an attack on this post will occur tonight. I think it would be foolish to ignore that warning, don't you?"

"I think presumptive actions based on unfounded rumors are foolish. Do you have any proof that this attack will take place?"

"Well, we could have brought two dead FBI agents to show

you," Jinx interrupted, "but they are so awkward to carry around."

The mention of dead bodies got his attention. Stephenson sat up. "Dead FBI?"

"That's right," Jinx continued. "Two agents were killed this evening in a house in Austin. We found another body with them. We believe him to be a Soviet Spetsnaz soldier. Other information we have indicates that the dead Russian's friends are very interested in the motor pools here at Ft. Hood."

"That's very interesting, Mr.—?"

"Jenkins."

"Mr. Jenkins, but I'm not sure—"

The major's speech was interrupted by a sudden yellow glare that filled the lobby of the building with light. A moment later, the loud BOOM rattled the glass on the west side of the building.

The sergeant at the front desk was standing next to the tall glass panels. "Holy shit! Look at tha—"

The glass wall broke into a million flaming shards, ripping the sergeant from head to toe, propelling him backward over the receptionist's desk. A thousand tiny fires covered the lobby.

"They're heeeerrrreeee!" BJ said loudly.

Pat had her 9mm out of the holster. She stepped to the door and took a quick look around the corner. "I can't see anything out there for the lights in here.

Jinx jumped to the door, hit the light switch, and rolled against the wall. The office was plunged into darkness, the glow from the many small fires in the lobby the only light.

"Pat, cover us to the car. Major, this is it. Now is your chance to be a soldier. Come on BJ."

BJ scuttled over by the door next to Jinx.

"Ready, Pat? Now!"

Pat swung around the door frame and fired two shots from her pistol into the darkness. Jinx and BJ were through the shattered glass wall when a rocket hit on the floor above them. Glass and fire burst from the second floor. The fire alarm and sprinklers went off. Pat fired again and ran after Jinx and BJ to the car.

BJ jerked the door open and handed Jinx the AR-15.

"I think I saw a flash over there," she said breathlessly. She pointed over her left shoulder. "There, next to that building."

As she spoke, a tongue of flame lit the side of the wood-frame building, clearly silhouetting two figures. Another rocket streaked into the headquarters building, setting the third floor ablaze. The two figures disappeared behind the building.

"BJ, I gotta get back to the MPs," Pat said, her voice breaking with excitement and fear. "You guys keep your heads down. You might get shot as terrorists in those outfits."

"Go on, Pat," Jinx said. "We'll go after those two. Don't worry about us."

Pat smiled at Jinx, winked at BJ, then said, "Cover me!" as she ran toward the MP station a block away.

KA-KA-BLOOM! The rocket slammed into the tank just below the top, right where he had been told to aim. The airspace was filled with volatile fumes. A huge orange fireball billowed into the cloudy sky. Globules of burning gasoline showered to the ground.

Sokolov began firing short bursts of tracers into the other tanks' thin skins, punching holes that pissed burning fuel.

Another rocket flashed, this one striking a diesel tank. The oily fuel spilled from the jagged hole. Votrin fired another rocket, lighting the spilled fuel. It continued to burn, finally igniting the tank's contents.

Several vehicles had stopped on the highway overpass two hundred meters beyond the blazing tanks. Sokolov adjusted his sight and swung the light machine gun in their direction. He fired several long raking bursts into the shapes of men, silhouetted by their vehicles' headlights, and watched people running and falling.

★39★

"Mother fuckin' shit!" Pfc Jacob Cummings grumbled out loud. He just knew his platoon sergeant had a hard-on for him. Some brother! Guard duty on Christmas Eve!

"Shit man! We need ya Cummings, I can trust ya. With all this shit about a heightened alert, we need somebody we can count on!" He mimicked Platoon Sergeant Heinz.

At least they had given him an M16 instead of that stupid club! But with only five rounds, big deal!

He reached the east end of the compound's fence and turned back toward the gate. He also had to lug this heavy-ass prick 119 radio and wear a stupid helmet!

"Colder'n a well digger's ass and now its startin' to snow!" he groused. "Shit!"

As Cummings contemplated his lousy luck, three dudes began walking up the road shoulder. They were wearing BDUs and carrying packs.

What's this shit? Must be some dumb asses who got lost in the training area, Cummings thought. On Christmas Eve? Nobody but him had to wear a fuckin' uniform on Christmas Eve! What's goin' on here?

Lieutenant Pavlenko could see the outline of the sentry ahead. He was almost to the gate. This will be perfect! He will be in just the right position, close to the sentry hut. All Senior Private Barchugov had to do was move in closer. Pavlenko and his other man hung back a little to give the gunman a clear shot.

Clack! "Halt motherfucker!"

Barchugov's P-6 came up fast. Cummings saw a glint of metal.

"Shit!" *BLAM! BLAM!*

The gunman fell backward as two 5.56mm bullets slapped into his chest from ten feet, the silenced pistol spiraling into the road. Pavlenko reached into the big leg cargo pocket and yanked on the small 5.45mm PSM pistol. It caught on the pocket flap!

BLAM! BLAM! The first slug penetrated just below his navel and severed his spinal cord. The second went through is right side below the floating ribs and grazed the other *reydoviki's* thigh. He fell sideways into the fence, still struggling to unsling his AKS-74.

Seeing the third man down, but still moving, Cummings stepped forward and fired his last round from the hip, disintegrating the man's right elbow.

Three big steps closed the distance to the man, who was now trying to get to his feet. Reversing his rifle, Cummings slammed its butt into the man's head; once, twice.

"Fuckin' shit! What the fuck, over!"

A towering column of fire rose in the western sky.

Jinx and BJ came up over the hood of the car, but there were no targets, no muzzle flashes. Pat made it without a shot fired at her.

"BJ, what's over there, behind that building?"

"The field house, I think."

"Get in the car, let's flank 'em."

BJ looked skeptical, but slid into the driver's seat. Jinx slipped into the cramped back seat. He took up a firing position out the right window. BJ gunned the engine, then shot out of the drive, jumped the curb, and tore across the lawn, finally landing back on Support Ave. As they hit the pavement, they saw a figure disappear into a side door at Abrams Field House. A Chevy Suburban was parked next to the building.

* * *

Subunit 10 strolled toward the small sentry standing idle by the gate. He did not move, seemed to be preoccupied in thought. This is too easy! thought Karmasov.

In the distance several sharp shots sounded.

The sentry looked in the direction of the shots. Hearing a crunch of gravel, he suddenly turned around.

Karmasov whispered, "Now!"

As Zalmanson's pistol rose they saw the fireball leap skyward beyond the sentry. He looked in the direction of the explosion when it's muffled boom reached them. The startled sentry now turned back to them and began to unsling a rifle.

A too high-pitched "Halt!" came from the sentry.

Zalmanson fired, the 9mm bullet hitting dead center in the sentry's solar plexus. The rifle dropped to the ground and he sat down hard, not falling over.

The *ikhotniki* moved in closer. Straightening his arm, he took careful aim and popped two rounds into the confused sentry's young face. The body flopped onto his back.

Zalmanson had killed before, but this somehow seemed like murder! He stepped over the body and grasped the helmet's front lip. The Americans are so like the Fascists, he thought, that they even use the same helmet!

He pulled it off and strands of long blond hair fell over a girl's mutilated face! He froze.

"Move!" Karmasov hissed, grabbing Zalmanson's pack and shoving. "Dymshitz, let us get him in the hut!" As Dymshitz was reaching for the legs, he realized that he and the captain were picking up a dead woman.

"The bastards. Using girls for soldiers' work!"

"Move!" shouted Karmasov.

Zalmanson grabbed the helmet and put it on. He picked up the M16A2 rifle, chambered a round, and slung it. Where was the radio? It was not on the girl. The captain and Dymshitz picked up the girl and gently laid her in the hut. The radio was there. He slipped it on. Dymshitz jumped to cut the gate chain and Karmasov followed him through.

Zalmanson felt something wet running down his forehead. Blood! From the dead girl's head! Zalmanson wiped the inside of the helmet with his sleeve, disgusted.

* * *

"Quickly, Ensign, the girl." Bodnya said as they ran for the gymnasium building. They had discarded the RPO-A launcher after firing the last rocket at the headquarters building. Bodnya had been surprised to get return fire, even though it had been wildly inaccurate.

Kovpak veered over to the back doors of the truck, jerked them open and pulled out the struggling girl. She collapsed on the concrete, and Kovpak simply pulled her up like a sack of potatoes and threw her over his shoulder. Bodnya, covering, held the door open for Kovpak and both entered the gymnasium building.

"How shall we effect her martydom, Major?" Kovpak asked as they entered the huge basketball court.

"When we are ready to leave, we will leave her outside the building with a weapon. Dead, of course."

"Of course," Kovpak smiled.

The ringing phone startled Alice Holbert out of a deep, dreamless sleep.

"General Holbert's residence." she answered automatically. Thirty-two years of military life with Bill and she still felt uncomfortable with the forced formality.

"Ma'am, this is Captain Nelson, SDO. Is the general in?"

"Yes, just a moment," she answered, placing her hand over the mouthpiece. "Bill, its the staff duty officer."

"Damn, what time is it?"

She handed him the phone. "12:10."

"General Holbert."

"Sir, this is Captain Nelson, SDO. There's been a big explosion west of here on the highway! We also have reports of gunfire from the motor pool area."

"Are you certain of this?" Holbert asked, shaking the fog of sleep from his head.

"Yes sir. I sent the runner outside and he can hear the shots. There's a lot of them, sir!"

"Okay, alert all the CQs! Have you called the MPs?"

"Yes sir! They're on the way! Do you want me to send a car?"

"No, Captain. I'll be right there!"

"What is it, Bill?" Something wasn't right, she could tell by his voice.

"I think we've got trouble, Hon', maybe terrorists," Holbert answered, rolling out of bed toward the closet. "I'm going to the HQ. Get dressed and stay put! And don't turn on any lights!"

William C. Holbert, Commanding General of the 1st Cavalry Division, pulled a pressed set of BDUs off a hanger and began pulling them on. His fingers fumbled with his bootlaces in the dark. This was taking too much time! Reaching up to the top shelf of the closet, he brought down his issue 9mm M9 pistol in its black leather holster. Strapping on the belt, he snatched up the single loaded fifteen-round magazine he kept on hand.

Finally dressed, he sprinted down the stairs and through the kitchen. The car keys were on the ornate key rack that one of his nephews had given them last Christmas.

Opening the back door, he saw a man's shape in the shadows of the garage! His hand dropped to the holster. The shape moved a little.

He flung the screen door open and leaped to the right off the concrete steps. Hitting the ground rolling, he came to both knees with the heavy pistol out. Pops came from the shape, still in the shadows. Loud whacks came from the wall behind him.

The general squeezed the trigger four times, the weapon bucking in his two-handed grip. The shape crumpled.

Alice was at the door.

"Stay inside, Alice! I think—I hope I just bagged a bad guy!"

Beyond the overpass, coming up Base Road from West Ft. Hood, were three fire trucks of the Gray Army Airfield fire station. Sokolov reached into his backpack and removed an RPG-22 rocket launcher. Extending its tube, he took aim at the crest of the overpass. He fired a high explosive anti-tank rocket at a truck parked on the overpass. There was a flash, but no fire. Behind him, Votrin launched another of his rockets into the depot, rewarded by another scorching fireball. The heat was so intense, that seven hundred meters away they felt it. Sokolov fired another of the U.S. LAW rocket copies into the parked cars. This time, one began to burn.

* * *

Senior Private Toshkin held his RPKS-74 and used it to steady himself as the van slowed to a stop. Instantly, the sliding door was opened and the remaining passengers spilled out. They made for the roadside shadows as the van moved quietly away. When the white van disappeared in the darkness, they made their way quickly to the airfield's fence. There seemed to be no activity at all on the field. The *reydoviki* on his left touched Toshkin's arm and pointed. On the hardstand in front of a row of parked AH-64 Apaches, a sentry paused to stretch. Toshkin looked to see if the others had seen. They had. When the guard walked farther down the line, the helicopters hid him from their view, and them from his.

The six shadows darted across the road to the fence. The West German cutters went through the chain link in an instant. A dozen soft clips, and the subunit was through, onto the field itself. Splitting up into teams of two, the men made for the neat rows of parked helicopters.

Toshkin and his partner crawled slowly forward, looking for the sentry. Toshkin finally saw him, standing behind an Apache, relieving himself on the grass. His M16 slung over his shoulder, the sentry had his head back, lost in relief. When the ball of flame leaped up into the western sky, his head snapped back down.

Toshkin rolled onto his side to get the RPKS-74 into play, but before he could even get the weapon off his back, he heard the soft popping of a silenced PB pistol off to his left. The sentry, mesmerized by the tower of flame, suddenly twitched and spun to the ground, a stream of steaming piss arcing over him.

Toshkin and his partner leaped to their feet and sprinted toward the line of Apaches. They started in the middle, working their way to the ends of the row.

Toshkin jumped up on the side sponson and pulled the canopy release lever as he had been taught. He almost fell off when the latch refused to budge. It was locked! Toshkin stared at the canopy for a moment, then shrugged his shoulders, pulled the fuse lighter, and set the thermite bomb on the fuel cell. He then jumped down and ran to the next gunship, repeating the process.

He was at the third helicopter when he heard the first shots from across the runway. An unseen sentry had discovered one of the pairs and opened fire. A burst of AKR fire had cut him down, but now there was no time to dally. He pulled the igniters on several charges and ran from ship to ship, tossing them on the fuel cells. The engine intakes would have been better, but they had red nylon covers on them. When he had placed all twenty charges, he untied the RPG-22 from the empty pack, slung it across his back, and sprinted for the hangars across the runway.

Cummings crouched beside the bodies. "This ain't happnin' man!" He finished pulling the weapon off the last man he had killed. A fuckin' AK! They were wearing BDUs, but there were no patches, no rank. Not even a name or U.S. Army tape!

He pulled the AN/PRC-119 radio handset off his harness.

"Home Guard, Home Guard, this is Post One Six, over."

"One Six, this is Home Guard, do not transmit! We have traffic!" A pause. *"All Home Guard posts, there has been weapons firing reported. Report any activity in your area. Stay in place and stay alert. Over."*

"Home Guard, this is One Six. That was me, man! I just whacked three dudes! Over."

"One Six, say again, over!"

"I shot three people tryin' to kill me, over!"

"One Six, are you injured? Over."

"That's a big negative, over."

"One Six, stay in place. We are dispatching assistance. Home Guard, out!"

He heard a sound down the fence. Three men were moving around down there too! Picking up the AKS-74, he fiddled with the selector level until it moved down a notch. He rose and moved down the fence toward the next gate. Would he get in trouble for leaving his post? Fuck it! There's some serious shit goin' down!"

Subunit 2 heard the rapid succession of shots from the first motor pool. All three men dropped to the ground behind the sentry's still warm body. He had been no problem at all. But, now there seemed to be a problem.

"Cut the chain!" commanded the sergeant.

One man did so, reaching up from a kneeling position. He pushed it open and went in on his hands and knees.

The sergeant tapped the other senior private with the toe of his boot. "Stay alert!" A figure was coming down the road shoulder. Both *ikhotniki* aimed.

"Do not fire! It is one of our men!" The sergeant whispered. He could see the helmet and the AKS-74's large flash suppressor.

"Nyandoma!" he challenged. The use of Soviet town names for challenges and countersigns had long been a tradition.

"Fuck you!" Cummings squeezed the trigger hammering twelve rounds into the prone figures dancing them across the driveway. He had not realized that the selector lever's first position was full automatic.

The man inside ducked behind a stack of wooden pallets. He shoved his assault rifle's muzzle between a space in the pallets to cover the gate.

Cummings swung the gate open wide and darted through at a crouch, then rolled to the right. The thin pallets kept the Soviet's rifle from tracking him, but a short burst came from the stack anyway.

Rolled half over on his side, Cummings emptied the remainder of the thirty-round magazine into the pallet stack.

Splinters and bullets drove into the man's face and chest. By chance, one of Cumming's tracer rounds passed through the man's shoulder and into the thermite charges in his pack. The blocks ignited with almost explosive effect turning the Soviet and pallets into a blazing white column of sputtering flames.

On the far side of the runway, one of the other subunits was engaged in a firefight with two American MPs, whose car was skewed across the road at the base of the control tower. The third subunit worked its way down a row of UH-60 Blackhawks, chucking their charges up on top of the big troop carriers.

Toshkin slung his machine gun over his shoulder and climbed atop a metal CONEX container. He pulled the RPKS-74 off and flipped the bipod down. Dropping prone near the edge of the CONEX, he began putting short bursts into the

MP car. His magazines held half ball, half tracer. The red tracers slammed into the car and ricochetted off the concrete up into the night sky. On the fourth burst, the car exploded with a muffled *WHUMP*! The two MPs were knocked away by the blast, one covered with burning gasoline. The other, trying to smother the flames on his partner, was cut down by a burst from the other pair. The firefight over, the *reydoviki* went back to work on another row of Apaches. They waved their thanks at Toshkin, who continued to cover them from the CONEX. Behind them, the AH-64s across the runway were bursting into flame as the thermite charges burned into their fuel tanks. The flames lit the field with a wonderful flickering light.

The lights came on first upstairs, then some minutes later, in the kitchen. A tall figure appeared at the back door. He spoke to someone inside. The door opened and the bare-headed, BDU-clad man, came down the steps two at a time. The young sergeant raised his pistol.

Not yet, not yet! The man came rapidly across the damp grass as snowflakes drifted across the yard. Almost to the garage, the sergeant aimed carefully and fired three muffled shots.

The man collapsed to the edge of the driveway. The back door suddenly flew open and a woman in a pink robe came down the steps.

"Frank, you forgot—" Two low pops and she stumbled back into the concrete steps, her head thumping like a ripened melon.

He stepped to the man's body and shot once into the head before walking over to the woman. Another pop.

The sergeant reached down and pulled from her clutched fist a BDU cap with three polished silver stars on its front. Jamming his own cap into a pocket, he placed the trophy on his head.

The first fire truck roared under the highway overpass with sirens wailing. Yellow coated firefighters leaped off before it came to a complete stop, hauling hoses from the back. Votrin did not hesitate even a moment. Bracing the RPG-16 on the steel railing, he fired a rocket that went streaking toward the red truck. A small flash caused the running men to fall to the ground. Water began pouring from the pumper's ruptured onboard tank.

Sokolov rattled a few short bursts into the men while Votrin hastily reloaded. This time he aimed at the cab. The rocket hit a fuel tank that detonated in a fiery flash. The other trucks stopped under the overpass.

An MP patrol car, blue and red lights flashing, swerved around the trucks and slid to a halt at the base of the overpass. Sokolov directed a tracer stream into the flashing vehicle. One man bailed out the car's left door. Sokolov tracked the rolling man across the road until he stopped rolling.

The two *raydoviki* crouched among the shrubs on the north side of the Officer's Club. Their orders were to wait fifteen minutes after the attack was launched before they were to pounce, or to attack immediately if the partygoers were alerted. They had heard several shots across the way in Wainwright Heights. But the closed building and the revelers' noise kept them oblivious to what was going on. Individuals and small groups were trickling out, their cars' headlights sometimes sweeping over their hiding place.

As the time approached, the two rose and simply walked down the sidewalk on the brick building's windowless east side. Keeping their AKSUs to their sides, they rounded a fenced lawn with a walkway leading to a patio. Overlooking this was the main ballroom, still filled with people, around a large, decorated, artificial tree. As a man with a young girl came out the glass doors and headed for the parking lot, they stepped aside, into the shadows of an oak tree. The two soldiers looked at each other. There were still children inside. They had their orders though.

An empty four foot deep concrete pot, meant for flowers, was encircled by a section of the sidewalk in the center of the lawn. Using it for support, they pointed their submachine guns at the plate-glass windows and squeezed the triggers.

Glass shattered, sending shards flying through the room. People screamed in fear and anger. Changing magazines, they emptied another into the room.

Then they ran. Out the gate and past the black-plastic-covered swimming pool. Behind them was utter chaos.

* * *

Bathed in the glare of the Russian's funeral pyre, Jacob
Cummings went back through the gate and picked up another
AK. Rolling one of the bloodied bodies over, he pulled four
magazines out of a canvas pouch and stuffed them into his
cargo pockets. "What the fuck's goin' on?" he asked the
dead man.

"*All Home Guard stations!*" The handset crackled in his
ear. "*This installation is under attack! All posts report their
status! Post One report!*"

Cummings was Post Sixteen. He didn't have time to wait
his turn. He struggled out of the radio's shoulder straps and
dumped it by the gate. Breathing hard, he rushed across the
compound and crouched behind a tank, peering into the next
compound.

The young *ikhotniki* crouched behind the sentry hut,
searching for movement up the fence. There had been a lot
of shots from the next motor pool and a blazing white fire
had burst just inside the compound. It was so bright it dazzled
his vision.

Cummings reached up and placed the rifle on top of the
CONEX. Using stacked rolls of concertina wire, he climbed
to the top of the steel shipping container. On the far side of
the next compound, small white fires flared on the engine
decks of a row of tanks. Flames spewed from their gun muzzles. Taking a wide step to the pipe on top of the chain link
fence, he stepped over the barbed wire strands and climbed
down the other side to crouch behind another tank.

Small arms fire rattled farther away. Sirens wailed from all
directions. More fires were burning in other motor pools.

Peering across the wide lane to the next row of M1s, he
quickly scanned the big vehicles for signs of movement.
Nothing. He double-timed across the interval in a low crouch
just like he had learned in infantry training.

Two figures were making their way down the row of tanks,
one running on the engine decks and the other on the
ground. Both stopped at each vehicle and placed charges of
some sort. He would take the one out on the ground first,
since he had the most chance of getting away.

Aiming at the man's center of mass, Cummings squeezed the now familiar trigger, touching off a short burst. This bounced the man into a tank's rear and onto the ground. The other was gone!

The burst of AKS-74 fire that killed his partner completely stunned Senior Sergeant Savin. He leaped down between two tanks and scrambled to the front of one. Who was it? Where was he?

Still keeping low, he moved around the tank's front, and then to the next. The first thermite charge on this row suddenly ignited behind him. Startled, he turned around. Realizing what it was, he turned back and faced the biggest man he had ever seen!

Cummings jammed the rifle's muzzle down into Savin's right eye.

"Lookin' for me, asshole?" He tapped the trigger and one shot rang out. "Keep an eye out for me next time, dude!"

Charges were flaring white all down the first three rows of tanks and Karmasov and Dymshitz had not yet finished the final row. From his position on an engine deck he could see thermite flares in the next compounds, but there was also some automatic weapons fire down the way.

A car with its blue and red overhead lights flashing squealed around the corner of Hood Street and slid sideways into the compound's driveway. Zalmanson's AKSU rattled rounds into the car at close range. Karmasov caught a glimpse of two MPs piling out with M16s. There was no return fire.

A Hummer whined down North Avenue and screeched to a halt beside the patrol car. Two more M16-armed men came through the compound gate. Karmasov raised his AKSU high and fired several long bursts just to rattle the attackers. He leaped off the tank.

"Dymshitz! Over here!" Unslinging his pack, he began pulling out thermite charges. Dymshitz stumbled around the tank's back fender, out of breath.

"Watch our front and flanks! There are four with rifles!" He pulled off Dymshitz's pack and dumped his remaining charges on the ground.

Pulling igniter rings, he began throwing the charges as far

across the compound as he could, spacing them all through the area. Men, silhouetted against the blazing hulks, were darting from vehicle to vehicle. Dymshitz began firing short bursts as Karmasov threw the last charges.

Moving to the other end of the vehicle, he fired a burst at a man working his way toward them between the tanks and the fence. The figure ducked behind a hull. He pulled one of the RGN grenades from his belt pouch and tossed it high, hoping it would arc between the right tanks. *Clang!* It bounced off a turret. *BLAM!*

"I am moving forward!" he shouted to Dymshitz, who was firing rapidly.

In a crouch, he dodged from hull to hull until he came upon a body writhing between two sets of tank treads. It was missing a forearm and its uniform was tattered with fragmentation holes. He shot a three-round burst into the form.

Karmasov picked up the MP's rifle. It appeared operational, even with a few small fragment holes in the black plastic stock and forearm. He pulled four magazines from the dead man's pouch and shoved them into his pockets. He might need these before this night was over!

More sirens wailed to a halt outside the compound. Waiting a few seconds, he threw another grenade in the gate's direction. *BLAM!* The first thermite charges began igniting throughout the compound. He ran back to Dymshitz, who had just thrown a grenade.

"Go to the fence and cut a hole! GO!" *BLAM!*

He moved into Dymshitz's position and began firing at what muzzle flashes he could see among the blazing vehicles. Return fire rang off steel hulls on either side of him. He rose and fired another burst. Something zinged off a road wheel, hot needles stabbed into his face's right side, and he fell to the left, banging his head against a track skirt.

"Captain, it is done!"

Pulling the two remaining grenades out, Karmasov threw one at the next row of tanks. Moving on all fours, he crawled to the ragged opening. *BLAM!* Dymshitz was through. He threw the last grenade over the vehicles and clambered through. His partner rolled into a prone position in the hole and fired a long burst between tanks. *BLAM!*

They were out, in a shallow ditch beside Hood Road. Now

what? Across the road was another motor pool, full of engineer equipment. It had not been attacked, but there were scores of fires in the other 2d Armored Division compounds beyond it. Group 2 was doing well, much better than Karmasov's group. To the south, down the road, were barracks. North was the only choice. There was blood soaked around a ragged hole on Dymshitz's left shoulder, but he said nothing.

Crouching, they trotted up the ditch to North Avenue. Several MP vehicles were parked in disarray in front of the compound from which they had just escaped. Sprinting across North Avenue, they headed up a gentle slope toward a small cluster of white buildings. Pinpoints of muzzle flashes lit up a yellow truck parked on a side road three hundred meters to their left. They could dimly see Whisper leaping from the cab and crumpling to the ground. A Hummer and an MP sedan were pulled up fifty meters away from the truck, their occupants riddling it with full automatic fire. There would be no pickup for Group 1.

Both men were out of breath as they stumbled past a carved wood sign inscribed, "ROD AND GUN CLUB." As Dymshitz cut the gate's chain, Karmasov noticed that the snow was coming down more heavily.

Major General Baskins had been awakened by the sound of sirens. Laying in bed, still more asleep than awake, the realization that there were a lot of sirens slowly seeped into his consciousness. The sounds were faint, the central heat unit was humming. Quietly rolling out of bed so as not to disturb his wife, he went to a bedroom window and pulled the curtains. Over the roofs of neighboring houses, to the northeast, a scattering of red tracer dots winked into the sky.

"Oh shit!"

Dressing quickly, he bounded down the stairs without even awakening his wife. Opening the garage doors, he heard a tiny sound behind him. Turning, he stared into the muzzle of a pistol gripped by a determined young man. The general shut his eyes tight.

BJ cut his speed as he pulled into the parking lot, taking care not to get too close to the Suburban. He and Jinx were out of the car as soon as it stopped, Jinx slithering out like a big snake. They covered each other as first BJ then Jinx ran to the shadows next to the big building. They rapidly made their way down to the door, not wanting to be caught against the brick wall.

From every direction, the sounds of combat grew louder. M16 fire countered the distinctive barking of AKs. RPG rockets went off in the distance. It was amazing how each weapon had its own distinctive voice. Tonight, there were more Russian voices than American.

Cowboy slowed as they neared the storage area and maintenance yard. There were lights on the buildings, but no signs of life. The massive vehicle maintenance shop, a seventy-six thousand-square-foot, tilt-wall building, was dark. There seemed to be no guards of any sort. The *reydoviki* of Group 4 suspected a trap, and deployed five hundred meters south of the facility. Cowboy stopped the truck and killed the engine. He was to wait in the darkness for the soldiers to do their work. If it was a trap, they were on their own.

Silently, cautiously, the twelve dark shapes circled the chain link fence, coming up behind the equipment yard. They crouched in the dirt, searching the rows of vehicles for any signs of ambush. There was no sign of life. Finally, one trio slipped up to the wire and cut through, slipping like shadows into the yard. Another team followed, then another. Soon, ten men made their way quickly down the rows, waiting for the attack to begin. It was only four minutes later that a tower of flame shot up into the southern sky. Quickly, each man went down the rows, placing his charges and igniting the fuses.

Row after row of tanks, armored personnel carriers, self-propelled artillery, tank recovery vehicles, Hummers, and trucks went up in flames. When they ran short of charges, the men punched holes in gas tanks and lit the fuel as it poured out. They broke open fuel pumps and turned them on, letting the fuel feed the flames.

By the time the ten *reydoviki* slipped through the gate next to the road, the storage yard was an inferno. Row after row of vehicles were burning, scores of them reduced to smoking hulks.

Cowboy gunned his truck down the road, picking up the twelve raiders. They turned north on Highway 36. At Gatesville they turned left on Highway 84, then left again onto Farm Road which would take them south to Copperas Cove.

The attack on North Ft. Hood had gone so smoothly it scared the soldiers. They could hear firing from the main post. Why had there been no defenders on their target? It made no sense. Behind them, one of the fuel pumps exploded, its pillar of flame a small replica of the one that had signaled the attack.

★40★

Jinx reached up and gripped the metal knob. He nodded at BJ, then turned the knob and pulled the door open. BJ burst through the door into the shadows to the right of the doorway, crouching, listening more than looking. Jinx waited a beat, then wheeled around the door himself, sidestepping quickly to the left of the door so he wouldn't step on BJ. The door closed quietly behind them. There was no fire, no grenade.

The door was at the end of a long hallway. As they leapfrogged down the hall, going from one doorway to the next, the sound of voices came from an open double door halfway down the hall. Two men were talking and another voice, muffled and incoherent, was interrupting.

Jinx motioned to BJ, who joined him against the wall. The voices seemed to be coming from right behind them. Jinx nodded at BJ, then spun around the wall with BJ right behind them. As they cleared the doorway, they ran right into the two men coming from the other direction.

Jinx reflexively pushed away the man in front of him with his rifle, bringing the rifle up in a buttstroke at the man's head. He missed as the big man stepped back. Past his opponent, he saw BJ bounce off a bound figure being pulled by the other man. In the frozen combat-time, he saw the shorter man step back and fire his pistol at BJ's head. The gun made no sound. BJ spun to the floor. Distracted, Jinx didn't see the big man's hand coming up with a knife. As he thrust the knife out in front of him, the blade shot forward through the air. It stuck with a loud thunk in the plastic buttstock of Jinx's Ar-15.

"Freeze!" Jinx screamed, covering both men with his rifle.

The short man had his gun on Jinx, but the big man blocked his shot. Jinx tried to keep the big man between him and the little bastard who shot BJ.

A flare shining from outside lighted the scene. Jinx nearly didn't recognize Susan. Her eyes were puffy from crying and her face was raw from the abrasion of the Suburban's carpeting. The sudden hope in her eyes showed that she recognized Jinx, too.

"Hello, Susan, who's your friend?"

It had been weeks, but Bodnya suddenly recognized the stance, the face before him. He had last seen it singed and smoking.

"So, we meet again," Bodnya said. He moved slightly to give Kovpak a shot. The American moved with him, never taking the gun off Bodnya.

"Yeah, tell your little friend that if he shoots, I'll kill you anyway before I go."

"I am certain he knows that," Bodnya answered. "You are not the first man he has killed—tonight."

The sound of shooting outside grew louder. As they circled, Jinx saw that the little man was holding Susan around the chest with his left arm. In his left hand was a grenade, an RGD-5.

"Shall we do now as we did that night in Nicaragua?" Bodnya asked. "Shall we both live to fight again?"

"You got lucky that night," Jinx answered, knowing he had been lucky, too.

"Yes, perhaps—" Bodnya said, still circling.

Behind him, the other Russian spoke to Susan.

"Since I know that you like things stuffed between your tits," he hissed, "try this."

The little Ukrainian pulled Susan in front of him and stuffed the grenade down into her bra.

Bodnya then stepped back by Kovpak, who used the thumb of his gun hand to pull the pin from the RGN. The safety lever sprang up and off, firing the fuse. Sparks shot out of the fuse's vent slit, burning Susan's cleavage and igniting the pink rose on the front of her bra. Kovpak pushed her away from him, firing a quick shot at Jinx. With the woman between him and the Russians, he could not get a shot. The two Russians ducked through the double door.

Jinx had two seconds to make up his mind. If he pursued the Russians, the grenade would turn the woman's chest into a canoe. If he saved her life—again—he would lose the man he had tracked so far. He glanced down at the woman.

Susan's eyes widened even farther. They looked like they would pop out of her head. She was writhing, trying to dislodge the grenade. There was no chance of that, it was firmly wedged between her seared breasts. She was screaming behind the tape.

Jinx dived at her, tossing his rifle to one side. He dug into her bra, grabbing the grenade by the fuse and pulled. The body of the grenade caught on the smouldering nylon and slipped out of his fingers. He dug deeper into her bra, grabbing the body of the grenade and pulling it out. In one motion, he flipped it through the double door, and rolled with her toward the wall. With luck, the grenade would catch the two Russians in the hall, but Jinx doubted it. The grenade skipped out the door, across the hall, bounced off the far wall and went off under the water fountain. The explosion echoed through the empty gym.

Jinx and Susan ended up against the wall with Jinx's face pressed into her burned bosom. The smell of burnt nylon filled Jinx's nose. He pulled his face back and pinched out the tiny burning rose.

"We have to stop meeting like this," he said, looking up into her terrified face. He got to his feet, pulling her with him.

Once she was on her feet, Jinx pulled the tape from her mouth. She inhaled deeply, then deafened him with a piercing, long bottled-up scream.

"It's nice to see you too." Jinx said, wincing. He stepped over to the discarded AR-15 and pulled the black knife blade from the stock. He had heard of the Russian's flying knife before, but this was the first one he had ever seen, nearly the last. As he sawed through the cord around her wrists, he heard a sound from the floor.

"Ooouuggghh."

BJ rolled over, weakly feeling for his head.

"Beej, I thought you were dead!" Jinx yelled, cutting Susan's hand free. He knelt by his friend.

"You may be right," BJ answered groggily. "Who are you?"

BJ rolled his head toward Jinx, who saw for the first time the long gouge that the pistol bullet had made down the side of BJ's head. A chunk of his ear was gone, blown away by the passage of the 9mm slug. Blood covered the left side of his face, matting his hair.

"Can you stand up?" Jinx asked.

"Sure, Mom, why not?" BJ answered. His eyes were rolling, and he seemed to have a tenuous grasp on consciousness. Jinx helped him to his feet, put BJ's arms around his shoulders and turned for the door.

"Come on, Susan," He called over his shoulder.

She followed along behind like a zombie.

Votrin launched a final rocket into the flaming cauldron they had created. Sokolov had fired his last RPG-22 at the fire trucks under the overpass. Votrin picked up his AKSU and fired a long, raking burst in the direction of the burning traffic jam. He replaced the magazine and slung the RPG-16 over his shoulder. He had kept a single rocket, just in case. The two men shook hands against a burning backdrop, went to opposite sides of the road, and trotted to the pickup point.

Cummings could see the figure kneeling beside the sentry hut by the light of the few burning tanks. He slowly edged around one tank's prow. The figure moved behind the hut. He must've spotted him. Moving up to another tank, he could make out the man in the shallow ditch.

Red tracers zipped past him. He quickly fired a return burst, immediately answered by another. Something stung into his leg! Falling heavily on his back to the asphalt surface, he rolled under the tank's bow overhang.

Protected by the tread, he slipped a heavy plastic AK magazine out of his pocket. Raising to his knees, he hefted it and arched it over the fence to the man's right. The figure spun around, firing. Cummings triggered off a long burst and the man continued to spin into the ditch.

"Hot shit, man! Just like Eddie Murphy in *Beverly Hills Cop*!"

With the last of the charges planted, the group moved to the north side of the airfield for their escape from the field. They had some time to make it to the pickup point. The van would be parked on a secluded dirt road that snaked around the base of Castle Mountain, a brush-covered rock pile just north of the airfield. Toshkin came up on his knee to get a better stance, then raked a row of OH-58C helicopters. They had placed no charges on the small observation helicopters, but Toshkin saw no reason to leave them intact. Red tracers stitched their way down the line, each ship taking one or two hits. One OH-58 caught fire from a tracer and a moment later, blew up, demolishing the ship on either side with shrapnel and burning fuel. The magazine empty, Toshkin jumped down from his platform and ran to join the others. The six men were nearly to the open gate when the MP Hum-V turned the corner onto Murphy Road. A spotlight on top of it lighted the road ahead, sweeping from side to side.

Toshkin and two others hit the dirt and froze. The other three were caught in the glare and instantly a burst of M16 fire came from the open turret ring of the Hum-V. One of the *reydoviki* went down hard. Another was hit, but rolled back up, firing his AKR and limping across the road. The two others with Toshkin opened fire on the Hummer, while he unslung the RPG-22 and popped open the end caps. Extending the inner tube, he jerked it onto his shoulder and peered through the crude sight. As the Hum-V pulled through the main gate, Toshkin pressed the firing button. The rocket flashed out of the tube and hit the Hummer just behind the driver's door. Flame and smoke belched up out of the open turret ring. The MP who had been firing, standing up, screamed and fell back in the vehicle, which coasted by, stopping twenty meters away. There was no more firing from the Hum-V, no motion at all. It sat there, smoking.

As they sprinted through the gate, Toshkin checked the fallen *reydoviki*. Dead. The others were helping the wounded man. A second Hummer turned the corner, then slid to a stop. Rifle fire came from the doors. The wounded man and one of the men helping him fell. Toshkin fired the remaining rounds in his magazine to cover the raider still on the exposed road. From the ditch on the far side, a rocket flashed toward the Hum-V. It hit the windshield, knocking the two MPs away from the vehicle. They did not get up.

It was time to get away from here, to the pickup point. Toshkin looked back at the burning helicopters and smiled. They had done well. He sprinted to the far side of the road. The two others joined him as they ran for their pickup.

Outside, the fighting was still brisk. There was firing to the east, probably the airfield. Tracers streaked everywhere. There was sporadic firing from the 1st Cav. area, as well. Dyer and his MPs had run out of targets and were now assisting the firefighters, attempting to save the new, modern headquarters building. In the gym parking lot, Peterson sat on the hood of BJ's Camaro, tying a field dressing over her bleeding right hand.

"Pat, give me a hand," Jinx shouted. "BJ's hit!"

"Shit, man we're all hit," Peterson answered as she tied off the field dressing and walked over to support the stumbling BJ. "One of those fuckers that came out of the gym nearly took off my hand."

Susan sat down on the curb. Finally able to breathe, and in no immediate danger, she broke down, holding her head and sobbing. Around her, the world was burning. Men were screaming, sirens wailing, the sounds of weapons. It was over and she was alive.

Oh, God, she thought, how could this happen? They were going to kill me. I only wanted to help someone, just to help. Why did it turn out so horribly? Why did they hurt me so badly?

"Who's that?" Peterson asked as Jinx laid BJ down on the hood of his car.

"Susan Elliot, the lady in Austin I told you about," Jinx answered. "Her Russian friends brought her along to martyr her for the revolution."

"Too bad they missed."

"Now, now," Jinx scolded.

"No, you're right," Peterson snapped back. "Now that we're at war, we can hang this Commie traitor bitch."

It was obvious to Jinx that Susan would fall heir to all the punishment Jane Fonda had avoided two decades before.

BJ came to again and sat up, using one hand to steady himself. Gingerly he fingered the bandage on his face. He looked around at the smoke and fire, the burning cars and the flaming fuel storage tanks.

"Oh, man, this reminds me of what Adam said to Eve!" he exclaimed.

Jinx and Peterson turned to him. "What?" they both asked.

"Whoa, stand back, I don't know how big this thing's gonna get!" With that, BJ fell back on the hood of the Camaro, his head bonging on the sheet metal.

Jinx and Peterson looked at each other for a second, then howled with laughter. The old euphoric feeling was coming back. The fight was over, and they were alive. That might change soon, but tonight they were alive; more alive than ever before. One thing was sure, the cold war was over. Now there would be no more negotiation, no talks, no diplomacy. Fire and steel would settle this. Tomorrow, the world would be a different place.

It seemed that Sergeant Zherebtson had waited for hours. He was freezing! He had heard shots fired several houses away, sirens screaming, and in the distance, there was more gunfire. It seemed to be building in intensity. Lights had come on in most of the houses, some people were moving around outside, and cars were pulling out of driveways. An ambulance, its strobes flashing, wailed up the street and turned into a driveway in the next *cul-de-sac*. But, still, his assigned house remained dark. He was becoming nervous.

A man in uniform ran to the house next door and began pounding on the back door. A porch light came on and he went inside. A light green MP car cruised slowly up the street, its spotlight searching the shadows and shrubbery. He nestled down further between the bush and garbage can. Something was wrong! He could stay here no longer. Slowly he stood up. Looking around, he stepped onto the driveway and walked down it. Reaching the sidewalk, he turned left. A car quickly passed.

"Freeze!"

He stopped, a lance of fear driving through his heart!

"Place your hands on your head. Turn around, slowly."

He stood facing a middle-aged man wearing camouflaged trousers and a maroon bathrobe, aiming a sleek automatic shotgun at his midsection.

"What is it, Sam?" Another middle-aged man, this one in a complete uniform, came across the lawn. He had a deer rifle in his hands.

"This fella looked like he was out for an evening stroll. Came down General Beal's drive. Walking down the sidewalk without a care in the world!" said Sam.

"Let me see some ID, son," said the man with the deer rifle.

"Everyone to eat shit, Amerikanski!" shouted a defiant Zherebtson.

"Jesus Christ!"

The shotgun moved in. "Cover me, Fred." He put the shotgun's muzzle in Zherebtson's face and began patting him down. He pulled the silenced pistol from a jacket pocket and tossed it onto the damp lawn.

"It's a good thing the deputy corps commander's visiting his new son-in-law in Maine!" said Fred.

★41★

Hollis, in the truck with the remaining members of Group 2, was already in the warehouse. Only a security group was outside, hidden in the brush that filled the ravine. As the van and Suburban pulled up to the door, it opened and both vehicles drove on in.

Once the two vehicles were safe inside, Hollis pulled the overhead door down. Bodnya turned the Suburban around, then shut off the engine. Malinkov did the same with the van, the two vehicles pointed toward the door. Kovpak spoke to Cowboy, then checked the wounded men. Group 3 had taken its share of losses. Two of the assassins were missing. The airfield attackers had not been lucky. Of those six, three were dead. The other three were in the truck, one wounded.

Bodnya sat behind the wheel of the Suburban, his mind a racetrack of thoughts. Group 1 had been decimated. The firing from those motor pools had been heavy. There was no way to know how many vehicles they had destroyed, if any. None of them had returned. The truck was not seen again after it left the dropping zone. There was no time now to review the success or failure of the mission. The Americans had been far more prepared than they had expected. That was the fault of a failed *maskirovka*. The attack had achieved its objective. There were dozens of burning tanks on Ft. Hood right now. The *reydoviki* of Group 2 had wreaked havoc on the 2d Armored Division. Casualties in Group 2 were only three lost and two wounded.

The psychological effects of such an attack on the American homeland would be great, although Bodnya wondered if the effect would be the one sought by the planners in Moscow. He tended to think not. The Japanese had made such a mistake in 1941.

The sound of a truck outside the overhead door cut short this rumination.

Again, Hollis ran up the door, admitting another Ryder truck. Group 4 was intact. The twelve men had executed their mission without problems. Their calm demeanor and spotless condition was in sharp contrast to the other *reydoviki*.

The *feldsher* made the wounded as comfortable as possible for the trip to the airfield. There were blankets, litters, additional battle dressings, and cans of water in the warehouse. The men drank deeply from the cans to ease their combat-induced thirst. Bodnya got out of the Suburban and walked over to Kovpak.

"Comrade Major, we are ready to depart," Kovpak said. "Should we wait for Group 1?"

"I think not, my friend," Bodnya answered, his eyes looking back in the direction from which Ft. Hood was burning. "I do not believe any of them will be along. Send the signal." Kovpak slipped out the side door of the warehouse and activated the tone signal in Whisper's boombox. Ten seconds later, the confirmation tone and light came on.

Kovpak went back inside to Bodnya.

"They are on their way."

"Excellent, let us go meet them."

They pulled onto the blacktop road that would take them south to Copperas Cove and to the airfield. Speeding down Farm Road on Ft. Hood's western boundary, Bodnya saw fires still burning over the base. He rolled down the window to get a better look. The air was cold on his face, but the sight of that burning post warmed him. Working their way through the town's back streets, they turned onto Highway 190 and then onto a side street beside a convenience store. The burning fuel depot was still visible. They followed the winding road until it ended at Base Road. Here they turned right and followed the road down the hill to the West Ft.

Hood cantonment area. The airfield was hidden by a low rise. When they crested the hill, the gate was right in front of them, open.

Spec. 4 Knot was watching the flames still dancing up from the fuel depot and the dull glow that came from the direction of the main post. The airfield's fire equipment had screamed out of the fire station at the base of the control tower and gone racing off to fight the fuel depot fire, sirens wailing, lights flashing. The lone MP car had followed. He thought that the headlights approaching down the hill were the firefighters returning. It took him a moment to realize that the four vehicles entering the airfield were civilian, not military.

"Sir, we have some POVs on the field," he called to Lt. Cranston. Cranston was in the other room, trying to make contact with someone, anyone, on the main post.

"Of course we do, idiot," the frustrated officer barked back at Knot. "Everybody has a car."

"I don't mean cars, sir, I mean some civilian trucks," Knot called back, as the small convoy disappeared behind the hangars.

Cranston hung up the phone and came back into the control room. "What trucks?" he said, looking out the windows. "I don't see any—holy shit!" Cranston's gaze had drifted over to the radar screen which now showed an aircraft just off the south end of the runway, obviously on final approach. "Who the hell is this?" he screamed. "That's it, I'm calling the MPs."

Cranston returned to the phone and attempted once again to get through to the MP station. The line was still busy. Everyone on Ft. Hood was trying to call the MPs to report the painfully obvious.

Scheverard switched on the landing lights. They were so close to the runway now, it was useless to hide. He flared out over the numbers, and dropped the An-12 lightly onto the wide runway. Once the wheels touched, Scheverard reversed the propellers and began riding the brakes. It was imperative that the An-12 stop as quickly as possible. Scheverard rode the brakes, slowing the lumbering plane enough to turn on the third crossover.

"Sergeant Gregorian," Scheverard spoke into the intercom, "when we come around, I want you to engage the control tower with your guns."

"Yes, Comrade Colonel," the young gunner replied, the tension audible in his voice.

"Sergeant?"

"Yes, Comrade Colonel?"

"Only a few rounds, save some for the trip home!"

"Yes Comrade," Gregorian answered, chuckling. "I will save a few."

The whale-like An-12 turned onto the taxiway, headed back the way it had come. In the tail, Paili Gregorian centered the gunsight on the two figures in the glass enclosure atop the control tower.

"There it is, sir, it just touched down." Spec. 4 Knot reached for his binoculars. The black-and-green C-130 had stopped short, and was now turning onto the taxiway. "I can't make out any numbers. It looks like a Pave Spectre. It's turning around."

"Give me those binoculars," Cranston snarled. "Who the hell do these people think they are? This place is a zoo tonight. They told me this was going to be an easy shift!"

As Cranston focused the binoculars, flame engulfed the tail of the plane. A second later, the control tower shook under the impact of forty high-explosive 23mm shells. Knot dived behind the console when the guns flared, but Cranston was still standing when the fusillade hit. His torn body flew across the small control room, along with a cascade of glass and aluminum. An exploding shell sent fragments spearing into Knot's foot and lower leg, but the radar console took most of the punishment. Its screen, punctured by flying metal, blew out in a shower of sparks.

On the taxiway, Bodnya's convoy was just emerging from the hangar complex when the 23mms went off. Kovpak yelled, thinking for a second that the plane was shooting at them. When the control tower erupted in explosions, he looked sheepishly at Bodnya. Bodnya smiled and gunned the engine of the van. The trucks and the van sped up too, eager to be away. They caught up with the An-12 at the end of the taxi-way and followed it out onto the runway. The jumpmaster was already lowering the tailgate as the plane turned back onto the ten thousand-foot runway. Scheverard again stood on the brakes, bringing the plane to a stop. He locked the brakes and slowly pushed the throttles up, revving up the four turboprops.

As the plane stopped, the trucks fanned out behind it, the soldiers already jumping from the lift gates while the trucks were still rolling. The wounded were handed down and quickly whisked into the plane. As the remaining raiders of Summer Harvest hurried up the cargo ramp, Kovpak took a small pack from the van and walked to each vehicle, placing one of the incendiary charges in each one. It would be hard to use this end of the runway until the burned hulks had been removed.

When he was finished, he sprinted to the already moving ramp. Bodnya pulled him inside and nodded to the Air Force sergeant above him in the tail gun. The lieutenant spoke into his intercom and the plane jumped forward, straining to reach the sky. In seconds it was airborne, banking sharply to the left.

In the tail, Gregorian had seen the rows of parked Mohawk reconnaissance airplanes as they had turned around. Now he could see all of them, parked in rows on the apron below.

"Comrade Colonel, permission to fire at the parked air-craft!"

Scheverard smiled. "Granted, sergeant, remember—"

"Save some for the trip. Yes, Comrade Colonel."

Gregorian swung the guns down, aiming for the far end of the apron. He pressed his triggers in short bursts, watch-ing the tracers, correcting his aim. He walked a line of fire down the row of parked twin-engined Mohawk intelligence-gathering aircraft. He fired until his gun was blocked by the An-12's turning.

"Well, Sergeant?" the colonel's voice came over the in-tercom.

"Comrade Colonel, I damaged or destroyed four of the parked aircraft!"

"It is too bad we do not have Aces in our Air Force, Lieutenant," Scheverard said. "You would surely be one."

The An-12 would fly due west over Lampasas, then head southwest, crossing the U.S. border at Eagle Pass, well south of Laughlin Air Force Base in Del Rio and west of the fighters based at Bergstrom Air Force Base in Austin. Scheverard was sure the alarm would spread before he could reach Mexican airspace, but hoped that the length of the border, over five hundred miles, would let him slip through undetected.

"Comrade Dorroffeyev," Scheverard said into his mike, "what is our first terrain feature?"

"In fifteen minutes we should come up on a formation of three large rock domes off our port side," Dorroffeyev answered, looking at his map. "It is called Enchanted Rock."

★ Epilogue ★

Two weeks later, the world was indeed a different place. At the time Bodnya had given the order to attack, fourteen Soviet and East German Divisions of the first echelon had crossed the border into West Germany. Other Spetsnaz units attacked III Corps' pre-positioned equipment pools in the Netherlands and Germany. Denmark succumbed to a massive Soviet, East German, and Polish airborne and amphibious assault, securing the Baltic for the Warsaw Pact. The NATO forces, outgunned and outnumbered, struggled to contain the onslaught.

Jinx, BJ, and Peterson were in Germany. Peterson was with the 163d MI near Bielefeld, where III Corps had relieved a reeling I Netherlands Corps. Jinx was in the 588th MI Detachment attached to Special Operations Command Europe. Detached from the CIA, he was coordinating long-range reconnaissance patrol operations. BJ was healed and running those LRRP missions into East Germany with Company G, 143d Infantry, the Houston Light Guard.

The first elements of III Corps were not airborne until two days after the attack, twenty-four hours behind schedule. Losses of equipment after the Soviet attack on Ft. Hood ran to sixty percent of available vehicles. At Ft. Hood Airfield, seventy-eight helicopters were destroyed, an additional twenty-eight damaged.

Cited for preventing the destruction of a mechanized infantry's and two tank battalions' vehicles, Sgt. Jacob Cummings was awarded the Silver Star and Purple Heart. While covering the withdrawal of his squad from a burning warehouse in Bückenburg, West Germany, Sgt. Cummings received the Oak Leaf Clusters for both decorations, posthumously.

Bodnya and Kovpak had escaped to Cuba with the survivors of Summer Harvest. Now they were in East Germany, hastily forming a Spetsnaz pursuit unit to hunt down the many NATO LRRP teams. All members of the Summer Harvest force, alive and dead, and the air crew of the An-12 were awarded decorations for valor, even Lieutenant Plaski.

In the next few weeks, thousands would die. Europe again became a Hell on Earth. In America, vicious debate broke out over our role and our commitment abroad. Many wanted to abandon our allies, to save ourselves. Others saw the danger and pleaded for total commitment.